D0477501

700037720809

SHADOW FORCE

MATT LYNN
SHADOW FORCE

headline

First published in 2011 by
HEADLINE PUBLISHING GROUP

1

Cataloguing in Publication Data is available from the British Library

ISBN 978 0 7553 7168 6 (Hardback)
ISBN 978 0 7553 7169 3 (Trade paperback)

Typeset in Hoefler by Avon DataSet Ltd,
Bidford-on-Avon, Warwickshire

Printed in the UK by CPI Mackays, Chatham, ME5 8TD

Headline's policy is to use papers that are natural, renewable and
recyclable products and made from wood grown in sustainable forests.
The logging and manufacturing processes are expected to conform
to the environmental regulations of the country of origin.

HEADLINE PUBLISHING GROUP
An Hachette UK Company
338 Euston Road
London NW1 3BH

www.headline.co.uk
www.hachette.co.uk

To Angharad

Acknowledgements

Without the support, advice and encouragement of men who know far more about military matters than I do, the Death Force books would never be able to achieve any level of realism or accuracy. Thanks to Mitch who introduced me to some of the private military corporations now guarding merchant ships in the Somali Basin; the techniques they have developed for combating the menace of piracy proved an invaluable lesson in marine warfare. Thanks also to Jean who helped me through the French tradition of underwater fighting; the character of Henri, needless to say, bears no resemblance. Martin Fletcher at Headline and Bill Hamilton at A.M. Heath were constantly helpful. And, of course, my wife Angharad, to whom this volume of the series is dedicated, and my three daughters, Isabella, Leonora and Claudia, who provided a loving contrast to the rugged, masculine world I was immersed in whilst writing this book.

Matt Lynn, Goudhurst, Kent, March 2010

The Unit

Steve West A South Londoner, Steve served in the SAS for five years, fighting in Bosnia and behind the lines in the second Iraq War. After leaving the Army, Steve started freelancing for Bruce Dudley's private military corporation, Dudley Emergency Forces – an outfit known in the trade as Death Inc. for the high-risk, high-stakes jobs it is willing to take on. With the money he made in Afghanistan – a mission described in *Death Force* – Steve has bought out his uncle Ken's half-share in a vintage car dealership in Leicestershire.

Ollie Hall Once an officer in the Household Cavalry, the most blue-blooded of British regiments, Ollie was trained at Sandhurst, and was, for a time, one of the fastest rising young stars in the armed forces. But he had a problem with drinking and gambling, and eventually left the Army to make a career in the City. When that failed as well, he started trying to form his own PMC, before joining up with Steve for the mission in Afghanistan. At the end of *Fire Force*, he breaks off his engagement to Katie, a London PR girl.

David Mallet With twenty years' experience as an officer in the Irish Guards behind him, David is an experienced, battle-hardened soldier, an expert in logistics and military strategy and planning. He is divorced from his first wife, with two children at private schools to pay for, and his second wife has just given birth to twins.

Nick Thomas From Swansea, Nick spent two years in the Territorial Army before joining Steve on the Afghanistan mission. An only child, he was bought up by his mother Sandra, now working as a lap dancer, and never knew who his father was. He is the man with the least military experience on the team. But he is also the best marksman any of them have ever met, with an uncanny ability to hit a target with any kind of weapon.

Ian 'The Bomber' Murphy A Catholic Ulsterman, Ian grew up in Belfast, and spent ten years working as a bomb-maker for the IRA. He was responsible for several explosions that killed both soldiers and civilians, and was sentenced to life imprisonment. After spending years in the Maze prison, he was released as part of the Good Friday Agreement. He is no longer a member of the IRA, and has severed his connections with his old life. But he is still an expert bomb-maker, able to fashion an explosion out of the most basic components.

Dan Coleman A former member of the Australian Special Air Service Regiment (SASR), a unit closely modelled on the British SAS, Dan fought in Afghanistan as part of an SASR unit deployed to fight the Taliban. He accidentally killed two children, and spent a year in a military jail, although he always maintained his innocence. Haunted by the incident, he has left the Australian Army, and has taken up freelancing for PMCs. Dan is an expert on weaponry, always aware of the latest military technology, and desperate to try it out.

Ganju Rai A former Gurkha, Ganju served for eight years in C Company, in the 2nd Battalion of the Parachute Regiment, primarily staffed by Gurkhas. He comes from a small Nepalese village, and is fiercely loyal to the traditions of the Gurkha Regiments. Rai's brother, also a Gurkha, was killed in Kosovo, and his wife and children are not getting a pension. Ganju has become a mercenary to earn enough money to help support his extended family back home. He is an expert in stealth warfare.

Maksim Prerova A former member of the Russian special forces, the Spetsnaz, Maksim is a suicidally brave soldier. His father was killed in Afghanistan in the early 1980s, and he has a bad vodka habit. During the mission in Afghanistan described in *Death Force*, he was tricked into betraying the unit, but was forgiven because he proved himself the most ferocious fighter any of the men had ever seen. Fit, strong and courageous, Maksim is always ready for a fight.

Henri Colbert A sailor with the French Navy, Henri qualified for Commando Hubert, that country's formidable unit of underwater combat specialists. After five years in Hubert taking part in missions around the world, Henri left the French forces and became a freelance consultant specialising in marine security. Brave and resourceful, Henri is a tough soldier, but he is also proud and argumentative, and finds it hard to fit into a team.

Bruce Dudley A gruff Scotsman, Dudley is the founder and chief shareholder in Dudley Emergency Forces. A former SAS sergeant, he left the Regiment ten years ago, and soon realised there was money to be made from running a private army. He was a legendarily tough soldier himself, and doesn't see why anyone else should complain about terrifying conditions. He has an acute understanding of what makes his soldiers tick, and knows how to manipulate them into fighting every battle as ferociously as he did when he was younger.

Deceased

Chris Reynolds A veteran of South Africa's Special Forces Brigade, known as the 'Recce' unit, Chris spent fifteen years in the South African Defence Force, and regarded the Recces as the finest fighting unit in the world. But he left the armed forces after he became disillusioned with the post-apartheid regime. He bought himself a farm in South Africa, but when that went bust he was forced to work as a mercenary to pay off his debts, even though it is illegal for South Africans to work for PMCs. He was brutally crucified in Batota, a mission described in *Fire Force*.

Jeff Campbell A former soldier, Campbell came from South London, and grew up with Steve. The two men were best mates. He was the man in the unit with the greatest sense of camaraderie, always organising a party, and making sure everyone had enough to drink. He died from wounds on the mission in Afghanistan described in *Death Force*, despite the best efforts of the rest of the men to save him.

One

S TEVE WEST WAS LYING TRAPPED beneath a beam that had fallen across his chest, attached to a bomb that could detonate at any second.

Only two men could help him.

One of them was on the end of a mobile with a fading signal.

And the other was a bloke who'd been drinking the local beer since breakfast.

So what the fuck could possibly be the good news?

'I said, do you want the good news, pal?' repeated Ian 'The Bomber' Murphy, speaking over the mobile in a low, throaty growl that sounded something like a diesel engine stuck in first gear.

'Why not, mate?' answered Steve with a ragged sigh. 'It hasn't exactly been my day so far. I could use some cheering up.'

'If the bomb blows, the blast from that quantity of explosives will move faster than the signals within your nervous system,' said Ian. 'So you quite literally won't feel a thing.'

'Thanks, mate. That's a load off my mind.'

'Back in PIRA, there was a bloke called Mick O'Brian who used to show us boys how to make bombs. This was in Derry in the eighties, and there were always a couple of lads who got the shakes when they were handling high explosives for the first time. Mick would tell them that to try and calm them down.'

'Much as I'd love to stop and chat, Ian, there isn't much charge left on this mobile. Do you think we could crack on?'

'Right.'

Steve could feel the sweat pouring off his body. He was lying on the ground floor of an abandoned hotel on the island of Haikl, ten miles from the coast of Avila, a small Central American state sandwiched between Panama, Guatemala and Belize. The beam had trapped him, falling across his chest. And on top of that there was a two-hundred-pound bomb, packed with P4 plastic explosive: enough of it to destroy a decent-sized building, never mind the poor sod lying right underneath it. Ian would know how to make it safe, but he was trapped down the beach in a firefight. All he could do was give instructions to Ollie. And Ollie had been drinking heavily before the battle had kicked off.

Steve handed the phone back to Ollie. They'd arrived on Haikl only a week ago, after flying out from London to Avila. It wasn't meant to be anything more than a jaunt. Ian had been out here for a month, helping out a mate of his from his Provo days called Robert Finnan who was now working with what he described as the local businessmen but what most people would call drug dealers and gunrunners. They used the island as a staging post for secretly shipping contraband from South America into Europe, the same business the IRA had been in all through the troubles, before they dropped the politics and turned themselves into full-time criminals. They were worried about some other gangsters trying to muscle in on their territory, and Ian was helping out with securing the island against attack.

Steve had only come out with Ollie and Nick, two mates from the missions they'd run in Afghanistan and Africa, because he reckoned a few days drinking the local beer and eyeing up the girls would be good for him. He hadn't counted on getting mixed up in a full-scale turf war between rival gangs.

That was the last kind of trouble he needed.

'Speak to the sod, will you?' said Steve, as Ollie took the mobile.

Steve remained completely still. There hadn't been much work to do since they stepped off the plane. Ian's job had been to rig the bay with mines, and Steve and Ollie and Nick were meant to be advising on that, but most of the time was spent sitting around the pool drinking the Panamanian-brewed Balboa Beer and chatting to the señoritas. Ollie in particular had been putting in more work on the beer than the girls; the way Steve saw it, he was still moping after Katie, the fiancée he'd broken up with at the end of the African job. He kicked off with a few beers for breakfast, then got stuck into the local rum around lunchtime, before getting into some serious drinking at night.

It was fine for a holiday, reflected Steve. But this was work. Of the most deadly kind.

'I'll get this sorted,' said Ollie, taking the mobile and pressing it to his ear.

Steve flinched. Outside he could hear the rattle of gunfire, but he could no longer keep track of who was shooting who. A fly had landed on the side of his cheek. There was a deep cut where a nail from the beam had snagged his skin, and the creature was feasting on the blood that had seeped to the surface. There was a nasty stinging where it had clawed into his cheek. But there was nothing Steve could do about it. His right arm was pinned down by the fallen debris, and he could only move his left a few inches. And anyway, any kind of movement risked triggering the bomb.

'Sod it,' he muttered under his breath. Just get me out of here, and I'm packing in this lark for good.

The hotel had come under heavy bombardment at dusk. RPG rounds had pounded into the building. At first, they'd had no idea where the shots had come from, then it was clear that a couple of motor cruisers had pulled up in the bay and were putting some heavy-duty firepower straight into the building. Steve had rushed inside to rescue Midiala, the waitress he'd been knocking around with for the last couple of days. But as they'd tried to escape from the first floor, a shell had blasted the ceiling, bringing the beam down on Steve. And it just happened to be one that they'd already

3

rigged up with a booby-trap bomb to protect the building in case of attack.

Just my sodding luck, thought Steve. And this drunk is the only bastard that can help.

Ollie burped twice, wiped a film of sweat from his forehead and put the phone down. He was approaching the beam. He paused, then steadied himself before leaning forward. Steve took a deep breath. The bomb had a simple battery-powered detonator, designed to explode when the wires were tripped. It hadn't been fully rigged yet, because they weren't expecting an attack this soon. Even so, it was a miracle it hadn't blown when the beam came down; the chances were it would blow if they tried to shift it.

With one hand, Ollie flicked away a layer of broken plaster, and with the other he lifted the top from the device. The P4 was packed into a plastic container. The plan had been to lure any attackers into the old hotel, then blow them to pieces from a safe distance. But like most military plans, reflected Steve, it was a balls-up before it even started.

'OK, I see the wires,' said Ollie, putting the phone back to his ear.

'What colours are they?' snapped Steve.

Ollie looked down. 'No back-seat driving,' he said. 'Either I'm doing this or I'm not.'

He cupped the phone closer to his ear. Steve could hear talking but couldn't make out the words. He could feel his heart thumping in his chest. With time in the Regiment behind him, and then five years working as a fixer for Dudley Emergency Forces, he'd put his life on the line dozens of times. He'd been on two jobs with Ollie and together the two men had faced hundreds of rounds of bullets without Steve really worrying that any had his name on them.

But right now, he could feel death's damp, clingy embrace.

'OK, cheers, mate,' said Ollie to Ian, putting away the phone.

He leant forward. His hands were shaking slightly. With a knife in his right hand.

'You know what you're doing?' asked Steve.

'We reckon it's the right wire.'

'Which colour?'

'It's not a plug from B&Q,' snorted Ollie. 'There aren't any bloody colours.'

Steve felt another bead of sweat roll down his back. The right wire, he thought to himself. All Ian is doing is telling him left and right and to cut one of them. I haven't got any more than a fifty-fifty chance of surviving this.

And neither does Ollie.

Ollie steadied himself, and slipped the knife into the box. He paused. Then he looked down at Steve. 'I just wanted to say thanks, mate,' said Ollie. 'I mean, there have been some good times.'

Good times, thought Steve. He'd fished Ollie out of a brothel in Baghdad to sign him up for a mission in Afghanistan on which one of his best mates had died. He'd broken him out of jail in Africa before they'd headed off to assassinate Batota's President. A laugh wasn't exactly the way Steve would have chosen to describe it. Still, for the last two years, their lives had been intertwined, twisted together like the threads in a rope. It had never occurred to him that he might have to say goodbye.

'Let's just sodding do it,' growled Steve.

Ollie leant forward. His finger was on the knife.

'Shit,' he muttered.

Steve looked into his eyes. He could see the fear there, like a pale, ghostly shadow.

'You can piss off if you want to,' he said. 'I mean, there's not much point in both of us dying.'

Ollie shook his head. 'We're like brothers, old fruit . . .'

Steve permitted himself a brief, tight smile. He had a brother already. A guy who lived close to his mum and dad in Bromley and commuted to work at a bank every day and washed the car and looked after the kids at the weekend. But that was just blood.

With Ollie, along with the rest of the blokes in his unit, it was something different.

'In arms . . .' muttered Steve, drawing a long, deep breath of the humid, salty air that he sensed could well be his last.

Ollie steadied his wrist and flicked it forwards. There was a short, snapping sound as the wire was severed.

Then silence. You couldn't even hear either man breathe.

The building shook. Another RPG round had smashed into the second floor of the building, detonating with a brutal thud, shaking up a fresh layer of plaster that dropped down on to Steve like snow. Out on the beach, they could hear the rattle of machine-gun fire, and the sound of a hand grenade exploding.

But it was impossible to tell how many men were taking part in the scrap. Or who was gaining the upper hand.

'Lift the fucking beam,' yelled Steve. His voice was raw and harsh, shot through with the shattered emotion of a man who knew he had just survived death by the narrowest of margins.

'There's another wire to cut,' said Ollie bluntly. He was cradling the mobile in his neck. 'Ian,' he hissed. 'Ian . . . where the bloody hell are you?'

Another RPG round. Another layer of plaster. The stuff was coating Steve with a dusting of debris. Another pair of flies had settled on his cheek.

Ollie looked down at Steve. 'Listen, old fruit, I don't suppose you've got a credit card on you?'

'What do you mean, have I got a sodding credit card?'

Ollie held up the phone apologetically. 'Out of credit. Un-bloody-believable the amount Vodafone charge you for calls from abroad. I put twenty quid on already this week.'

Steve rolled his eyes. 'Breast pocket,' he snapped.

Ollie looked down.

The beam was lying right across Steve's chest. There was no way they could get the card without moving it. He wiped another bead of sweat off his forehead, and burped again.

'Looks like we're fucked, pal,' he muttered.

'Two wires left?' said Steve.

Ollie nodded.

'You piss off, mate, I'll be allright.'

Ollie shook his head.

'I sodding mean it,' said Steve. 'Get down on to the beach, sort these fuckers out. Then bring Ian back here to dismantle the bomb.'

Ollie took five steps towards the window. The glass had been shattered and was lying in shards across the floor. As he looked out, he could see the two boats dominating the harbour. On the closest vessel, a man was on deck, putting RPG rounds into the building, but five more men had landed ashore in an inflatable dinghy and were advancing steadily towards the building.

Each of them was carrying an AK-47, clearing the way ahead of them. A round of incoming gunfire chipped at the concrete and blasted the glass out of the windows. Ollie ducked, shaking a few shards of glass out of his hair. 'There's no time,' he said.

He ran back towards Steve, and plunged his knife into the box of explosives.

Steve felt something he'd never felt before. Not in the SAS, not as a mercenary. A beat of panic close to his heart. 'Leave it,' he insisted. 'I'll take my chances.'

But Ollie was already holding up a severed piece of wire.

'Too late, old fruit,' he said with a rough, sly grin. 'Job done.'

He leant towards the beam. Ollie was a big man, six feet tall, with jet-black hair, and thick, broad shoulders. He grunted, then spat as he pushed hard on the five-hundred-pound block of wood. It moved a couple of inches. He grunted again, then with a roar he lifted it clear away from Steve's chest, tossing it contemptuously to one side.

He pushed down a hand, grabbed Steve's fist, and yanked him hard upwards.

Steve shook the dust free from his body. There were bruises

and cuts running up from his chest to his neck. His sweatshirt was torn down the middle. The muscles in his chest ached and his shoulders rippled with pain. But so far as he could tell, nothing was broken.

Both men rushed towards the window. Two men had stepped into the building, another three were standing guard outside. As they looked down the beach, they could see that Ian and Nick and the rest of the men were pinned down behind a makeshift barricade. They'd piled tyres into a stack, setting fire to them, but another group of men had landed on the beach, advancing steadily towards their position.

Ollie slammed a Brazilian-made Taurus 24/7 pistol into Steve's hand.

'Got a plan?' said Ollie, his voice tense.

'Yeah,' said Steve tersely. 'Regiment rules.'

'You mean run like fuck and shoot anything that moves?'

Steve nodded just once.

They started to advance towards the stairs. Midiala had already escaped out the back of the building, so at least they had only themselves to take care of. The staircase led up from the reception lobby, curving round in a ninety-degree arc. And as he looked down, Steve could see a single man advancing towards him.

About five foot ten. With curly orange hair, angry brown eyes, and his finger on the trigger of his AK-47, he looked like a mad, aggressive carrot.

Steve raised the Taurus level with his eyes.

The man hadn't seen him yet.

Squeezing the trigger, Steve fired once, then twice. Regiment training. The double tap. One to kill the opponent and one to make absolutely sure he was dead. It was drilled into him, an instinct by now.

The man reeled backwards. The Taurus's 9mm bullet had plenty of punch on it and at fifteen yards its impact was deadly. The first shot split open the man's chest, breaking a pair of ribs, and chewing into his lungs. The second smashed into the side of his face, knocking out most of one cheek before slicing into his brain.

He staggered back, blood seeping up from his mouth, then collapsed on to the floor.

Behind him, a man was shouting. 'Feckin' move, boys, feckin' move . . .'

Steve recognised the accent immediately. In the SAS, he'd done a couple of tours along the cold, damp fields that made up the treacherous border zone between Southern and Northern Ireland.

An Ulsterman? What the hell were those mad bastards doing out in Avila?

There was no time to worry about it now. He was the enemy, that was all that counted.

Steve started to run down the stairs, kicking aside the dead man.

The lobby looked straight out on to the beach. The glass doors had already been shattered, and the wall had been hit by a shell, so that the back door was blocked off. They could escape through the restaurant. Or else they could go straight through the front door.

Two men were firing into the lobby from the beach. Two more had gone round to the restaurant.

'Let's take the bastards,' said Steve.

Ollie nodded.

Cautiously, they started to advance through the lobby, their guns raised.

Steve looked towards Ollie. 'Shall we just forget anything we said in there, mate?' he said tersely. 'I mean, you're still a wanker.'

Ollie nodded, then grinned. 'And I should have left you to die.'

Two

STEVE CHECKED THE CLIP IN the Taurus.

Four bullets. And there were five men lined up in front of him.

Sod the maths, he told himself grimly. You can fight your way out of here.

The lobby of the old hotel led directly out on to a wide veranda, leading down to a pool, and then on to a beach. It had been built as a casino complex during the prohibition era, when rich Americans would fly down to the island for a week of gambling and drinking, but it had closed down during the Second World War and was now just used by the gangsters running drugs and arms from here to Europe. Since then, it had been falling apart, buffeted by the high winds blowing in off the Atlantic, and slowly chewed apart by the lizards and rats.

And, today, being blown apart by whoever the hell had decided to pick a fight with Ian and his mates.

Steve was crouching behind what had once been the pool bar. You could still smell the rum and vermouth, although it must have been forty years since anyone last mixed a cocktail here. He glanced at a row of bottles. Empty. 'Sod it,' he muttered under his breath. I could use a drink.

As they'd come out of the lobby, they'd come under an intense barrage of fire. Ollie had dived down into the old pool. Steve had hidden behind the bar. Further down the beach, they could see the battle raging where another dozen men had pinned down Ian and Nick and the rest of the boys. But before they could go and help them, they had to deal with the men straight in front of them. Or else die trying.

A pair of shots slammed into the front of the bar. It was made from bamboo, Hawaiian-style, but had chipped and rotted over the years. The bullets were taking great slugs out of its side. Steve gripped the Taurus tight into his fist, and peered cautiously around its edge. The five men were advancing towards him, in a steady line, their AK-47s firing on automatic, putting round after round into the bar.

Another minute at most, reckoned Steve. And then that barrage of hot, angry steel is going to smash this bar to pieces.

A grunt. One of them staggered forward, blood foaming from his mouth, then collapsed on to the ground.

Glancing up, Steve could see Ollie rising up out of the pool, his hair and clothes soaking, his pistol held out in front of him like some grisly mermaid of death. Another shot, another man down. The three men left standing turned, releasing a volley of fire from their assault rifles. Ollie fell backwards into the pool, a splash of green, murky water rising up into the air. Whether he'd been shot or was diving to avoid the oncoming fire, it was impossible for Steve to tell at this distance. There was no time to think. The shot had created a split second of confusion, an advantage that was not likely to be repeated. Steve raised both hands, the Taurus gripped between his fists, and levelled it straight at the man still facing him. He squeezed the trigger, smashing a bullet straight into his face. He fell to the ground, his finger jammed into his gun, spraying the bullets left in his clip into the air.

The remaining two men were caught in a pincer.

One spun, the other remained steady.

But neither of them was quick enough to avoid Steve's fire.

One of them was hit in the shoulder, the other in the back. Both started to scream in agony, but neither was dead yet. Steve kicked back with his heels and started to run hard towards them. One bullet left in his clip. And two men ahead of him, wounded but not yet dead.

'You feckin' cunt!' roared the first man.

Another Ulsterman, noted Steve. He'd shot a few of his kind during his tours across the water back in the Regiment, and he knew from bitter experience there was plenty of fight in the sods. Two, three, sometimes four bullets were needed to drain the last miserable dregs of life from them. He slotted the last bullet from the Taurus straight into the man's chest, sending him staggering backwards. In the same moment, the AK-47 dropped from his hand. Steve tossed the pistol aside and lunged for the weapon.

Too late.

The one man remaining alive stamped his foot down hard on the weapon. He pointed the barrel of his gun towards Steve. 'Hold it right there, son,' he growled.

Six feet tall, with a shaved head, and a black beard, blood was spitting from his mouth as he spoke. He'd taken a bad wound to the shoulder, but was still standing, the pain under control.

He put his finger to the trigger of his weapon.

Behind him, Steve could see Ollie rising out of the pool.

Steve ignored him. If the man could see anything other than fear in Steve's eyes, he would shoot immediately.

A shot. Ollie loosed off the two remaining bullets from his Taurus, both of them striking the man in the back, splitting open his spine. Even as he died, he slammed his finger into the trigger of his AK-47, but Steve had already started to roll across the ground, avoiding the 7.62mm rounds peppering the broken concrete surface of the ground. As he moved, he grabbed the assault rifle from the dead man, and fired a short, rapid burst of fire up into his assailant.

He collapsed dead on to the ground.

Steve paused for breath. His heart was thumping viciously, and he could feel the adrenalin surging through his veins.

Ollie was walking towards him, his hair and clothes dripping from the pool. No one had cleaned it in thirty or forty years, and a thick layer of green algae was clinging to Ollie's skin.

'That Incredible Hulk impersonation is shaping up nicely,' said Steve, glancing up towards Ollie. 'Only not so good-looking, obviously.'

'Well, you needed something incredible, mate,' said Ollie, reaching down a hand and hauling Steve to his feet. 'You were dead on the ground. Maybe you're slowing down.'

Christ, thought Steve. What if he's right? That's the second near-death experience of the day. I'm not sure how much more of this I can handle.

Steve glanced first left, then right.

Five corpses, including the man on the stairs.

They'd dealt with the immediate danger. But they still had to get a mile down the beach to rejoin Ian and the rest of their mates.

'Who the hell were they?' asked Ollie, picking up an abandoned AK-47 and jabbing it towards the corpse.

'Boyos,' said Steve, slipping into the slang the SAS used to describe Ulster terrorists during the troubles. He'd done two tours in Ulster, but Ollie had been in the Household Cavalry, and although he'd seen plenty of action in Bosnia and Iraq during his time in the Army, he'd never fought in Northern Ireland. 'But they're a long way from home, that's for bloody sure.'

Ollie was about to speak. But the sound of a hand grenade exploding blasted away the words before they could form on his tongue.

Both men crouched, looking down the beach.

A mile away, Nick and Ian and the rest of their unit had barricaded themselves behind a couple of upturned rowing boats and some old tyres. Now set alight, they were hiding behind the thick black smoke rising up out of the flames.

But a dozen men were advancing on them, letting rip with their assault rifles. One man had just put a hand grenade into their defences, blowing away a chunk of upturned boat and sending a plume of sand and smoke kicking straight up into the air. There was sporadic fire coming back from behind the barricade. But it was sparse, and fleeting.

Steve knew precisely what that meant. He'd been in the same position himself a dozen times.

They were low on ammo.

'Looks like they need help,' said Steve, his tone tense.

Ollie wiped away some of the green algae still clinging to his face with the back of his hand. 'Then let's sodding move . . .'

Steve grabbed a couple of spare clips of ammo from the dead men, picked up an AK-47, then started to run. Dusk was already turning into night and the sun was setting over the horizon, smudging the sky a dark orange. A hazy light was wafting over the golden sand and the deep green leaves of the palm trees. Paradise, thought Steve bitterly, as his lungs gasped for air, and his feet pummelled against the sand. So long as you don't have a bunch of mad Ulster bastards trying to shoot you.

The distance was closing by the second. Six hundred yards, then five hundred separated them from the battle.

They could see the backs of the twelve men advancing on the barricade. Another grenade had been lobbed into the air, but it was caught by the thick flames rising up from the tyres and exploded with a deafening crack fifty feet upwards. Shrapnel was flying in every direction, and even the advancing wall of men threw themselves to the ground, aware of the lethal danger from the falling shards of hot metal.

Steve signalled to Ollie to take shelter behind a bank of palm trees. The two men started to run furiously, taking cover behind the wood. Steve looked straight forward. The column of men had broken up, four running in one direction, eight in the other. The plan was obvious: to storm the sides of the barricade, trapping the men behind it in a murderous barrage of fire. It was street fighting, the kind you learned on the dark alleyways of 1990s Belfast. But no less effective for that. Steve locked his AK-47 into position, nodding to Ollie to do the same. From the watermark on the barrel of the gun, Steve could see that the AK was one of the newly produced Venezuelan weapons, but it was far from a cheap knock-off. The Venezuelan factory was built by Russia's Izhevsk Manufacturing Plant, which had been making the assault rifle for decades. The weapon was as lethal, fast and simple to operate as one of the originals from the old Soviet Union.

Squeezing his finger into the trigger, Steve loosed off a volley of fire. On automatic, an AK can fire six hundred rounds a minute, but its effectiveness is limited by its thirty-round mag, as well as by its poor accuracy at any range over five hundred metres. The bullets rattled from the barrel, the spent shells spitting from the side of the weapon. Steve was holding it rock steady in his arms, putting round after round into the group of eight men. Two went down immediately, the bullets smashing into their backs. Two more stumbled as the wounds felled them. The remaining four men turned, unleashing a volley of fire in the direction of the trees. Steve dived behind the palm, using the fraction of a second of cover to discard the clip and slot a fresh one into place.

He glanced over to Ollie.

With deadly efficiency, he'd finished off three of the men in the group of four advancing on the far wing of the barricade. Two of them were already dead, one down wounded, probably fatally.

The final man from the group was running along the beach, back towards the dinghy he'd landed in.

Bullets were still chattering against the tree trunk, chipping away at it, sending slithers of bark flying in every direction. Steve tried to look round. Three men had pulled away from the side of the barricade. He recognised all of them: Robert Finnan, the old Provo mate of Ian's who'd brought them all over here, plus Michael Flannery and Declan O'Brian, two more of his IRA pals. They had American-made M-16s held tight into their chests, with bayonets fixed underneath them. They fired one bullet, then two into the men confronting them. One man went down, but the second managed to get a bullet straight into O'Brian's chest. Steve jumped forward, raised the AK with the fresh clip to his eyes and slotted a single bullet into the forehead of the one man remaining standing.

The shot was a good one.

His knees buckled, then he fell.

Steve nodded towards Ollie. The two men started to run towards the flaming barricade. It was a distance of three hundred yards. The sun had already dipped below the horizon, and only the flickering light from the burning tyres illuminated the beach. Steve's lungs were bursting, but as far as he could tell, the battle had already ended.

For now, anyway.

Ian and Nick were crouched behind the upturned boats. Both of them were sweaty and grimy. The burning rubber had created a thick, swirling smoke that seeped into the skin and clothes. Both of them had knives in their hands, but no guns. Finnan, O'Brian and Flannery had taken their only guns, and even those had only a couple of rounds of ammo left in their clips.

Steve dropped down to the ground, followed swiftly by Ollie. Finnan and Flannery were retreating behind the barricade, a look of wary triumph in their eyes. They were hard men, noted Steve. Boyos of the oldest and roughest school. They knew how to stand their ground, how to improvise a defence out of nothing and, most of all, how to enjoy delivering a lethal blow to their opponents. They'd been killing men all their lives and they weren't about to lose the taste for it now.

Finnan stepped out carefully, hoisted O'Brian over his shoulders and brought him back behind the barricade. Blood from the wound had seeped all down his chest, but it was too late to do anything for him now. He was already dead.

'Who the fuck were they?' growled Steve, looking across from Ian to Finnan.

'A bugger called Jack McDongell,' answered Finnan, putting down the corpse. 'One of the hardest men in the Ulster Volunteer Force. He did ten years in the Maze with us boys, and we'd see him sometimes across the yard. He's a mercenary now, just like the rest of us. There are some businessmen from Belize who like to use this island as well, and the way I heard it, McDongell's working for them.'

'It's just like sodding Belfast in nineteen ninety-five out here,' said Ian, standing up and looking down the beach.

'Except with better weather,' said Ollie.

'And decent grub,' said Nick.

'And girls you might want to shag,' said Steve.

Ian grinned. 'OK, it's nothing like Belfast. But it's still bloody dangerous.'

'Which is why we're getting the hell out of here,' said Steve.

'There's still a battle to be fought,' said Finnan. He was slotting a row of fresh bullets captured from the dead men into the clip of his M-16, and pointing down the beach. 'That bastard will be back soon with more men, we can be sure of that.'

Steve shook his head curtly. 'I don't know whose battle this is,' he said. 'But it's not ours.'

Finnan took a couple of steps forward. 'Scared of a fight, are you, Englishman?' he said. There was a tone of low menace threaded through his voice. 'I came across a few of you Regiment men in the old country, and they were all talk. When it came to a fight, they'd piss off.'

Instinctively Steve's fists started to clench into a ball. He'd lost a couple of mates in Ulster, and although he had grown used to Ian over the couple of years they'd been fighting together as mercenaries, he wasn't about to stand for this kind of taunting.

'That's a fucking—'

'Leave it,' snapped Ian, stepping between the two men.

Ian was a small man, with dusty brown hair that had started to turn orange in the sun, skin that had turned a blotchy, freckled red, and a squashed nose that looked like someone had slapped it on in a hurry. But he had thick, bruising muscles, and Steve had never seen him back out of a fight.

Steve started to push him aside, lunging towards Finnan, but Ollie grabbed his shoulder. 'We're getting the hell out of here,' he said. 'There's been enough fighting for one day.' He nodded towards the one small rowing boat still tied to the jetty twenty yards away.

'He'll be back,' said Finnan, pointing up the beach. 'We're not finished yet.'

But Ian was already pushing him away. There was a hint of remorse in his eyes. They had spent years together in the Maze, and the way he described it, Finnan had been the man who kept him sane. But Steve, Ollie and Nick were men who'd come out here for a holiday, with a bit of military advice thrown in. They hadn't reckoned on getting plunged into a full-scale battle. 'Our war is over, Robert,' he said. 'We're just hired guns, and none of us signed up for this kind of shit.'

'You're as bad as the bloody English,' roared Finnan.

From his pocket, he pulled out a flask of rum and swilled it down his throat. There was a tanked-up malevolence in his voice, and a look of wild anger in his eyes. He was a man in his early fifties now, with greying hair, and skin that was ragged and blotchy, but he was still as strong as an ox.

'We're leaving,' said Ian tersely.

The M-16 in Finnan's hand was raised level with Ian's chest. 'I said, there's a war to fight . . .'

Nick stepped forward. The Welsh boy was still only twenty. He'd lied about his age to join the unit, and he had no more formal military experience than two years in the Territorials. He was tall and gangly, with dusty orange hair and ears that stuck out of the side of his head. But he'd proved himself as able and resourceful a fighter as any of the hardened special forces soldiers in the unit and, Steve reckoned, had just as much right to make himself heard as any of them.

'There's three of us, man,' he said, glaring straight at Finnan.

He didn't need to finish the sentence. Its meaning was clear enough.

Get into a fight with Ian, and you take us all on.

Gently, Nick pushed the tip of the M-16's barrel away. 'So save your bullets.'

Ollie had already run to the jetty and was unhooking the small boat. It was a simple wooden rowing vessel with two oars and space for six men. There was an outboard motor, but they wouldn't want to risk the noise that would make until they had slipped clean away. Ian, Nick and Steve clambered in behind him. There was some water collecting at the bottom of the boat, and a bucket for bailing it out. Steve grabbed one oar, and Ollie the other, whilst Nick took the rudder, and Ian used the bucket to ship water over the side.

As they pushed away from the jetty, Steve grappled with the oar to get some grip on the heavy swell of the sea. Darkness had fallen, and there was a harsh, damp wind blowing in from the east. The waves were breaking all around them, spitting up into their faces, and leaving salt on their skin and lips. Off in the distance they could see the lights on the two big boats McDongell had moored in the cove, they could see men scurrying around on the deck, and they could hear gunfire coming from the hotel.

But there were no lights on their boat. And within seconds, they slipped away into the darkness of the Atlantic, invisible and unnoticed.

'Christ,' muttered Ollie, using the oar to kick out into the heavy swell of the sea. 'They've got a bit of work to do on their sodding tourist industry. Next year, I'll book us two weeks in Malaga.'

Three

THEY HAD NO MAPS OR charts to guide them, and only the compass Ollie always carried with him to steer by. Right alongside the island of Haikl was a nineteen-mile coral reef, one of the reasons it had once been a popular resort area. A couple of times they scraped the bottom of the boat on the coral, but they soon learnt to recognise the swell of water around the rocks and steer past them. Within an hour, they were out into the Atlantic proper. A stiff breeze was blowing, and there were some spits of rain from the dark clouds hanging in the night sky, but it was nothing they hadn't experienced before.

'We used to do the Liverpool-Belfast run all the time back in my old outfit,' Ian had commented halfway through the night. 'We would bring weapons in and out of the country by hiding them in the laundry bags on the night ferries. Now that is a rough bastard of a sea.'

They took it in turns to get some sleep. Two men crashed down on the bottom of the boat, whilst one man steered using the outboard, and one man kept watch. Steve checked the time just after they broke free of the coral reef on his Luminox Navy Seal diving watch: originally developed for the American special forces, his uncle Ken had given it to him the day he was accepted into the SAS, and it was the one thing he had that was designed for these conditions. It was just after ten at night. He tried to grab some rest between twelve and two in the morning. But he was dressed only in jeans and a sweatshirt, and those had been torn when the beam had trapped him. The temperature dropped sharply at night, and the winds blowing across the sea made it feel close to zero. Occasionally a big wave would crash into the side of the boat, splashing water right across them, which meant he was not just cold but wet as well. And even though he was exhausted from the battle they'd left behind them, the conditions meant it was impossible to do much more than lie down, shut his eyes, and hope he'd be landing safely at Heathrow by this time tomorrow night.

As he lay in the dark, Steve remembered something a bloke from the Special Boat Service had said to him when their unit had been on joint exercises with his SAS squadron. 'If you've got a problem with being damp and uncomfortable, then there's no point being in this business.'

Too sodding right, thought Steve. I've spent ten years in the regular Army and the Regiment, then five years as a fixer and mercenary for Dudley Emergency Forces. I've got a vintage car dealership back in Leicestershire which is just about breaking even. The last thing I want to do is start getting into firefights on remote Central American islands. We'll get back to the mainland, make our way up to the capital, then get to the Virgin Airlines office and on to the first flight back to London.

It was after two when Steve looked through the soupy night sky and saw the lights of a small harbour glowing in the distance. From the island of Haikl to the Avila mainland was a distance of forty miles, and they had made the journey in just under seven hours. Not bad going for a small rowboat with only a fifty-horsepower Yamaha outboard engine to power it.

The shoreline drew closer by the minute. They were just a couple of hundred yards from it now, and as they sailed closer, the swell of the sea dropped, allowing them to steer gently into the twin jetties lined with fishing boats and yachts. They ditched the AK-47s over the side; there was no point in taking those ashore, they would look way too suspicious. Each man had a Taurus tucked inside his belt, and even though Steve's was out of ammo, it might still come in useful if there was any trouble. At a hundred yards, Nick killed the engine, and Ollie and Steve grabbed the oars, guiding the boat gently along the sea walls and towards the harbour. It was just after four in the morning. Within the next hour, the fishermen would be up, getting their nets and the ships ready, but at this time of night, the port and the small town of Murugo behind it were completely empty. Only a few lights shone from the street lamps, and even though somewhere in the distance they could hear a dog barking, no one seemed to be about. Perfect, thought Steve. We can slip quietly ashore, keep our heads down in a back alley for a couple of hours, and in the morning re-emerge as tourists looking for a train back to the capital.

Ollie grabbed for the jetty, holding the boat steady as the men clambered up on to the pier.

Ian went first, followed by Steve and Nick before Ollie hauled himself on to the pier and tied up the boat. There were two wooden walkways leading fifty yards out into the sea, one with fishing boats tethered to it, the other with yachts and pleasure cruisers hired out to the tourists. Up ahead of them was a small square, with a fountain at its centre, and a couple of seafood restaurants flanked by a bar. Probably a nice enough place, thought Steve. I'll check it out on the Lonely Planet website sometime. But this morning I just want to get the hell out of here.

'Alto!' shouted a voice.

'Shit,' muttered Steve under his breath.

The Spanish word for stop.

They had just walked into the square. The headlamps from two Toyota Land Cruisers flashed on to hi-beam, creating a dazzling light that struck them straight in the face. Steve shielded his eyes, then looked straight forward.

A man was walking towards them, dressed in military uniform.

A major, reckoned Steve from the stripes on his shoulder.

'Shit,' Steve muttered again.

'*Alto*,' the Major repeated.

He was standing five yards in front of them. A square, bull-headed man, he had black hair and one of the thick Saddam Hussein moustaches that seemed to be compulsory for mid-ranking officers in Third World armies. His eyes were hard and unyielding. He was flanked by two men on either side, a total of four soldiers, each of them carrying the Belgium-made FN FAL assault rifles that were standard issue in the Avilan Army.

The five men stopped, all of them standing in a line.

The Major scanned each face in turn, a twisted smile on his face. He pointed towards the second SUV. 'I must ask you to come with me,' he said, speaking in heavily accented English.

'We're tourists,' said Steve.

The Major looked at him closely. 'I don't care what you are,' he answered crisply. 'You are on Avilan soil, and that means you obey my orders.'

'We're—' started Ollie.

The Major had already nodded towards his men. There was a clicking sound as the safety catches on the rifles were released. You don't need to translate that, thought Steve bitterly. It means the same thing in any language. The bastard is about to execute us if we don't do what he says.

Ian's eyes swivelled forward, then he stepped towards the SUV. 'We better go, boys,' he said. 'There's no point in arguing with the big fella.'

The four men started to walk towards the Land Cruiser. 'Search them,' snarled the Major.

'Back off,' snapped Nick as one of the soldiers started to push him towards the side of the SUV, kicking his legs apart.

A fist swung into the side of his face. Instinctively, Nick's knuckles clenched into a ball, and he stared to swing a punch in the direction of the soldier who had just hit him. Two more men jabbed their rifles into his chest.

'Leave it, Nick,' growled Ian, grabbing hold of him.

'He bloody . . .' started Nick, his face reddening with anger.

'I said leave it.'

'Come on, English, punch my soldier,' said the Major, a hint of a laugh in his tone. 'Then I can shoot you all, right now.'

Ian glowered at the man. He pulled the Taurus pistol from his belt, and tossed it to the ground. Steve reached into his belt and threw down his own weapon, followed swiftly by Ollie. Steve looked towards Nick. The Welsh boy was still shaking with anger. He was the best shot he'd ever met, and a natural soldier. But Steve was always aware he didn't have the training of the rest of the men. When to fight and when to surrender was one of the first lessons any soldier learnt; unless you knew that, you were just a pub brawler with a uniform. And this was a moment to surrender. They were outnumbered and outgunned, and all they could hope for right now was to live to fight another day.

'Drop it, Nick,' said Steve quietly.

Reluctantly, Nick tossed the weapon on to the ground.

The Major stooped to pick up the four pistols, checking the numbers of bullets in each clip. 'Four pistols, recently used,' he said. 'I know the British have a reputation for being troublemakers as tourists. But that's a little excessive, don't you think?'

Four

THE HEAT OF THE CELL was unbearable.

Steve walked the six yards to the row of bars that sealed them off from the dark empty corridor, gripping the chipped, rusted iron with his fists. It was at least thirty-five degrees down here, and humid, with enough moisture in the air to keep a rainforest going.

He glanced left, then right.

Nothing.

The corridor stretched ten yards in either direction, with a wall at one end, a door at the other. Two more cells led off it but both were empty. There were no windows, and no ventilation; the air just filtered down from the main prison into the basement and sat there for years, growing as stale and dirty as the men it surrounded. Steve wiped a film of sweat away from his forehead, noting the grime on the back of his hand. 'Sod it,' he muttered under his breath. How the hell did we end up in this craphole?

He walked the six yards to the rear of the cell, then back again, retreading the same path he'd taken a hundred times already. From the marks worn into the flagstones, it looked as if plenty of other men had paced the same relentless route before him. Maybe for years. Anything to keep yourself sane, he reflected bitterly. Steve wasn't afraid of many things. He'd faced bullets and RPG rounds, parachuted out of planes, and tumbled out of choppers into oncoming fire without fearing anything worse than a quick death.

But incarceration? That ate into his soul in a way he had never quite been able to explain to himself. A couple of mates from the Regiment had got mixed up with some bank robbers and wound up in Wandsworth nick. Steve had been to see them twice, and he could still recall the snap of fear that ran through him as he heard the bolts shut behind him, and the tired, defeated faces of the men waiting in the visiting room. Still, better Wandsworth than this place, he told himself grimly. At least the parole board let the boys out halfway through their sentence so they could get back to robbing post offices and banks. In this place, a man could lose hope within days, never mind weeks.

'You're doing your nut in, pal,' said Ian, looking across at him anxiously. 'I did years of this in the Maze, and you look like you're ready to break after twenty-four hours.'

Steve knew the Irishman was right but that didn't make it any easier to take. It was a tiny, cramped space. There was a double bunk bed along one side of the cell, with a wire frame but no mattress or sheets. Ollie and Nick were getting their heads down: there was only space for two men to sleep, while the other two men had to either pace around or sit on the slabs of old stone that made up the floor. In the corner, there was a bucket to crap into. Ollie's insides had been playing up from the vast quantities of beer and rum he'd been putting down his throat, and there was already a vile stench from that corner that made Steve queasy every time he walked past it. They had been here for twenty-four hours now. No one had offered them food or water, and nor had they heard any sounds from beyond the door at the end of the corridor. Forgotten? wondered Steve. Or abandoned?

'What the hell are they doing with us?' he growled.

'They'll be here soon enough,' said Ian.

Steve walked back to the bars, gripping them with his fists. He shook them as violently as he could, but they were drilled hard into the floor and ceiling and there was not a millimetre of give in them. 'I bloody hope so.'

Another hour passed, then another, before the door finally creaked open. Two soldiers advanced steadily towards them, FNs cocked and ready to fire. They silently gestured the men towards the door.

'*Pasar*,' growled a soldier.

Move it, translated Steve silently. You don't need to tell me, pal. I'm ready to get out of here.

The four men started to walk along the corridor. They were unwashed, and unshaven, and their clothes reeked of sweat and sea salt. Nick looked wide awake, but the rest of them were all dog tired, their heads close to going down. The door opened, and the soldier pointed towards a narrow corridor, then towards another door. They stepped inside. The room was bare, except for a wooden table, with one chair next to it. On the walls, there were traces of blood, some of it, Steve judged, no more than a few days old.

He didn't need to be told what it was.

An interrogation room.

'Good morning, English,' said the Major, stepping through the door.

The two soldiers flanked him, guns still cocked and ready to fire. The Major smelt of aftershave, its pungent aroma punching through the sweat and blood that filled the small room. It was just after ten in the morning, but it was even hotter up here than it was down in the basement, reckoned Steve. At least thirty-seven, thirty-eight degrees with not a whisper of a breeze in the air.

'I need to know who you are and what you are doing here,' said the Major, sitting down on the single chair.

The four men stood opposite him, on the other side of the table. They recited their names one by one: Steve West, Oliver Hall, Ian Murphy, and Nick Thomas.

Stick to the drill, Steve reminded himself. Name, rank and serial number. And sod all else.

The Major put a cigarette into his mouth, holding it steady without lighting it. 'My name is Luis Duarte,' he said. 'You are being held in the Rodas military jail.'

'On what charges?' said Ian.

The Major smiled, then lit his cigarette, blowing a puff of cigarette smoke into the air. 'No charges as yet. We're investigating.'

'We've been given nothing to eat or drink,' said Ian.

'You won't be,' snapped the Major. 'Not until you tell me what you are doing in Avila.'

'We already told you, we're tourists,' said Steve. His throat was so dry he was croaking out the words, and his stomach was starting to ache from hunger.

The Major pushed back from the table. He stood a couple of inches from Steve's face, close enough for him to smell the toothpaste on the man's yellowing teeth.

'I warn you not to lie to me, Mr West,' the Major growled. 'One way or another, we'll get to the truth, and when we do, we'll know what to do with you.'

'We're British citizens,' said Ollie. 'We need a lawyer, and we need representation from the Embassy.'

A smile slowly started to crease up the Major's face. 'And I'd like to fuck Jennifer Lopez's brains out,' he said. 'But I don't suppose that's about to happen either.'

He walked along the line of men, stopping in front of Nick. He tapped the ash from his cigarette, so that it fell down the front of Nick's sweatshirt.

'Just tell me what you are doing here,' he repeated.

'We're tourists,' answered Nick, his voice blunt.

With a sudden movement, the Major dropped the cigarette to the floor. He pulled back his right hand and levelled a punch straight into Nick's gut. The Welsh boy was strong, with muscles that he trained into rocks, but the blow had a savage force to it, and his face crumpled. Instinctively, his fist curled into a ball, but he steadied himself, and held the punch, looking back up at the Major, his eyes calm, even though he was gasping for breath.

'Pick it up,' snapped the Major, pointing down to the cigarette he'd dropped on the floor.

Nick knelt, lifted the smouldering tobacco, and passed it back. 'We're tourists,' he repeated. 'We have rights.'

The Major chuckled. 'This is Avila,' he said. 'The only right you have is to do exactly what you are told.'

Five

STEVE WAS STARTING TO RECOGNISE the smell of the blood streaked across the wall. It hit him straight in the face, a brutal reminder of the suffering and pain that must have been inflicted on men in this room in the past few weeks.

A torture chamber, he thought grimly. Where you screw a confession out of a man.

They had just been led back into the same interrogation room where they'd been questioned twenty-four hours earlier. They'd spent the night back in the same cell, given one bucket of water to share between them, but still nothing to eat. It was three days now since any of them had had any food and, with the sweat, the heat and the fear, the weight was starting to melt off them. Steve could feel a couple of ribs starting to poke through his chest, and the gnawing endless hunger was making the mood tense and edgy, as each man tried to cope with the growling from his stomach.

The Major walked into the room, the same two soldiers flanking him on the left and right, their FNs ready to fire. Up above, Steve could hear barking from the courtyard as the prisoners were taken out for a morning run, but so far, since they'd arrived in this jail nearly forty-eight hours earlier, they hadn't seen a soul apart from the Major and his two thugs.

'Feeling rested, English?' said the Major, a half-smile on his lips. 'Enjoying your holiday in Avila?'

He chuckled to himself, as if delighted by his own humour,

33

then nodded towards one of the soldiers. The man slipped outside, and returned with six wooden chairs, placing them around the small wooden table.

'We want to see someone from the Embassy,' said Steve, his tone harsh, and his eyes looking straight into the Major's face.

'I give the orders around here,' he snapped.

He raised his fist, as if he was about to throw a punch, and instinctively Steve flinched. But then the hand stopped. 'You wait here,' he said, turning round and walking swiftly from the room.

The two guards followed, snapping the bolts behind them. Steve pulled up a chair and sat down. He felt weak and exhausted and confused. 'What the hell does he plan now?' he said.

'A trip round the islands,' said Ollie, trying to sound cheerful. 'Maybe some deep-sea fishing?'

'A tour of a rum factory,' said Ian, grabbing his own chair.

'Or a night out with Miss Avila,' said Nick.

Steve grinned. 'Some sodding holiday this turned out to be.'

He looked at his watch. Ten past ten. There was a single light bulb in the centre of the ceiling, casting a pale light through the small room, but no windows, and the confined space was airless and stuffy. An hour stretched by. Ollie and Nick were discussing the football, wondering what might have happened in the Liverpool-Man U game at the weekend, and Ian was speculating on what the Major might have in store for them if they didn't cooperate, but Steve couldn't get engaged with the conversation.

I just want to clean myself up and get out of here.

It was twelve when the door swung open. They had been there for close on two hours, with no idea what was to happen to them. The water they'd drunk overnight had already sweated from them, and Steve could feel himself dehydrating fast.

'You wanted to talk to the British Embassy,' said the Major. 'Well, here you are.'

Two men were standing behind him, peering into the small cell with expressions of lightly disguised contempt.

Steve glanced up. The older man stepped in first. With neatly combed sandy hair, and a thin, gaunt face, Steve reckoned he was about fifty. He was wearing a light-blue suit, and a white shirt, with no tie. He was followed by a younger man. About thirty-five, judged Steve. He was short, no more than five foot five, with the pugnacious, sod-off manner of a parking warden. He was dressed in chinos, and a blue open-necked shirt, with a silver chain round his neck, and a grey jacket that he'd slung over his left shoulder.

'We're told you wanted to see someone from the Embassy,' said the older man, sitting down. His voice was cultured, public school, but with a grating edge to it.

'And it's a four-hour drive from the capital,' said the younger man. 'So there better be a bloody good reason.' His voice had the melodic, sarcastic inflection of a Liverpudlian, noted Steve.

'Major Duarte tells us you've been asking for representation,' said the older man. He'd pulled up one of the wooden chairs. 'Perhaps you'd care to explain why.'

'We've been arrested,' said Steve.

'And we're British citizens,' butted in Ollie.

'I can see that,' said the older man.

'Maybe you're criminals,' said the younger man. 'It's not our job to go around bailing people out of jail.'

Steve already didn't like the man. In fact, neither of them seemed very sympathetic.

'We're tourists,' said Steve. His throat was so dry, his voice had been reduced to little more than a rasp and, with the temperature climbing all the time, he could feel the sweat dripping off the side of his face and seeping through the stubble growing across his chin. 'We were out on a fishing trip. The Avilan Army arrested us, threw us into this jail, but they haven't told us about any charges.'

'We've been here for more than two days,' said Ollie. 'Just water to drink, no food . . .'

'Major Duarte says you are foreign mercenaries,' said the Scouser.

The older man pulled a pair of reading glasses from the breast pocket of his jacket and started playing with them. 'Is that true?'

Ollie was about to speak, but Steve raised his hand to stop him. He caught Ian's eye, and could see that he was thinking exactly the same thing he was. There was something funny about these two guys.

Something suspicious.

'Who did you say you were exactly?' he said.

'Like we told you, we're from the Embassy,' said the younger man.

'And your names are?'

'Our names?' said the older man.

'That's right,' said Ian, leaning forward on the table. 'We didn't catch them.'

The younger man leant forward on the table as well, so that his face was just three inches from Ian's. The stifling heat of the room was starting to get to him too, and a bead of sweat was running down his face into the side of his neck. 'You can call him Ant and me Dec,' he said, with a nod of the head towards the older man. 'And you know why? Because we're bloody irritating, and there's no getting away from us.'

Shit, muttered Steve silently. Whoever these blokes might be, one thing is sodding clear. They're not here to help.

'Good cop, bad cop,' said Ian sourly. 'That's the routine, is it?'

'Not quite,' said Dec, with a sly half-smile. 'More like bad cop, and really bloody bad cop.'

Definitely not here to help, thought Steve, his spirits deflating. We're not going to be on the next flight to London, that's for sure.

The older man – Ant – opened up an attaché case and pulled a sheaf of papers on to the desk. He balanced the reading glasses on his nose and looked down, his eyes squinting slightly. 'Let me see what we have here,' he said, a sarcastic drawl to his voice. 'Steve West. Ex-SAS, now a dealer in used cars—'

'Vintage cars,' interrupted Steve. 'We're talking Jags, the Mark II and Mark III, Aston Martins, the DB4 and DB5, Austin-Healeys and—'

'Yes, well, so far as I know the DB5 is no longer in production, so *used* cars will suffice for the purpose of these records, thank you, Mr West.'

'We're not talking a bloody five-year-old Astra—'

'That will do, Mr West.' He looked back down at his notes. 'Oliver Hall. Formerly of the Household Cavalry. Sandhurst trained. Then a brief stint in the City, and currently of no fixed abode or income.'

Ollie shot him a look of burning anger.

Ant ignored him, and kept on looking at the sheaf of papers.

'Ian Murphy,' he started. He rubbed his eyes, as if in disbelief. 'Once a bomb-maker for the IRA, and sentenced to life imprisonment for causing the deaths of more than thirty people in Dungiven and Strabane. Released in two thousand and five as part of the Good Friday Agreement.' A brief smile flashed across his face, then vanished. 'And Nick Thomas. A twenty-year-old who served two years in the Territorials. Last known job, McDonald's in Swansea, but that was three years ago.' Ant looked up from his papers. 'A strange group of men to be holidaying together, don't you think?'

'We like deep-sea fishing,' said Steve. 'Tuna, marlin, that kind of thing.'

They ignored him.

Instead Dec pulled out his own sheaf of papers. Placing them down on the desk, he started to read.

'In two thousand and nine, a group of ten mercenaries staged a raid on a drugs baron in Helmand, Afghanistan, getting away with several million dollars in gold and diamonds,' he said, pronouncing the words in a flat, nasal drone. 'In two thousand and ten, a band of mercenaries was responsible for the assassination of President Kapembwa in the impoverished African state of Batota.' He leant back in his chair, the smirk returning to his lips. 'You boys wouldn't happen to know anything about any of that, would you?'

Sod it, muttered Steve silently. They're on to us.

'Are you planning to help us or not?' he snapped.

'Wrong question,' said Ant. The older man folded his reading glasses back into his breast pocket. 'The issue is whether you're going to help us.'

'We're British citizens,' shouted Ollie, starting to bang his fist on the table.

The two soldiers stepped forward, their FNs clicked into firing mode. Then the door swung open and Major Duarte barged in, flanked by two more soldiers.

'Move it,' he barked. 'This meeting is over.'

Six

THERE MUST HAVE BEEN AT least thirty men crammed into the cell, judged Steve. He'd seen some ugly, nasty-looking brutes in his time, from the raw recruits in the SAS to the teams of cheap muscle used by the PMCs as cannon fodder on convoy protection in Iraq and Afghanistan, but these men appeared to have stepped out of their own private compartment of hell.

The soldiers pushed him roughly on to the floor, then slammed the door shut, turning the key in the lock.

Steve slowly levered himself up with his forearms.

A man was already leaning down, looking into his eyes.

At least six foot two, but weighing only about a hundred and fifty pounds, he looked like a wrestler who'd been starved. There were tattoos across his arms, chest and neck, and his head was shaved. There were two scars running down the side of his cheeks. His eyes were like rocks of coal, dark and brooding and stupid, but with a strength to them that gave him an aura of malevolent power. Around him, another half-dozen men were starting to gather. They were different sizes, and with ages ranging from twenty up to forty, but they all looked much the same: shaved heads, tattoos and scars, like a pack of wild dogs turned into human form.

The man closest to Steve reached down a hand and pulled him to his feet.

'Thanks, mate,' said Steve casually. Act friendly, he reminded himself. You could be penned up with these hooligans for a while. And they don't look like the kind of blokes you'd want to get into a scrap with.

'Let's hope they're Chelsea supporters, then you'll have something in common,' said Ollie cheerfully. 'They certainly look like they might be.'

'Watch it,' muttered Steve.

He'd supported Chelsea since he was boy – a ball signed by Kerry Dixon was among his most prized possessions – and although like every fan he had his doubts about what had happened to the team since the Russians had taken over, he wasn't about to take any lip from Ollie.

'You're American?' growled the prisoner. He spoke in a heavily accented voice, but the words were clear enough.

'English, old boy,' said Ollie. He nodded towards Ian. 'Except this bloke, he's Irish, and Nick here, he's a Welshie, but he does a passable impression of a member of the human race.'

'Bloody leave it out,' snapped Nick.

The prisoner in front of them broke into a smile, revealing just two yellowing stumps where his teeth used to be. 'It doesn't matter who or what you were,' he said, his tone turning sombre. 'Once you're in this place, you're dead men, and we're all the same under the ground.'

'Thanks for the heads up, mate,' said Steve. 'Good to get that sorted out.'

He looked through the cell. It measured thirty feet in length by ten across. Right at the end was a small window, just bars, with no glass. Ten double bunk beds were lined up along the right-hand wall, with metal frames and boards to sleep on. No sheets or blankets. There were three slop buckets to crap in, and another couple of buckets of drinking water. There was some straw on the floor, thick with dirt. Otherwise the cell was bare, filled only with the brutal, demonic men who looked to have grown used to living out their lives in this cramped, ugly space.

One of the inmates was approaching Nick. He wasn't the largest of the men – five nine, judged Steve – and nor was he the strongest. But he looked like one of their leaders: he had a confidence in his step that told you he wasn't a man used to being on the wrong side of any trouble. He glanced towards Steve, then Ollie. 'Whose *chica* is the boy?' he growled.

Chica? thought Steve. What the fuck . . .

The man put his arm across Nick's shoulder. 'I take him,' he said, a rough grin on his lips.

Suddenly Steve realised what was going on. 'I've known you for two years, mate, and this is the closest you've come to a shag yet,' he said, looking at Nick.

But he could see a look of tight fear on Nick's face. The man was pulling him towards his chest, and Steve realised it wasn't a joke. Hard though it might be to comprehend, the bloke really did fancy Nick. And there was nothing funny about that.

'Piss off,' snapped Nick, pushing the man away.

He whipped into action. The prisoner was compact but lean, and stronger than he looked. He grabbed Nick's right arm, and twisted it savagely behind his back. His left hand slammed into the centre of Nick's throat, temporarily knocking the oxygen out of it, leaving him gasping for breath. He squeezed hard, gripping Nick from behind, making it impossible for him to move.

Instinctively, Steve and Ollie stepped forward, but already a dozen men had crowded around them, and as he started to move, Steve could feel a couple of hands on his shoulders, holding him back.

Ian had also stepped forward. He looked straight into the prisoner's eyes, a steely thread of determination in his eyes. 'The boy is mine,' he said softly. 'You want him, you fight me for him. That's only fair.'

Steve could see the prisoner was thinking for a moment. Thinking clearly wasn't what he was best at, though, and you could see his brow creasing up as he weighed the challenge. Ian was smaller than him, by at least an inch, but he was heavier, and he looked better fed. There was no way of knowing what kind of fighter he'd be. But to turn back now would be to lose face. And in this place, face was all you had. Lose that, and you were nothing.

He let Nick go, leaving him gasping for air on the floor.

'OK, we fight,' he said, his tone rasping, like metal being pulled over rocks.

'One man against one man,' said Ian.

The prisoner nodded.

A circle formed. Composed of all the men in the cell, they stood in formation, making a wall of muscle and bone that created a makeshift ring. Ian was standing ten feet away from the prisoner. He wiped a bead of sweat from his forehead, then spat on the ground. The prisoner was starting to move, just inches at first, grinding his fists together. Steve was watching both men, judging their skill. He'd seen plenty of fights in his time, both in the Army and on the street, and reckoned he could tell the winner as soon as the scrap kicked off. It wasn't about strength, both blokes had plenty of that; it was about guile, and speed, and the instinctive ability to force a punch into the place it would do most damage.

Let's hope Ian knows what he's doing, he thought grimly. If he loses this fight, it's not just Nick that's buggered. It's the lot of us.

The prisoner ducked, and flew forwards. He was fast, like a whippet, full of wiry, pent-up energy. He was using his head as a battering ram, aiming to smash it into Ian's groin, a move which, if it came off, could finish the fight in seconds. A man knocked in the balls by a flying skull is going to drop to the ground in agony, and then he can be finished off with a hard kicking. But Ian was already wise to the move. Probably seen it before in the Maze, reckoned Steve, and he'd anticipated the attack when it was still just a signal somewhere inside his enemy's nervous system. That spilt second gave him the chance to respond. He'd already swerved, flinging his body sideways, and at the same time raising his fists high into the air and pulling them together so they formed a hammer of knuckle and skin. The prisoner was trying to change direction, but it was too late. The momentum was too great. In the same moment, Ian brought his fists crashing down into the back of the man's neck. The blow was timed to perfection, hitting the prisoner in the soft mass of veins and nerves between the skull and the shoulders. He shuddered in pain, then roared. Ian followed with a knee that flew straight up into the man's stomach, kicking the wind out of his gut. A hand swung round, the fingers clenched into a punch, and hit Ian in the side. There was enough rage and fury in the prisoner for even such a wild uncoordinated blow to have the power to rock Ian on his feet. He absorbed the pain, grimaced, spat, then unleashed a volley of punches into the sides of the man's face. For the next minute, there was a ruck of flailing fists and arms. The two men were pummelling into each other, the crack of bone on bone echoing around the confined space. The fighting was brutal, and unforgiving. But Ian had the upper hand, reckoned Steve. He'd taken the first points, put in the first hard blow, and he was crafty enough not to lose that advantage once he had it. After ninety seconds, the prisoner was lying flat on the stone floor, still breathing but only just.

Ian drew back.

'I think that's settled,' he said.

He spat again on the ground, his saliva mixed with blood. There was sweat all over his face, bruising to his right eye, and a nasty gash down his right arm where the man's teeth had ripped straight into his flesh.

Steve glanced around the prisoners. There was a grudging respect in their eyes, and although there might well be more trouble ahead, they'd done enough to ensure themselves a relatively peaceful twenty-four hours.

'Let's get you cleaned up, mate,' he said, steering Ian towards the water buckets.

He tore a strip off his own shirt, and dipped it into the drinking

Matt Lynn

water. There were a couple of bugs sitting on its surface, and if they didn't carry a dozen diseases Steve would have been surprised. But there was no time to worry about that now. He dipped the cloth into the liquid, then washed out Ian's wound, before tightening the makeshift bandage round it. It wasn't much, but it would stop him bleeding through the rest of the day.

'Jesus, even in the Maze, he'd count as a tough little sod,' said Ian, still wheezing slightly. He gave Nick a playful punch on the shoulder. 'Still, they reckon you're my *chica* now, so you'd better play the part.'

'I might fight you for him,' snorted Ollie. 'Now I come to think about it, Nick's always been quite cute . . .'

'I'd have been allright,' growled Nick.

'We know you would, lad,' said Ian, wiping some blood from his face with the back of his hand. He looked towards Steve, and nodded to the back of the cell. 'Reckon we're OK?'

Steve could see the prisoners hauling their man off the ground and cleaning him up. They were muttering to each other in Spanish, but he couldn't figure out a word they were saying. The man had lost face, that much was certain. He wouldn't be one of the leaders anymore, not after starting a fight he couldn't win. But another man would take his place and sooner or later another challenge would be issued. Those were the only rules this jail knew, a constant battle in which a man could never be the victor for more than a few hours before the next round kicked off.

'For a bit,' he said quietly. 'But I reckon we take turns to get some kip tonight. One of us should be keeping watch at all times. Otherwise we'll wake up with our throats cut.'

The four men sat down, taking sips of the drinking water from the single tin cup. They remained silent for five minutes, then ten, each of them lost in their own thoughts.

'I just can't work out those blokes from the Embassy,' said Ollie. 'Why the hell won't they help us?'

'They were from Six,' answered Ian.

The slime, thought Steve, slipping into the term used within the SAS for the secret intelligence agency that was constantly calling on special forces soldiers to do its dirty work for it.

'They would pull the same trick in Ulster,' Ian continued. 'Bring in some of our boys, rough them up, put them in jail with a bunch of Orange nutters, threaten their families, then they'd offer them a deal. Start working for the British and we'll let you go. A lot of good men were turned that way . . . and a lot of them regretted it in the end.'

'Why the hell would they do that?' asked Ollie.

'There's a job,' said Ian. 'A job no man in his right mind would take. So they've decided to make us do it.' He spat some of the blood still in his mouth on to the ground. 'The bastards.'

Seven

STEVE HAD TAKEN PART IN some rough games of football as a kid. Twenty aside, with a punctured ball, no referees, and extra marks for kicking the hell out of the boys from Chislehurst, that had been how he'd spent much of his schooldays in Bromley. But Christ, he thought to himself, looking out on to the exercise yard. Even Mad Mick, a brute of a boy who used to make tackles that would have disgraced Millwall on a bad day, might have thought twice about joining this ruck.

There were at least thirty men on each side, although amid the swirling tumult of bodies and the dust kicked up from the playing ground, it was impossible to make any accurate count. There were playing on the jail's exercise yard, thirty square metres of cracked mud, surrounded by a high wall of yellowing brick, and overlooked every fifteen metres by a soldier equipped with a local knock-off of the Israeli-manufactured Uzi machine pistol: a formidable weapon capable of spewing out six hundred rounds a minute from its stubby barrel, more than enough firepower to turn the whole prison into a graveyard in the space of a few seconds. Not that the blokes kicking the ball between the goalposts needed much help in that department, reflected Steve. They were doing a good of job of ending each other's lives already.

'I thought these Latin chaps were meant to be good at the footie,' said Ollie, looking out on the pitch. 'The beautiful game, and all that.'

'Maybe these are the reserves,' said Steve.

'I reckon Chelsea might sign the left back,' said Nick, nodding towards an ugly brawl that was developing where a striker had been scythed down by a two-footed tackle that had been aimed straight at his groin. 'John Terry would like the bloke's style.'

'What is it with the sodding Chelsea jokes?' snapped Steve, looking at Nick. 'At least it's not thirty years since we last won the league like bloody Liverpool.'

'Next season—' started Nick.

But the sentence was cut short by one of the guards. He tapped Nick and Steve on the shoulders and pointed towards the left side of the pitch. 'You and you,' he barked. 'That team.'

With a curt nod, he placed Ollie and Ian on the other side.

'I'm more of a sub myself,' said Ian. 'Sick note, that's me. Like Joe Cole. Talented but not available to play.'

'Move it,' barked the guard.

Steve didn't reckon there was much point in debating the issue. It was just after eleven in the morning, and the sun was already high in the sky, the temperature had climbed past thirty, and it looked as if it would get much hotter as the day progressed. They'd managed to grab some kip in their cell, taking turns to keep a watch on their cell mates, but when the breakfast of bread and oatmeal had been pushed through the door, they hadn't been offered any and didn't feel like starting a fight for it. They were tired and weak, certainly in no state for a kick-about. Not that it made any difference to the guards.

'The English, they think they good at football,' the soldier said, grinning through his stubbly black beard. 'Let's see you play.'

A couple of the men grunted towards Steve, but without any strips it was hard to tell who was on which side. There was no organisation to the team. One bloke was staying back in goal, and a few more guys were hanging back in defence, but apart from that it was one team with twenty strikers, much the same way it had been back in Bromley. Every time the ball landed on the ground, at least fifteen guys pounced on it, creating a dust-up, from which the ball would emerge a couple of minutes later.

'I reckon this is like the rugger at school,' said Ollie. 'Just keep as far away from the bloody ball as possible and you might live until lunchtime.'

Nick found the ball at his feet. He managed to make ten yards, swerving past a couple of lunging tackles before a two-footed sliding challenge brought him crashing to the ground. He winced as another three men swerved for the ball, ignoring the man down, kicking him out of the way. Another bloke was running with the ball now, before Ollie stepped in front to body-check him. There was a nasty thud as the men collided, and yet, while Ollie didn't have much in the way of skill, he was as solidly rooted to the ground as an oak tree, and he was no more likely to crumple in a one-on-one collision than an armoured vehicle. The prisoner bounced off him, tumbling to the ground, and the ball flew up into Ollie's face. He nodded it forward, but no sooner had he done so than the man had scrambled to his feet, a knife pulled from his boot. He was lunging towards Ollie, the blade in his hand.

Christ, thought Steve bitterly. We're not exactly settling into this rathole.

Ollie had already moved a couple of steps back, but the man was still coming for him. Like a bull in full charge, once his blood was up there was no stopping him. Steve stepped forward, putting himself between the knife and Ollie, and Ian had come across to help them. 'The English, dirty fucking players,' growled the prisoner, slashing the blade through the air.

Up ahead, the game was still going on, but at least twenty of the men had stopped, deciding to watch this sport instead.

'It was a fair challenge,' said Steve, putting up a hand.

'It was a foul,' growled the prisoner.

'Listen, mate, you can have a sodding free kick, for all I care,' said Steve. 'Just talk to the ref, if there is one . . .'

But the prisoner ignored him, nodding towards Ollie. 'We fight right now,' he said.

Suddenly, the sound of a shot blasted across the exercise yard. The bullet had been fired harmlessly into the air, but the crack of a hammerhead against steel had brought the game to a stop. Major Duarte was striding towards them, his pistol still in his hand.

'You're lucky,' he said. 'Your friends from the Embassy are here to see you.'

'I didn't imagine I'd ever be saying this, but I might actually be pleased to see those two sods,' said Steve.

The Major nodded towards a pair of guards, who barked a few words in Spanish to the prisoners, then led the four men back inside the main prison building. There was no air conditioning, but with thick stone walls, and few windows, it was a few degrees cooler inside, and Steve was grateful for that. They went down one flight of stairs, then were shown into the interrogation room. Ant and Dec were already sitting at the small wooden table. Neither man looked up, nor made any attempt to speak.

The Major slammed the door shut.

They were alone.

'Settling in, are you, boys?' said Dec. 'Making some friends?'

'Not exactly,' said Steve, with a curt shake of the head. 'They don't seem to take to us. I reckon it's Ollie here.'

'No, well, it's not exactly the friendliest jail in the world,' said Ant, with the same languid, public school drawl to his voice that had grated on Steve's nerves yesterday. 'Still, there were only thirty deaths in here last year, out of almost five hundred men, so it can't be that bad.'

'And you boys only have another thirty or forty years to go,' said Dec, with a rough chuckle. 'You'll be out by twenty fifty—'

'We've examined your case,' interrupted Ant. 'Major Duarte says he has evidence that you were in Avila as foreign mercenaries helping gangsters who use the islands off their coast to run narcotics and weapons into Europe. As you no doubt know, the British government takes the war on drugs very seriously. We certainly can't help anyone involved in that traffic, especially when they are as guilty as you appear to be. You'll be tried and sentenced in the next few days. Unless—'

'Unless we do a job for you,' interrupted Ian.

The four men had sat down on the wooden chairs on the other side of the table. There was a jug of water, but only glasses for the two Embassy officials. The air was stifling, and sweat was starting to pour off the Irishman's face.

'You catch on quick,' said Dec, leaning forward on the table and taking a sip of his water.

'I was a Provo,' said Ian. 'We know how you operate.'

Neither man bothered to contradict him, noted Steve.

Ian was right. They were the slime.

'What's the deal?' Steve asked.

'You'll be released from here, taken to the capital, and flown straight to London,' said Ant. 'You'll be given the details of the operation there.'

Dec stared hard at each man in turn. 'This is a single, one-off, non-negotiable offer,' he said flatly. 'If the operation is a success, then the slate will be wiped clean. You boys can get on with the rest of your lives. But it's take it or leave it.'

'And if you don't like our offer, then you're welcome to stay here and take your chances with the local judge,' said Ant. 'No one's forcing you to do anything against your will.'

'I don't suppose there's any point in asking what the job is?' said Steve.

Ant just shook his head. 'Like we said, this is take it or leave it.' He rapped his knuckles against the tabletop. 'And we'll have an answer right now please.'

Steve glanced at each man in turn. He could see they were all thinking the same thing.

'If we could think of any other options, any at all, then we'd take them,' he said, looking back across the table. 'But as it is, it looks like we're in.'

Eight

AS THE TRUCK PULLED UP at the airport, Steve was already beginning to feel like a human being again. One in plenty of trouble, admittedly. But at least he wasn't a caged animal anymore.

'I hope there's a McDonald's,' said Nick, glancing up at the terminal building. 'I'm bloody starving.'

After agreeing to Ant and Dec's demands, the Major had led them away to a shower room. They'd washed, shaved, and by the time they'd dried themselves off, some fresh clothes had been laid out for them. Each man changed into the jeans, sweatshirts and deck shoes, got as much water down their throats as they could, then stepped outside to the truck that was waiting to drive them the forty miles to the main airport just outside the capital. Ant and Dec rode up front with the driver, whilst a pair of soldiers, both of them carrying Uzis, sat with the men in the back. No chance of escaping, reckoned Steve, watching the way their fingers were sliding up and down on the triggers. Even if we wanted to.

'We're catching the Iberia flight that leaves for Madrid at four this afternoon,' said Dec as the men stepped into the departure lounge. 'We'll be there by the morning, then connect straight on to a flight to London.'

Steve glanced around the terminal. It was a hot, shabby place. Avila didn't get much tourist traffic, and if you excluded the narcotics business, there wasn't much of an economy either. Only the Spanish airlines made daily flights to Europe; apart from the Madrid plane, there was a flight scheduled for New York, and a couple of short-haul flights up to Mexico or down to Brazil, but not much else on the departure board.

'Let's eat,' he said, nodding towards the restaurant. 'We've got a whole hour.'

While Nick ordered in a round of burgers and chips, and Ollie helped him collect them from the counter, Steve slipped away to the gents, followed swiftly by Ian.

'What do you reckon?' said Steve, as soon as he made sure neither Ant nor Dec had followed them. 'Maybe we should make a run for it. Down to Brazil, perhaps. Plenty of beer and birds, and the local football teams can't be too bad either.'

'There isn't any point,' answered Ian. 'I've known Provo boys who tried that after the slime put the squeeze on them. Ten years later, they're still on the run. They have to cut themselves off from everything and everyone they've ever known. That's the only way you can evade capture. But it's no life for a man, no life at all.'

'It's going to be sodding dangerous, whatever it is they want us to do.'

'That's something we can be certain of,' agreed Ian. 'But I've spent a chunk of my life in prison already, and let me tell you, that's no life for a man either. We can die quick or die slow, that's the choice they're offering us, and I think they've already guessed which side of that coin we'll choose.'

Steve shook his head. 'It's going to be sodding Helmand, I just know it. Jesus, I swore I'd never go back to that hellhole. Not after what happened to us the last time.'

'There's plenty of other rough spots the British might want to send us to.'

'Like where?'

Ian dried his hands, but paused before the door. 'I only know this,' he replied quietly. 'They aren't even checking on us. They know we aren't going to run, and so do we. Let's just see what the job is, and take it from there.'

It's true, thought Steve as he walked back to the table. They've got us by the balls.

The bastards.

He finished his food in silence. It was three days now since he'd had a proper meal, and at least it felt good to get some protein inside him. Nick had already finished off his burger, and even though he was complaining it was nothing like as good as a quarter-pounder with cheese from Maccy D's, he'd already gone back to get another one, whilst Ollie had polished off a bottle of the local beer in one swig. By the time their flight was called, they were fed, with a couple of beers inside them, and although their mood was still sour, they were a lot better off than they had been when they woke up this morning. And that, at least, was something, decided Steve.

The next ten hours slipped by quickly enough. Steve watched a bit of the film showing on the Spanish Airbus A-340, gave the meal he didn't feel like eating to Nick, shared another beer with Ollie, then dozed off for most of the rest of a quiet flight. They spent an hour in transit at Madrid's Barajas International Airport, then got on the 8.50 a.m. EasyJet flight to Gatwick, which touched down at 10.15. There was a stiff breeze blowing across the airport when they got off the plane, and the skies were grey. None of that made any difference to Steve. He was just pleased to be back on home soil.

Ant and Dec steered them through passport control and customs. They had no special clearance, noted Steve. MI6 could get anyone through an airport in an instant, but they only did that when they had to, and they never drew attention to themselves unnecessarily. Two cars were waiting for them in short-term parking: a silver-grey Ford Mondeo, and a black Toyota Avensis, each equipped with a driver. Two of the most anonymous cars on the road, noted Steve. They were keeping this low-profile. Steve and Ollie climbed into the back of the Ford, with Ant up front. Ian and Nick joined Dec in the Toyota. As they steered away from the terminal, the driver took them up on to the A25 towards Guildford.

'Where're we going?' asked Steve, leaning forward to Ant.

'You'll find out when we get there,' he replied.

Steve already had a pretty good idea, and it was confirmed when the car pulled up in an ordinary, tree-lined street on the eastern side of the city. MI6 ran a network of safe houses, and they were mostly in the quiet towns of the south-east, or else in the immigrant suburbs of north and east London, depending on the skin colour of the assets they wanted to hide away. They were simple, ordinary houses maintained for storing prisoners, or refugees, or just people they used for jobs. But the fact they weren't being taken to MI6's Vauxhall Cross headquarters already told him something. This job was so far off the books they didn't even want to talk about it on their own premises.

And that was hardly a good sign.

Ant led them inside. It was a modest semi-detached house, with four bedrooms, and a small garden, but well-maintained, clean and with a kitchen that was stocked with food. From what Steve knew of the drill, there would also be a set of handguns hidden underneath one of the floorboards, and a concealed fridge in the cellar with basic medical supplies, plus a dedicated secure phone line that would put you straight through to Vauxhall. But none of that was going to be used today. 'There's toast if you want some,' said the woman who led them through the hallway and into the kitchen. 'Or some fruit, as well as coffee.'

Steve couldn't help but be struck by her appearance.

She was five eight, with black hair cut neatly so that it curled around the side of her neck. Her skin was lightly tanned, with just a few freckles across the side of her cheek, and her eyes were a light brown. She was dressed in black cotton slacks, and a white blouse, one button open, with a single string of pearls round her neck, and another pair studded into her ears. But it was the smile that Steve noticed. It only lasted for a fraction of a second, but it was both knowing and mischievous at the same time.

The day is looking up, he decided. If they'd told me I was meeting this looker at the end of it, I might have been a bit happier about getting shot at, tossed into jail, then carted off half-way round the world to be thrown into a mission where the only return ticket probably comes with a free coffin. Wouldn't have complained at all.

'Some coffee, Mr West?' she said.

'Call me Steve.'

The smile again.

'Some coffee, Steve?'

'Maybe a muffin or something,' interrupted Nick. 'I'm starving.'

'Or a full English would be good,' said Ollie. 'After all that South American muck, then the airline grub, some bacon and eggs would go down a treat.'

Christ, I could do without these blokes around me, thought Steve. Maybe talk to her one to one.

'We'll see what we can do.'

Steve helped himself to some coffee, and waited while Nick and Ollie grabbed several slices of toast and spread them with thick piles of butter and jam. Ant was exchanging a few words with the woman, but Steve couldn't make out what they were saying. By the time he had drained his mug and stuffed a slice of toast down his throat, she was calling them to attention.

'My name is Layla Thompson,' she began.

The smile, noted Steve again. It was there, then it was gone, like a breeze on a hot summer's day.

'Like my two colleagues,' she continued, nodding towards Ant and Dec, 'I work for MI6. We've been to a lot of trouble to get you boys out of Avila, and now we'd like to make sure it was worth it.'

This is it, thought Steve. The deal. And we're about to find out where it is exactly we're going to get our arses shot off.

Layla opened up a Dell laptop, but left it a few inches in front of her, not showing anyone what was on the screen. 'The shipping industry is crucial to world trade,' she began. 'About ninety per cent of world trade is carried by sea, which amounts to seven point seven billion tonnes of cargo. There are around fifty thousand merchant ships sailing internationally, and a million people work on the crews. It's a big business. It's crucial to world trade, obviously enough. But it's also crucial to the British economy. Most of that shipping is insured at Lloyd's of London.'

She paused, glancing at the Dell, but avoiding eye contact with any of the men.

'And it's getting hit by piracy. Hit hard. I'm sure you've heard all about the pirates off the coast of Somalia. Well, it's a problem here in Britain because it's playing havoc with the insurance market. Tens of millions are being paid out in ransoms and the pirates are getting bolder all the time. Lloyd's is getting hammered. We've already seen the banks in the City of London get into trouble. We can't afford to bail out the insurance markets as well. And we can't afford to see that industry go down either.'

Finally, she made eye contact first with Steve, then with Ollie, Ian and Nick.

'We need to hit the pirates and hit them hard. It's an issue of national economic survival.'

'Last time I checked, you had a bunch of blokes with funny hats sailing around the world,' interrupted Steve. 'Called the Royal Navy, as I recall. When they aren't too busy chauffeuring Prince Charles around the place, perhaps they'd like to have a crack at it.'

'They've tried,' said Ant. 'There are patrols from all the major navies off the Somali coast. We're there, the French, the Americans, the Russians . . . everyone. But there are two point two million square miles of ocean within easy striking distance of

Somalia. Protect one part of the sea, and the pirates just strike somewhere else. They know these waters like the back of their hand, and they can hit the ships at night if they want to. There is no way the Navy can protect all of them.'

'We need to hit them hard, and the only place we can do that is on land,' said Dec. 'Out at sea it's useless. Even if we do catch them, under international law all the Navy can do is arrest them, and then the bastards start calling their lawyers. Believe it or not, under the Human Rights Act, they can apply for asylum in Britain, and they'll probably get it as well.' Dec chuckled softly to himself. 'Then we'll just have the bastards robbing people in south London rather than Somalia. It's not exactly solving the problem, is it?'

Layla turned the Dell round. On the screen was the face of a strong black man. His eyes were dark and brooding, and his jaw rugged, with white teeth that were sharp and hungry. Even in a picture you could sense the strength of his character, noted Steve; you could see the determination built into every muscle, and the anger burnt in his expression.

'This man is called Ali Yasin,' said Layla. 'According to our intelligence, he is the warlord who controls the Somali pirates. Everything goes through him. He decides which boats get hit, and who does the job. He supplies the arms and equipment. He handles the ransom money, negotiates with the ship-owners. Once the money gets paid, he splits it up, and takes care of laundering it into the European banking system. He's the linchpin.'

'And we want him captured,' said Ant. 'Alive.'

'Alive?' queried Ian. 'Why not just kill the fucker?'

'This man knows the network, and it's the network we need to break,' said Ant. 'Killing one man doesn't make any difference. There will just be another Somali thug to take his place.'

'The pirates aren't working by themselves,' said Dec. 'A bunch of Somali peasants don't suddenly have access to power-boats, weapons, sophisticated radar systems, the works. And they don't have access to banks in London or Frankfurt or Dubai that can launder the money for them. These guys are linked to gangsters in Britain, Russia and Italy. This is the deadliest criminal conspiracy operating in the world today . . . and we need to break it.'

'Yasin is the key,' said Ant. 'Everything is inside his head. The gangs, the routes, the bankers. He knows how it all fits together. We need to bring him in, break him, then we can start clearing up this mess.'

'Let me guess,' said Steve warily. 'You want us to do it.'

'We can't make a military strike in Somalia,' answered Layla. 'We wouldn't ever get authorisation from the UN. And even if we did, we wouldn't want to be responsible for clearing up the mess afterwards. We've still got too many problems to deal with in Iraq and Afghanistan. So we're forming a small, secret military force, totally off the record and off the books. We'll give you all the logistical support you need, all the training, all the kit, and back-up. And then we'll send you in to capture Ali Yasin and bring him out alive.'

'I thought you lot gave up press gangs in the eighteenth century,' said Ian sourly.

'We've already told you, this is your choice,' said Dec harshly. 'You can take the job or you can go back to Avila to stand trial.'

Ollie leant forward on the table, his brow creased. 'Why us?'

'We may not like you much, or you us, but the fact is we need you,' said Ant. 'No one else could have pulled off that heist in Helmand like you boys did. And no one else could have taken out President Kapembwa in Batota.'

'You're the best,' said Layla. 'And that's what this job needs.'

'Actually, we're crap,' said Ian. 'Don't know our arse from our elbows.'

'You wouldn't want us clowns messing about with a boat,' added Steve. 'We'd sink it.'

'You're the best, and that's final,' snapped Dec.

Layla looked up at Steve, pushing a lock of hair away from the side of her face.

That smile again.

'Welcome to the Shadow Force,' she said.

'What the hell's that?' asked Steve.

'It's a name we use sometimes,' Layla explained. 'It's a top-secret unit that operates in the grey, shaded area between legit and black ops. And you've just signed up.'

'Are we getting paid?' said Ian.

'Two hundred and fifty a day, plus expenses,' said Layla crisply. 'With tax deducted at source, of course. I know that's a bit of a change for you boys, but if you think we're rough, wait until you meet the Revenue.'

'Any chance of a government pension?' said Steve. 'Index-linked? I hear they're a pretty good deal.'

Layla smiled. 'Somehow the men we recruit for the Shadow Force never seem to need pensions,' she said. 'And I think you can guess why.'

Nine

'THE SHADOW FORCE,' SAID IAN with a snort, cradling a mug of hot, milky tea in his hand. 'Since when did the slime get into giving their units a sodding brand name? They'll be giving us all freshly designed uniforms soon.'

They were standing in the kitchen of the safe house in Guildford. Steve glanced from the window into the well-kept suburban garden. Over the fence, he could hear one of the local mums telling a toddler to be careful on the trampoline. Normal life was going on all around them. Tell any of the people on this street you were planning a strike on the nastiest, deadliest pirate operating on the world's oceans, and they'd just laugh at you.

We could still make a run for it, thought Steve. But like Ian says, they know we won't. Layla Thompson knows us as well as we know ourselves. Possibly even better.

The bitch.

After describing the task ahead, Layla had given them twenty-four hours to bring the unit together and get their lives sorted out. Then she left for London with Ant and Dec. Steve had already called Bruce Dudley. A tough, former SAS sergeant, he was the founder of Dudley Emergency Forces, a private military corporation that was known on the circuit as 'Death Inc.' for the reckless way it took on jobs nobody else in the business would touch. They'd been working for DEF on both the Afghan and African jobs. Dudley was sympathetic. And just like Steve, he reckoned they didn't have much choice but to take the mission. 'Get the unit together and get it done,' he said. 'And let me know if you need any help.'

Right now, the only help they really needed was getting the rest of the men together.

'Pirates,' said Nick, finishing his own mug of tea. 'It's exciting anyway. Better than sitting around on our arses.'

'You're sodding crazy,' said Ian. 'There nothing exciting about drowning.'

Steve glanced at the boy's face. That was the trouble with Nick, he reflected. It was just one big game to him. If he wasn't working for a PMC, he was getting rat-arsed down at Wetherspoon's in Swansea, and sending increasingly desperate text messages to girls who'd already given him the brush-off. Even after a couple of jobs, he still hadn't figured out that each one took you closer to the grave. Maybe he never would.

'At least we'll be back doing something we believe in,' said Ollie. 'I mean, the woman is right. The pirates are a threat to the British economy.'

'Christ, spare us the Sandhurst crap,' groaned Ian.

'It's only crap to a sodding terrorist,' growled Ollie. 'Just because you never believed in anything.'

'I believed in freeing my people from the feckin' British,' snapped Ian. 'And I wasn't too busy getting drunk to stick with it.'

Steve glanced from man to man. He had a sense what was going on. Ollie had been one of the fastest-rising young officers in the Household Cavalry, the poshest regiment in the British Army. He'd been talked about as a certainty for general one day. But he had a weakness for drinking and gambling, had dropped out, and tried and failed to make it in the City. He'd been at a low ebb when Steve signed him up for Death Inc. Since then, he'd broken off his engagement to Katie and had been kicking his heels ever since. The way Steve saw it, he was itching to get back into the Regular

Army again. It was the only thing that had ever meant anything to the man.

'They won't have you back, you know,' said Steve.

'What do you mean?'

'He means we're just cannon fodder to them,' said Ian. 'This Shadow Force bollocks, it's not an official unit. It's a suicide job, otherwise they'd get their own boys to do it.'

'Maybe you should stop being so sodding chippy,' said Ollie.

There was a rasp to the man's voice, noted Steve. A sound you generally heard before a fight was about to start.

'At least we're going to see Ian working for the British government,' he said, trying to defuse the row that was brewing. 'Maybe it's worth it just for the look on his face.'

Ian grinned. 'Don't rub it in,' he said with a laugh. 'Jesus, who'd have thought I'd ever end up working for Six. It's like Ryan Giggs transferring to Man City.' He looked at Steve. 'And you?'

'I just want to crack on, get this thing done, and get back to my dealership,' said Steve. 'There's a Jag Mark II in the garage that hasn't sold yet and I want to take her out for a proper drive before some moron of a footballer buys it and spills Cristal all over the leatherwork.'

'So maybe we should stop arguing among ourselves and start getting organised,' said Ollie.

They all knew the first task was to get their team together. Jeff had died in Afghanistan, and Chris had been killed in Batota. Half of them were already on board, but that still left another four to get hold of: David Mallet, a former Irish Guards officer, now living with his second wife Sandy and their twins just outside Woking; Ganju Rai, the former Gurkha; Dan Coleman, the big Australian, who'd been in the Special Air Services Regiment, Australia's equivalent of the SAS, but who'd spent time in a military jail after being wrongly accused of killing two kids in a firefight in Afghanistan; and Maksim Perova, who'd been in the Spetsnaz, Russia's special forces unit, and a man who was, beyond question, the maddest, most dangerous, most lethal individual Steve had ever fought either with or against.

'You two boys round up Dan and Maksie,' said Steve to Ian and Nick. 'Ollie and I will get hold of Ganju and David. We'll meet up for breakfast in London tomorrow morning.'

Layla had left them a rented Vauxhall Astra and the kit they'd need for the next twenty-four hours. They each had fresh clothes, a pre-paid mobile phone with fifty quid in credit charged to it, a wallet with five hundred in cash, and a credit card loaded up with £2,500 to pay their expenses for the next few days. Say what you like about Six, thought Steve, they were at least professionals. The job might well be impossible, but at least they would have all the equipment they needed.

It took Steve and Ollie almost two hours to drive down to Baslow Road, the quiet street of mostly retired couples down on the south-east coast where Ganju had lived with his grandfather Gaje, another fearless old Gurkha warrior, and a man who could keep you entertained for hours with stories of the Italian campaign in the Second World War. Ganju's brother, Lachniman, had been killed while serving with C Company in the 2nd Battalion of the Parachute Regiment, a unit mainly staffed by Gurkhas, and now it was up to Ganju to look after his wife and two children back in Nepal.

When they arrived at the house, there was an estate agent's sold sign outside. That wasn't what Steve had expected. And it could only mean one thing.

'I'm going home,' said Ganju simply, offering Steve and Ollie some tea and biscuits as they stepped into the small, immaculately neat house.

His grandfather had died last year, and his sister-in-law Kani needed a man about the place to help raise the children, Ganju explained. Steve wasn't about to question the decision. The Gurkhas had their own code of honour, and the obligations it imposed were unbreakable. That was what made them so special.

'There's been too much death in the family,' said Ganju quietly after Steve explained they were about to embark on another mission.

'But—' started Steve.

'Leave it,' said Ollie stiffly.

The two men said their farewells, wished Ganju the best of luck, promised to stay in touch, and climbed back into the Astra. It was another two hours' drive up to Worpledon, the village near Woking where David Mallet lived with Sandy and the twins. They drove mostly in silence. Not having Ganju on board was a blow, Steve reflected. He was their Frank Lampard, Mr Reliable, the first name on the team sheet every Saturday. The Gurkha was the finest stealth fighter Steve had ever seen, a man who could use guile and cunning to overcome odds that seemed impossible. He had the quiet confidence of his people, the self-belief that came from knowing they'd been born into the finest warrior nation on earth. He was a quiet man, sometimes solemn, and he didn't join in the banter with the rest of the lads, but he was part of the glue that held the unit together. He'd be missed, Steve reckoned. Probably more than they could yet judge.

'Maybe Ganju's right,' said Ollie, as he steered the car up the driveway of David's modest, semi-detached house.

'About what?'

'Too much death. First Jeff, then Chris, and now we're taking on sodding pirates.'

'Losing your bottle, mate?' said Steve.

Ollie just scowled, pulling the keys angrily from the ignition.

Even as Steve said it, he regretted the remark. The same thought had been running through his own mind. Maybe there had been too much death, just as Ollie said. Every guy in the unit was brave and strong, they'd proved that dozens of times. But every soldier knew there was always one battle too far. And maybe this was the battle.

Dusk had already fallen as Steve rang the bell. Sandy answered the door, a toddler in one arm, and a tin opener in the other. A blonde of thirty-five, with a pert, warm face, her figure had completely recovered from the birth, and she looked better than Steve had ever seen her before. Maybe it was the bright smile. Usually Steve found his married mates' wives were about as pleased to see him as they were an arrears letter from the mortgage company. Trouble, they usually called him, and he could see their point: their husband was about to spend the night drinking with the boys while they were stuck at home with the babies. Not Sandy. Not this evening anyway. 'You boys get down the pub,' said Sandy, pushing David out the door. 'I'll get the twins off to bed.'

'Blimey, maybe the family thing isn't so bad after all,' said Steve as they walked the few yards down to the Ox & Bull. 'Nice-looking woman to send you off to the boozer while she reads Peppa Pig to the babies.'

David just laughed. 'She's just trying to fool you, that's all,' he replied. 'Part of the grand conspiracy. They're all in it together.'

Half an hour later, they were finishing off a round of steak pies and chips, and putting away the second pint in the pub. They'd caught up on each other's news. And they'd told David precisely what the mission was, and why they had no choice but to accept it.

'Jesus, pirates,' said David, blowing away the froth on his third pint. 'They're mean bastards.'

'You OK financially?' asked Steve.

Even though they'd made some money in Afghanistan and Africa, he knew David was always short of cash. He had two kids by his first wife Laura, both at public schools, and what with the fees and the alimony, and the cost of the twins, the man ripped through a fortune every year.

'Sandy's brother has the Skoda dealership over in Woking,'

David answered. 'I sank a pile of cash into that. He gave me a fair share, but with the credit crunch, sales have been flat. There won't be any profits this year, maybe not next either.'

'There won't be a fortune in this job,' said Steve.

'But with the slate wiped clean with Six, we could be back in business,' said Ollie.

David grinned.

Steve sensed he was about to accept.

Then, behind David, he saw Sandy walking through the pub. Her coat was pulled up around her neck, and her expression was serious. She put her hand gently on her husband's shoulder and looked straight at Steve. 'We need him here,' she said.

'Honey, we're just talking about a few days,' started David.

'He's been having dreams,' she said simply, her eyes still fixed on Steve. 'The bad sort.'

Steve knew precisely what she meant.

Back in the SAS, post-traumatic stress disorder was referred to simply as 'bad dreams'. It was an accurate enough description, even if the psychologists weren't happy with it. Most of the men would automatically dismiss anything the shrinks said as bollocks, and most of it was. But not the 'bad dreams'. They were real enough, and everyone knew about them. Back in the First World War, it was called shell-shock, and it could get a man shot for cowardice, but these days even the SAS recognised it as a serious condition. The intense stress of combat put so much strain on the nervous system that a man would simply turn in on himself, making it hard to return to any kind of normal life. They couldn't sleep, they couldn't get out of bed, they couldn't work. A couple of guys Steve knew in the Regiment had suffered from the 'dreams', and when Steve had been to see them in the care home it had been among the most tragic sights he'd ever witnessed. Strong, brave men, with hearts of oak, reduced to shambling, nervous figures, without even the willpower to get themselves out of bed in the morning. Better to get a leg or an arm blown off, Steve had decided at the time. At least you could still have the spirit to fight back from that.

'I'm bloody allright,' growled David.

But Sandy's hand remained on his shoulder. And the look on her face said that wasn't true.

'It's just a few nightmares,' he continued, taking a swig on his pint, gulping back the beer in a rush. 'That time we saw Chris crucified in Africa . . . it preys on the mind. But I'll be OK, really.'

Steve reached across for the keys to the Astra.

'You look after yourself, mate,' he said with quiet determination. 'We're going to be gone for a few weeks, but when we get back we'll have a few quid in the bank, and we'll take you away for a few days R and R.'

He stood up and, with Ollie at his side, started to walk back towards the car. David didn't bother to reply. He knew there wasn't any point in arguing, and Steve reckoned he didn't really want to either. Once the dreams started, the way Steve had heard it explained by the shrinks, a fear started to take hold of you. Men became scared to go out of the house, scared even to talk. Combat was out of the question.

As he opened the door to the Astra, he felt Sandy touch his shoulder. He turned round, and could see the smudge of a tear in her eyes. 'Thanks,' she said, with that note of quiet determination that Steve had noticed military wives used to get them through the inevitable adversity their man's choice of career dealt them.

Steve just nodded, unable to think of anything to say.

'And you boys make sure you get back allright,' she continued, reaching out to squeeze Steve's hand. 'He needs his mates more than ever.'

Ten

THE PRICES HAD GONE UP at the Starlight Café since Steve had last been there, but it was the only place with an SW in the postcode where you could still get a full English for less than a fiver and as many refills of your cup of tea as you wanted. Which might be quite a few, decided Steve as he spread some butter on his toast then speared a sausage. There's a long day ahead of us.

They'd driven up to London last night, and kipped down at the flat on the Battersea side of the river that Bruce Dudley made available to the men who worked for his firm. As he put his head down, Steve was thinking about David, and how lucky he was to have a women like Sandy to look after him. And he reflected briefly on how there was no one who'd stand by him if he was in that kind of trouble. He'd knocked around with plenty of girls, but only one of them had been someone he could imagine spending his life with. Sam, the girl who'd been on the mission in Africa with them. She'd told him she loved him, and he'd been sure he felt the same way, but he was too stupid to say so, and then Ollie had shot her brother for betraying them, and after that Steve had been certain he'd never see her again. There will be plenty of regrets in my life, he'd thought to himself as he drifted off to sleep. But that will probably be the greatest of them.

First thing this morning, they'd texted Ian and Nick to meet them at the café at eight sharp, but when they walked through the door they could already tell the news wasn't good.

'Two more breakfasts,' grunted Ollie to the elderly lady behind the counter.

'With extra beans,' said Nick. 'And four sausages. I'm starving.'

'Get that grub inside you, because it looks like we'll need a double-sized Nick,' said Steve. 'We're going into this job short-handed.'

He explained briefly about Ganju and David. The men were all silent. Post-traumatic stress disorder was what many of them feared most. It struck mercenaries just as hard and just as frequently as regular soldiers – stuck out on convoys and protection jobs with no back-up, they were just as likely to witness carnage – but they didn't have any specialist doctors they could turn to. They'd all heard of blokes turned into wrecks after mental breakdowns, thrown out by their wives, and losing their jobs and their houses. You could find a few of them sleeping rough around Waterloo Station most nights, and none of them were men you wanted to get too close to. The world turned its back on them very quickly.

'We'll sort out some money for David when we get back,' said Ian. 'Make sure he's OK, and Sandy sticks with him.'

Steve nodded. 'In the meantime, what about Dan and Maksie?'

'I've been calling and texting their mobiles, but nothing,' said Ian.

'Sod it,' snapped Steve, spooning more beans on to his fork. 'We need more than four blokes.'

'I could always call Roddy,' said Ollie.

Steve grinned. Roddy Smarden was a mate of Ollie's from the Household Cavalry, signed up for both the last two missions, but both times he'd failed to show up for the job itself. 'Watching Woddy the wanker walk the plank might be good for a laugh.'

'He's a good bloke if you give him a chance.'

'He's a public school tosser.' Steve looked across at Ian. 'Would any of your mates be up for it?'

'We've got enough terrorists on this unit,' grunted Ollie. 'The IRA sods will probably just join up with the pirates.'

'Right, like we can trust the British—'

'I know where Dan is,' said Nick suddenly, interrupting Ian before he could finish the sentence. 'My mum's with him, out in Majorca.'

'Why the hell didn't you say?' asked Ian.

'And what the hell is she doing with Dan?' Ollie wanted to know.

'I had a bit of a bust-up with Mum,' answered Nick. 'She won't give up the lap dancing.'

'Why the hell should she?' said Ollie. 'She's bloody good.'

'How would you like it?' growled Nick. 'Having your mum take her kit off for everyone.'

'Nick, Nick, we know what you mean,' said Steve quickly. Nick was turning bright red and had speared his last sausage furiously. 'But we need to get hold of Dan.'

Nick pushed his mobile across the table. 'She texted me yesterday,' he said sourly. 'You can call her if you like. I'm not speaking to her.'

Ten minutes later, Ian had spoken to Sandra and sorted out the rest of the day. It turned out Dan was working on the beer bar he was opening out in Majorca, and Maksim was helping. Sandra was out there for a few days, organising some lap-dancing nights for the bar. Ian had called EasyJet, and got them a booking on the twelve fifteen flight from Gatwick. It cost them six hundred quid for the last-minute tickets, but it was MI6's money, and they'd be there by mid-afternoon.

'Pack your suntan lotion, boys,' said Ian with a grin as he returned to finish off the remains of his breakfast. 'We're going on a holiday.'

*

It was six by the time the cab from the airport pulled up outside the sign saying 'Dan's Beer Bar'. It was nestled into a cove just before the village of Portocristo, a half-hour by car from the airport at Palma, with a view of the crystal-blue sea, and hidden from the road and the string of budget package hotels a bit further along the bay by a row of palm trees.

As Steve stepped out of the taxi, Dan slapped him so hard on the back, he was briefly winded, then Maksim locked his hand in a vice-like shake so tight he was sure a couple of bones had been twisted out of position. But it was great to see both men. They looked tanned and fit, and they had the quiet smiles on their faces of men who'd found a purpose in life that didn't involve carrying an AK-47 on their backs or having a knife slipped into the inside of their boots.

And good luck to them, thought Steve. They deserve it.

'Just what we bloody need,' said Dan, practically knocking Ollie over as he thumped him on the back with his massive strong hands. 'This place is just about done, and we need a few blokes to break open some beers and give the place the kind of christening it deserves.'

As Dan showed them around, Steve was amazed at the job the Australian special forces man had done. The main bar had been completely refurbished, with a long sweeping saloon, equipped with a dozen big TV screens tuned constantly to Sky Sports, leading out on to a terrace where a grill served up burgers, hot dogs, grilled seafood, and chips. Maksim had shipped over a crew of five Russian guys, and although their skin had turned the colour of a beetroot in the sun, they'd worked hard through the last three months, and the job was almost finished. Around the back there was a disco that doubled as a lap-dancing club two nights a week, which was why Sandra was out here. She had volunteered to help kit out the place and run the dancers. 'There's nothing but Ukrainian and Polish sluts on this island,' she complained as she helped Dan show them round.

'What this place needs is some proper Welsh strippers.'

'Beer, sport and strippers,' said Ian, looking at Dan. 'I think maybe you're going for the bloke market.'

'We've got seafood salad on the menu, and we can mix up a shandy if we have to,' said Dan. 'The babes can't complain they're not being looked after.'

Dan had rolled out some sleeping bags for the boys to kip down in the disco, close to where the Russian builders were sleeping while they finished the job. Steve went for a quick swim in the ocean, washing some of the exhaustion of the past few days away in the fresh, clear waves breaking in from the coast, and by the time he'd got back to the bar, Sandra and Ollie had got a barbecue going. The smell of burgers and seafood was mixing with the salty smell of the Mediterranean, and a soft, orange dusk was settling over the horizon. Dan was busy explaining to Nick how he'd put in orders from all around the world for different beers. 'The widest selection of beer anywhere in the Med, that's what we're going to put in the adverts for this place when we get all the work finished.'

'Any chance of a Stella?' asked Nick.

'Sod the Stella, lad,' said Dan. 'Look what we've got here.' He reached behind the bar for a bottle. 'Rooftop Red Lager brewed by the Matilda Bay Brewing Company and shipped all the way from Oz. We've got Czech beers, Russian beers, German—'

'I'll be fine with a Stella, mate,' said Nick.

Steve broke open a bottle of the Rooftop Red and drank half of it on the first gulp. It tasted cool and refreshing, a world away from the Foster's you got in pubs back home.

With darkness falling, Dan put down a couple of crates of cold beer, Ollie and Sandra put down the plates of hot food, and the men pulled a few tables together to settle in for a long night of drinking. The talk was of old battles, of victories snatched from the jaws of catastrophe, and of death cheated at the last moment. They knocked back toasts to their two fallen comrades, Jeff and

Chris, saluting their bravery, and wishing them well wherever the gods might have sent them. And they looked forward to challenges and triumphs still to come.

'This is the life you've got sorted for yourself out here, mate,' said Steve to Dan, as he finished off his plate of food, and cracked open his fourth bottle of the evening. 'Dan Coleman's big payday.'

'You reckon?'

Steve nodded. 'Every man is working for a big payday, that's my theory anyway. Something he can build for himself. For me, it's the vintage car dealership. For you, this place.'

'I don't know,' said Dan, turning thoughtful. 'I've sunk every penny I made out in Africa and Afghanistan into the bar, and I've put two hundred thousand euros on the mortgage just to get the work finished. Who the hell knows when it'll turn a profit.'

'You don't measure a payday in money.'

'Then how?'

Steve took a long hit on the beer. He needed to think about that one. He'd always imagined it was a place, like this bar, or the dealership, but maybe it was women, like Sandy, or Sam.

'You'll know it when you see it.'

'That's sod all use,' spluttered Dan. 'What if you're not sure?'

Sandra was putting down another plate of grilled prawns, a bowl of chips, and a couple of jars of mayo to dip them in. Maksim was breaking open the second bottle of vodka to share with the Russian workmen: one of them was starting up a round of Cossack drinking songs. Nick and Ian were lugging across another crate of beer; Nick was even sampling something other than Stella.

'Not bad,' Nick muttered as he tried the Rooftop. 'I'll suggest they get it on draught down at JD Wetherspoon's in Swansea.'

'There's a job,' said Ollie, suddenly leaning across the table.

Dan put his beer down.

Maksim looked across, ignoring the singing from the workmen

behind him. 'Christ, man, I thought we'd put all that crap behind us.'

Steve started to explain what had happened to them in Avila, and how they didn't have much choice. 'They're on to us, boys,' he finished. 'They know what we've done, and they're not going to let go until they get what they want.'

'But, Jesus, pirates,' said Dan, with a shake of the head. 'Those bastards are animals.'

'I know,' said Steve. 'But I don't reckon we have much choice.'

'Payback time,' said Dan, his expression turning solemn. 'There's always a price to be paid, and I guess we're about to find out what the bill is.'

Eleven

NOT EVEN THE BRIGHT MORNING sunshine could pierce the hangover.

Steve sat for a moment on the beach, letting the waves break right over him. It was still only seven in the morning, but he hadn't been able get much sleep. It was partly the alcohol, and partly the sound of Maksim and the Russian workmen snoring and belching through the night. But it was mostly the look on Dan's face when he'd told him there was a job, and that they didn't have much choice about whether they accepted it or not. He plunged into the water, letting the waves crash over him, and pushed out into the sea. Just keep moving, he told himself, as he swam furiously into the cold water. Get this job done, and we can all get back to enjoying our big paydays. Whatever they might turn out to be.

As he walked back up to the bar, he saw Ollie slipping out of Sandra's apartment. No, he thought to himself. They couldn't have got together last night. Not possible. He's probably just taking her a cup of tea.

Ian was already up, brewing up some tea and coffee and frying bacon and sausages and eggs. Bruce Springsteen's *Working on a Dream* album was humming away on the speakers.

The sea had washed most of the beer out of Steve's system. He grabbed a coffee, piled some bacon and eggs on to his plate, and watched the fishing boats come back into the harbour down below. It's a fine spot Dan has picked for himself, thought Steve. Until us blokes came along to spoil the view.

'Where you been?' said Nick, rubbing his eyes, looking towards Ollie whilst heaping three well-fried eggs on to his plate.

Steve's eyes flitted from man to man. No, not possible, he repeated to himself. You can't shag a mate's mum. It's just not the rules. Even if she is a lap dancer.

'Just enjoying the early-morning sunshine,' said Ollie, a chipper note in his voice.

Nick sat down grumpily. 'I tell you, I'm sticking to the sodding Stella from now on. That Aussie lager doesn't half leave you feeling like crap in the morning.'

Maksim sat down next to them, a broad grin on his face. 'Pirates,' he said, slapping Steve on the back. He roared with laugher, then burped, the smell of beer and vodka still lingering on his breath. 'Maksim Perova working for the British government. Who'd have thought that possible? Maybe I'll get to meet the Queen.'

Good old Maksie, thought Steve to himself. There isn't a scrap in the world the bloke doesn't want to get stuck into.

'I'm sure she'd be charmed,' said Ian.

'I don't know, mate,' said Dan, sitting down next to them. He had a big mug of tea in his hand but hadn't collected any food. So far as Steve could remember, it was the first time he'd seen Dan lose his appetite. 'I want to help you boys out, but the bar needs looking after. I've sunk so much money into this place, I'm not sure I can afford to take any risks with it now.'

'They'll come after you in time,' said Ian. 'Six never give up, and they don't take no for an answer. Sets a bad precedent.'

'I'm an Aussie, and I'm living in Spain,' said Dan. 'What can they do?'

'You do what you think is right,' said Steve. 'David and Ganju aren't coming, and no one's being forced into anything.' He grinned, taking a mouthful of food. 'We've got old Maksie here, and he's an army all by himself.'

Dan was staring up the driveway. A police car had pulled up, and two officers had stepped out. They were from the Cuerpo Nacional de Policía, the national Spanish police force, directly controlled by the Ministry of the Interior, not the local police. Dan walked up towards them, talking for a few minutes in a mixture of broken Spanish and English. Steve couldn't make out very much of the conversation, but he did hear the word 'tax'. Not a phrase you ever want to hear, he thought to himself. Not in any sodding language.

When Dan sat back down at the table, there was a dark frown creasing up his brow. 'Apparently I owe fifty thousand euros in taxes on this place,' he sighed. 'The last owner pissed off without clearing the debts.'

On the table, Steve's mobile was ringing.

'I thought your friend might need a little persuading,' said Layla, when he picked the phone up. 'Tell him that so long as he's on the mission, he won't be hearing any more about the Spanish taxes.'

'You bitch,' snapped Steve.

'Language, language, Mr West,' she said lightly. 'There's an easyJet flight leaving Palma at five past twelve. Make sure you and your friends are all on board. We'll pick you up at Gatwick.'

He was about to speak but the line had already gone dead.

'That was Six,' he said, glancing up at Dan. 'Take this job, and the tax boys will be off your back.'

Dan looked up. Suddenly he broke into a broad grin. 'Looks like I'm on the bus, then,' he said. 'And those pirates better watch out, because right now I'm in the mood to kill some people, and they look like being the first in the queue.'

Twelve

LAYLA WAS STANDING A DISCREET distance away when the team stepped through the arrivals hall at Gatwick. It was a Saturday afternoon, and the airport was heaving, but it still took only a fraction of a second to pick out her face amidst the crowd of people waiting to collect their friends and relatives.

She smiled. That smile he'd noticed the first time he met her.

But this time Steve didn't return it. He just nodded curtly, standing with the rest of the unit whilst she walked across to fetch them. Layla reached out a hand to Dan and Maksim. 'Mr Coleman, and Mr Perova,' she said. 'Welcome to the Shadow Force. A car is waiting.'

The unit walked in silence, their bags slung over their backs, towards the car park. Ant and Dec were waiting for them in a nine-seat Renault minibus. As soon as they were all inside, Dec took the wheel and steered the vehicle cross-country towards Winchester, then down towards Bournemouth.

'Let me guess, we're visiting the shaky boats?' said Steve, looking towards Layla, as he noticed a signpost for Poole, the small naval and port town just to the west of Bournemouth.

She nodded. 'The headquarters of the Special Boat Squadron, that's correct,' she replied. 'We'll get a full briefing on the piracy threat when we arrive.'

'A few laughs as well,' said Steve. 'Those clowns always crack a bloke up.'

'Now, now, Mr West, we can drop the special forces rivalries. We're all one big happy team now.'

Steve remained silent for the rest of the journey. It was close to six by the time they reached their destination. Unlike the SAS, which had its own purpose-built regimental barracks up in Herefordshire, the SBS base was blended into the Royal Marines base in Poole. The naval equivalent of the SAS, the SBS kept a much lower profile. It was woven into the fabric of the regular armed force, and never drew attention to itself. There was plenty of rivalry between the two units, mainly because they were competing for the same meagre resources and the same high-profile missions. But when their backs were against the wall, they had plenty of respect for one another; the selection for the SBS was every bit as rigorous as it was for the SAS, and the training just as arduous.

Rain was starting to fall as the minibus pulled up at the gates of the sprawling military complex. The SBS shared it with 1 Assault Group of the Royal Marines, 148 Commando Forward Observation Battery, and the Royal Artillery. As the windows were wound down, a stern-looking marine put his head through the window, checking how many men were inside.

'Big Mac and fries, please, mate,' said Nick with a grin.

But nobody smiled. And certainly not the soldier.

'You're in a proper army now,' said Ollie. 'They don't do jokes.'

Layla showed her papers. He clearly recognised her, as well as Ant and Dec, but studied the passes meticulously before waving them through. Glad to see the Army is still concentrating on ticking boxes and filling in forms, thought Steve, as the Renault drove through the gates and started to steer round to the back of the complex. So long as the Ruperts get their paperwork sorted, everyone's happy. You could lose a whole battalion, but so long as the right procedures were followed, no one would mind.

'You'll be staying here,' said Layla, showing the men into a small wooden barracks building. 'Enjoy.'

As she shut the door behind them, Steve glanced around. It was a single-storey building, thirty feet long and fifteen wide, with eight metal-framed beds arranged in two rows of four. There was a single electric heater, but it wasn't doing much to take the damp and the chill out of the air. The base was close to the harbour, and there were seagulls flapping everywhere, and a gale blowing in from the Channel that slanted the rain sideways. A window looked out on to a row of barrack huts and beyond that to the parade ground, and even in the early evening, with the light fading, Steve could see a bunch of fresh recruits being drilled into shape by a sergeant with a yell that seemed to shake the foundations of every building each time he opened his mouth. As he looked into the wet, tired faces, Steve could see himself, more than a decade ago, being drilled into shape in his first few weeks in the Parachute Regiment, years before he'd been chosen for the SAS. And he could see the same mixture of hope and fear in each of the boys' eyes that he remembered feeling himself.

'Christ, we're still here, aren't we,?' he said, glancing across at Ollie. 'Looking out on to some parade ground in the pouring sodding rain, listening to some arsehole of a sergeant give everyone hell. We haven't exactly progressed with our lives, have we?'

'We're doing what we were made for,' answered Ollie stiffly.

'What you're made for, maybe, pal.'

'You too, Steve,' said Ollie, his tone suddenly serious. 'And the sooner you accept that, the sooner you'll stop being such a right royal pain in the arse.'

Steve shook his head. 'I was made to sit around Dan's gaff waiting for the first planeload of lap dancers to show up.'

'Stop kidding yourself.'

Steve ignored the remark. There was fresh linen on each bed, but they were unmade, and for a few minutes he busied himself with the sheets. Better polish my boots as well, and get a haircut, he reflected with wry amusement. I don't want that sergeant coming in here and giving me a bollocking.

At seven, Ant escorted them across the parade ground towards the main SBS building. It was a single-storey concrete building, with a flat roof, and two main corridors running through it. There were offices where the Ruperts ran the show, and, at the back, a briefing room. It felt familiar to Steve as soon as he stepped inside. Just like being back in Hereford, he reflected. The same sense of quiet, efficient purpose. The same pride in excellence. The same qualities of endurance and fortitude. They were all qualities you found within any special forces operation, and they seeped even into the bricks and mortar of the building itself. And they were qualities you couldn't find in any other walk of life.

Maybe Ollie's right, he thought. Maybe this is what I'm made for.

'Find yourselves seats, gentlemen,' said Ant.

A second later Layla walked into the room, accompanied by a man in uniform. About forty-five, reckoned Steve, with brown-grey hair just starting to thin out, cold blue eyes, and a half-smile that looked as if he enjoyed giving orders, the tougher the better. Steve wasn't an expert on the Navy, but he recognised a commodore's stripes when he saw them. Just below rear-admiral, but above a captain, a commodore was the equivalent of a captain in the Army, and the stripes on the cuff consisted of a small gold circle, with a four and a half inch gold stripe underneath it. Next to him was another man. Thirty-five, judged Steve. With dusty blond hair, reaching down to his collar, and slightly too long for the bloke to be any kind of regular soldier, he was wearing black jeans, a plain black polo sweater, and deck shoes, with no socks. He was at least six three, and powerfully built, with a rugged jaw and a chest and shoulders that looked as if he'd be the first man you'd pick if you were looking for a prop for a scrum. Both men remained silent as Layla walked up to the front of the briefing room.

'This is Commodore Daniel Bamfield,' she said. Her tone had changed, noticed Steve. She sounded like a supply teacher taking detention, and not looking forward to the task. 'He's the Royal Navy's key expert on piracy. He's been out off the Somali coast on patrol for much of the last six months, and he knows more about the challenges you are about to face than any other man in the country.' She glanced sideways. 'Commodore . . .'

Bamfield stepped forward. He spoke in the clipped tone Steve recognised from the Ruperts in the Army. But there was no bullshit in there, he noted. The guy clearly knew what he was talking about, and wasn't afraid to level with them. How much Layla might have told him about their backgrounds, Steve didn't know. But it was clear from the start that he knew they were experienced soldiers, and he could talk to them as equals.

'For starters, gentlemen, and I'm sure I don't really need to tell you this, forget anything you might have read in the papers about piracy,' he began. 'These aren't just Somali peasants, and they certainly aren't any kind of swashbuckling heroes. These are vicious, well-organised criminals, who know precisely what they are doing, and they're bloody good at their job.'

He pointed to a map that had been flashed up on the wall. A jagged stretch of coastline, sticking out into the Gulf of Aden. 'This is Somalia,' he said. 'A country that started out as the armpit of the universe and went steadily downhill from there. It's dirt poor and completely chaotic. From the eighteen eighties until the Second World War, a big chunk of it was part of the Italian empire, and the fact that even the Eyeties were able to colonise the place gives you a fair idea of how crap it is. They don't make anything, there aren't many resources, and fishing is about the only honest way to earn a living. For the last ten years since our American friends pulled out, it's been a nominally Islamic state. But the authority of the central government has completely collapsed. In their place, al-Queda have been moving in hard. We've been making life hard for those boys out on the Afghan-Pakistan border, so they've moved a lot of their training camps to Somalia instead. If you're a young Muslim hothead from Bradford who fancies a bit of jihad, the chances are you'll be sent here. That's one reason we have to stop the pirates, and stop them now. They are being integrated into a global network of crime and terror, and they're taking to it like fish to water.'

The Commodore paused, took a sip of water, and pointed at a fresh map.

'This is Puntland,' he said. 'God probably created it just so the rest of the Somalis could go around saying, well, at least I'm not in bloody Puntland. Its name is taken from the ancient Egyptian territory known as the "Land of Punt".' He stopped and grinned. 'And no, that's not a place full of betting shops. It was the place the ancient Egyptians regarded as their ancestral homeland, although its precise location has never really been identified. Anyway, it's not hard to see why they left. There's not much there, except for the dried-up scrubland. And this.' He ran his hand along the edge of the map.

'Sixteen hundred kilometres of coastline, which just happens to look out over some of the most important shipping lanes in the world. There isn't any oil or gold or even tin or copper in Puntland, but there is coast, and plenty of it. They used to fish a lot of lobster and tuna, but since the government collapsed, they haven't been able to protect their territorial waters, and big fleets from the rest of the Gulf and even India have come in and nicked all the fish. So they turned to the one trade coastal peoples have always turned to when times are hard.' He paused, and seemed to be looking straight at Steve. 'Piracy.'

The Commodore pointed at the map again. 'Ships coming out of Europe and through the Mediterranean go through the Suez Canal, past the Gulf of Aden, and come out right here, off the coast of Puntland in an area we call the Somali Basin. Likewise, cargo ships and the big oil tankers leaving Saudi Arabia, Iran and the rest of the oil-rich Middle East sail through here to get up to Suez or across into Asia. It is, quite simply, the richest sea lane in the world. And these bastards are looking right at it.

'Forget anything you've heard about dirt-poor fishermen. This is a technically sophisticated operation. The pirates know precisely what ships they are going to hit and when. Every modern cargo vessel has an AIS, or an automatic identification system, on board. It's a regulation of the International Maritime Organisation, so they don't have any choice. It allows coastguards and navies to know who they are and what they are carrying, and it lets other captains know what other boats are in the area. It's a big help, both on safety and sea-lane management. But it makes it a lot easier for the pirates. You can get all this information on the web, so you know precisely which ships are on their way. On top of that, they use dickers in Dubai, and along the coast of Egypt and Eritrea, to keep an eye on vessels going past. They keep tabs on what the cargoes are. The more valuable, the better, obviously enough. Grain isn't worth much. Neither are the cheaper raw materials. But an oil tanker is worth taking. So is a boat full of finished manufactured goods – cars and TVs on their way from Japan or China, that kind of thing. The dickers report back to the pirates, so they have a couple of days' advance warning of a juicy target and can prepare their strike.'

'So how do they get on to the boats?' asked Nick. 'If you've got a height advantage, it should be easy just to shoot down into the bastards.'

The Commodore nodded. 'Easy enough, if you have the right kit. But the maritime organisations don't allow their members to employ armed guards. Makes sense when you think about it. A ship might call in at a dozen ports on its way from Hamburg to Japan. The local police aren't going to be too happy if every cargo boat has half a dozen heavily armed Ukrainian boys on board. They have enough trouble in the bars already. Then they'd have to deal with all the legal fall-out if their guys did get involved in a firefight. The shippers are big commercial organisations. It's not the kind of thing the health and safety monkeys in human resources want to get involved with.'

'So they don't carry weapons?' said Steve. 'That's crazy!'

'It might be, but that's the way it is,' answered Bamfield. 'Plenty of ships are carrying security these days. All the thugs, psychos and chancers who were making out like pigs in the shit out in Iraq have rebranded themselves as maritime security consultants. They'll put four or five guys on a boat, and quite a few of them stash away a few AK-47s in case any rough stuff kicks off. Even unarmed, there's stuff they can do. They rig barbed wire around the deck. And they rustle up a few Molotov cocktails. If the pirates try and come aboard, they lob those across the deck. You try climbing up a moving steel wall with barbed wire and a wall of flame at the top of it.'

'But it doesn't stop all of them?' asked Dan.

'It has a deterrent effect, and it scares off the amateurs, but it doesn't stop the professional pirates.'

'They just ratchet up the violence,' said Ian.

'Precisely,' said the Commodore. 'Put up too much resistance, and they'll start firing RPG rounds into the ship. They don't mind how many people die, and they are perfectly capable of steering the boat back into port if the crew get killed. It's like any fight. Once you start it, you have to be prepared to do whatever it takes to finish it, and most of the shipping companies aren't willing to get into that kind of a scrap.'

Bamfield flashed another picture on the wall. It showed a minor port, with crystal-blue water, bright sunshine, and a dusty road behind it. 'This is Eyl, in Puntland, Somalia. Pirate central. When they attack a boat, they climb on board using grappling hooks, threaten the crew with guns, tie them up, then they steer the ship into the harbour in Eyl, or moor it in one of the dozens of coves running up and down the border. So long as there isn't any trouble, they treat the crew pretty well. These are businessmen, not murderers. A message is sent to the ship's owner, and a ransom demanded. It's usually one to two million dollars, more if there is anything really valuable on board.'

Another picture flashed up on the screen. The same strong, powerful figure Layla had shown them back in Guildford. Ali Yasin.

'This is the man who controls the whole operation.' He's tough, cunning and well-connected. The pirates are plugged into gangster networks in Russia, in Italy, and here in Britain. Yasin is the linchpin, the man who connects the boys in the skiffs to the rest of the world.'

'How are they getting the money?' asked Ollie.

'Forget about choppers dropping in suitcases stuffed with dollars,' said Bamfield. 'This is all done electronically. A middleman in London or Moscow or Milan arranges a discreet bank transfer. And, hey presto, the ship is released.'

'Can't you trace the funds?' asked Ian.

'Believe me, we've tried. A whole team of Special Branch officers have been trying to crack the pirate networks. But Yasin is the key. He knows how it all operates, and that's why we need to bring him in.'

The Commodore's eyes flickered across each man in turn. 'We don't know where he is, and we don't have an easy way of finding him. He moves along the coast, using small boats, and he seldom stays in one place for more than forty-eight hours.'

'But you're going to tell us how to get him?' said Steve.

The man who'd been standing at the Commodore's side stepped forward, speaking for the first time.

'No,' he said, in a crisp French accent. 'I am.' He looked straight at Steve. 'My name is Henri Colbert. And in the morning we will discuss the plan of attack.'

Thirteen

AN HANDED AROUND CUPS OF tea, and the thick cheese sandwiches that had been left behind in the barracks room. 'Where's the vodka?' growled Maksim.

'This is the British Army,' said Ollie stiffly. 'We don't drink on base.'

'In Russia, that's *all* we do,' said Maksim

Steve looked through the window. The rain was still falling heavily, and the wind was whipping through the barracks. The electric heater hardly warmed the room; there was a coal-fired brazier in one corner, but no one had left any fuel. They weren't allowed into the mess, nor the canteen, and they were under strict instructions not to leave the shed. Get a good night's sleep, Ant had told them as he led them back from the briefing. We'll reconvene at seven sharp and start getting this operation planned.

'So who the hell was that French bloke?' asked Nick.

'Commando Hubert, I reckon,' answered Steve. 'They're the men for this job.'

'What the sod is that?' asked Nick.

'The French have the finest special marine forces in the world,' said Steve. 'The boys in this place will tell you it's the SBS, but they are mainly specialists in beach landings, naval intelligence, that kind of thing. When it comes to combat swimming, the French have always been the business. They formed Commando

Hubert in the nineteen fifties, and they fought in Vietnam, in Algeria, and in every other scrap the French have been mixed up with ever since.'

'We came across them a few times in the Pacific,' said Dan. 'Sinking the *Rainbow Warrior* out in New Zealand, that was one of their jobs. Within NATO, and its allies, if there was a job that needed working underwater, then it was always old Jacques and his garlic-munching friends who got the call.'

'He's still a bloody Frog, though, isn't he?' said Ollie. 'I mean they're the damned enemy, aren't they?'

'I'd rather trust them than the sodding British,' said Ian.

'And I've had just about enough of your lip, mate,' snapped Ollie.

He moved swiftly across the floor, his fists raised, as if he was about to punch Ian, but Nick grabbed hold of his arm. Ian had put down his tea, and there was a malevolent look in his eyes: the look of a man who would welcome a punch, and the fight it would inevitably start.

'Drop it,' said Nick, holding Ollie back. 'The Frenchman will be just fine. So long as he knows what he's doing, that's all that counts.'

'This is the Army, mate,' said Steve with a sour chuckle. 'The one thing we can take for granted is that no one knows what they're sodding doing.'

The unit finished their food, and kipped down on the bunks. Steve put his head down and pulled the thin, grey blanket over him to protect himself against the chill in the air. The shed had a corrugated iron roof, and the rain was beating down hard now, creating an incessant rhythm like a drum machine gone crazy.

As he closed his eyes, Steve's mind drifted back more than a dozen years, to a seventeen-year-old getting the bus up from his parents' house in Bromley to the Army Recruiting Office in Lewisham. Twenty minutes later, he'd signed up for the Parachute Regiment, and he walked out with a train ticket that in three days' time would take him away to a new and completely different life. His dad had been furious, his mum had been in tears, and his younger brother – the same brother who now worked in a bank and was the apple of his parents' eye – had just laughed and called him a 'sodding wanker'. But Steve had never regretted it for a minute. Even now. In the background, Maksim was snoring, and the wind was rattling the pane of glass in the window. They were about to be shipped off to the armpit of the universe, facing an uncertain battle against a fierce enemy. And yet, despite that, Steve could feel a contentment that only came over him when he was about to embark on a mission. Maybe Ollie was right, he thought again. We're fighting men, doing what we're made for. That's why we keep doing this. And with that thought he drifted off to sleep.

The rain had stopped by the morning, but there were still heavy clouds hanging over the harbour, and stiff winds blowing across from the Channel. Ant woke them up at six fifty, gave them ten minutes to wash and shave, then led them through to the canteen. The base was already humming with activity, but the six men were led to a separate, isolated table, away from the rest of the troops. A few shot them curious glances, no doubt wondering what six blokes in jeans and sweatshirts were doing in a military canteen, but they were used to having the SBS men mixing with them, and their eyes didn't linger. Henri was already sitting at the table, a croissant, some fruit and a yoghurt in front of him. One of the cooks arrived with a pair of trays, putting down six full English breakfasts. Two sausages, two rashers of bacon, tinned mushrooms warmed up in the microwave, lots of baked beans, and a couple of slices of white bread and margarine, with a big cup of tea next to it.

'Christ, this is crap,' said Nick, taking his first bite of the murky grey sausage on his plate. 'Even worse than the Wetherspoon's one ninety-nine all-day breakfast in Swansea when my mate Darren is doing a shift in the kitchens. I'm bloody glad I didn't join the Regular Army. I don't think I could handle this sodding grub for five years.'

'You're lucky, mate,' said Steve, a smirk playing on his face. 'It could be a growler.'

Out of the corner of his eye, he could see Ollie smiling. The only other bloke here who's done time in the proper Army, thought Steve. He knows what a growler is.

'We'll introduce you to one soon, Nick,' said Steve.

At his side, Ollie was already laughing so hard he was starting to choke.

'What's a bloody growler?' demanded Nick.

'Easy, boy, don't get too excited,' said Ollie.

'I think it's good,' said Maksim. He leant across the table, speared one of Nick's sausages, and swallowed it in one gulp.

'Hey, watch it, that's my sodding grub . . .'

'There's no time for arguing, chaps,' said the Commodore, standing at the head of the table. He nodded towards Henri. 'This man's in charge of you for the next forty-eight hours. I know you are all experienced soldiers, but this is marine combat, and that takes a few special skills. You'll spend two days getting up to speed, then we'll let you know how to get those pirates.' He seemed about to turn away, but then he looked back at the men. 'There's just one thing I want to tell you,' he said, his tone suddenly serious. 'Listen to what Henri says. He spent five years in the regular French Navy, and then five years in Commando Hubert, and they are the finest marine combat troops in the world. Take note of everything he tells you. And remember, if you screw up at sea then it's much more serious than screwing up on land. Because you are going to drown.'

Steve drained the last of his tea. Thanks for reminding us, sir, he thought sourly.

'OK, let's go,' growled Henri.

He was a big man, with piercing eyes, and a no-nonsense manner. He spoke with a thick accent, but his English was good enough.

'Where to?' asked Steve.

'Just follow me. You'll find out.'

As they stepped out of the canteen, the rain was once again falling in thick sheets. Henri ignored it, the same way a duck might, walking straight down to the harbour used by the Marines and the SBS. An open-topped fibreglass speedboat was sitting tied up to a small metal jetty positioned to the left of the main harbour, and next to that were three canoes. Steve recognised them at once from one of the occasional bad-tempered joint exercises held between the SAS and the SBS. The Klepper Aerius II was a two-man collapsible canoe, with a lightweight wooden frame, a canvas and rubber skin, and an aluminium rudder. It could be packed into three bags for easy transport, and could take a payload up to 500 pounds. The canoes had a low silhouette that made it extremely difficult for them to be spotted by enemy observation points, they were quiet, there was no risk of mechanical failure, and they could be transported easily. For marine special forces, they were the perfect way of inserting and extricating troops. So long as you knew how to use them.

'Slightly rough day for a bit of canoeing, isn't it?' said Ollie, glancing up towards Henri. 'I mean, I like to splash about on the lake as much as the next man, but . . .'

'Today is good enough,' grunted Henri.

Ian was looking out into the Channel. Inside the harbour wall, it was calm, but as you looked into the grey horizon there was a lot of white water churning up the sea. 'We'll be OK in the harbour, I reckon.'

Henri took a step closer, so that he was leaning into Ian's face. The rain was beating down but Henri just ignored it. 'We're going to France.'

'France?' spluttered Ollie. 'You're bloody crazy.'

'I need to see what you're made of. And how much work I have to do.'

'In this bloody thing?' Ollie was pointing down at the canoe.

'This is a Klepper,' snapped Henri. 'In nineteen fifty-six, Dr Hannes Lindemann made the first solo crossing of the Atlantic in one of these. The Atlantic. *Solo.* There's going to be two of you in each one, and it's only crossing the Channel. Now get a move on.' He looked at Ollie, a sneer curling his lips. 'Or maybe you're scared, Englishman?'

Ollie's face darkened but he remained silent.

'Let's get a bloody move on,' said Steve. 'The sooner we get moving, the sooner we'll all be sitting down to a nice plate of snails and a big carafe of the vin rouge.'

Fourteen

IT TOOK THEM TWENTY MINUTES just to prepare for the voyage.

As they worked, Steve could feel the rain lashing into him, and the wind blowing hard into his face, and, as much as he tried not to show it, he couldn't help feeling nervous. He'd been on the ferry often enough to know that the Channel could cut up rough when the weather was poor. It could be bad enough with 3000 tonnes of P&O ferry around you. In a canoe . . . *Christ*.

'Staying dry, that's the first thing you have to concentrate on,' said Henri.

Each man was handed a lambswool sweater and, to pull over that, a LIFA thermal top, made by the Norwegian company Helly Hansen, a brand used by the majority of the world's marine special forces. It was light, lasted well, and retained forty times less water than standard polyester. On top of that, they slipped on a windproof coat, with a knife, a whistle, a torch and a compass attached to it.

Next, they had to prepare the canoe. In combat, you'd store your weapons up in the front, but since they weren't actually planning to invade France, they didn't need any munitions. Instead, they packed their personal possessions into a waterproof bergen and secured that to the inside of the Klepper's frame. The seats had been removed, as they were from all the SBS canoes, and in their place was an empty bergen and a roll mat to sit on.

'Right, pair yourselves off,' barked Henri.

Steve glanced around. With the big waves bashing around you, who would you want holding the other paddle? he wondered to himself. Dan for his strength, perhaps. Maksim for his courage, Ian for his guile, Nick for his agility, and Ollie for his dogged perseverance. They were all good men. Ian had already paired up with Nick, and Maksim and Dan were putting their canoe down into the water.

'Looks like you and me, old sausage,' said Ollie, grabbing hold of the Klepper. 'Last one in's a rotten egg.'

'The C team,' grunted Steve. If he were putting money on it, he'd back Maksie and Dan to hit the shore first, and Ian would probably hitch them a ride from a cargo ship. Which leaves us.

Henri had already climbed into the speedboat and was gunning up the engine. 'I'll be keeping a close eye on you, and if you run into real trouble, I'll fish you out,' he said. 'But just keep heading south-south-west and don't overtire yourselves, and you'll be fine.'

Steve jabbed his paddle into the water, pulled back, and steered the Klepper up through the harbour. Maksim and Dan had already kicked off, with Nick and Ian following on behind. Ollie was riding up front, with Steve behind. Ahead of them, Henri had already left the harbour, and was waiting for them in open sea. There was a regular ferry service from Poole to Cherbourg, and that took four and a half hours, but there was no way they were going to make that kind of speed, decided Steve. It was a total of seventy-three miles across the Channel at this point, and the Klepper with two strong men on board was capable of four knots, or five miles an hour. Christ, thought Steve. That's fourteen hours' rowing. If we're lucky.

The first couple of hours weren't too bad. There was some wind blowing across the sea, but they were heading straight into it, which meant it didn't rock the canoe too much, and although it was kicking up some waves, none were higher than two or three feet. Steve kept paddling steadily, holding himself in position with his legs and putting all his upper body strength into the strokes. By the third hour, he reckoned he and Ollie were starting to work up a rhythm, coordinating their strokes so that they squeezed the maximum power out of each one. Dan and Maksim were pulling ahead, a testament to the brute strength of the two men, but they were keeping pace with Nick and Ian. We should be there by nightfall, reckoned Steve. And so long as I have about four days to sleep it off, I might just survive.

By two in the afternoon, he could feel himself starting to flag. They had kicked off at just after eight in the morning, so they'd been going for six hours now. With any luck, they should be hitting halfway soon. The compass showed them keeping a steady enough course, and Henri was in view. A couple of cargo boats had crossed their path, but they hadn't paid any attention to the small craft.

'You OK?' grunted Steve, up towards Ollie.

'I could use some sodding lunch.'

By four, the skies were darkening, and the seas were cutting up rougher. The glimmers of light that had still been evident back in Poole had long since vanished, replaced by a soupy, grey mix of cloud, spray, and heaving water through which it was impossible to see more than fifty yards ahead. The rain was turning from spit to sheets, and the wind was picking up strength. The waves were getting higher and they had more bite to them. Steve could feel them kicking into the hull of the Klepper, and although they were riding straight into them, they were still thumping into the prow of the craft with a relentless force.

'You holding it steady?' Steve shouted up towards Ollie.

Ollie just grunted.

The man wasn't speaking anymore. He'd put his head down, paddling hard into the waves, ignoring everything around him. That was his way of handling everything: get his head down, grit his teeth, and bash on relentlessly. As Steve glanced around, he realised he couldn't see the other canoes anymore. Neither could he see Henri's speedboat. 'Shit,' he muttered under his breath. We're alone out here.

He checked the compass.

They were holding a true enough course, south to south-west, and despite the weather they were making a decent enough clip. The wind was blowing in from the French coast, and so long as they could head straight into it, the waters were navigable. Any change in direction, thought Steve, and we're in real trouble.

By eight, the last of the light had vanished. The rain was still beating into them, and the waves were rough. Visibility was down to a yard, sometimes two. All they could see was the churning flecks of the waves, and they had only the compass to give them any sense of movement or progress. They'd been rowing for at least twelve hours now. Steve felt as if every muscle in his arms, neck, and torso was about to break. The tendons were stretched thin, and even the bones seemed to be creaking. The water kept shipping on to them, and even through the waterproofs, his legs felt damp, cold and exhausted. There was a numbness in his feet, and a throbbing inside his head.

Ollie paused. He held his paddle to the water, trying to steady the Klepper as it was rocked violently from side to side in the churning seas. He looked round slowly at Steve, his blue eyes suddenly bright, lighting up like a fox's on a dark country road at night.

'Bugger this, mate,' he growled. 'This is sodding ridiculous.'

'Well, if you see a taxi, let's hail it,' said Steve.

Ollie took a deep breath.

Steve reached across and thumped him on the shoulder. The Klepper was rocking in the waves, and the wind was whipping through them, shifting direction, so that it was coming in from the north. Steve checked the compass. They had to change course, so they were tacking straight into the wind. Let it come in from the side, and it would knock the canoe straight over. That meant it was going to take even longer to reach the shore. Somewhere on the far horizon, he could see the dim lights of a cargo ship. They had a couple of flares tucked beside the bergens they were sitting on. If the worst came to the worst, they could always send out a distress signal.

Except for one thing. It would be humiliating.

'Crack on, mate,' he said. 'It's only a couple more hours. We don't want that French bastard thinking we can't do this.'

Steve dug his paddle into the water and the Klepper started to move forwards. And as Ollie grunted once, then twice, then joined in, they picked up a steady rhythm again, crashing through the swell and the darkness as they ploughed closer to their destination.

Another hour passed. Then ninety minutes. Steve was keeping his head down, focused only on the task. Occasionally his mind flitted back to the selection course for the SAS: a week tramping through the Brecon Beacons, with no food, no proper shelter, and only the relentless, unending exhaustion to keep you occupied. He'd thought that was tough at the time. But he'd swap places instantly if offered the chance. At least we were on dry land, he reflected to himself as he fought back the tiredness.

The wave struck unexpectedly.

They were adjusting their course all the time, but the wind was still shifting, reshaping the pattern of the waves as it did so. Steve could feel it lifting them unexpectedly, felt a surge as the heaving swell of white water pushed them up into the driving rain, then felt a cold, ugly spasm of fear as he realised that even the stable Klepper wasn't going to hold itself upright against a blow of that force. In the next second, his head was plunged deep into the salty, ice-cold water. He slammed his mouth shut, protecting his lungs from the sea. The wave was washing them sideways, dragging the canoe forwards. Steve was already struggling with his strap, freeing himself from the hull. He dropped into the sea as he sprang loose, then desperately pushed a hand upwards, grabbing hold of the canoe with his right hand. Opening his eyes, he looked around for

Ollie, but in the dark water he could see no sign of him. Sod that French bastard, he told himself grimly. *If we die here . . .*

Kicking back with his legs, he pushed himself through the water, just in time for a wave to break straight over him. Still holding on to the hull of the Klepper, he looked feverishly around, until suddenly Ollie broke to the surface, spitting white foam from his mouth. He was ten yards away. Steve pushed forward, steering the prow of the upturned canoe towards him until he grabbed hold of it.

'What the fuck do we do now?' shouted Ollie above the din of the waves.

'Get her upright,' said Steve.

It was easy to say, he reflected, hard to achieve. Even in calm water, righting a Klepper took skill, experience and practice. In rough seas, it could prove impossible. He grabbed the side of the hull, dragging backwards with all his strength, and yelling at Ollie to do the same, but each time they managed to break it free of the swirling water, the waves knocked it straight back again. There was nothing to grip on to, nothing to lever it against, and as the fifth, then the sixth attempt failed, Steve could feel his spirits sinking.

'This is sodding useless,' he shouted.

Ollie nodded just once.

Steve knew precisely what he meant.

There was no point in dying here.

Steve reached inside the boat, ripped the bergen free and dragged out the flare gun. He held himself steady, then shot the missile up into the sky. There was a delay of a second, then the flare burst open, a crescendo of white, hot light suddenly breaking through the rain and wind.

They waited, counting the seconds.

Ten, fifteen . . .

They were holding on to the Klepper, using it to stay afloat, but they were wet through, and Steve reckoned that in water this cold they wouldn't have more than half an hour before they started to lose consciousness.

'So where is that French bugger?' growled Ollie.

'Probably pissed off for a pint of Kronenbourg.'

'What did I tell you? You can't trust the fuckers.'

Steve was worrying about the second flare. There was one more in the Bergen, but he wanted to hold on to that if he could. If Henri hadn't seen the first one, it would be their one remaining hope of getting picked up. The Channel was the busiest shipping lane in the world, he reminded himself. *Someone must see it . . .*

The water was chilling his bones. The Klepper was bobbing on the rough waves, and it took all Steve's strength just to keep hold of it. His arms were already aching, now they were being stretched every time the waters pulled him downwards. His lungs were as sodden as his clothes and his eyes were stinging from the salt water constantly washing over him.

The speedboat broke through the darkness, a hi-beam flashing across the waves until it settled on the Klepper. Henri was standing at the wheel. He slowed the engine and tossed out a lifeline. It was five yards in front of them. Steve swam desperately towards it, waiting for Ollie to grab hold of it as well, then he clung on as Henri hauled the line back in towards the boat. Steve reached up for the hull, kicked back with his legs to propel himself out of the water, then grabbed hold of the side railing, using the last remaining strength left in his shoulders to lever himself on to the deck. He lay still for a moment, panting for breath, letting the water drain off him.

Slowly he stood up, looking around the speedboat. Henri secured the upturned Klepper with a grappling hook, and, with the canoe in tow, started steering back towards the shore.

There was no one else on board.

Either the others have made it, Steve decided, or else they are dead.

'You should have steered straight into the waves,' said Henri, still gripping the wheel as the speedboat bounced into the waves, but glancing sideways at Steve and Ollie. 'Then you'd have been OK.'

Steve stepped behind the wheel. The boat was open-topped, but with the wind driving the rain in sideways, its window offered some protection. 'That's what we were doing,' he said sourly. 'It was bloody hard out there.'

'The others made it.'

Steve remained silent.

Henri's eyes were still on him.

'You failed,' he said curtly.

Steve stifled the urge to punch the man. He'd failed at plenty of things in his life. Exams mostly, even if that was because he'd been bunking off school. But they hadn't been things he cared about. When he'd joined the Army, he realised he'd finally found something he was good at. Endurance, stamina, fighting. Those were his skills, and he'd never been found wanting when they'd been put to the test.

Until tonight.

'Just get us to the sodding beach,' snapped Ollie.

Steve leant back exhausted against the side of the boat. He was wet through and shivering, and his spirits were down. The boat was crashing through the waves. Within a couple of minutes, he could see the lights of Cherbourg off to the left, but Henri was steering them east of it. We weren't far, Steve thought bitterly. Another hour or so and we'd have made it.

'Here,' said Henri. He'd already dropped the anchor.

The boat was moored in a small cove, with jagged rocks at both sides, and a small pebbled beach. The seas dropped within the inlet, and although the wind was still blowing hard, it wasn't cutting up the water. Henri jumped straight in and started wading towards the shore.

'Looks like we've arrived,' said Ollie.

He jumped down, and Steve followed swiftly behind him. A

flashlight was beaming from the beach, and on the wind Steve could hear Dan and Ian laughing. At me? he wondered. I sodding hope not.

'We made you a nice hot cup of Bovril,' said Ian, handing a warm mug across.

Steve grinned. He took the hot cup in his hand, cradling it close and letting its warmth flood through him, whilst the beefy smell of the drink slowly revived him. He didn't much care for Bovril, but just at this moment it was about the most welcome drink he'd ever had.

'Any chance of a Pot Noodle?' he asked.

'Funny,' said Nick. 'That's just what I was saying. I could murder a Bombay Bad Boy. All we've got is this crap Bovril.'

'So what kept you, boys?' said Dan.

Ollie just shrugged. 'A wave . . .'

Behind him, Henri was shaking his head.

'Dan and Maksim were good,' he said. 'Ian and Nick I can work with . . .' He paused, looking towards Steve and Ollie. 'But as the English put it, you were shit.'

'It was bloody rough,' snapped Steve.

'For the Channel, that was nothing.'

'I was SAS . . .'

'And I was Household Cavalry,' added Ollie belligerently.

'Was, was, was,' growled Henri. 'Right now, you're a couple of raw recruits who aren't making the grade. We've got three days to get you into the kind of shape where you might just be able to take on the pirates and live for more than five minutes.' He chuckled to himself, wiping the rainwater out of his face. 'And let me tell you something. By the time those three days are over, you're really going to hate the French.'

Fifteen

STEVE STEADIED HIMSELF ON THE prow of the dinghy.
His legs were swaying from the combined force of the waves and the wind buffeting the small craft, and he had to keep adjusting his position to hold his balance. He raised the Bushmaster Leupold to his right eye, lining up the night-vision goggles strapped across his face to its telescopic sights. The Bushmaster was a decent enough gun: a lightweight high-precision rifle, semi-automatic, manufactured from aircraft-quality aluminium for strength and durability. American-made, it was the kind of weapon you could pick up at any decent hunting supplier. Six aren't taking any chances, noted Steve when it had been handed to him; if anything goes wrong while we're out here training – and since we're using live rounds, plenty could – then they don't want us carrying any kit that can trace us back to Britain.

'Fire,' barked Henri.

Steve steadied his shoulder, concentrating on the target. The dinghy was bobbing in rough water, half a mile off the coast of Brittany. It was close to midnight, and the sea was pitching hard as the winds blew in from the east.

'I said fire,' repeated Henri.

The target was standing on the deck of the boat thirty yards away: three old tyres roped together with a life jacket slung over the top to make it look like a person. A gust of wind whipped into the side of the dinghy, but Steve ignored it, squeezing the trigger.

The retort of the Bushmaster rattled through the night air.

Steve looked through the blurred, green haze of the goggles. Missed.

'Crap,' spat Henri. 'Listen, if there are pirates you need to attack, they are going to have lookouts posted on the skiff. You'll need to take down any men on the deck before you try and board. You're only going to get one shot, so you have to make it count.'

He turned towards Nick.

'Fire,' he said curtly.

Nick took a moment to line up his Bushmaster. The wind was dropping. 'Kill,' muttered Nick, squeezing the trigger.

A piece of plastic spat out of the life jacket as the bullet ripped into it.

Henri glared at Steve. 'We'll keep practising until you get it right.'

It took another hour. Steve had plenty of experience as a marksman, but only on dry land. At sea, your brain had to process a whole new set of calculations, compensating for the movement of the boat beneath you as well as for the way your target would shift around on the waves. It wasn't impossible, but it had to be hard-wired into your brain until it became an instinct. Nick could do it automatically, but then the Welsh boy had a gift with guns. Steve had to relearn everything he knew about shooting.

It was two in the morning by the time they made it back to the pair of tin huts where they were staying for the next two days. From the landing near Cherbourg, they had been driven two hours down the coast, to an old abandoned Commando Hubert base that was now used by Henri's PMC contacts for training its men. They'd been allowed to sleep for a few hours, then they'd been taken for their first drill of the day: a ten-mile run across the beaches, then a five-mile swim. After that, they'd been introduced to their instructors, a pair of former Hubert commandos called Jacques and Jean-Paul. Both of them were in their early forties, fit and strong, with a manner that Steve reckoned would leave even an SAS sergeant wondering if he wasn't being a bit soft with his men.

As he struggled back into the hut, Steve threw himself down on the iron cot and went straight to sleep. He didn't reckon he'd been this tired in his life before.

They were woken at six sharp, and given ten minutes to wash and dress whilst Jacques handed around bowls of steaming hot black coffee and hot, fresh baguettes with jars of strawberry jam to spread across them.

'Any chance of a nice cuppa?' said Ollie, grinning. 'We're English, you know. We drink tea in the morning. With milk in it.'

'If you start passing a few tests, maybe we'll let you have some,' said Henri, chortling.

He started to run through the drill for the day.

For the morning, Jean-Paul was going to take them to a seawater pool used by French commandos five miles away. There they would be taught the basics of 'drown-proofing': both their hands and their feet would be bound, and they'd be taught how to swim for at least ten minutes with nothing but body motion to keep them afloat. Next, they'd spend the afternoon on 'cold-water conditioning'. Even out in the Gulf, he explained, the water would never get above fifteen or sixteen degrees, and they needed to acclimatise the body to long periods at those low temperatures. They had to get used to withstanding the water for hours at a time, and the only way they were going to do that was by spending as many hours as possible naked with the rough waves of the English Channel washing over them.

'And then tonight,' said Henri with a grin, 'we'll show you how to get on board a boat. And that's where the fun will start.'

By the time they were back out at sea, Steve was already wet through and exhausted. But he was starting to get to grips with the training. He'd survived the swimming exercises, and even the cold-water conditioning hadn't been too bad. It was hard and brutal, the same way his first few weeks in the SAS had been, but there was one thing he'd learnt when he'd moved from the training camps to live combat, and he'd never forgotten it. No matter how bad the training was, it wasn't ever as bad as finding yourself facing a determined enemy intent on killing you and not knowing how the hell you were going to deal with him. And that was what made the training worthwhile.

There were some much-needed steak sandwiches for supper, then they were back out at sea again. Jacques had run through the basics of storming a boat. The pirates lived on the water, and the chances were they'd have to hit them on their own territory. Go in at night, he explained. Wear thick black wetsuits, and black up your faces with boot polish. That way they won't be able to see you. They'll still be able to hear you, however. 'So this is what you do,' Henri explained. 'Use a plastic inflatable dinghy, and kill the engine at least one hundred metres from the target. Use night-vision goggles. Then use your paddle to approach the boat directly from the rear. The engines will be kicking up so much noise, that's the blind spot. They won't see you coming and they won't hear you either. Use a grappling hook, lever yourself up to the edge, and rush on board. You'll have about three seconds to kill everyone before they have a chance to reorganise and hit back.'

It looked fine on the drawing board. It was a lot harder when you had real waves around.

Steve was sitting at the side of the dinghy, alongside Ollie. It was one in the morning, and although the waters weren't as rough as they'd been last night, there was still enough swell to make holding any kind of balance a real challenge. Dan was proving the best sailor among them, so he was at the back controlling the outboard motor, with Maksim sat alongside him holding the grappling hook. Ian and Nick were directly opposite Steve, using their weight to balance the small craft. The dinghy was bouncing like a Frisbee across the surface of the sea, and there was some fog coming down, but eventually Steve could make out a rough grey shape through his night-vision goggles. Jean-Paul had organised a fishing tug for them to practise on, and that was their target. A hundred metres, reckoned Steve.

'Kill the engine,' he hissed. 'We're close enough.'

Steve slashed his paddle into the water, and started to pull forwards. The rest of the men did the same and the dinghy moved quietly into the tug's slipstream. Dan was steering them straight into the churning water cut up by its propellers. White foam was starting to splash up all around them, the salt spitting into Steve's lips, leaving his mouth dry. The dinghy moved relentlessly forward.

'Steady her, steady her,' called Maksim from the prow.

Steve watched as the Russian slung the hook forward. He'd watched him make that move fifty times during the afternoon, but that was on dry land, just practising, and it was difficult enough then. All four men were holding their paddles straight, trying to balance the dinghy. The hook hit the stern of the boat, and Maksim instantly started reeling them in, dragging them hard into the water churned up by its engines. 'Get ready to board her,' he yelled into the wind.

All five men stood up. Suddenly a wave rocked over them, its power amplified by the swirl of the engines. It rolled across the dinghy, knocking into Nick's side, and suddenly he was falling, collapsing straight into Steve, knocking him off balance and plunging him hard into the icy water. Steve could feel himself falling. Five feet, then ten he dipped downwards. He could feel the pull of the propellers tugging him towards them, and his brain snapped into action. Propellers will drag you into their blades, Henri had warned them. And then chew you up like the grass in a lawnmower. Steve kicked away hard, putting all his strength into the strokes, until he broke through the surface, ten yards back from where he'd fallen. He ripped off his night-vision goggles and looked around.

'Christ,' he muttered.

The dinghy had capsized. And all six men were in the water.

'I hope the fate of the world doesn't rely on you lot,' said Henri as he pulled the last man out of the water. 'Because if it does, we're all in deep trouble.'

'We can keep practising until we get it right,' said Steve tersely.

'There's no time,' said Henri. 'We only have one more day.'

The final sessions were taken up with the basic tradecraft of marine combat. The instructors taught them how to pierce holes in their boots so that they wouldn't drag them down if they were plunged into the water with their footwear still on. They were shown how to put on waterproof body armour, and how to turn water bottles into makeshift life jackets by emptying them and tying them to their ankles and wrists. Ian was shown how to blow up a boat from underwater. A sock of C-4 plastic explosive was attached by a swimmer to the hull of a vessel encased within a waterproof cover. Into the base of the sock you drilled a blasting cap, and on to that an M-60 underwater fuse igniter, a device that encased the fuse inside a plastic tube and gave the diver at least three minutes to get clear of the boat before the explosive blew a hole in its side.

'It's a shame our mates in Libya never gave us any of these back in the IRA,' said Ian with a shake of the head as the technique was explained. 'We could have blown up a couple of Navy ships. Now that would have been quite something.'

The rest of the men were drilled in what kit would work underwater, how to keep their guns and ammunition dry, and how to pack body armour over waterproof clothes.

'We've trained,' Henri announced eventually. 'And since this is France, now we eat.'

An hour later, they were sitting at a small table at a restaurant in the village of Landemer, looking out over the coast. It was a Tuesday night, and there wasn't much trade. The proprietor turned out to be a cousin of Jacques, and was pleased to suddenly have nine paying customers filling a pair of his tables.

'Try these escargots, Nick,' said Henri as he tried to explain the menu.

'What's that then?'

'It's a kind of small sausage, Nick, but it comes in a shell,' said Ian.

Steve and Ollie both laughed.

'Sounds OK,' said Nick. 'I like sausages. Me mum always makes those for me.'

'Double escargots for the boy, then,' said Steve. 'And the rest of us will have the smoked salmon followed by the steak frites. And plenty of bottles of the red.'

'I don't suppose there's any chance of getting some Stella,' said Nick. 'I don't fancy any sodding French lager.'

Ollie looked across the table. 'Nick, Stella *is* French lager.'

'You're kidding? I thought it came from Luton.'

'Actually, it's from Belgium originally,' said Henri.

Nick shook his head. 'I've been drinking sodding French lager all these years. Well, well . . . I'm right posh, I am.'

'Belgian lager,' repeated Henri. 'Not French . . .'

'Who cares?' said Maksim. 'So long as you can drink it.'

'We'll stock some in the bar,' said Dan. 'Especially for when Nick and the Swansea Patrol come and stay.'

'We'll be there,' said Nick. 'Straight off the EasyJet flight from Cardiff.'

The waiter put down a round of beers, and a couple of carafes of the house red.

'To Dan's Beer Bar,' said Steve, raising a beer glass and taking a swig of the lager. It was the first drink he'd had in days, and with his muscles still aching from the toughness of the training, it felt about as good as any beer he'd ever sunk. 'Once this job is done, we'll go straight back for a right proper piss-up.'

All the men cheered, raising their glasses.

'Maybe Nick's mum will have got the lap dancing organised,' said Dan. 'Beer, sunshine, girls . . .'

'Good to see you've got your priorities straight,' said Ian.

Steve tucked into a side of smoked salmon before glancing across at Nick's starter.

'Bloody funny place to hide a sausage,' said Nick, looking at it suspiciously.

'Just get it down your throat, mate,' guffawed Ollie.

'Not bad,' said Nick. 'Sort of chewy, a bit like the Breakfast McMuffin.' He popped a second one into his mouth. 'Not bad at all.'

'Nick, it's a snail,' said Ollie.

Everyone was laughing, even Henri.

'A snail? Who the fuck eats snails?'

'The French,' laughed Henri, slapping him on the back.

'Well, they're not bad,' said Nick. 'I might order them again.'

'Blimey,' said Steve, with a shake of the head. 'Nick's turning into a gourmet. We'll make sure we bring along a Jamie Oliver book on our next job.'

By the time the steak and chips finally arrived, several rounds of the beer had been finished off, along with a few carafes of the red wine. Maksim's head was rolling from side to side drunkenly, Dan was listing all the different beers he wanted to stock in the bar, Ollie was still laughing over the escargot joke, even though Steve reckoned it had fallen a bit flat, and Ian was discussing improvised incendiary devices with Jean-Paul, whilst Jacques was impressing Nick with stories from the five years he'd spent in the French Foreign Legion.

'We'll miss you, Henri,' said Ollie when the last of the food was cleared away. 'You're as good a man as any in the British Army.' He raised his glass. 'To Henri.'

But Henri's glass stayed in his hand.

'No need for toasts, guys,' he said, his tone turning serious. 'I'm coming with you.'

Steve was caught with half a glass of red down his throat and struggled to stop himself spitting it back up all over the table.

'This unit fights its own way,' he said. 'And we fight with the men we know and trust.'

Henri glanced towards him, a sharp look in his eye. 'The lady already told you the score,' he said. 'I'm the leader of this mission.'

'The leader?' spat Steve. 'We fight by Regiment rules, pal. No leaders, just men.'

Henri chuckled, nursing his wine glass in his fists. 'That may be fine on dry land. At sea, you need captains. That's the way it's always been and will always remain.'

'There's no leaders,' snapped Steve.

Henri leant forward. 'Listen, Englishman,' he growled, his tone suddenly deepening. 'This unit isn't in any shape to take on pirates without some experienced muscle in charge. And you know who that's most true of? You.'

Steve stood up angrily. He drew his fist back and started to wing a punch towards Henri, but before he could deliver the blow, Dan had grabbed hold of him, using his massive strength to restrain him. Ollie stood up, holding Steve back. 'Leave it,' he snapped

At the table, Henri remained completely still. But he was looking up at Steve with a crooked half-smile. 'I should have left you to drown in *la Manche*.'

Sixteen

L AYLA'S HAIR WAS BLOWING HARD in the wind from the powerful rotors of the Eurocopter EC225. She'd wrapped a scarf round her neck, and was wearing a green waterproof jacket to protect her against the light rain blowing in off the Channel.

'Good morning, gentlemen,' she said, shouting to make herself heard above the din of the engine. 'I hope you enjoyed your training.'

'If you like being shouted at by some mad French bastards,' said Steve grumpily.

'And half-drowned,' added Ian.

'Not to mention being tied up and tossed into a freezing cold sea pool,' said Ollie.

'Or being sucked up by the propellers of a tug boat in rough seas,' said Dan.

'Still, the grub was bloody good,' said Nick. He flashed Layla a broad grin. 'Snails. Ever tried them? Sodding great.'

'I believe I have, yes,' said Layla, looking slightly puzzled.

'I'm getting me mum to cook some. Make a change from the McCain's oven chips.'

'You mean Sandra does chips as well as lap dancing?' said Ollie. 'I think I'm in love.'

'Bloody leave it,' snapped Nick. 'She's giving up the dancing.'

Steve led the way up to the Eurocopter. The EC225 was a big, dignified chopper designed for passenger transport, which could hold up to twenty-four people along with two crew and the pilot. It was used by rescue services, as well as for short-haul business flights. He sat back in one of the seats, and snapped the safety belt into place. It was just after seven in the morning. His head was still aching from the amount of wine and beer they'd downed last night, his muscles were still sore from the training regime of the last three days, and his mind was still buzzing from the confrontation with Henri. The way it felt now, the job could only get better. But somehow he wasn't feeling optimistic it would.

'Where the hell are we going now?' asked Steve, looking across at Layla.

'Paris,' said Layla. 'Then we're connecting on to a flight to Croatia. You'll be getting your final briefing there.'

'And Henri? Whose idea was it to put him on the team?'

'Mine,' said Layla flatly. 'You boys are tough and resourceful, but this is sea fighting, and none of you have trained for that.'

'And what do you know about combat, exactly? We're six blokes who are all mates. We know each other's strengths and weaknesses and we'll pull together. Put a stranger into the mix and it all starts to fall apart.'

By the time he'd finished the sentence the engine had roared into life and the Eurocopter was pulling up into the sky. It might be a passenger machine, and it didn't make the deafening roar of the military helicopters Steve was used to, but it was still a struggle to make himself heard over the racket.

'What's this about, Steve? *You* being in charge?'

Steve remained silent.

'He's on the team, and that's final. You need him.'

It was only a forty-minute hop up to Charles de Gaulle Airport. The Eurocopter dropped them down at the back of the main terminal building, then Layla led them into the transfer hall. They were booked on to the eleven ten Air France flight to Split, down on the southern Croatian coast. It seemed Layla had secured the cooperation of the Direction Générale de la Sécurité Extérieure, or DGSE, the French equivalent of MI6, because they were whisked straight through security and on to the waiting plane without anyone asking for their passports.

'Interesting,' noted Ian to Steve, as the DGSE official took them through security clearance. 'The DGSE don't usually co-operate with anyone, and certainly not MI6. They must want this Yasin guy pretty bad.'

'If I'd known we weren't going through a scanner, I'd have brought a gun,' said Dan. 'We could hijack the plane and get the hell out of here.'

It was a short, two-hour flight. Steve flicked through the in-flight magazine, ate the whole of the meal to help cure his hangover, then dozed off for an hour. At least the training is over, he thought to himself as he closed his eyes. Now we can crack on.

At Split airport they were met by Ant and Dec, along with a minibus to drive them down to the coast. As soon as the bus turned south of the airport and started driving along the main road that led down the Adriatic coast, Steve had a pretty good idea where they were heading.

'Peljesac,' said Ollie at his side.

Steve nodded. 'Makes sense.'

During the Bosnian war, a NATO base had been built on the peninsula of Peljesac, close to the southern tip of Croatia where it bordered war-torn Bosnia. It was a naval base, designed to keep control of weapons run into and out of the country, but it was also used as a staging post for NATO special forces being inserted into the region. Steve had been there three times during his time in the Regiment. So had Ollie, whilst serving in the Household Cavalry. It wasn't much of a secret to anyone in the military, but the existence of the base, on the far side of a peninsula that was largely deserted, was never officially confirmed. For a job that was off the books, Peljesac was precisely the kind of place Six would use.

Discreet, decided Steve. And, if necessary, deniable.

It was four by the time they checked into the hotel in Ston, the only town of any significance on the peninsula. It was a simple mid-market place, catering to the cheaper end of the package tour market, but only a third full at this time of year. Each man had his own room.

'R and R tonight, chaps,' said Ant, after he'd checked them in. 'We'll pick you up at seven tomorrow morning, and that's when this mission starts for real.'

'Get some fun in now, lads, because you won't be having any more for a while,' added Dec.

'But no hangovers in the morning,' said Ant sternly. 'And if any of you get arrested, this time we're leaving you to rot in jail.'

Ston was typical of Croatia's Adriatic towns. Cobbled streets lined with whitewashed houses with red slate roofs banked down to a small port. At its centre was a small square, with a fountain, some restaurants and bars, and a few shops. It was pretty enough, but there were plenty more spectacular towns only a few miles further up the coast, which explained why it didn't get many visitors.

'Right, lads, your first job is to research the Croatian beers for my bar,' said Dan as they left the hotel. 'Anyone who finds a good one gets a free lap dance from Nick's mum.'

'And a sodding kicking from me,' growled Nick. 'I'm fed up with jokes about me mum.'

'And your second task is to find a girlfriend for Nick here,' said Dan, slapping the Welsh boy on the back. 'A nice Croatian girl. We need to calm him down a bit.'

Ian looked around. 'It's pretty much the back of beyond,' he said. 'But surely the girls aren't that desperate.'

They kicked off at the café on the square. The weather was far better than it had been back in Britain: there was some hazy, late-autumn sunshine, and a mellow sunset streaking the sea and hills with a brilliant orange light. They were just settling into the second round of beers before finding a restaurant desperate enough for business that it didn't mind taking a rowdy bunch of mercenaries when Steve got a message on his mobile. 'We should talk, alone,' it said. 'Meet me at the Kapetanova Restaurant in half an hour.'

He paused for a moment before replying.

Layla? Alone?

Why?

Then another thought flashed through his mind.

Why the hell not? It's no worse than an evening watching these boys get the worse for beer once again. And watching them trying to find a girlfriend for Nick could quickly turn into a desperate affair. He'd seen the Welsh lad trying to talk to some girls at the South African mansion of the billionaire who hired them for their last job, and he'd seen Regimental ties less tightly tied than Nick's tongue when he was standing in front of a woman.

'I'm getting an early night, boys,' said Steve, as Dan organised them to move on to the second bar of the evening. 'My head's done in.'

'You're getting old, mate,' said Dan.

'Maybe,' said Steve, slipping away before anyone could try to dissuade him.

Half an hour later he'd showered, washed his hair, put on a fresh shirt, and was sitting opposite a single candle at a table overlooking the sea.

'I had a feeling you'd scrub up OK,' said Layla, sitting down opposite him.

'And so do you.'

It was just banter, but this time it also happened to be true.

She'd changed into a white cotton dress, through which he could see the outline of matching black bra and panties. There was a twirl of lace around the bra, where it cupped her breasts, and in the fading autumnal light it was plainly visible through the thin fabric. She was wearing a purple shawl that just covered her shoulders, her hair was tied back in a bow, and there was a single row of pearls round her neck.

'I'm doing you a favour, Steve,' she said.

Steve took a sip of the red wine. He'd had more than enough to drink last night, but what the hell. Tomorrow he'd be plunged into the most brutal fight of his life, with no way of knowing whether he'd get out of the scrap alive. Another bottle wouldn't hurt.

'For shipping me out to fight the maddest bastards on the high seas? I'll try and return that favour one day. Maybe put you into a ring with a couple of sumo wrestlers.'

Layla looked at the waiter hovering at their side, ordered the soup of the day and some grilled fish for both of them, then looked back at Steve. 'For showing you the way back to who you really are,' she said, putting the menu aside. 'For allowing you to be a warrior.'

That smile again, he noted. But different this time. There was a softness to it. Flirtatious? Maybe. He couldn't yet be sure. But she certainly seemed to care for him. This wasn't just work.

They talked casually for the next couple of hours, the time flying by. The wine was finished, and Steve had hardly noticed the food, but that was gone as well. She had a way of talking to him that Steve found rare in a woman. She understood what made men fight, why they were compelled to march towards the next battle, and she didn't criticise him for it. There was a connection there, he felt certain of it. He'd found that with Sam as well. But he'd lost her forever, and that level of understanding from a woman was something he hadn't imagined he'd ever be able to find again.

'You said you needed to talk,' said Steve finally, as they finished the coffee. 'So what was it?'

'This mission depends on you, Steve,' she said.

'There's six of us. Seven if you count the French tosser. But we've yet to see how the bastard shapes up when the sound of real gunfire is close by.'

'But you're the leader.'

'Henri reckons it's him,' said Steve firmly. 'But really there are no leaders. Just blokes fighting for each other.'

Layla shook her head. 'You're the one who holds it all together,' she said. 'Ollie's just a big kid. Nick is only a boy. Maksim is a madman. Dan wouldn't be here at all except he doesn't want to let his mates down. And Ian is just playing the angles, figuring out what he needs to do to survive in a world that doesn't like him very much. It's you, Steve, that's the gravity, the force that keeps the whole thing in orbit.'

'I just want to get it done, and get home.'

'But there could be a future for you in this, Steve. The Shadow Force is real, a black ops team that works for the whole of Nato—'

'One job, that's all I've signed up for,' interrupted Steve. 'And then I'm done.'

'We'll see.'

Layla stood up, and wrapped the shawl round herself. 'Walk me home,' she said.

They started to walk through the streets. There was still some warmth in the evening. Her arm slipped into his as they strolled along the seafront.

'That's what I like about you Regiment boys,' said Layla. 'A girl always feel safe.'

Layla was staying at a different hotel, a place with at least two more stars than the one they'd booked the men into, noted Steve.

They walked into the hotel together as if it was the most natural thing in the world. Layla collected her key from the desk, and then nodded towards the lift. He followed her, as if dragged forward by her scent alone, up to the first floor, then waited as she pushed open the door. It was her lips that she wrapped round him first, the red wine still evident on her tongue as she flicked it across his face. Then her arms, then her legs. Within moments, Steve had pushed her down on to the bed and pulled up the white cotton dress so that it was scrunched messily around her shoulders and arms. He buried his face into her bra and knickers.

'Fast, make it fast,' she muttered huskily. 'Don't make me wait.'

Steve unbuckled his trousers. She grabbed hold of his torso, flicking her tongue up to his chest and nipples, biting hard so that her teeth stung his skin, then caressing each tiny delicate wound. He lay on top of her, pushing hard inside her, whilst she started to writhe and moan.

'Faster,' she hissed again. 'I told you not to make me wait.'

Within minutes, she was lying across his arms, her passion spent, a sleepy cat-like smile of sensual satisfaction playing across the smudged lipstick on her face. Steve could feel her sweat mixing with his, and he could feel his muscles ache, but this time it was a pleasant, mellow ache not the brutal, harsh pain of training.

'Perfect,' purred Layla. 'There's only one thing I'd change.'

'What's that?' asked Steve.

'Next time I want you to fuck me on the beach.'

'I'm sure it can be arranged,' said Steve with a broad grin.

Back at the bar, the beers were still flowing. Dan had organised dinner, but no one had rated the Croatian food very highly.

'I haven't tasted crap like this since I left Sherborne,' said Ollie. He prodded at one of the dumplings in his veal stew with the end of his fork.

'You need to get back to Sandra's cooking,' smirked Ian.

'And not just the cooking,' grinned Ollie.

'What the fuck does that mean?' demanded Nick.

'Nothing, lad, nothing,' said Ollie quickly, before kicking off an extended discussion about whether Andrew Flintoff or Mike Atherton had been a better captain of the England cricket team. But Nick wouldn't let it go. They moved on to another bar, sank a couple more beers, asked a taxi driver to take them to a nightclub but ended up in a dismal strip club where a single dance from an ageing stripper cost a hundred euros, then wound up in the same bar where they'd started, mixing vodka, rum and beer in equal measures. And at each stage, a sullen, drunker and drunker Nick kept asking Ollie questions about what he'd been up to back at Dan's bar, and where he'd slept.

'Why don't you just tell him you shagged his mum?' said Dan eventually.

'And no shame in that, we'd all shag her if we got the chance,' said Ian drunkenly.

'Maybe we will,' chipped in Henri. 'If she'll sleep with Ollie, she can't be too fussy.'

'I'd shag my own mother,' grunted Maksim. 'And her sister . . .'

'You fucking tosser,' shouted Nick.

His face was red and there was a raw anger in his voice. He grabbed hold of Ollie's shoulders and hurled him with an unexpected ferocity through the doors of the bar and out into the cobbled courtyard. Ollie staggered backwards. He was a strong man, but he was also a ferocious drinker, and he'd put the equivalent of a bottle of hard spirits down his throat in the last couple of hours. Even Ollie, with all his experience of drinking too much and getting into fights in mess halls, didn't have the stamina to hold out against Nick with that much alcohol swilling around his bloodstream. He wobbled, snagged his heel on the ground, and crashed hard into the cobblestones. 'Fucking fuck it,' he shouted as he hit the ground. Nick was on him in a flash, jumping on to his back, putting a series of brutally hard punches straight into his torso. Ollie kicked back ferociously, catching Nick's shoulder with the side of his boot, sending him reeling backwards. Ollie got unsteadily to his feet. 'Come on, you fucking taffy peasant,' he growled. 'It's time you had a lesson in proper fighting.'

Ian and Dan and Maksim watched grim-faced. Ollie deserved a few punches, none of them would dispute that. But they needed both blokes to be fighting fit in the morning, and once they got stuck into each other, it didn't look like either man would stop until one or possibly both of them were hospitalised.

'It's not really on to shag a mate's mum, is it?' said Dan, glancing across at Ian. 'I mean, not after you've left school.'

'Never a problem I've really had to contend with,' said Ian. 'Not the kind of thing that happens in Belfast. Too sodding cold.'

'We'd better not let them kill each other, though,' said Dan. He nodded towards Maksim. 'I think we better step in,' he said quietly.

'I was just starting to enjoy it,' said Maksim ruefully. 'Shall we give them a few more minutes?'

'We could bet,' said Ian. 'My money's on Nick . . .'

'Better break 'em up,' said Dan. 'Otherwise we'll be starting this mission by ourselves.'

He stepped forward and grabbed Ollie by the shoulders. Ollie lashed out, pushing Dan away, but the Australian grabbed his right arm and yanked it hard behind his back.

'I'm fucking taking him,' yelled Nick.

Ian and Maksim allowed Nick to land one vicious blow straight in Ollie's stomach while Dan held him back, then they stepped forward smartly and, grabbing a shoulder each, dragged Nick back five paces.

'I'll sodding finish this,' spat Nick, his face still red with fury.

'You'll sodding get to bed,' said Ian. 'We've got a job to do. Once we get back from Somalia, you can kill the bloke if you want to, but not until the job is finished.'

Still holding on to Nick, they started to steer him back towards the hotel.

Steve and Layla had made love for a second time, but Steve knew that he shouldn't spend the night. It would only create tensions within the group, and that was the last thing they needed. He dressed quickly, kissed her passionately, and then slipped quietly into the street.

It was past two in the morning, and Ston was largely empty. The waiters were clearing away the tables and chairs outside the cafés and bars, and the few tourists had long since gone to bed. There was a lightness in Steve's step as he used the moonlight to walk back along the seafront towards his hotel. There had been a couple of girlfriends since he'd broken up with Sam at the end of the African mission a year ago. Girls he'd met in the villages around Leicestershire. They were pleasant enough women, but they were small-town and small-time. There was no edge to them, no mystery, and no challenge.

He hadn't met anyone who excited him in the way Sam had. Not until tonight.

The punch landed as if from nowhere.

Steve was hit from the side, the blow winding him, and in surprise he staggered down on to the beach, only just managing to keep his balance. He lashed around, raising his fist up towards his face, only just in time to deflect the blow that was crashing towards him. He felt the knuckles smashing into his skin, and winced. A knee snapped upwards, crunching into his balls. Steve gasped in pain, struggling to compose himself for long enough to take the fight back to his assailant.

He glanced up.

Henri.

'What were you doing with Layla?' growled the Frenchman menacingly.

'Boy, girl, middle of the night,' said Steve. 'I think you'll find there's a word for it in French, pal.'

Henri's right hand reached out, grabbing hold of Steve's new shirt, but Steve spun away, ripping a strip off his shirt in the process.

'Layla, she's *my* woman,' Henri grunted aggressively.

'Then you should keep a better eye on her, mate,' said Steve.

He curled his fist into a tight ball and swung a vicious brutal punch that connected hard with Henri's ribcage. There was a crack of bone that suggested the punch had been a good one, and the Frenchman roared, then lashed out again with his right hand. But Steve had had far less to drink than his attacker, and there was a nimbleness in his step that allowed him to dance away from the punch before delivering a sharp return right into the underside of Henri's jaw.

'Easy, boys,' barked Dan.

Together with Ian, he was running down towards the beach. Dan grabbed hold of Steve, while Ian pulled Henri sharply backwards.

'What the hell are you doing?' shouted Dan.

'He started it,' said Steve.

He wiped the sweat off his face and spat on the ground. He'd have a few bruises on him when he woke up in the morning. But as far as he could tell, no real damage had been done.

'Layla and I have been together for six months,' growled Henri. 'I saw him walking back from her hotel.'

'And how the fuck was I meant to know that?'

Henri just shrugged. He thrust Ian away, and started walking towards the hotel. 'We'll finish this properly when the job is done,' he said.

Ian stepped up to Steve, checking he was OK, then glanced across to Dan. 'I wonder if there's a bookies anywhere around here,' he said. 'Because the way this unit is falling out, I wouldn't mind putting a tenner on the pirate boy coming out on top.'

Seventeen

THE COMMODORE LOOKED RELAXED AND confident as he sat down in front of them in the briefing room.

I'm glad someone does, thought Steve. Because right now this unit hardly knows how to tie its own bootlaces.

It was just after seven in the morning. They'd been woken at six sharp, allowed ten minutes to grab some breakfast, then driven straight across to the naval base ten miles away on the other side of the peninsula. It was protected by a high wire fence, with NATO forces patrolling the perimeter. Inside, there were a dozen barrack buildings, two mess halls, an operations centre, a stores room, and an arsenal, all of it facing a secure harbour where NATO boats kept a watchful eye on the coastline leading down towards Bosnia and the rest of the Balkans. There was more trouble potentially brewing in the hundred square miles south of here than in the rest of Europe combined, Steve reminded himself. And everyone on the base would be well aware of that.

Ollie had a cut on the side of his face, covered up with a plaster, and Nick had some bruising to the side of his left eye. Henri was nursing his ribs, and Steve had a stiffness in his shoulder where he'd taken a bad blow last night. The rest of them didn't look much better. The alcohol had been flowing too freely, and Steve reckoned that their ability to snap straight back into action in the most testing of circumstances was about to be stretched the limit.

Only Maksim was grinning. But then a skinful of alcohol and

the prospect of a nasty scrap always put a smile on the Russian's face.

Up on the screen, the Commodore flashed a series of maps showing the Gulf coastline leading down towards Somalia. 'You boys are leaving tonight,' he said. 'So we'll be spending today going through the drill and getting you kitted up.'

Out of the corner of his eye, Steve could see Henri glancing at him, a menacing smirk in his eye. There was no sign of Layla. What the hell was she playing at? he wondered. How could it make any sense to start an argument among blokes you were about to send into a mission of this importance? Steve wasn't kidding himself that he was so irresistible to women that she couldn't keep her hands off him, nor did she look like the kind of slapper who couldn't keep her knickers on. In fact, she didn't look the kind of woman who did anything without calculating its consequences with the precision of a laser beam.

So what was her game?

'So here's the plan,' said Bamfield.

The sound of his voice jerked Steve out of his line of thought.

As he spoke, the Commodore's eyes were surveying each man in turn, and his expression suggested he wasn't too impressed. Up on the screen, he flashed a picture of a standard-looking cargo ship, the kind you saw in every harbour in the world.

'This ship is currently sailing towards the Somali coastline. The owner and the captain have been paid to cooperate with this mission. It's not carrying anything more valuable than grain. But on board we've placed three full-size safes, and we've switched the AIS records to say it has a high-security, high-value cargo on board. The dickers watching the coastline in Dubai, and the hackers monitoring the AIS system, will be fooled into thinking there is some good stuff on board. The pirates will attack it, I'm certain of that. It is the perfect target for them.'

He paused, taking a sip of water from the glass on his desk.

'They'll discover the grain in the hold, and they'll be pissed off about that, but they'll also discover the three safes, and my hunch is they'll take them because they will assume there must be something valuable inside. One man from this unit will be on board guarding the safes. The pirates will take him with them, for the simple reason there won't be time to open them there, and they'll assume the guard knows how to get into them. That man will have a secret tracking device implanted into his tooth.

'The rest of the Shadow Force will follow at a safe distance in a fast motor launch. The guard and the safes will be taken to the pirates' HQ, the base for Ali Yasin. The tracking device will have a radius of twenty kilometres: it has to be low-powered so it won't be easy to detect with any kind of scanner. The Shadow Force will follow behind, and you'll be led straight into the pirates' lair. Then you organise an attack, and go in and capture the bastard.'

'So have the health and safety monkeys okayed this plan?' asked Steve, glancing up.

'No,' answered Bamfield sternly. 'And I don't suppose they would either. We're well aware that the man who is the bait is going to be taking a hell of a chance. But this Yasin guy is a bastard to track down, and this is the only way we could figure out to do it.'

'Why not just put a tracking device inside the safes?' asked Ian. 'Then we can follow that.'

'Won't work,' answered the Commodore crisply. 'They have to be made to believe there is something genuinely worth having in those boxes, and if it was worth anything, there would be a man to protect it.' He looked around the room. 'Now, all we have to decide is which of you is going to be the bait on the end of the hook.'

Steve glanced around the seven men. The Commodore was right, he reflected sourly. One of them was going to have to put their life on the line. And there was only one fair way of deciding that. By letting fate make the call.

'We draw lots,' he said.

'Cards,' said Ian. The Irishman drew a pack from his pocket.

'We all cut the pack. The man with the highest card drops out, then we carry on until only one bloke is left.'

Steve nodded. It sounded fair enough. 'Let's draw,' he said.

He reached across and cut. A nine. Not bad, he thought ruefully. There was no question that the man who protected the safes was putting himself in maximum danger. The pirates weren't going to put their hostage up in the local Hilton, that much they could be certain of. It would be a rough ride, and the odds of coming through the job with blood still running in your veins weren't what any sane man would accept.

'Not Henri,' said the Commodore. 'I don't mind which of the rest of you is the bait, but you'll need Henri to get you into Somalia.'

Steve shot the Frenchman a malevolent glance. 'If he's not man enough to take his chances along with the rest of us, then he has no place on the sodding team.'

Henri leant forward to take a card. 'I'm man enough.'

'No,' snapped Bamfield, stepping forward. 'Henri is the best sailor among you, and you'll need him to follow the tracking the device. He's not going.'

Reluctantly Henri withdrew his hand.

'Looks like we'll have to find out if you've got any balls another day, Frenchie,' grinned Steve.

Ollie leant forward and drew a card. A four. By the time they'd finished the round, it was Dan with a queen who dropped out. On the next round, it was Ian, then Steve, then Maksim. A shame, thought Steve. With the Russian as a hostage, the pirates might decide to turn themselves in peacefully.

'It's me or you, Nick,' said Ollie. He was shuffling the cards in his hands.

Christ, thought Steve. Not Nick. Of all of us, he's the one bloke we wouldn't want to send into a trap like this.

'Cut,' said Nick.

There isn't a trace of fear in the boy's voice, noted Steve. I always suspected that boy was a nutter. But now I know for sure.

Ollie was still flicking the cards into position. Steve knew he'd been a gambler for much of his life and had frittered away far more money than he could afford at poker tables. And although he couldn't quite tell how he was doing it, he was sure that Ollie was fixing the deck. Steve glanced at Ian, and could tell he was thinking precisely the same thing. Then he looked back at Ollie. There was a crooked smile on his face.

'Go on, mate, draw the sodding card,' he said, looking at Nick. 'We haven't got all day.'

Nick drew.

An eight.

Instantly, Ollie turned up his own card. 'A six,' he said flatly. 'Looks like I'm the lucky one today.'

The Commodore stepped across. 'Good man,' he said, slapping Ollie on the back. 'Now, let's crack on.'

Steve started to walk from the room. 'Well done, mate,' he said, patting Ollie on the back.

Ollie just grinned, but although the smile was broad, there was no mistaking the hint of nervousness behind it. Ollie was a fine, determined soldier, but he was a team player, a man who worked best as part of a unit. On this job, he'd be operating solo.

'After the fight last night, I didn't reckon I could let Nick be the bait,' he said.

'You might never get another shag off his mum.'

Ollie grinned. 'There's that to consider.'

'You think you'll be OK?'

'Just make sodding sure you come in and get me.'

'No worries, mate. You just put your feet up with those pirate boys and work on your tan. We'll do all the hard work.'

Eighteen

'YOU HAVE TEN HOURS TO prepare yourselves,' said Layla. She was standing at the front of the canteen, looking over the unit as the men piled their plates high with what might be the last cooked meal before they went into action. The base was a multinational NATO facility, which meant there was food from a whole range of different countries. 'Sort of like the food court at the shopping centre,' said Nick, as he surveyed the buffet. Steve and Ollie were tucking into some Bratwurst prepared for the Bundeswehr, Ian and Dan were taking heaps of pasta cooked for the Esercito Italiano, whilst Maksim was polishing off some big, greasy Spanish omelettes served up for the Fuerzas Armadas Españolas. 'Shame the French Army isn't here,' said Nick cheerfully. 'I wouldn't mind a few more of those escarwotsits.'

'Stick to the German grub, mate,' said Steve. 'Say what you like about the Krauts, they know how to make a sauasage.'

It wasn't the best food he'd had ever tasted, Steve decided as he finished off his second Bratwurst. But it was tastier than anything the British Army served up for its men, and it was better than anything they were likely to find in Somalia, so they might as well enjoy it.

'You'll get a military helicopter from here and fly out across the Med towards Oman,' Layla continued. 'Ollie is going to be dropped from the chopper on to a cargo boat called *The Starfish*.

The rest of you will be flown on to the Omani coast, where a motorboat has been prepared for you.'

Her hair was tied back, and neatly combed, and her make-up hid any trace of tiredness from the night before, noted Steve.

'Finish your food, then we'll take you down to the quartermaster, and you can get yourself kitted up.' A half-smile played across her face. 'Take whatever you need, but remember this is the "new austerity", as the Prime Minister puts it, and even if this mission is off the books, that doesn't mean it doesn't cost money, so don't take anything you don't need.'

'Need?' muttered Dan, glancing up from his food. 'Seven blokes up against a whole sodding country shouldn't be stinting on the arms or the ammo.'

As they finished their food, Ant and Dec joined them, then led the way out of the canteen, past the barracks, and towards the stores room. Steve hung back for a moment, peeling away from the rest of the group. As Layla started to leave, he grabbed her arm. 'What the fuck were you playing at?' he hissed.

She brushed his hand away. 'You should know. You were there as well.'

'But I didn't know you were seeing Henri. The bastard flattened me on the way home.'

'That's the trouble with Frenchmen,' Layla replied. 'Too possessive. It's the Mediterranean culture, I suppose.'

'Bollocks. You knew it would cause trouble.'

'The one thing I know is how to get boys fighting,' she said. 'I learnt about that in the playground and I've remembered it ever since.'

'I reckon you're a bitch,' muttered Steve.

'But a dirty one,' said Layla. She ran a hand through Steve's hair. 'Bring me back that pirate, and maybe I'll let you fuck me again.'

Up ahead, Steve could hear Dan shouting at him to hurry up. There was no time to deal with this now. Just get the job done, then forget about her, he told himself as he hurried to join the others.

The woman was trouble.

By the time Steve made it into the stores room, Dan was already wide-eyed. The Australian was purring like a cat locked up overnight in a dairy. They were used to dealing with the black-market conmen and sharks who sold weapons to the private military corporations in the nastiest corners of the world. You ended up paying over the odds for a Turkish knock-off of an AK-47 when you wanted to get your hands on the real thing. But this was a secret NATO armoury, designed to equip special forces being deployed into Bosnia, and there was enough kit here to take apart a medium-sized nation and still have plenty left over.

If it went bang, and it hurt people, they had it. And it was all free.

'Looks like Christmas Day has come early, boys,' said Dan. 'Let's fill our sodding boots.'

They had already run through a list with Dan of the basic kit they needed. They were going to have to be self-sufficient and mobile, and they'd need food and water as well as ammo to keep them going for at least four days. They had to stay light and quick to follow the pirates, and get Ollie out before any harm came to him, but they also needed enough firepower to make sure they could capture Ali Yasin alive. Too much kit, and they'd lose mobility. Too little, and they'd be short on firepower. Between the two, they'd have to find a balance and hope they got it right. Their lives would depend on it.

They took eight British made SA-80 assault rifles, one for each man, and one spare. They'd have preferred to carry AK-47s, because that was what the pirates would have, and there would be ammo they could nick locally, but the SA-80 was a weapon all the men were familiar with, and its 5.56mm cartridge was a NATO-standard munition, making it common enough, so the chances were they could resupply themselves if they needed to. Each man would carry a spare mag, and a hundred rounds. Anything else would weigh him down too much.

Steve picked out eight Browning Hi-Power pistols, again standard British Army issue, and all the quartermaster was willing to give them. With a black metal barrel and brown stock, the Browning had been the service handgun for the SAS for most of the years since the Second World War. Simple and reliable, and with plenty of punch in its 9mm round, it was a safe and familiar choice. It wouldn't let them down.

The kit needed to be waterproofed, and Henri took care of that. They stocked up on webbing, body armour, helmets, ropes, knives, C-4 explosives plus underwater charges, compasses, boots, gloves and fins in case they had to swim long distances.

Whilst Ollie and Ian were sorting that, Dan and Henri were quizzing the quartermaster about some of the other kit in store. A gruff Yorkshireman called Dave, he wasn't planning on giving away any more gear than he had to. But like any specialist, get him talking about his own private enthusiasm, and he soon warmed up. Dan knew more about military equipment than anyone Steve had ever met, and within minutes he was discussing the merits of different weapons as if he and Dave were old mates.

'Any chance of an HK P-11?' said Dan.

The P-11 was an underwater pistol developed by the German manufacturer Heckler and Koch in the 1970s, but so secret that its existence was never confirmed in any of the company's official literature. A compact handgun, it was designed to fire lethal darts both above and below water; above water it was accurate up to thirty metres, and below water up to fifteen. The low visibility under water meant the range was more than enough to cope with most opponents. The weapon had been ordered in limited quantities by Commando Hubert, the German Kampfschwimmer, as well as the British SAS and SBS and the American Navy Seals. It was an expensive piece of kit, however, since every time it was fired it had to be sent back to the Heckler and Koch factory to be reloaded. As a result, it was kept in storage, and used only on the most crucial missions.

'We've only got one,' said Dave.

'We need it,' said Dan.

Dave glanced across at Ant, standing at the back of the stores room. He shook his head.

'Bloody hell,' snapped Dan. 'I thought this Yasin bastard was a major threat. So why can't we have the kit to go and get him?'

'The P-11 is authorised for hostage rescues only,' said Ant quietly.

'If Dan says we need it, we need it,' said Steve.

'Not without authorisation from Whitehall,' said Ant.

Dan looked away in disgust. 'Typical bloody British Army,' he muttered. 'It was the same when I was out in Afghanistan. None of your blokes had enough kit. They had to hit the sodding Taliban just to nick their ammo.'

Dave quickly cheered him up with some less expensive kit. They collected a GREM, made by the Israeli company Rafael Advanced Defence Systems. Short for 'grenade rifle entry munition', the GREM was a rifle-launched device designed to blow down doors at a safe distance. Its specially designed head generated a shock wave that could force even a steel door to buckle and yield. The Israelis had designed it for clearing the heavily fortified basements of the Lebanon, but Ian reckoned it could be just as useful for breaking and entering a pirate headquarters. They took three corner-shot rifles, another piece of Israeli-designed kit that used a video system to allow you to shoot round corners: the rifle split into two pieces, and the video camera allowed the shooter to hide safely behind a wall whilst taking aim. Nick was particularly impressed with them, and anxious to try them out. Next, Maksim picked out the Russian made GSh-18 pistol, which came complete with its specially designed 9mm PBP AP ammo for special applications. The bullet pierced body armour, perfect for bringing down men at close range.

'Shooting round corners, blasting through body armour,' exclaimed Ollie. 'Jesus, it's hardly a fair fight.'

'And this,' said Dave, moving on, will make it even less fair, which in Somalia is exactly the way you want it.'

The quartermaster explained. They had in a batch of 'stealth paint', a high-tech body coating that damped the amount of heat escaping from your skin, and so made it far harder for night-vision goggles, which operated by detecting heat, to see you.

'I like it,' said Dan, the satisfaction evident in his voice. 'If we'd had some of this stuff in Afghanistan, we could have crept straight up on the Taliban and slotted the bastards before they even realised we were there.'

Before they'd finished in the stores room, Ollie was taken away to have the signalling device fitted in his tooth. Ian went with him, saying he wanted to make sure it was done properly. They were going to be relying completely on the signal; lose it, and they had more chance of finding Elvis in Somalia than they did Ollie. There was a dentist inside the camp, and a quick check revealed that Ollie had a single crown on the left side of his mouth. The dentist opened it up, inserted the microscopic transmitter inside, then sealed the crown back into place. An hour later, Ollie was back with the rest of the unit, collecting the remaining supplies, and making sure all the kit was working. Nick had zeroed all the weapons on the shooting range, making sure each one was true, whilst Dan had been trying out the stealth paint, and Maksim was reacquainting himself with the formidable punch on the GSh-18, a weapon he'd trained with in the Spetsnaz but which wasn't yet widely available in the rest of the world, despite its ability to defeat the powerful body armour now routinely worn by battlefield soldiers.

'We need some grub,' said Steve. 'Last time I checked a map, Somalia was right next to Ethiopia so I don't suppose there's much chance of living off the land.'

'It's rat packs, I'm afraid, boys,' said Dave.

'Christ, not even any MREs,' said Ollie.

MREs were the American 'meals ready to eat', standard issue for US troops. Using chemical compounds, as soon as you peeled back the pack, the casserole or pasta bake inside would heat itself up. They weren't a culinary feast, but they were edible and nutritious, which was more than could be said for the traditional British Army ration pack, or 'rat pack' as they were known to the men.

'Sorry, guys, that's all we've got.'

Ollie started to rummage through the crates. None of the food was fresh, and although the boiled sweets and chocolate were edible, the rest made a 1950s school lunch look like something Gordon Ramsay might rustle up. 'It looks like baby's heads, cheese possessed or truncheon meat.' He glanced across at Henri. 'To translate for our French friend here, a baby's head is a tinned steak and kidney pudding, cheese possessed is processed cheese, because you'd have to be possessed by the devil to eat the stuff, and truncheon meat is luncheon meat, but it's more useful for hitting a bloke on the head with than actually eating.'

'I think I'm loosing my appetite,' said the Frenchman with a broad grin.

Steve held up a pair of tins, nodding towards Nick. 'This, in case you were wondering, is a growler. And it's probably the reason you fight for a PMC and never bothered with the Regular Army.'

'What in the name of sod is it?' asked Nick.

'A tinned pork sausage, packed in white grease,' said Steve. 'It looks something like a Frankfurter with chickenpox.'

'I think I'll pass.'

Henri, meanwhile, had loaded up his iPod with music, and bagged a pair of portable speakers. 'The complete works of Bruce Springsteen, Coldplay and U2,' he said proudly. 'The best fighting music ever written.'

'There was a bloke called Jeff who always made sure we took along the right kind of music,' said Steve. 'Springsteen, just like you, but also a lot of Prince and Stevie Wonder.'

'What happened to him?'

'Killed,' said Steve simply.

Henri nodded sagely, and turned back to the computer where he was downloading music. 'I'll add some Stevie Wonder.'

'And some Stereophonics,' said Nick.

'And the Pogues for Ian,' added David.

'Aye, whatever,' replied Ian, walking away with a curt shake of the head. 'I want to send a few emails before we sail into what sounds like certain death.'

Nineteen

THE MERLIN CHOPPER LIFTED SMOOTHLY from the Ahmed Al Jaber Air Base. Steve glanced from the side of the craft as it rocked up into the air, rolled with the south-westerly winds, then started to steer east. He'd never liked Kuwait, not from the first time he'd set eyes on its sandy highways and sun-blasted skyscrapers. He'd been there during the second Gulf War, preparing for Regiment missions into Iraq, and he'd been back plenty of times after he'd started working for DEF, using the Emirate's international airport as the safest way into the region, the same way most of the PMC guys did. But he'd never warmed to the place. Rich and soulless, it had none of the tacky exuberance of Dubai to the south, or the wild, rugged danger of Iraq to the north. Like Switzerland, as Bruce Dudley had put it on one their trips there for DEF. Except with more sand, and less alcohol. And, Steve reckoned, that just about summed the place up.

'I don't like it,' said Ian at his side.

'Neither do I,' answered Steve, nodding down towards Kuwait City. 'It's a sodding craphole.'

'Not that,' said Ian tersely. 'This mission. There's something they're not telling us.'

'Like what?'

'Like why they aren't using their own guys. There's the SBS, Hubert, the Kampfschwimmer. They could be using any of them.'

Ian might be right, thought Steve. But it was too late to discuss it now. They were about to be thrown into the thick of the action, and the only way they were getting home was with the pirate chief as their prisoner. From Croatia, they'd flown down to the Ahmed Al Jaber Air Base, a nominally Kuwaiti facility that was still in reality controlled by the Americans, in a Hawker 4000 private jet that had been leased just for the trip. They'd been given a few minutes to grab coffee and some food after landing, then transferred immediately to an RAF Merlin that was already prepped and waiting for them on the runway. From Kuwait, it was a short hop across the desert to drop Ollie on to the boat, then put the rest of the men down on to the waiting launch.

Steve glanced around. It was just after nine in the evening, and the light was starting to fade. All seven of them were sitting strapped to the side of the Merlin, with two pilots up front. Layla, Ant and Dec had said farewell and wished them luck as they climbed on board back in Kuwait. They were on their own now, with nothing apart from a few hundred miles of sand and ocean separating them from their target.

They completed the journey in silence. The Augusta Westland Merlin was kitted out as a transporter rather than an attack chopper, but it was still a military machine, and that meant it was built for speed and aggression rather than comfort. You couldn't make any conversation above the roar of its blades. All you could do was hunker down, roll with the vibration of the craft, and wait to be put back down on the ground again.

It was close to ten when the pilot announced over the radio pieces attached to each man's helmet that they were homing in on *The Starfish*. Steve looked down, but it was a cloudy night, and although he could see the lights of a few merchant ships slowly cruising up through the Gulf of Aden, nothing was clearly visible. Some were going up to the Suez Canal, some to the Gulf, some across to India, but they were moving so slowly that from up here they looked like specks of light strung out across a heaving mass of black water. The Merlin dropped hard out of the sky, and Steve could feel his gut heaving. Ollie had already harnessed himself up, and was standing next to the winch. He nodded at each man in turn, then smiled briefly.

'Good luck, mate,' said Steve tersely. 'You'll need it.'

'I was at public school. Survive that, and a few pirates are nothing.'

And then, with a brief salute, he stepped out. The pilot had brought the chopper down to fifty feet, and Steve could now see the deck of *The Starfish*. There were six crewmen flashing torches up into the sky, and the winch was lowering Ollie on the end of a metal rope. The air was relatively calm, with no more than a slight breeze, and the seas were steady, making this a routine drop. Ollie swung briefly as a gust of wind caught him, but one of the crew men caught his legs, and pulled him to the ground. Ollie unhooked the harness, and without even looking back up, walked away with the captain.

'So far so good,' shouted Steve, above the roar of the blades.

'Makes a change,' said Dan. 'Usually our jobs are fucked up in the first five minutes.'

'We'll get to that bit soon enough,' said Ian flatly.

The pilot pulled the winch up, then flew on. It took only another twenty minutes to fly back to the coast of Oman. They'd already been briefed on the location. A small, sandy cove, close to the town of Dalkut, on the southern tip of Oman, near the border with Yemen. A long coastal strip, directly underneath the Arabian Desert, the region was marked by long, sandy beaches, with mountains behind them, and cliffs that tumbled straight into the sea. Along the coast, the climate was temperate, with a few fishing villages, but inland there were only harsh mountains and barren desert, making the region virtually empty of people. There were miles and miles of coastline where you could moor a boat for days without anyone noticing it.

Steve tumbled out on to the wet sand of the beach, crouched down low to avoid the whirlwind of sand and spray being sucked up by the Merlin's rotor blades, then checked that each of the six men were in place. As Henri bought up the rear, he waved up to the pilot, and the Merlin spun up into the air, its lights quickly disappearing into the sky. Steve took a moment to look around. The beach was half a mile long, with two ranges of cliffs at either end, making a natural cove. The waves were crashing in against the shore, and there was a three-quarters moon, creating plenty of light to see by. Moored twenty yards out to sea was the distinct shape of a boat, anchored to the seabed.

'Let's go,' grunted Henri.

The unit advanced through the crashing waves. The water wasn't particularly cold, nothing like the English Channel, noted Steve, nor were the waves that strong. Within minutes, all six of them had clambered on board and secured themselves a berth. It was a simple black vessel, with a fibreglass hull, three plastic benches, and a Yamaha 350-horsepower outboard engine controlled by a steering wheel up front. From the scuffs and the marks, Steve reckoned that Six had bought it second-hand somewhere nearby and moored it here. He had no problem with that. Second-hand meant it would have been well run in, and so long as it was seaworthy, it would get the job done.

From his rucksack, Henri unpacked a small hand-held radar.

'There,' he said, pointing at the screen, and showing it to the rest of the unit. 'Ollie.'

It was clear enough. An illuminated dot showed clearly where Ollie, or at least the bloke's tooth, was located. Seventeen kilometres to the south-west of them.

'Move it,' said Steve. 'More than twenty and we'll lose the sod.'

Henri kicked the Yamaha into life. With a throaty roar, the vessel started to cruise out into the ocean. A course south-south-west was set, which would take them directly into the wake of *The Starfish*.

Steve could feel the damp clinging to his wet clothes. As he looked up, he could see the stars glinting menacingly in the jet-black sky. The waves were rocking into them as Henri steered a course straight out across the Gulf of Aden, and splashes of water were kicking up over the prow of the boat.

'Next stop, Somalia,' said Dan, his tone resolute and cheerful. 'Maybe they've got some beer we can try out for the bar.'

Twenty

ANJU RAI LOGGED ON TO the laptop one last time.
It was just after seven in the evening. He'd spent the final day in the small house going through the last of his grandfather's possessions. There was memorabilia from the campaigns he'd fought through in the Second World War, particularly the Battle of Monte Cassino where the Gurkhas were involved in some of the heaviest engagements of the entire Italian campaign, but also memoirs and medals from other members of the long-since disbanded 2nd King Edward VII's Own Gurkha Rifles, a regiment that had seen action in North Africa, Cyprus and Burma.

Just dusty old pieces of brass and strips of braided cloth, reflected Ganju sadly. But each one was a testament to the will, determination and indestructibility of his grandfather. It was still hard to believe that the old boy was finally gone, and even though, according to the Gurkha tradition of samsara, he would by now have been reborn into a new body, with a status that reflected his achievements and qualities in the life he had just departed, his absence was something Ganju felt every waking minute.

The house had already been sold, and the estate agent was expecting the keys to be dropped off tomorrow. Another day, and the house would have been cleared. And Ganju would have caught a plane back to Nepal, planning to spend the next few years looking after his sister-in-law Kani, left behind after his brother

Lachniman had been killed in action, and her two young children Gurung and Israni.

At least that was the plan.

Until he read the email.

Ganju read it twice. Once to see what it said. And once again to make sure he could really believe it.

He took the printer out of its packing box, hooked it up to the laptop, made three printouts, then stepped outside to the BMW 3 series that was also due to be dropped off to the dealer he'd bought it from.

From the sea up to Worpledon was a drive of two hours, with some heavy mid-evening traffic along the way, but although Ganju's head was buzzing for most of the drive, he didn't for a second have any doubts that he was doing the right thing.

There were only two qualities a Gurkha really cared about. Duty and loyalty. Tested on either, they would never be found wanting. And there was no question what both demanded he should do tonight.

It was just after nine thirty by the time he pulled up outside David Mallett's modest house. There were still lights on as Ganju rang the doorbell.

Sandy answered the door. She looked tired and stressed. There was a baby in one arm, and another screaming for its mum in the background.

'I need to speak to David.'

'He's . . .' She hesitated. Ganju's pale brown were eyes looking straight at her and she could see the quiet determination in them. 'I'll get him.'

'Ganju, me old mucker,' said David, bouncing through the hallway. There was still a kid's storybook in his hand, and he was dressed in his pyjamas, but he looked in good shape, and the grin on his face suggested he was genuinely pleased by the distraction. 'The twins are just nodding off, honey,' he said, turning towards Sandy. 'We can slip off to the pub for a couple of quick pints.'

'No drinking,' said Ganju.

'Right, mate, I forgot you don't. We can still grab a juice—'

'It's about this.' He handed across the printout of the email.

David read it just once. 'Shit,' he muttered. 'Is this what we think it is?'

'Bruce Dudley will know.'

'He's in Scotland.'

'We could fly there.'

David shook his head. 'Too late,' he answered crisply. 'But if we drive through the night, we should be there by dawn.'

'David, you're crazy,' said Sandy. 'You can't drive to Scotland tonight. You're—'

But David cut her short by handing her a copy of the email. 'We haven't any choice,' he said simply.

Twenty-One

LARS VOGEL WAS A BIG, strong man, with the evidence of a thousand ocean voyages cut into the grooves running through his tanned, weatherbeaten skin. He shook Ollie by the hand, and offered him a cigarette.

'No thanks, mate, I've given up.'

Vogel chuckled. A Danish seaman, with thirty years of crewing and captaining merchant ships under his belt, he didn't look as if very much would surprise him. Until tonight, that is.

'We're going to be attacked by pirates, apparently, in the next twenty-four hours. It's hardly the time to be worrying about your health.'

'We'll be fine,' said Ollie. 'We're giving in without a fight, and that's always a piece of piss.'

The captain just shrugged. He was approaching fifty, wearing a thick lambswool sweater, with a sturdy leather jacket over it. *The Starfish*'s deck was huge, stacked with metal containers, and with two grain silos underneath, and although there wasn't much of value on board, there was plenty of weight. Her big engines were churning up the water, propelling her forwards, but Vogel didn't reckon there was much to worry about yet. He led Ollie past the bridge, towards the main cabin area. There was a small kitchen, then a canteen, and the sleeping quarters for the crew. The ship was staffed by ten men in total, two Croatians, three Turks, and five Filipinos. One of them handed across a cup of hot, sweet tea, and a thick sandwich made from sliced bread and processed cheese, before returning to a TV room thick with cigarette smoke and the sound of grunting from the porn playing on the television.

'Got the entertainment sorted, I see, chaps,' said Ollie. 'And I thought this was going to be boring.'

Vogel held up a stack of DVDs with pictures of naked women on the covers. 'German. American, Russian. Take your pick.'

'Better not,' said Ollie. 'I'll get down to the safes, and kip down. If the pirates come aboard, it needs to look like I'm on the job.'

The captain led him down another flight of metal stairs, taking him deeper into the hold. The three safes were pieces of high-security office equipment, designed mainly for storing wages on building sites. Five feet high and eighteen inches wide, each one was made from reinforced fire-resistant steel. They were sealed with digital locks, and only Ollie had the code, but that was staying firmly locked up in his head. One of the crewmen had put down an inflatable mattress, and a sleeping bag.

'Get some rest,' said Vogel. 'You'll need it.'

'Does the crew know?'

The captain shook his head. 'This has been arranged between myself, the shipowners, and your people. The fewer people know about it the better.'

'They won't fight?'

'Our standard instructions are not to take on the pirates,' he replied. 'It sounds crazy, but the insurance companies won't allow us to start shooting people. It's cheaper just to pay the ransom.'

By the morning, Ollie was feeling rested. He'd slept well enough, once he'd got used to the hum of the engines and the gentle rolling of the ship as it ploughed its steady course towards the Somali coast. The captain's assurances that the pirates were unlikely to attack at night made enough sense for him not to worry about being disturbed; the pirates were so cocky and confident in these waters, they didn't even bother to conceal their movements.

He made himself some coffee and toast in the kitchen area, and glanced through to the small living room. The Croatian who had just finished the night shift was relaxing with a beer, a microwaved hotdog and a DVD called *German Goo Girls Volume Seven*.

'Want to watch?' he said, glancing across at Ollie. 'Is good.'

'Love to, pal, but I think if you haven't seen the first six it's hard to pick up the story.'

He walked up to the deck. It was just after seven in the morning, and the sky was already a brilliant blue. There was a small walkway outside the bridge of *The Starfish*, with a lifeboat, a bench, and an untidy heap of cigarette butts. Ollie leant on the railing, took a hit of his coffee, and looked far into the horizon. They must have done thirty to forty miles overnight, he reckoned, which was taking them straight into the combat zone. Somewhere to his east was the coast of Somalia, though it was too far away to be visible. The seas were light to moderate, and the wind gentle. A couple more cargo boats could be made out in the distance, but there was no sign of any of the navy patrol vessels that were meant to be policing these waters.

Come on, boys, he thought to himself. What's keeping you? We want to get this show on the road.

He spent twenty minutes up on the deck, enjoying the sea breeze, and composing his thoughts. From what he'd heard, the Somali pirates treated their prisoners well enough. It was ransoms they were interested in; bloodshed, and beatings and killings would just slow down a trade that was proving very lucrative.

But if they find the tracking device?

Then I'm a dead man.

It's worth it, thought Ollie as he drained the remains of his coffee. This job can get me working for Six. And from there, maybe I can work my way back into the Blues again. This PMC lark is all very well for a man like Steve. He's a lone wolf, unable to fit into any organisation. Maksim's just a psycho, Ian doesn't have any other options, Dan's career was finished when he got sent to jail after those kids got killed in Afghanistan, and Nick doesn't have a clue how the world really works. But I was considered a certainty for general in Sandhurst. And maybe I can get back on that track again. If I can pull this job off.

He grabbed another coffee and a roll from the kitchen, caught five minutes of *German Goo Girls* with the Croatian, then went back downstairs to the safes. He'd changed out of his combat kit into black jeans and a sweatshirt. He'd put a knife into his belt, and a satphone, because he reckoned he needed to look like a proper security guard, but he decided against carrying any kind of weapon. There were a few PMCs that supplied armed guards to merchant ships, since there was no law to stop a man carrying a gun in international waters, but they had to get clearance from the local police for every port they stopped at, so many of them didn't bother. A weapon was only going to start a fight. And that was precisely what he didn't want.

Ollie checked his watch. Just after nine. There was nothing to do but wait. He closed his eyes, and for a few minutes imagined himself back in the mess of the Blues Combermere Barracks close to Windsor. There would be more than a few glasses raised if he ever went back, Ollie reckoned. And a deck of cards being shuffled. But this time around, he wouldn't be joining them. He knew more than enough about what drink could do to an officer's career already.

The first he knew about the attack was the rattle of gunfire and the sound of men shouting.

Ollie sat tight. He knew his role. To pretend to be guarding the safes.

The pirates had sprung from nowhere, like spirits that danced out of the sea itself. Two skiffs powered up into the wake of *The Starfish*, then pulled alongside its hull. Their seamanship was expert, holding their vessels steady even in the churning water around the hull of their target. Each skiff carried six men: five for the attack, and one steering with an outboard motor. As they pulled alongside, they raked the deck with a murderous barrage of fire, shooting high into the air at first, as a warning, then along the rim of the deck to clear it of anyone mad enough to put up any resistance. A pair of grappling hooks were thrown up on to the rails, and in the same instant they caught, the men started to climb. It took less than thirty seconds for all ten men to clamber on board. They were dressed in khaki shorts and bright orange and purple T-shirts, with no body armour: either they couldn't afford it, or else it just slowed them down, Ollie reckoned when he finally laid eyes on them. They hardly needed it anyway. They were as fast and aggressive as any special forces unit, and in less than two minutes from the start of the attack, they had the ship firmly under their control.

They were led by a tall, dark man in sunglasses, with a thick, fake Rolex watch round his wrist, and a collection of gold chains hanging round his neck. He gave his name as Omar Mustaf, barking the words in rough, heavily accented English. Do exactly what you're told and you won't get hurt, he commanded. The crew were terrified, offering no resistance. They were huddled into the small living room, where two pirates kept their AK-47s trained on them, while Mustaf demanded that Vogel let him inspect the ship. A blast of swearing, and a rattle of gunfire that even Ollie could hear down below, greeted the news that the main hold was filled with nothing other than grain. Nor were the containers any better. Most of them were empty, shipping out to China and the Far East to be filled with manufactured goods, whilst the few that had anything inside were filled with cheap raw materials.

'Below,' Ollie heard Mustaf bark.

He tensed himself.

The captain stepped through the steel door, with Mustaf and two more of his men following smartly behind him. They were carrying AK-47s and wearing shades, but they had made no attempt to disguise themselves. These were their seas, and they could do what they liked on them. The second he marched through the doors, Mustaf's eyes latched straight on to Ollie, then on to the three safes right next to him.

He pushed Vogel aside, taking two steps forward. Ollie was standing bolt upright, his arms folded, a look of determination on his face. His hands were resting on his belt, and the knife tucked into it was clearly visible.

'I was told there was something of value on this ship,' said Mustaf, his voice dripping with menace. 'And I think I've just found it.'

Ollie remained silent, his face immobile.

'What's in the safes?'

'That's the business of the people who own them and theirs alone,' said Ollie stiffly.

A thick smile spread across Mustaf's lips. It hadn't been much of a fight so far, and he'd found nothing of value, but even so he was starting to enjoy himself. 'Everything that sails through these waters is our property,' he said.

Ollie didn't respond.

'What's in the safes?' barked Mustaf.

Again silence.

'Open them.'

Two of the pirates stepped forward, pushing Ollie roughly aside. The butts of their rifles were jabbing into his side. It was pointless to resist. The pirates examined the safes and quickly saw the digital locks fitted to their thick steel doors.

'Open them,' barked Mustaf.

Ollie remembered his drill. Stay calm, tell them you don't know anything, and force them to take you prisoner. That was what Bamfield had told him and he planned to stick to it precisely.

'I don't have the the code,' he said, his tone flat. 'My task is to watch these safes until they reach their destination.'

'I don't have time for this,' snapped Mustaf. 'Open them.'

'I already told you, I couldn't even if wanted to.'

Mustaf took a step forward. There was a bead of sweat dripping down his face but Ollie remained completely calm. The pirate reached down, took the knife from Ollie's belt, and lifted it up to his throat. Ollie could feel its blade pressing tight into his skin. 'Don't think for a moment I won't kill you.'

'I've no doubt you will. But it won't make any difference.'

'Open the safes.'

'I can't.'

Ollie winced in pain as Mustaf twisted the blade a fraction, piercing the skin. Five drops of blood slid down the edge of the blade, wetting its handle.

'Tell me,' Mustaf growled.

'I can't,' spluttered Ollie.

The tightness of the blade against his throat was making it hard for him to speak. The man's eyes rolled up to meet Ollie's, so for a brief second they were locked on to one another. For the first time Ollie felt a shiver of fear. He could see only a cold, murderous fury in the pirate's expression. The plan hinged on being taken captive, reflected Ollie bitterly. But they might just as well decide to kill him and take the safes anyway. My life's hanging on a guess, the way it might on a poker table. And right now, I'm not sure my luck is any better than it was on the gaming table.

'Then prepare to die.'

The blade pressed closer. Ollie closed his eyes, ignoring the steel slicing into his nerves.

Then suddenly the knife clattered to the steel floor. The ship was rolling slightly in the waves, and there was some shouting from the deck above, but it was only one of the pirates barking at the crew to stay still. Mustaf turned around, jabbing his AK-47 into Vogel's chest.

'You open them, then,' he barked.

Vogel shook his head. 'I'm just a merchant seaman. I don't know the codes any more than this man does.'

'Where's it going?'

'Singapore.'

Mustaf nodded. Three heavily protected safes on their way to Singapore, the financial capital of the Far East. Whatever was inside, he wanted them. He glanced at his watch, his expression anxious for the first time. Ollie was aware that the ships sailing through these waters put out emergency signals as soon as there was a pirate attack and they would be picked up by any of the NATO or Russian naval patrols in the region. The ships weren't fast, so it wasn't like making a 999 call, but there was never any way of knowing how close a patrol might be, and the pirates couldn't hang around too long. They came on board and, if they were taking the ship, steered it towards Puntland as fast as possible. If not, they scarpered.

'Take the safes and the man,' Mustaf barked to his men. 'There's nothing else here worth having, and nobody will pay a decent ransom for it.' He looked towards Ollie. 'You're coming with us.'

Ollie's face remained expressionless. But inside he was smiling. The cards just came good, he thought to himself.

Mustaf jabbed him with his rifle, and started to push him upstairs. The rest of the men were lifting the safes. They were big and heavy, but the pirates were strong men, with powerful muscles, and the safes were shifted easily enough.

As they passed the kitchen area, Mustaf grabbed half a dozen of the porn DVDs and stuffed them inside his sweatshirt. The man let off a burst of a dozen rounds from his AK-47, laughed viciously, then prodded Ollie hard in the back with the still warm steel of his gun barrel.

'Move it, white boy,' he snarled. 'You're going to be our guest until we find out what you're protecting in those safes.'

Twenty-Two

HENRI HAD EQUIPPED HIMSELF WITH a pair of military-standard Oberwerk Mariner binoculars. With a rubber-armoured heavy-duty construction, they were sturdily designed for use at sea. They magnified an image ten times, and with a one-kilometre field of view, it was simple to observe any naval encounter at a safe distance.

He watched closely, the glasses pressed in tight to his eyes to prevent the spray blurring his vision. 'They're taking him,' he said flatly.

Steve leant forward in the boat, squinting his eyes.

It was a hot morning, with a blazing blue sky, and he was starting to sweat inside his heavy waterproof kit. They had spent an easy enough night out at sea. The waves kept the motorboat constantly moving, but he'd still managed to grab a few hours' kip. Through the night, Henri maintained a steady distance of ten miles behind *The Starfish*, close enough to make sure they were well within range of the vessel but far enough behind not to be spotted by the pirates coming out to attack it. As dawn arrived, Nick and Dan had broken out some breakfast. There was no space to brew up, so it was just water and biscuits, and they had to take a piss over the side of the boat, but by the time they had all eaten, the unit was in decent shape and ready for the task that lay ahead of them.

They just had to wait for the attack. And ignore the nagging worry that the pirates would shoot Ollie and take the safes to open at their leisure. In which case, there wouldn't be anything to do apart from take his corpse home.

And give the poor sod a decent funeral, reflected Steve.

'Let me take a look,' he said to Henri.

The Frenchman handed across the binoculars. 'Don't drop them.'

Steve stifled the urge to snap. Henri had been needling him ever since their fight. There was unfinished business between the two men, and sooner or later they would need to sort it out. Not today, but soon. And when the moment came, Steve sensed he'd enjoy it.

He put the Oberwerk to his eyes. The view was magnificent, a crystal-sharp image of the bright blue sea, with the imposing hulk of *The Starfish* right in front of it. Two pirate skiffs were alongside it, each one manned by a single sailor. The captain had killed the engine, and the ship was just drifting under its own momentum, the skiffs riding alongside it. Up on the deck, the winches were being used to lower the three safes on to the skiffs. None of the crew was resisting.

Up by the railings, Steve could see a man with a gun at his back.

Ollie.

Steve felt sure that Ollie was looking straight at him, an expression of grim determination on his face. But then he started to move.

'Let me see,' snapped Henri.

As Steve passed the Oberwerk back, he could see ropes being slung from the side of the ship. And Ollie was being pushed down, lowering himself into one of the skiffs.

Henri waited.

The engine was still idle, the boat bobbing gently on the waves rolling into them. Apart from *The Starfish* on the far horizon, the sea was almost empty. In the far distance, an oil tanker steaming up towards Kuwait was just visible. Apart from that, nothing. Not even any seagulls, a sure sign the oceans were quiet.

'OK, they're off,' said Henri, putting down the binoculars.

He checked the radar screen. The tracking device was transmitting clearly, and began to move as the two pirate skiffs powered up and started to sail back towards the coast of Puntland.

'Some of us know what it's like to be a prisoner,' said Ian. 'Good luck to the poor bastard.'

'He'll need it,' said Dan. 'I can still remember my first day in a military jail. I felt like an animal and—'

But the rest of his remark was drowned out by the noise of the Yamaha engine as Henri fired it into life and started to steer them in the direction of the pirate skiffs that had already disappeared over the far horizon.

Twenty-Three

BRUCE DUDLEY WALKED SLOWLY THROUGH the morning mist.

His border terrier was barking at the rabbits, and there was a light drizzle drifting through the trees. Bruce always got up early, and walked the dog before breakfast. A legacy of his Regiment training, he'd sometimes reflect. The money he'd earned out of Dudley Emergency Forces made him rich enough to sleep until whatever hour he felt like. But he enjoyed the freshness of the foggy, early air. Through the trees, he could see the shores of Loch Kinord, fifty miles from Aberdeen in the wild interior of Scotland, dominated by lochs, rolling hills, and forests of tall birch. There was a brooding, rugged power to the landscape, tough and disciplined, and Bruce had felt he belonged here the moment he set eyes on the place.

Down by the loch, the dog disturbed a pair of fat pheasants, and as they fluttered into the air, Bruce reckoned he'd get his shotgun out later on. But not yet. For now, he just wanted to be alone with his thoughts.

Business wasn't as good as it had been. And certainly not as good as it had been for the last five years. If I was starting out today, I certainly wouldn't be able to afford a manor house, or the thousand acres of farm and woodland that came with it, Bruce reminded himself. Not even up here in Scotland.

Iraq was winding down, now that the British were out, and the

167

Americans were off soon. There was no longer the flood of foreign aid money pouring into the country, which for a time meant every nutter who knew one end of an AK-47 from the other could get himself a job out there. Afghanistan was nothing like as lucrative as Iraq had been at its peak. There weren't any raw materials to interest the private companies, and the place was getting so dangerous the United Nations crowd huddled together in the relative safety of Kabul, protected by the American troops. The downturn in the global economy meant there was less close protection work for corporate bigwigs, and the oil companies weren't pouring money into putting up rigs in every hellhole on the map the way they had been a couple of years ago. The lean years had arrived, of that there was no question.

But the good men would always be allright. The world was always at war with itself, and, over a couple of millennia, there had always been work for mercenaries who knew what it took to win a fight. That wasn't likely to change now.

We'll be OK.

Bruce paused by the two oak saplings.

Each time one of his men was killed, Bruce planted an oak tree for them right here in the woodland. Jeff Campbell, read one. Chris Reynolds, read the second. They'd had a good summer, with plenty of fresh growth on them, even if they looked small and bare now that winter was settling in. Jeff's was two years old now, and was above a foot, Chris's slightly shorter. Both good blokes, reflected Bruce with the same momentary sense of sadness he experienced each time he walked past them. Solid, dependable warriors, with bodies of iron, and spirits that flamed into life at the first rumour of battle. They didn't make many men like that. And there wasn't a day that passed when their mates wouldn't miss them.

'Bruce,' shouted David, from the edge of the woodland.

He turned round, startled. The dog was barking wildly, the way he always did at visitors. Bruce could see David Mallet running down towards him, with Ganju Rai following on close behind.

What the hell are they doing here?

Bruce marched back up the hill to meet them, shouting at the dog to shut up as he did so. Both men looked tired. They had driven through the night, taking turns at the wheel of Ganju's BMW. There was a day's worth of stubble on their chins, and you could see the traces of a couple of gallons of motorway coffee in their eyes. And that was enough to tell Bruce that something was wrong. David and Ganju were men who took pride in their appearance, the way all decent soldiers did. They must be in a hell of a hurry to turn up looking like this.

'Christ, what's going on?' he demanded.

David took a moment to catch his breath. They'd parked the car up at the front of the twelve-bedroomed mansion. Dudley was unmarried, and lived by himself, but there was an elderly Scottish lady who cooked and cleaned every morning, and she had told them he was down in the woodlands with the dog. They'd run straight there.

'Take a look at this,' said Ganju. He handed across a printout of the email.

'We reckoned you were the one man who'd know for sure what it meant,' said David. 'And we didn't want to put it on a fax, or even an email. It was dangerous enough for Ian to send it from Croatia.'

Bruce took the single sheet of paper and held it in his hand.

His expression slowly turned from serious to scared.

'Shit,' he muttered out loud. He looked at Ganju. 'When was this sent?'

'Yesterday.'

'Where are they now?'

'How the hell should we know?' said Ganju.

It was the first time Bruce had ever heard the Gurkha swear. He'd spent his life in the company of British squaddies, and no race of men cursed more than they did, but Ganju always remained calm and dignified even under the most intense pressure.

Until today.

'Somewhere off the coast of Somalia, I reckon,' said David.

Bruce looked straight at him. 'Then we'd better find them as fast as possible,' he said, his voice threaded with a note of quiet determination. 'Because if this means what I think it means, there are going to be six more oak trees planted in this sodding piece of ground in the next couple of days.'

Twenty-Four

OLLIE COULD FEEL THE HANDCUFFS cutting into his skin, and the seawater splashing against his face had turned his lips salty and dry.

They had been cruising for at least six or seven hours, he reckoned. The two skiffs kept in close formation, never more than a hundred yards apart. Driven by big Honda outboard engines, there were six men in each one, steering through the swells and currents of the open seas with an expertise that made it clear these men had been born into these waters and could navigate them as easily as a child could find its way around its own back garden. The men were lined up along either side of the skiff, with the captured safes in the middle of the boat, strapped down with metal chains to prevent the occasional big wave that kicked over the top of the skiff from knocking them into the water. Ollie was sitting at the back of the boat. There were handcuffs across his wrists, and his feet were manacled to a metal ball that weighed at least a hundred pounds. Let's just hope I don't get tipped overboard, he thought to himself as he looked out into the bright blue sky for any sign of bad weather. With this weight attached to me I'll sink straight to the bottom of the ocean. Shark food. At best.

The air was wet with spray that clung to skin and clothes, but the sunshine was bright and intense. The first couple of hours weren't too bad, but as the journey wore on, Ollie was starting to perspire badly from the mix of damp and heat, and his clothes were starting to cling to his skin. A couple of times he asked for water, but Mustaf ignored him, concentrating on scanning the seas around them for other ships.

Maybe they're not done for today, thought Ollie. Let's just hope they don't start any more firefights before they take me in. I just want to get to Yasin's headquarters, so the boys can come in and rescue me as fast as possible.

At four in the afternoon, one of the men up front started to shout and wave.

Ollie craned his neck forward.

Land.

The skiff turned, and started to head directly towards the shore. One of the pirates loosed off a few rounds from his AK-47 into the air, but that was the first sign of ill discipline that Ollie had noticed. They were strong men, with a ferocious appetite for battle, and a hardened camaraderie born from long periods spent together on small skiffs, and when the moment came, that was going to make them a formidable opponent.

Slowly, the port of Eyl came into view. Ollie recognised it from the videos they'd been shown during their briefing. What had started out as a small fishing village, with an old, cracked sea wall to help the natural harbour protect the ships from the weather, had been turned by the pirates into a major shipping hub. They passed one big oil tanker that had been taken last night and was now being anchored half a mile out to sea while a ransom that would run into millions was negotiated with its owners. A couple more big cargo boats were anchored nearby, racked up like buses in their depot, and their crews were sitting bored on the decks as their weeks of captivity stretched out before them. The skiff steered its way between them as it approached the harbour. Inside its walls, Mustaf killed the engine, and ropes were thrown out to the dock, where a couple of ten-year-old boys grabbed hold of them and pulled them on to a rickety wooden jetty.

It was just after four in the afternoon when Ollie finally got his feet on dry ground. The dock was bustling with life. Skiffs were steering their way in and out of the narrow channel, some of them taking food and water out to the captured ships, others heading down the coast to other pirate hideaways; a few, judging by the assault rifles and rocket launchers brandished by their crews, setting out on fresh attacks. A crowd had gathered further down the docks, waving and cheering as the oil tanker was moored out at sea, a crew of pirates on its bridge, and a small flotilla of armed skiffs alongside it. Payday, thought Ollie. The oil in the tanks of a big beast like that was worth a hundred million dollars minimum. And the owners would pay plenty to get it back again.

'Move it,' snarled Mustaf, grabbing him roughly by the arm.

Ollie was hauled up on to the jetty.

'Water,' croaked Ollie. 'I need some damned water.'

Mustaf grinned into his face. He was an ugly man, with cold, malevolent features, and breath that smelt of rotting bananas. Instinctively, Ollie winced every time he got close to him. 'You'll drink when we say you drink.'

The pirates began to unload the big safes from the skiffs and carry them to a Volkswagen van which was waiting for them at the side of docks, its doors already open.

'Forward,' snapped Mustaf, shoving Ollie with the butt of his rifle.

Ollie stumbled down the jetty, and finally up on to the road that ran alongside it. Walking with his hands chained and the ball attached to his feet was close on impossible, but no one offered to help, or to loosen the chains. Mustaf just jabbed him with the rifle as he took the tiny pigeon steps that were all that was possible with the chains on his ankles. The dock was crowded with people, but none of them paid any attention.

I guess blokes with chains being marched along by men with AK-47s are just what you see everyday around here. Nothing to get excited about.

He looked up. Eyl was made up of a main road that stretched around the harbour. Behind that was a maze of small, narrow streets that stretched back for half a mile, before running out into red, sandy scrubland, and behind that some low-lying hills. The houses were dirt poor, square blocks made out of concrete, with rough plaster, flat roofs and no windows. The streets were narrow, and cut out of the dirt; there were piles of rubbish everywhere, and stagnant, foul-smelling water collecting in fly-covered puddles. And yet there were signs of wealth as well. New Toyota and Mercedes SUVs muscled their way noisily through the streets, and the market stalls were filled with electronics, DVDs, and designer T-shirts, belts, watches and jeans. There were food shops, and gold merchants who doubled up as bankers, and bars with neon lights that flashed on and off even in the afternoon sun.

Imagine a sewer that just won the lottery, thought Ollie to himself. That's what it looks like.

'Get inside,' snapped Mustaf, whacking Ollie in the back with his rifle.

Bruised, Ollie started to climb into the van. It was cramped and hot next to the three safes. 'Where are we going?'

But the door slammed shut with no reply.

Twenty-Five

WHEN HENRI STILLED THE ENGINE, the shoreline was only just visible in the distance.

Steve looked out across the expanse of blue water. At last, he thought to himself. Dry sodding land.

It was just after four in the afternoon, and they had been tracking Ollie at a safe distance all day. At one point they'd closed in to seven miles, but then they'd seen what looked like a pirate skiff in the distance and, anxious to avoid any kind of confrontation, Henri had changed tack, putting fifteen miles between them and the target.

The hours had started to meander by.

Nick rigged up the speakers, and kicked off a series of Coldplay tracks from Henri's iPod, and by the time they'd finished lunch most of the boys were lying back in the boat, stripped of their vests, body armour and sweatshirts, and getting a skinful of the hot sun.

'Sod it, boys, this job doesn't look so bad after all,' said Dan, halfway through the afternoon. 'Maybe we could rig up a satellite system and see if we could find out what's happening in the cricket back in Oz.'

'Or the footie scores,' chipped in Nick.

'Maybe we should ask the local boys whether they have any fake Sky cards,' said Ian. 'That's one kind of piracy we don't mind.'

As the engine died, Steve looked across to check the radar monitor. Right now, Ollie was eight kilometres away but starting to move at a speed that meant he must be on dry land. It looked as if he'd docked at Eyl, and was now heading inland.

'We better get ashore, mate,' he said to Henri.

'In daylight? Too risky.'

'What time's sunset?'

'Seven thirty,' chipped in Ian.

'Then we wait until dark.'

Steve jabbed a finger down on the monitor. 'He's twelve kilometres away from us already, and travelling in a car or a van,' he said, his tone turning harsh. 'Another few minutes and we're going to lose the sod. This signal has a range of twenty kilometres.'

'Steve's right,' said Ian. 'Without the signal, we're lost. I don't think we want to start wandering around Somalia, stopping people in the street and asking if they happen to have seen our mate.'

'At night,' repeated Henri firmly. 'We need to get ashore safely, and we need to find somewhere to hide this boat.'

'And the sodding signal?' demanded Steve.

'We'll track it down. We know what direction he's travelling in. Get on the same road and we should pick it up.'

'Too risky. Lose the signal and we're done for.'

'And I say its too risky to go ashore. And since I'm in charge of this mission, that's final.' He glanced at each man sternly. For a brief moment, Steve thought about challenging him. Unless Henri learnt how to play in a team, there wasn't much chance of pulling off this mission. None of them was going to stand for some arrogant French tosser pulling rank on them for several days. And certainly not me.

'Do it your way,' he said eventually. 'But we're a team, remember.'

Henri chuckled to himself. 'Teams are fine with me. So long as they know how to obey orders.'

They waited half a mile offshore for the next three hours, restarting the engine at just after seven. The sun was setting right behind them. The wind had dropped to nothing more than a whisper, and the sea was completely still, allowing the dazzling orange light to bounce off its surface, creating a hazy mix of near-red sky and blue sea that merged straight into the dusty yellow shoreline. Henri motored up to three hundred metres from the beach, then killed the engine again, telling the unit to use their paddles to bring them inshore. Henri scanned the beach with his binoculars, making sure the cove was completely empty. A few yards out, Nick and Maksim jumped out into the splashing waves and pulled the small craft up on to the beach.

Dry land, thought Steve as he stepped ashore. Thank Christ for that.

He looked around. The cove was just a dip in the shoreline, where the beach curved in on itself, protecting the land from the beating waves. The beach was long, a mixture of sand and shingle, pitted with shells, and great clumps of sticky, pungent seaweed. Behind it, a set of hills rose gently from the ground, made up of dry, dusty scrubland, broken only by big chunks of red rock. A few trees were visible in the far distance, but they were twisted, shrivelled stumps, offering little shade, and doing nothing to break up the sunburnt desolation of the landscape.

Welcome to Somalia, Steve thought to himself. Jesus. This job has taken me to some real crapholes in the last couple of years, but this place looks like Craphole Headquarters.

'I've always wondered why I never saw Somalia in the tourist brochures,' said Ian, glancing around. 'Now I'm starting to understand why.'

There wasn't any time to look around, however. Henri had already sketched out the plan, and Steve couldn't see anything wrong with it. Seven white guys couldn't move through Somalia without attracting attention. They needed to nick a vehicle, and get a trace on Ollie as fast as possible. Two men would go up to the road and hijack the first car or truck that passed. The rest of them would stay behind and hide the boat. Once they'd captured Yasin, they'd bring him here and head back towards the coast of Oman with their prisoner. Layla had given them a satphone; contact her on that, and a chopper would be dispatched to take them back to Kuwait. With any luck, they'd be in and out of the country in forty-eight hours.

'Who's up for the hijack?' said Henri, looking around.

'I'll go,' said Steve immediately.

Henri looked at him harshly, then grinned. 'OK, time you did something useful.'

Steve ignored the remark. 'Maksie, you on for it?' he said, looking towards the Russian.

Maksim nodded just once.

'Two men enough?' asked Dan.

'We'll keep it simple. We'll sling a roadblock across the road, then turn our guns on them when they pull up to see what's happening. Two guys is enough for that.' Steve turned round and started to walk. 'If you haven't heard from us in a couple of hours, assume we're dead,' he said.

It was half a mile from the beach to the road. From Eyl, the route snaked inland towards Quardo, then twisted back to the coast, towards the small fishing village of Bandarbeyla, before eventually making its way to the tip of the Puntland peninsula, up by Culula. Steve trudged through the darkness. The sky was clear, and the moon was providing plenty of light to see by. As far as he could make out, this stretch of the coast was completely deserted: there was no fresh water, few trees, and no industry, so it was hardly surprising no one lived here. Even Somalis drew the line somewhere, Steve decided, and this tip was on the other side of it.

The road was nothing more than a track scratched into the dirt. It cut its way through the rocky landscape, its surface made up of pebbles, stones, and baked earth. In heavy rains, it probably turned into a stream, reckoned Steve, but the rest of the time it would be passable by any strong vehicle. He looked left and right. There was no sign of anything approaching. He nodded towards a small hill. 'Let's get to work.'

Both men stared to build a simple roadblock. Lifting boulders from the ground, they stacked them on top of each other to construct a makeshift wall that stretched across the track. A vehicle couldn't drive through it, and although it could swerve round the barrier by driving off the track and into the dry, open countryside, the chances were they'd slow down to see what was happening.

And they'd find out soon enough, thought Steve. A hold-up.

It was sweaty, back-breaking work. The night air was humid, thick with the salty moisture of the nearby sea, and the rocks were like lumps of iron. The redness of the soil created an eerie, desolate landscape, like suddenly finding yourself on a different planet. The waves down on the beach echoed through the still air, and the light wind whistled through the dust and stones with a creaking, whispering, moaning sound that appeared to make the hills come to life. Somewhere far away, Steve heard the cry of an animal, but although his Regiment training had taught him most survival skills, and he recognised most predators from their roar or snarl, he was buggered if he could identify it. 'What kind of animals you reckon they got around here, Maksie? Lions? Tigers?'

The Russian looked around. He dropped his boulder, and drew his Browning handgun.

'I don't know, and I don't like them,' said Maksim. 'Maybe we shoot them.'

'Easy, boy,' growled Steve. 'They're miles away.'

They resumed their work. By eight, the roadblock was built, but there was still no sign of a vehicle. Steve and Maksim crouched down behind the hill, their Browning handguns drawn, and their SA-80 assault rifles ready for action. Inwardly, Steve was cursing the fact they hadn't been supplied with Kalashnikovs. Nobody carried SA-80s except for British soldiers on official business, and anyone who saw them with one was going to be instantly suspicious. An AK was normal around here but the SA stood out. First chance we get, we'll nick ourselves some rifles, he told himself. That way at least they won't know we're British. Not until we open our mouths anyway.

The minutes ticked by.

Steve leant forward to scan the horizon, but there was no sign of a vehicle in either direction. He kept his ears close to the wind, but he could hear only the beating of the sea a half-mile back and the wail of an animal in the far distance. The sun had long since set, and a chill was starting to bite into his skin. He could feel the sweat that had soaked through his clothes and body armour whilst lifting the boulders turn cold and clammy. He took a bottle of water and some biscuits he'd tucked into his webbing, chewed slowly on them, then swigged the liquid down his throat. Christ, he thought to himself. We could be here all night. And then we'll never get a lead on where the hell they've taken Ollie.

It was close to nine before Maksim nudged him in the ribs. 'Look,' he hissed.

Steve glanced up.

Headlamps. About a mile distant.

Steve crouched down low, his finger poised on the trigger of the SA-80. Maksim was standing ready at his side. The plan was a simple one. As soon as the vehicle stopped, rush them, and turf them out. With any luck, the occupants would just be some fishermen heading up to the next village and they'd get this done without a shot being fired.

'Steady,' hissed Steve, glancing towards Maksim.

Steve craned forward, trying to get an idea what kind of vehicle it was. He knew a fair bit about engines from running the garage up in Leicestershire, but those cars were all vintage, and from the rumble now echoing out across the flat landscape, he could tell it was a modern car. A diesel, he reckoned, from its low throaty growl. And as it drew closer, he recognised it. A Toyota Land Cruiser with a big 4.7 litre V8 engine. It was the same rugged SUV the Taliban used out in Afghanistan, a machine so solidly built, it could be turned into a semi-armoured vehicle by any half-competent welder.

'Christ,' he muttered to himself. The Toyota was a classy piece of kit. Not something that was going to be driven by some local fishermen.

It was drawing closer. Three hundred yards, reckoned Steve, then two hundred. Its headlamps were on hi-beam, and from the way it was flooding the desolate hillsides with great wedge-shaped shafts of pure light, Steve reckoned the driver had souped the machine up with some extra illumination.

Which is just what you need for night runs along this track.

Definitely not fishermen.

The Toyota was down to a hundred yards. Steve ducked as the beam of light flashed across his face, temporarily blinding him. The driver was doing a steady forty, about twice the speed any sane man would attempt on this track. But his grip was good, and he was turning into the bends and riding the bumps with a precision that suggested he knew the road like the back of his hand.

'Move, move,' snarled Maksim.

But Steve grabbed his shoulder. 'Hold it.'

Maksim turned to him. 'What?'

'These guys look like sodding pros,' hissed Steve. 'Sit this one out. We'll take the next vehicle.'

'There might not be another one.'

'Take this one and we're kicking off a war,' said Steve. 'There could be a dozen heavily armed blokes inside.'

Maksim grunted, then dropped to the ground.

Down below there was a squeal of brakes.

The Toyota was skidding along the ground, kicking up a huge cloud of red dust as its big wheels scratched open the rock and dirt embedded into the track. It stopped a few inches short of the makeshift wall, its headlamps remaining full on, filling the road and the hills with the fierce, artificial light.

Steve remained still. He caught his breath.

A single movement might cost me my life, he told himself sharply.

But Maksim was edging his eyes upwards. The SA-80 was level with his right eye as he peered over the rock. 'Down, Maksie, down,' hissed Steve.

He sneaked a quick glance.

Three men had piled out of the Toyota. They were big strong blokes, dressed in jeans and bright orange T-shirts with body armour strapped to their chests. They had AK-47s in their arms, and ammo slung around their necks. Into their belts they had stuffed knives and handguns. Steve couldn't tell what make at this distance, but it didn't much matter. The bullets would kill you all the same.

None of the men were inspecting the wall. They were looking up into the hills. Trying to figure out where the ambush was coming from, realised Steve grimly.

'I can take them,' hissed Maksie.

Suddenly there was a raking burst of gunfire. The rock they were hiding behind shook as round after round of lethal munitions splintered its surface. Maksim's voice must have carried on the wind, alerting the men to their presence, and now all three had turned their fire straight into their position.

'Sod it,' muttered Steve. There wasn't any choice now. All they could do was stand and fight. And die with their boots on if they had to.

He glanced at the Russian.

'OK, mate,' he said sourly. 'Give 'em all you've got.'

'How many are there?'

'Three on the ground, could be more in the vehicle.'

Maksim nodded just once, an expression of implacable

determination settling into his rough, brutish face. 'I'll move, you fire.'

'Go then,' snapped Steve. 'We haven't got all sodding night.'

Maksim slammed his SA-80 into position. He rolled a dozen yards towards the next rock, opening up a burst of fire that pummelled down into the men below. One bullet caught a man on the shoulder, spinning him round like a top, but he still had plenty of fight left in him, even as the blood started to seep from the wound, and he crouched down, unleashing a barrage of fire from his AK-47 that smashed straight into the hillside. The distraction was enough for Steve to get a shot clean away. He lined up the man in the sights of the SA-80, then pulled hard on the trigger. The bullet connected with the side of the man's head, punching a clean hole in his skull that took out a quarter of his face. With a grimace, he tumbled to his side, already dead.

First blood, for this sodding country at least, though Steve grimly. But there will be more before this job is done.

The two remaining men dived for cover behind the Toyota. The driver had tumbled out, and was lying behind the vehicle. Whether there was anyone else inside, it was impossible to tell from here. Maksim had taken up position behind a rock, and was putting a few rounds down into their opponent, but the bullets were skidding off the bonnet of the Toyota. 'Don't damage the car,' hissed Steve across the fifteen yards that separated them. 'That's what we're bloody here for.'

He took a moment to assess their position. They were fifteen feet above the track, sheltered behind rocks, and well dug in, but so were their opponents. The three men left in the battle were sheltered behind the Toyota, and the way the bullets were bouncing off its surface, it looked to have been armoured with steel plating. They could hammer away at it all night without making any sort of dent in it, and if the blokes had a satphone, they could call in reinforcements, and then they'd be done for.

'Cover me,' hissed Steve. 'I'll get behind them.'

He started to crawl along the ground. They had darkness on their side, and the roughness of the terrain meant there were channels in the ground through which a man could slip unnoticed. Maksim put down a steady barrage of fire, distracting the marksmen, whilst Steve crawled ten, then twenty yards behind them, before creeping down silently on to the track. He slipped a full mag into the SA-80, giving him a fresh thirty rounds to fire on automatic. As he glanced forward, he could see two men crouching down behind the Toyota. The driver was still hidden from view. One of them was putting covering rounds into Maksim, whilst the other was unhooking a hand grenade from his ammo belt.

'Fuck it,' muttered Steve.

A grenade from a few feet would blow the Russian to pieces.

He braced himself, then started to charge, the SA-80 stretched out in front of him. He could feel the blood pumping furiously through his veins, and the adrenalin swimming up to his brain. Fifteen yards, then ten. He could see the man with the grenade looking towards him, an expression of horror on his face, but Steve had already opened up with a short burst from the SA-80 that shredded the man's face. He kept running, readjusting the rifle, so that the next dozen rounds smattered into the back of the second man, shredding his spine, until he fell face forward to the ground, blood seeping out of a dozen different wounds.

Just then, a hand reached out. It grabbed Steve's ankle, sending him clattering to the ground. The rifle spun out of his hand as he collapsed on to the ground.

The driver.

'Sod it,' muttered Steve.

The man was on him in a flash, grabbing his right arm and twisting it hard behind his back. He jabbed a Czech-made CZ-110 pistol into the side of his head. 'Stand,' he growled.

Steve remained motionless.

'Stand, I said.'

Steve looked briefly into the man's eyes, and realised he had no choice. Around him, the ground smelt of blood and spent shell casings.

He struggled to his feet, his right arm still twisted behind his back.

'Come down, or your friend dies right now,' shouted the driver, looking upwards.

Steve scanned the hillside, looking for some sign of Maksim.

'Now,' repeated the driver.

Steve could feel the sweat pouring off him. The man would execute him on the spot, of that there could be no doubt.

'Come down now,' shouted the driver.

Silence.

Steve could hear nothing except the murmur of the wind. Even the animals in the distance were quiet, frightened off no doubt by the noise and ferocity of the firefight.

Has Maksim pissed off? wondered Steve. Or gone to get reinforcements?

'He dies right now.'

The driver pushed Steve down on to his knees. He was gripping his hair with his right hand, forcing him to the ground, whilst his left hand was waving the CZ through the air, ready to take a shot at Maksim.

Steve could feel a cold bead of sweat drip down the inside of his body armour.

If you are going to kill me, just bloody get on with it.

A shot.

Steve winced as a portion of blood, skull and muscle splattered into the side of his face. A bullet had gone straight into the back of the man's skull, drilling a neat hole through his face and blowing the remnants on to Steve. The man managed half a pitiful moan before he died, falling with what little remained of his face into the dusty earth.

Steve looked around.

Through the blood that had drenched him, he could hardly see a thing. With the back of his sleeve, he wiped away the debris of the gunshot wound, then blinked a couple of times to flick away the soft tissue that had landed on his eyelid.

'Tough bunch of bastards,' said Maksim, with a rough grin. 'This is going to be fun.'

Steve spat on the ground, careful to stop any of the blood getting in his mouth. 'Well, I'm glad you're enjoying yourself, Maksie. Because if this is the kind of ruck they put up when we try and nick their Toyota, I hate to think what they're going to do when we try and grab their leader.'

There was no time to clean themselves up, nor to dispose of the bodies. The vultures would have to see to that. Steve climbed into the big Land Cruiser and turned the keys that were still in the ignition. The big diesel engine started with a throaty roar. There was plenty of fuel in the tank, and as long as you ignored the bullet marks that now peppered its sides, the machine was in good condition. Maksim slammed the door shut behind him and Steve drove up and off the track and down on to the beach where they had left their mates.

The boat had been carefully concealed behind a mound of sand and beneath a covering of brushwood and dried seaweed. Unless you were looking for it, or bumped straight into it, you wouldn't know it was there. Steve stepped down from the vehicle and strode straight into the sea. He stood still for a moment, letting the waves break over his feet and splash up his thighs, then jabbed his hands into the foam and splashed the water across his face. There was still blood on his skin, and he didn't like the smell of it.

'What kept you?' said Dan.

'Seems they don't like lending out their vehicles around here,' said Steve, stepping back out of the water. 'Can't imagine why.'

'Christ, you look terrible,' said Ian. 'How many blokes?'

'Four,' said Maksim. 'I thought the Chechens were tough fuckers, but I'd never met a Somali who thinks his Toyota is being stolen . . .'

'You should see what happens in Swansea, mate,' said Nick. 'When Darren's Fiesta got bashed, half an estate got wrecked, he was so pissed off.'

'Swansea, Somalia, I'm sure there's many ways in which they're alike,' said Ian.

'What happened to them?' demanded Henri.

'We told them we just needed their vehicle for a couple of days and if they gave us an address, we'd get it cleaned up for them and return it in good nick,' said Steve, looking at the Frenchmen irritably. 'They're sodding dead, aren't they.'

'They might have raised the alarm before they died. If anyone knows there's a foreign military force in the country, then we're in big trouble.'

'Then I suggest we get a sodding move on,' snapped Steve. 'Because the sooner we get a fix on Ollie, the more chance we have of getting out of this craphole alive.'

Twenty-Six

RUCE DUDLEY'S JAGUAR XJ PULLED up on a side street within Imperial Wharf. A huge new development of apartments on the Thames between Chelsea and Fulham, it was quiet at this time of night. Only about half the flats had been finished, and many that were completed weren't sold yet, so there were few cars around, and even fewer people.

'Wait here,' said Bruce to David and Ganju in the back of the saloon. 'I'll go and talk to her.'

He stepped out of the car, ignoring the light drizzle falling from the cold, cloudy sky. Pulling the collar of his coat up around his neck, he checked the apartment numbers on the door buzzer. Layla Thompson's apartment was number fifteen, fourth floor. From years working closely with the Ministry of Defence, on missions that were both official and covert, Bruce had plenty of contacts within the intelligence community. There were favours that could be called in, and secrets that had to remain under wraps; DEF had taken on plenty of jobs that were meant to stay off the record for a very long time. It hadn't taken long to find out Layla's home address. Nor had it taken long to decide that that was the best place to confront her with the information he was holding in his hand. This was too explosive to be dealt with in the office. And the information was too dangerous to be dealt with through any official channels.

No, he had decided grimly. This would have to be dealt with unofficially. Or else six good men would die.

He looked both left and right down the street. Bruce preferred not to ring the bell. She might tell him to piss off, or pretend not to be there. Briefly, he inspected the entryphone, wondering if there was time to hack his way in. No time, he told himself. They'd flown straight down from Scotland that afternoon because there wasn't any time to waste. They couldn't waste time trying to break in either. This was a modern, upscale development. There would be a stack of alarms, CCTV, security guards, the works. They could find a way in, there was no doubt of that, but it would take an hour or two, and time wasn't on their side.

Up the road, he saw a Domino's Pizza Delivery motorbike.

He ran towards the man. 'Want to earn yourself a quick hundred quid?'

The delivery boy, a young Moroccan, looked startled. 'Sure, mate.'

Bruce nodded towards Layla's apartment. 'Got a delivery for that block over there?'

The boy shook his head.

'Anyone order pizza regularly?'

'Number eight and number twenty-seven.'

'Buzz them,' said Bruce. 'When they say they didn't order anything, tell them it must be a mistake, but they can have the pizza for free if they want. OK?'

The boy nodded.

Five minutes later, number eight had accepted the offer of free pizza, and Bruce was inside the building. He peeled off a row of seven crisp twenties from his wallet and folded them into the boy's hand. 'Job well done, lad,' he said gruffly. 'Now there's a bit extra for you to piss off smartish and forget you ever saw me.'

Bruce ignored the lift and walked up the stairs.

There were four apartments on each floor. He scanned the numbers, then stood for a fraction of a second outside number fifteen. One knock, then two, delivered in quick succession, like the rounds from a machine gun.

Inside, he could hear movement. Then the turning of a latch.

Bruce hadn't met Layla before but he'd asked around as soon as Steve had mentioned her, and built up a picture of the women. Still in her early thirties, Cambridge educated, she was one of the rising stars within the intelligence service. A troubleshooter: someone they sent in to sort out a cock-up or a catastrophe, and there were always plenty of those to deal with at MI6. Cool, intelligent, and intensely ambitious was the way one contact had described her. 'She reckons she's the next Stella Rimington, the director general of the service, and a public figure after that.'

Although he hadn't met her, Bruce reckoned he knew the type: the men on the ground were just chess pieces, lumps of ivory to be deployed in a game someone else was playing.

But to me they are flesh and blood. Mates.

'Miss Thompson?'

The door was half open. Bruce had already stuck a foot into it before she had a chance to slam it shut in his face.

'Who are you?'

'Bruce Dudley, Dudley Emergency Forces,' he said, sticking out a hand.

There was a half-smile on her face. 'Death Inc. I've heard of you.'

'And you'll be finding out why we got that name if you don't let me in right now.'

'Is that a threat?'

'Just a statement of the facts.'

The door opened.

Bruce stepped into the hallway, then through into the living room. It was sparsely furnished, pristinely tidy, with a magnificent view stretching out across the river. A Brahms violin sonata was playing in the background, and her laptop was open on the glass dining table, a tumbler of whisky and soda next to it.

Putting the printout of the email down next to the computer, Bruce looked her straight in the eye. 'What the fuck is that?'

As Layla picked it up, Bruce took the open bottle from the stand and poured a generous measure into a glass. It was Famous Grouse, a blended whisky, and not a brand he cared for. But right now he was in no mood to discuss malts. Anything with some alcohol in it would be fine.

'You know what it is, don't you?' she said, looking straight back at him.

Bruce nodded curtly. 'It's a guidance system for a cruise missile.'

She blinked.

'The question is,' he continued, knocking back the whisky, 'what the fuck is it doing inside Ollie's tooth?'

Layla turned away. She was standing with her back to him, staring through the sheet of plate glass that looked down on to the river below, but he could see her reflection in the window, and he could see the cold set of her eyes and lips.

It was a look of cruel indifference.

'We planted it inside the man who is going to be captured by the pirates,' she said. 'We've got a submarine in the Gulf of Aden right now. As soon as we're certain that Mr Hall is inside Ali Yasin's headquarters, we're going to use that guidance system to bring a dozen cruise missiles straight into his camp.' Layla turned round so that she was facing Bruce directly. 'And we're going to blow that fucker right off the face of the planet.'

Twenty-Seven

OLLIE FELT HOT, STICKY AND uncomfortable.
He'd lost count of how many hours they had been travelling. Four, maybe five. His hands were still cuffed together, and he'd been sandwiched between the safes in the back of the van, with no water, and not much in the way of ventilation. The roads had been rough, the van bouncing along them, each jolt and judder shaking straight through his body.

But they'd been stationary for the last ten minutes. And Ollie could hear voices from outside.

The door opened.

It was the middle of the night. The moon was in the sky, and somewhere in the distance Ollie could hear the crashing of waves. The barrel of an AK-47 was pointing straight at him. 'Thanks for the welcome, pal.'

'You,' snapped the man. 'Get out.'

He was tall and strong, dressed in the cargo pants and bright orange T-shirt that seemed to be a uniform among the pirate forces. Ollie struggled to his feet. There was cramp in his thighs, and pins and needles in his feet from being cooped up in the van for so long, and he walked unsteadily.

'This way,' barked the guy with the gun.

Ollie took a second to get his bearings, taking in his surroundings. He knew about blokes with guns, and they hadn't brought him all this way to shoot him on sight, so there was no hurry, he reckoned. Delay, stall, play them along, those were the instructions. Give Steve and the rest of the unit time to catch up and plan their counter-strike.

It's the only way I'm getting out of here alive.

The van had pulled up at the end of a track. As Ollie's eyes adjusted to the pale moonlight, he could see a small cove five hundred yards away. Around its perimeter was a barbed wire fence, with two sets of flashlights rigged up to flood it with light. Making a quick count, he calculated there were five armed guards on patrol. The cove led down on to a beach of shingle and sand. Right in the centre of it was the hull of an old cargo ship that had either run or been forced aground. There were lights on in its portholes, and more men patrolling its deck. The waves lapped around it, but the old boat had plenty of strength left in it and looked capable of providing comfortable accommodation for as many as fifty men.

This is it, decided Ollie. Ali Yasin's headquarters. Pirate central.

'Forward.'

The pirate was jabbing at his back with the barrel of his AK-47. Ollie started to walk forwards, led by Mustaf. There were two men alongside him, while the rest of the blokes were unloading the safes from the van, and starting to carry them into the compound.

A gate had been cut into the barbed wire protecting the cove; Mustaf nodded at the two men on guard, and they opened it, letting them through. As he walked, Ollie was assessing the defences, making notes on how Steve and the rest of the unit would come and get him out. It's going to be a bugger, that much is certain, he decided glumly. The headquarters was built for mobility. If there was any real threat – an attack from a foreign navy, for example – the pirates would no doubt scatter into the hundreds of coves and beaches that filled the coastline. They fought mobile warfare; they wouldn't dig in for a long battle. But that didn't mean it wasn't well defended. There was the wire, then the patrols. And if you got through that without raising the alarm, you were going to have to get up and into the boat and overpower it to have any chance of getting both him and Yasin out alive. 'Sod it,' muttered Ollie to under his breath. Definitely tougher than we imagined.

'Welcome.'

A tall man had just walked down the long wooden plank that led down from the boat on to the beach. The waves were lapping around his sturdy boots, but he ignored them, the way most men would ignore a breeze while striding across an open field.

Ollie recognised him at once. Ali Yasin.

Well, at least we're in the right place, he thought.

'Come aboard.'

The barrel of the AK-47 jabbed him again in the back, and Ollie started to walk up the plank. Yasin was a powerfully built man, noted Ollie, with the natural air of authority about him you found in the best generals. At Sandhurst, he'd have been put in the fast stream on day one. He spoke clearly and directly, with complete certainty, in a way that Ollie could already guess would command total respect from the men. He was wearing shades, pulled down over his eyes, and a black sweatshirt, with a thick gold chain round his neck, but there was nothing showy or ostentatious about him. He was a soldier, not a gangster. Ollie paused on the deck. The boat might be old but it was kept in good condition, the deck scrubbed clean, floodlights fixed to provide it with light, barbed wire around the edge of the deck to deter an assault, and at least a dozen armed men on patrol.

'Come,' snapped Mustaf.

Ollie was led forward to what had once been the captain's quarters. It must have been a cargo ship, he decided, with most of the hull filled with containers, a bridge at the back and, directly below that, living quarters for the captain and a crew of perhaps two dozen. The door swung open and Ollie was led inside. Yasin stepped forward, looking straight into Ollie's eyes. In his right hand, he was holding a knife. The room was illuminated with a couple of bulbs run from the ships' diesel-powered generator, and the blade glinted in the pale light. With a sudden movement, Yasin grabbed hold of Ollie's arms and slashed the blade forwards. Instinctively Ollie steeled himself, expecting the metal to slice into his skin. He closed his eyes. It's starting, he thought. The rough stuff.

The knife cut open the plasti-cuffs, freeing Ollie's hands.

'We treat our prisoners as we would wish to be treated ourselves,' said Yasin, glancing up into Ollie's eyes as he chucked the cuffs into the bin.

Ollie remained silent. But he rubbed his hands together to try and ease the numbness where his wrists had been bound together.

'Tell me your name.'

Ollie said nothing.

'You are my guest here, now tell me your name.' Yasin repeated the command firmly, but his tone was level, with no sign of anger in it.

'Oliver Hall. British citizen . . .'

Yasin smiled. 'Then you'd probably like some tea.' He glanced towards Mustaf. 'Get some.'

Mustaf turned and left.

The room was sparsely furnished. There was a desk at one side, next to its only porthole, with a pair of laptops open. There were five satellite phones out on the desk, plus a set of nautical charts. On top of them was a Sig Sauer P22 compact handgun, a German-Swiss weapon, also known as the M11 when it was used by the American armed forces. On the other side of the room was a small metal bunk, with a sleeping bag neatly folded across it.

There was no fussiness, no luxury, and no ostentation.

Again, like all the best generals, thought Ollie.

Mustaf returned.

'Here,' said Yasin, handing across the hot tea in a clean mug.

Ollie put it to his lips.

There had been plenty of moments in his life when he'd been damned grateful for a hot cup of tea. But not quite as grateful as he felt now. After the hours of confinement, the thirst and the hunger, and the nagging fear of the beating he felt was almost certain when he arrived, the sweet, sugared, milky tea started to revive his spirits the moment it hit the back of his throat and made its way into his bloodstream.

'PG Tips,' he said, looking across at Yasin. 'Bloody good cuppa.'

'As you might say in your country, it fell off the back of a boat,' answered Yasin. 'We have food from all around the world here, kindly donated by the crews that spend time as our guests.'

Ollie laughed. Good cop, he thought to himself. That's what he's playing here. Trying to soften me up, get me on his side, so that he can get me to open those safes.

But the bad cop will be along in a minute.

As he finished the tea, Mustaf and a handful of men carried in the safes.

The pirate walked across to them, ran his hands across their steel casings, and examined the locks. 'Our intelligence tells us that a ship is carrying a valuable cargo. We take the vessel, and find nothing apart from a hull full of grain and some empty containers. Except for these three safes, protected by a British security guard.' A slow grin opened up on his face, exposing his immaculate white teeth. 'I think there might be something interesting inside.' He turned to look at Ollie. 'Open them.'

Again, Ollie remained silent. He put down the empty mug of tea, already wishing he had another one.

'I said open them.'

But Ollie remained silent.

Play for time, he reminded himself. It's the only card you have.

Twenty-Eight

THE LAND CRUISER WAS BOUNCING over the rough surface of the track, but the big wheels and powerful suspension of the Japanese machine were designed for the most brutal terrain, and it could easily handle it. Ian was driving up front, with the headlamps switched off to make it harder for any bandits to detect them. Fighting with the IRA, he'd spent years out on patrol in the wild, dark countryside dividing Northern Ireland from the South, and of all the men, it was his eyes that were the most acclimatised to the task of steering a vehicle using nothing but pale moonlight.

'At least it's not pissing down with rain,' muttered Ian. 'That was always the trouble back home. You'd get a lead on a British patrol, then you couldn't see the fuckers through all the water.'

'Any sign?' said Steve, leaning forward.

Henri was sitting up front, along with Steve, whilst Nick, Dan and Maksim were in the back seats. The radar was switched on, scanning for the tracking device fitted to Ollie. They were driving due north, right into the heart of Puntland, where the peninsula jutted out into the Gulf, and the twisting coastline with its complex maze of coves and hidden caves allowed the pirates to move in and out of the shadows at ease. The road took them ten miles inland, before heading back towards the sea again, and right now they were driving through the harsh interior of the country, where the breezes and vegetation of the coast had long since faded away, replaced by nothing except the baked red earth and the flaking, crumbling rocks that were scattered across its surface.

'No,' answered Henri, with a curt shake of the head. 'But he'll be up here somewhere, I'm certain of it.'

'Let's hope so,' said Steve, glancing out of the window at the dry scrubland. 'I don't fancy wandering around this place in daylight.'

They drove steadily through the night. The state of the road, and the unexpected twists in the track, meant that Ian couldn't risk going above fifteen miles an hour. Twenty max when he hit a straight track bathed in moonlight. It was turning into a slow, arduous journey. And they still didn't have any idea where the target was.

It was just after three in the morning when Nick cried, 'Stop.'

'What is it?' asked Steve.

'Kill the sodding engine,' said Nick, ignoring the question.

Steve scanned the horizon through the windows of the Toyota but couldn't see anything apart from the empty scrubland. There was a harsh cruelty to the landscape, he reflected briefly. A place of death. Nothing could grow in this arid soil. Steve had spent time in the Arabian desert, training with the Regiment, and that had a serene beauty to it. Lifeless, sure, but by choice, as if the land didn't want anything spoiling its pristine surface. But the emptiness here was ugly, as if a plague had swept through the country, destroying everything it touched. Only the skeleton of the earth remained.

'A light,' said Nick.

He was pointing straight ahead. Ian had killed the engine, and the windows were down, but they could hear nothing. The night was completely still.

'It was some kind of flashlight,' said Nick. 'Three or four hundred yards ahead.'

'This vehicle is a tempting enough target,' said Steve. 'We nicked it, so there's no reason why someone else shouldn't as well.'

'Give it five minutes,' said Henri.

They waited.

Steve was keeping an eye on the illuminated clock on the dashboard, his eyes darting between that and the hills to either side of them. Three minutes passed, then four. Nothing.

'I'm telling you, I saw a flashlight,' said Nick. 'Somebody's watching the road.'

'Then we'll deal with them when we see them,' said Henri impetiently.

'I'm not driving on,' said Nick. 'There's an ambush.'

Ian had already started the engine. The Toyota was inching carefully along the road.

But Nick was standing up, flinging open the door. There was an expression of fierce determination on the boy's face. 'I'll track up into the hills,' he said, his face turning red. 'Then I can at least give you covering fire when the assault kicks off.'

Steve and Dan exchanged glances. Nick wasn't an experienced soldier, and a light could have come from anywhere. It might just be a flash of moonlight bouncing off some mineral traces in the rocks.

Then again, this was pirate country. In a land of thieves, you had to be prepared for an attack at any time. And none of them wanted to leave Nick wandering around by himself in the darkness.

'I'm going with him,' said Dan, climbing out of the Land Cruiser. 'We'll meet you a mile up the track. If we haven't seen anything by then, we'll catch you on the road.'

'We're not waiting for you,' snarled Henri. He looked sharply towards Ian. 'Now drive.'

Steve had already steadied his SA-80 in his hand, checking the mag was full. He could feel the anxiety in his stomach as he scanned the horizon. I don't like this place, he told himself. Then again, I haven't liked it since I set foot on land, but a funny feeling tells you sod all.

Ian was starting to pick up speed, pushing up into second gear, taking the Toyota to fifteen miles an hour. The burst of gunfire that shattered the windscreen hit them with a ferocity that was no less savage for being expected. Splinters of glass were blown back into the cabin like hail in a storm. Ian slammed hard on the brakes, putting the Toyota into a spin that kicked up a cloud of dust, the engine revving wildly as the wheels cut into the ground.

'Out, out,' yelled Steve. He flung the door open, rolling straight on to the ground, ignoring the pain, focusing only on the need to get out of the car before it turned into a slaughterhouse.

He hit the ground, the back wheels spinning towards him, as Ian flung himself from the cabin. Steve kicked back with his legs, pushing himself a few yards forwards, creating just enough space to avoid being crushed by the Toyota before it skidded into the hills and stalled. He slammed his finger into the trigger of the SA-80 and loosed off five rounds, paying little attention to where they went. That didn't matter now. They just had to start returning fire, putting down enough rounds to make their opponents take cover. Maybe then they could regroup and start fighting back.

In the hills, twenty yards above the track, there was a sudden explosion. A burst of light flashed across the desolate hillside, followed a split second later by the crash of an explosion. Steve could feel the sudden hotness of the air on his skin and, in his nostrils, could instantly sense the acrid, fierce smell of the charge. A grenade. It had landed straight in their assailants' position, lobbed from the hillside behind them. Nick and Dan, realised Steve. The hit was a good one, it sent a shower of body debris clean into the air. Twenty yards in front of Steve, a severed hand landed in the dust, blood seeping from the wrist, but otherwise in perfect condition.

'Up, up,' yelled Steve.

He gripped his SA-80, clicked the trigger into automatic, and started to run straight up into the hills. His lungs were bursting, the sudden exertion making sweat pour off him, but the adrenalin of the battle had kicked in, speeding his heartbeat, and banishing everything else from his mind apart from the need to survive the next few seconds. The grenade had disrupted the attack, killing at least one man, and putting the rest into a flap. Steve lunged forward, with Ian, Maksim and Henri at his side, a tight, controlled unit moving in close formation to finish off their opponents. There was no other choice: their enemy had the high ground, and knew the terrain, and there was nowhere for them to take cover. If they didn't take advantage of the disruption caused by the grenade, they would never win the fight.

Steve could see two men moving ahead of them.

'Fire, fire,' he yelled, his voice ragged with anger.

He unleashed a volley of bullets from the SA-80. One man tumbled forward, the munitions splintering open his chest, whilst incoming fire from the rest of the unit took care of his mate. Amid the maelstrom of bullets, it was impossible to tell who was shooting whom. Not that it matters, thought Steve grimly. So long as it's the blokes on the other side that take the bullets.

Ten yards behind them, another man stood up and started to run, but a sniper shot from Nick on the hills on the other side of the track took care of him, sending him flying back into the scrubland as the bullet split open his forehead.

Steve paused.

The fight was ending as quickly as it had begun. Four bodies were dead in front of them. One more had been blown apart by the grenade, and his remains were scattered over the tracks.

Five blokes. Maybe that was it.

Then a noise.

He spun round.

Nothing.

With his rifle still outstretched, he peered into the darkness. There were only three rounds left in the clip but he didn't want to waste time changing the mag; a sniper might still be there, dug into the ground, just waiting for a moment to loosen off a shot.

'There,' he hissed, glancing anxiously to Ian at his right.

Ian nodded.

Steve glanced towards Maksim at his left.

Silently, the three men started to advance. The hills folded away in front of them, creating a series of dips and ridges, spaces into which a man could nestle, like a snake lying up in the long grass, waiting for the moment to pounce on its prey. The air was still and cold, the heat of the battle having faded as fast as it had flared up, and Steve couldn't hear any whisper of a breeze.

Then a sound.

To the right, closer to Maksim.

A burst of fire rattled from the Russian's rifle. A man suddenly leapt upwards from the ground, his face red with an ugly mixture of fear and fury. He was wearing body armour, and Maksim's first couple of shots had bounced harmlessly off his chest.

Silence. The Russian had run out of ammo.

The man had fired one shot from his AK-47, but it was wild, fired before he had any chance to take aim. Now he was steadying himself. Preparing for the next shot to be a good one.

Steve raised his SA-80, putting the sights to his right eye, and levelled a single shot straight into the man's windpipe. It cut open his throat, causing a massive, sudden loss of blood. The crimson liquid spilled down his neck on to his chest, he gurgled and spluttered, whimpered just once in agony, then collapsed on to the ground. Maksim had used the few seconds available to ram a fresh mag into his rifle, and quickly slotted another pair of bullets into the man.

Steve spun round. Henri had hung behind, protecting their rear, but one more assailant had jumped onto the Frenchman, knocking him down. The SA-80 had been knocked clean from his hands, and they were tussling on the ground, a vicious sprawl of arms and fists. Steve and Ian started to run. The Frenchman was strong but his attacker was wiry and agile and that made him a formidable opponent. '*Koos, koos,*' he was screaming each time a blow landed on him. Steve didn't know much Arabic, but he'd learnt the word for 'cunt' out in Iraq. Saddam's boys used it all the time, sometimes about the enemy, but usually about their own officers, and given the way they were led, Steve didn't reckon he could blame them. But an Arab? What was the sod doing out here?

With one massive heave from his legs, Henri pushed the man backwards, sending him flying into the dust. He crashed into the ground, but was holding himself steady. Steve started to run towards him, but the man had already started to draw a pistol from his belt. Ian placed a shot straight into him, then another. By the time Steve was on top of him, he was already dead.

'Christ, these people will nick anything,' said Ian, putting his gun down and standing next to Steve. 'Do you think they might be Scousers?'

'They're Arabs,' said Henri.

Whether he was ignoring the joke, or didn't get it, Steve wasn't sure.

'I know,' he said. 'But where the hell from?'

Henri shrugged. 'The Somalis have their own language, a member of the Cushetic branch of Afro-Asiatic languages. These guys are speaking Arabic. Yemeni, I think, from their accents.'

'So what the hell are they doing here?' asked Ian.

'I don't know,' answered Henri crisply. 'Yemen is an al-Queda stronghold. Osama bin Laden's father came from there. It's dirt poor and home to thousands of terrorists.'

'They'll feel right at home around here then,' said Steve. 'I suggest we get the hell out before any more nutters descend on us.'

They stopped to check that each man was dead; one man was still just breathing, but Maksim finished him off with a single tap to the head, as much out of mercy as any concern about a threat he might pose. They collected the weapons. There were four AK-47s, each with up to fifty rounds of ammunition, and they'd be useful. Then they walked back down to the track where Nick and Dan had already rejoined the stalled Toyota.

'Maybe you'll bloody listen to me next time,' said Nick crossly.

'Sure we will,' said Steve, giving him a friendly punch on the shoulder. 'Except when you start banging on about how Liverpool can still win the league.'

'Or Wales the rugby,' added Dan.

Ian was inspecting the damage to the vehicle. The windscreen was shot out, and two tyres had been punctured. There was one spare, and within minutes Dan had the jack out and had changed the wheel, but they would have to complete the rest of the journey with one flat.

'The state of this track, and the speed we're making, it's not going to make much sodding difference,' said Ian grumpily.

The six men clambered back into the Toyota, Ian gunned the engine and they started to bump along the track. It was still pitch black, and their lights were out, and with a tyre gone the ride was even rougher than before. They were all relieved to have survived the attack, yet remained wary of another assault.

'We've learnt one thing about Somalia, and we've only been here a few hours,' said Steve grimly. 'The place is crawling with criminals. Pirates, bandits, al-Queda. This place has more villains than Lewisham, and I didn't reckon I'd ever be able to say that about anywhere.'

Nick was fiddling around with the iPod, connecting it to the Toyota's speakers, and suddenly the vehicle was filled with the booming opening chords of Bruce Springsteen's 'Hungry Heart'. 'It's like Jeff told me, out in Afghanistan,' he said. 'When you've just killed a man, only the Boss will do.'

They drove for another half hour before they finally picked up the signal.

Nick had scrolled his way through a dozen Springsteen tracks and was humming along to 'Racing in the Street' when Henri switched the sound down and pointed towards the radar screen.

The drive had been uneventful enough. Ian was pushing forward carefully, and they kept a close lookout for any lights, but either they were into an empty stretch of country, or else the trail of corpses they'd left in their wake was deterring any of the local bandits from taking them on. Either way, the road was clear.

'How far?' asked Ian.

'Fifteen kilometres,' answered Henri. 'North-north-east. Just stay on the track.'

In the back seat, Steve breathed a sigh of relief. Nothing had gone right since they'd first set foot in Somalia, but they'd located Ollie, they had transport, and none of them had any injuries worse than a few scratches and bruises. They were on track. But they were about to go into the hardest phase of the mission, the moment when all their resources would be tested to maximum. And there was something about this place he didn't like. The country was swirling with enemies, like a room full of shadows where you could never be sure where the next attack was coming from. And that was always the worst kind of environment for a soldier to operate in.

It was just before five in the morning when Ian pulled the Toyota up.

The night was still dark, but soon the first glimmers of dawn would start to break over the horizon. They'd stopped a mile short of the target. Ian drove into the scrubland, eight hundred yards off the track, and steered the Toyota behind a ridge of rocks. It wouldn't be visible from the road, and they could tab the rest of the way in on foot. They certainly didn't want to drive up to Ali Yasin's compound. It wasn't as if the pirate was going to welcome them with open arms. The only chance of making this work was to hit with total surprise, and they could only do that if they remained hidden until the last moment.

'What do you reckon the chances of it still being there when we get back?' said Steve as they climbed out of the vehicle.

'Less than sodding zero,' said Ian with a rough grin. 'There are some streets in Belfast where you have to take the wheels with you if you want your car to have a chance of surviving the day. I reckon it's a bit like that.'

They started to walk. They kept well away from the track to minimise the chances of detection. It was rough ground, empty even of vegetation, and after they covered the first couple of hundred yards, Steve could hear the crashing of the waves in the distance. We're back by the coast, he realised. Looking at the radar, he reckoned Ollie was another eight, nine hundred yards away. He hadn't moved in the last hour since they'd tuned back into the signal, suggesting he was inside Yasin's lair. Either dead or alive, thought Steve grimly. We'll find out soon enough.

'Down,' snapped Dan. The Australian was walking a few paces ahead of the rest of the unit.

As Steve dropped to the ground, he looked straight ahead.

The lights of the base were clearly visible: a string of electric flashlights illuminated a barbed wire fence and, behind that, where beach hit water, the hull of an old cargo ship.

'That's the target, boys,' said Steve. 'Looks like we're about to find out how much fight these pirate boys have in them. And may God help us.'

Twenty-Nine

'THOSE ARE MY MEN,' SNAPPED Bruce, looking straight at
Layla.

He was not an emotional man. Ten years as a sergeant
in the SAS, followed by ten years building up his own private
military corporation, had taught him to keep his feelings under
control. Anger didn't get you anywhere in either job. Only guile,
cunning, strength and determination.

But his own blokes? Wasted as if their blood counted for
nothing? That was worth raising your voice for.

'They are mercenaries,' said Layla, her tone arch. 'They're
expendable.'

Bruce paused. It was going to take all the iron discipline and
self-control he'd learnt in the Army to stop himself from losing his
rag in the next few seconds. 'They are my boys,' he growled.

'Oh, please,' said Layla. She looked away, her expression exas-
perated. 'For Christ's sake, Bruce, every soldier is some mother's
son. That doesn't mean we don't ever put them in harm's way.'

'Jesus, you're a cold bitch.'

'This is a war. If you've grown too old and too soft to fight, and
to understand that blood sometimes has to be spilt, then I'd
respectfully suggest you're in the wrong fucking business.'

'And I suggest you've picked the wrong fucking fight,' Bruce
snapped. 'Respectfully.'

'Damned well grow up.'

'I know too much about too many black ops.'

Layla poured herself a stiff whisky, then another for Bruce. She took a sip, leaving a trace of red lipstick across the glass. 'Are you threatening me?'

Bruce nodded just once. 'They're my boys,' he said crisply. 'Piss them around, and there are plenty of embarrassing secrets that could suddenly find themselves leaking into the public domain. Some of the jobs that DEF have worked on in the past few years. Jobs that the British government paid for.'

Layla took another hit of the whisky.

Bruce remained expressionless but, inside, he was pleased. You could always tell when a threat was working in the first second after you delivered it. And she looked rattled.

She walked across to the desk.

A dossier was lying carefully folded next to the laptop. She opened it, and pulled out a shipping chart. Bruce recognised it immediately. The Gulf of Aden, leading into the Somali Basin. Then she pulled out a single black and white grainy picture showing a cargo ship and placed it next to the chart.

'A month ago, this British ship was sailing through the Gulf on its way to Japan,' she said, her tone controlled and slow, but with a note of tension audible within it. 'It was carrying reprocessed weapons-grade plutonium. It's not a trade many people know about because we keep it under wraps, but British plants take the plutonium the Japanese and other countries use in their nuclear power-generating stations, reprocess it so that it can be used in weapons research, then sell it back to the original owners. It's dangerous work, but it helps the balance of payments, and British industry isn't in such great shape these days that we can afford to turn down the money.'

She pointed to the picture of the ship. 'There was two hundred pounds of the stuff on board this vessel. Four weeks ago, the pirates hit it, overpowered the security team we had on board, and cleaned the ship out.'

'They got the plutonium?'

'Precisely,' answered Layla. 'I don't think they had any idea what they were taking. It was just a routine robbery, the kind that happens all the time, and we don't advertise the fact that a ship is carrying plutonium, for obvious reasons. But they aren't stupid, and they figured out pretty quickly what they had. Now Ali Yasin is auctioning it to the highest bidder. The Iranians, the Taliban, al-Queda, the North Koreans, they all want to get their hands on this stuff.'

'This is the raw material you need to make a nuclear weapon.'

'I'm afraid so. Just about any bright teenager sitting down with Google can make a nuke these days. The difficult bit is getting hold of the plutonium. Every terrorist group and rogue state in the world wants it. And we just lost two hundred pounds of the stuff to the greediest, best connected pirate in the world. It's probably the most embarrassing thing that has ever happened to the British government, and there's some pretty hot competition for that prize, believe me.'

She leant across the table, and pointed to the shipping chart. 'So we've put a tracking device on your man, and he's going to be taken prisoner by Yasin, and taken to his headquarters. Once we're sure he's there, we're going to send in a dozen cruise missiles and blow that bastard, and more importantly his plutonium, right off the face of the planet.'

Her eyes flashed up to meet Bruce's.

'Problem solved,' she said harshly. 'And a government saved.'

'You said this was about the insurance market,' said Bruce. 'They'll all die when those missiles go in.'

Layla drained her whisky. She turned away and walked back towards the window. Along the Thames the lights of the city were sparkling everywhere, but it was past two in the morning now and there was no traffic in the streets outside. 'Every war has collateral damage, you know that,' she replied. 'Like I said, they are expendable.'

Matt Lynn

'They're good men.'

'I don't doubt it. But we can't allow that plutonium to fall into the hands of terrorists.'

'You—'

'Leave it, Bruce,' she cut in. 'You're a soldier. You know all the arguments. You sacrifice one life to save a thousand. You made those calls in the Regiment, and we're still making them now. There's no point in complaining about it.'

Without saying another word, Bruce turned to leave.

'Don't get any funny ideas, Bruce,' Layla warned as he opened the door. 'They'll die in a good cause. Just be grateful for that.'

Thirty

'THE QUESTION IS A SIMPLE one,' said Yasin. 'Are you going to open those safes for me or not?'

Ollie remained rooted to the spot.

He'd been sitting in the cabin for a couple of hours now. Yasin had left the room, leaving just one armed guard behind to keep a watch on Ollie. He had been given no explanation as to where Yasin had gone, or when he might be coming back, so Ollie just sat and waited. An hour passed and then another. He knew precisely what they were up to. Back in the Blues he'd been through captivity training, it was part of the basic drill for every officer. The techniques varied; you might be tormented with knives, electricity, ropes or water. But one thing was always the same. The secret of torture, he could remember his instructor at Sandhurst telling him, was the same as the secret of Chinese cooking. It was all in the preparation. The torturer would keep his victim waiting, leave him alone with his thoughts, aware that it was in those lonely hours that his will would start to soften, and his resistance break. And then when you started to apply the pain, he'd be ready to talk.

Well, it makes no damned difference to me, thought Ollie. Time is all I'm playing for here. The longer they keep me waiting, the more time Steve has to organise his strike-back.

'As it happens, I don't know the codes,' said Ollie, his tone confident. 'But even if I did, I wouldn't tell you.'

He was sitting on a chair, slightly to the left of the three safes. Yasin was sitting directly opposite him at his desk. 'Do I look like a stupid man?'

Ollie shook his head. 'It's not my place to offer opinions.'

'Maybe not,' snapped Yasin. 'But it's hardly possible that a security guard would be protecting these safes with no way of accessing them. If the ship catches fire, hits rocks, whatever, you have to rescue what's inside them. So, please don't treat me like an idiot.'

'I'm not,' said Ollie. 'I'm telling you the truth. I don't know the codes, but I wouldn't give them to you if I did, so it makes no difference anyway.'

He glanced through the single porthole. It was four in the morning, and still dark outside. There were pirates patrolling the deck, well-armed and well-disciplined. Ollie hadn't yet managed to count how many men protected the compound. Thirty at least, he reckoned. For six men to overpower the ship and bring him out alive was going to be a hell of a task, he reflected grimly. Maybe even impossible.

'So the answer to your question is a simple one,' he continued. 'No, I'm not going to open them.'

'Do you know how we describe pirates in my country?'

Ollie shook his head.

'In Somalia, the word is *badaadinta badah*,' said Yasin. 'It translates as saviours of the sea.'

'I'm grateful for the language lesson.'

'We're tax collectors and coastguards,' said Yasin. 'The world uses our sea lanes, our coast. This is a poor country, and the sea is all we have. There is no reason why we shouldn't charge the rest of the world for using it.'

He stood, walked up to the safes and ran his hands over them again. 'So you see,' he continued, 'it doesn't matter how we are portrayed in the rest of the world. We are not bandits or brigands. We are not cruel men, and we mean nobody any real harm. As you may know, ships are brought into our harbours, but the crews are treated well, after which they are released—'

'You carry AK-47s and knives,' interrupted Ollie. 'It doesn't sound very peaceful to me.'

'Your policemen carry weapons, and so do your coastguards,' retorted Yasin. 'The point I am making is that we are just tax collectors. We have no other living we can make, not since our fish stocks were all stolen by the rest of the world, so this is how we support ourselves. We have no wish to harm anyone. We don't torture our prisoners or mistreat them if we can possibly avoid it. So one last time. You will be well looked after. But we need to open this safe.'

'It's my job to protect it.'

'And you are in my country, and the law here says you have to open it.'

'And I'm telling you, I haven't been given the combinations.'

Yasin took a step closer, and leant over, so that he was just inches away from Ollie's face. 'I've already told you, we are not cruel men. But we will break you if we have to.'

'Then do your worst,' said Ollie.

Thirty-One

D AWN WAS BREAKING OVER THE cove. Behind it the sea was flat and calm, its surface a brilliant emerald-blue, and the sun was still low over the horizon, gradually flooding the coast with a warm, gentle light as it inched into the sky.

Steve remained flat on the ground.

They were five hundred yards back from the wired perimeter of the compound, taking advantage of a small ridge to remain hidden. So long as none of them stood up, he was confident they would remain out of view; there was a sentry post on the fence, with a pair of armed guards manning it, but there were no watchtowers to scan the surrounding countryside for attacks.

A weakness, thought Steve. A properly trained commander would know that he needed men high up to spot any intruders.

He took Henri's binoculars and placed them to his eyes, taking a closer look at the compound. The pirates lived inside the old hull, and although they changed their shifts constantly, Steve reckoned there were thirty to thirty-five men on board. They were well dug in, they looked well organised, and well supplied; he could sense they'd be a far tougher enemy than he'd planned for.

'What do you reckon?' he asked, glancing toward the rest of the unit.

'Ollie's in there somewhere,' said Henri, checking the radar screen again. 'Inside the boat.'

Steve nodded. 'How are we going to get him out?'

'Run at the fuckers, and shoot them,' said Maksim with a wild grin.

'Thanks, Maksie,' said Ian. 'I was wondering if there might be something more subtle.'

'Such as?' asked Dan.

Ian took the binoculars and spent a few minutes scanning both the ship and the compound. 'Can we come in by boat?' he said, looking across at Henri.

Steve had unpacked a flask of water and some dried biscuits and was handing them around. The men had been up all night and they needed some food to give them the energy to carry on.

'How?' said Henri, taking a swig of the water.

'We could tab down the coast, get out into the water, then come at them from behind,' said Ian. 'Might be a lot easier than trying to get through that perimeter fence.'

Henri was staring straight at the compound. 'It's a possibility.'

'We're not here to decide anything this morning,' interrupted Steve. 'I don't reckon we can attack until night anyway, and we need to scout the whole area. We'll decide the best way in when we've looked at all the options.'

'You think Ollie can hold out until then?' asked Dan.

'Maybe we should be going straight in to get him,' said Nick.

'That's sodding barmy,' growled Steve. 'We need to scout the area.'

The men nodded, and Steve knew they agreed with him. Their mate was holed up in there somewhere, possibly taking a bad beating, and they all wanted to go in and get him out; if one of them had lost the card game, and gone in as the hostage, they'd be hoping to be rescued at the first possible moment. But there was a formidable opponent in front of them. And if they didn't plan the attack properly, they'd be throwing away their own lives, and quite possibly Ollie's as well. They were all professional fighters, and they knew the score. Your mates would rescue you, and they'd put their lives on the line if they had to. But they didn't commit suicide. That wasn't part of the code.

'Dan, you head round the perimeter, and scout out the ground overlooking the fence,' said Steve. 'Maksie, you get up into those hills behind the cove. We need to know where there's cover, where there might be reinforcements, and where we might go in.'

'And what are you blokes doing?' asked Dan.

'Getting some kip behind this rock and working on our tans.'

'Nice,' he grumbled. 'I owe you one.'

Dan dropped back two hundred yards and started to walk. He glanced inwards towards the compound, but felt certain he couldn't be spotted. The ground rose steadily as it retreated from the coast, but the surface was dry, and pitted with craters, like the surface of the moon. Dan was moving carefully, examining the territory. There was some high ground, he noted, from which they might be able to launch an attack. Under the cover of darkness, they could bombard the compound with grenades, and if they could find some piping, they could put together a simple mortar. That might soften the pirates up for a full-blooded assault. Then again, it would reveal their position, and might just provoke a counter-assault in which all of them could very easily be wiped out.

Dan kept going. It was getting close to nine in the morning. The sun was rising, flooding the surface of the sea with a brilliant yellow light and baking the dry ground with its heat. Sweat was starting to drip from his forehead. At this rate, he reckoned they'd all be perspiring like pigs in a sauna before it was even midday.

He stopped, dropping down to the ground.

He'd seen some men, he felt certain of it. Seen and heard.

He lay with his face down in a one-metre-deep crater cut into the dusty land. He peered up carefully over its lip. About five hundred yards away he could see a group of at least four men. They had thick black beards, and were wearing dishdashas: the loose, single-piece robes worn by the fighters Dan was familiar with from his time in Afghanistan. They were dug in behind a hill and, as far as he could see, two of them were keeping watch, their hands gripped tight to their AK-47s, whilst another two men were using small field telescopes to survey Yasin's compound.

He listened carefully, waiting to catch a whisper of their conversation.

Pashto. Again, he recognised it from Afghanistan. A rough, guttural language, like a bear spitting. He knew instinctively who they were. He'd fought them plenty of times, and learnt to hate everything they represented.

The Taliban.

What the hell are those bastards doing here?

Six hundred yards away, Maksim was climbing up into the hills. A ridge of high ground ran directly behind the cove, reaching a thousand metres above sea level half a mile inland. It was twisting, barren country, scattered with rocks and the occasional piece of scrub, but with no sign of fresh water. Maksim walked steadily forwards, keeping a wary eye out to make sure he wasn't visible from the cove, advancing a mile from where they were based in half an hour. As he looked back down, he could see the coastline more clearly. It twisted away from the cove, jutted out into a rugged, rocky promontory, then stretched into a long, sandy beach that ran for another mile or so. If they wanted to, they could kick off from the promontory and swim to Yasin's ship. It was a distance of half a mile or so, and although they would have some rough waves to contend with around the rocks, it wasn't anything that would present too much of an obstacle.

Maybe that was the way to attack. Crawl up out of the water, using some of the techniques they'd learnt in France.

He shrugged, scratching himself where the sweat inside his body armour was making him itch, and tried to figure out the angles.

They were more familiar with attacking from the land. But

coming in from the sea would spring a surprise. In the Spetsnaz, they'd storm the wire, and bring it down with an assault of bullets and steel. That was the Russian way. Crash into your enemy with overwhelming power and aggression, and let the casualties mount up on both sides. There were always more men, that was the solid rock on which Russian military doctrine was founded. Losses didn't matter, only winning.

But these Westerners were different. He was starting to learn their ways, and sometimes even respect them. Guile and cunning counted for as much as brute force.

Suddenly, the thought was interrupted. He dropped to his knees.

A voice. Two, maybe three voices.

Maksim crawled forward, positioning himself behind a boulder. There were three men seven hundred yards ahead of him. They'd taken up a position where two big rocks came together, creating a half-cave that provided some shelter from the baking sun and made it impossible to see them unless you were coming up the hillside along the route Maksim had just taken. They were slim, with dark, olive skin, short black hair, and wearing jeans and sweatshirts. As Maksim looked closer, he could see that the men must have been dug in there for several days. They were professional, he could see that at a glance; they had carefully cleared away all their rubbish, making sure they left no trace of their presence near the compound. But he could see food stacked up next to the kitbags, and traces of disturbed earth where they'd been burying their crap.

Listening hard, Maksim waited until he caught a few words of conversation. He recognised the language.

Persian.

And he reckoned he had a good idea who they were. The Quds Force.

What are those bastards doing here? wondered Maksim.

The special forces division of the Army of the Guardians of the

Islamic Revolution, itself a separate branch of the Iranian Army formed after the 1979 Islamic coup, and reporting directly to the Ayatollah, the Quds – or Jerusalem – Force was responsible for operations outside Iran. It was heavily involved in training Islamic fundamentalists around the world, and was permitted to carry out terrorist attacks. It was well plugged into every shadowy militant and terror group around the region. Maksim had come across them when he was in the Spetsnaz. They had clashed many times with the Quds, along the borders of Azerbaijan, Georgia, and Iran itself, all regions that the Spetsnaz referred to as the 'near abroad' and regarded as rightfully part of Russia's sphere of influence. They were tough and well-trained, and they operated with a fanatical ruthlessness that even the Russian Army regarded as bordering on the cruel. And they never flinched from a battle, no matter how impossible the odds or doomed the mission. For that, the Spetsnaz had learnt to respect them.

Maksim took a few minutes to observe the men, making sure at all times that he remained safely hidden behind the rock. They were an observation unit, he felt certain of it: a small patrol sent out in advance of a larger force to scout the land, assess the enemy, and probe for possible points of weakness. They weren't equipped for battle, and they didn't look to be planning an assault. They were just carefully monitoring the compound down below, getting to know precisely how many men were defending it, what kind of kit they were equipped with, and what their fighting capabilities might be.

But why? Why would the Quds be interested in some Somali pirates?

Maksim turned and started to scurry back down the hillside to the rest of the unit. It took him another twenty minutes to scramble down, making sure he remained out of view, and by the time he got back to Steve and the rest of the boys, Dan had also returned. He was crouching down, taking a long swig on a bottle of water and grabbing three of the dried biscuits that Steve had been handing round. Dan glanced at the men, his expression serious.

'There's a unit of Taliban less than a mile away, guys,' he said.

'Jesus, mate, Terry Taliban and his merry men,' said Steve. 'What the sod are those nutters doing here?'

'Are you sure?' quizzed Ian.

Dan nodded. 'Positive, pal. They've got dishdashas, black beards, they're talking Pashto, the works. I've seen those fuckers close up more often than any man really wants to. And that's who they are.'

'What are they up to?' asked Ian.

'Just watching,' answered Dan. 'Keeping an eye on the compound, maybe looking for a way in.'

'Same as the Quds,' interrupted Maksim.

'Spuds!' spluttered Nick. 'You met some spuds?'

'Were they chips or mash?' asked Steve chuckling.

'Quds,' snapped Maksim angrily. 'The Iranian special forces.'

Henri was looking at him sceptically. 'Really?'

'For sure,' said Maksim. 'I recognised them from my time in the Spetsnaz. Iranian special forces. Mean bastards. They're watching the compound, just the same as the Taliban that Dan saw.'

'Let me get this straight,' said Steve. 'There's a unit of Taliban out there. And another unit of Iranians. And they are both watching Yasin's headquarters?' He glanced towards the compound, his voice dropping a note. 'What the hell is going on in there that has suddenly got the whole world in such a flap?'

Thirty-Two

THE MORNING AIR WAS CHILLY in south London.
Bruce climbed out of the Jag and walked round the back of the small terminal building. Biggin Hill, between Croydon and Brixton, was the main private airport for the London area. Bankers, diplomats and businessmen used it all day long for landing their private planes, and a couple of dozen small charter firms operated out of the airbase, offering jets, complete with pilots and crews, for hire by the hour or the day.

But at five in the morning it was as quiet as a graveyard.

That's the advantage of flying private, reflected Bruce, as he stepped towards the small café used by the pilots, technicians and ground staff. You don't have to get up in the middle of the night to catch a six o'clock plane from Stansted like you do with Ryanair.

Jeff Roberston had a hot coffee waiting for him, and Bruce sipped it gratefully. It had been a long night, and it wasn't over yet. It had been after two in the morning when he'd left Layla's Chelsea apartment, and he'd spent the three hours since then discussing the options with David and Ganju, then working the phones to see if they could get the kit they needed.

Even in the daytime, it was a lot of favours to call in. In the middle of the night it was almost impossible. But one thing was certain. They weren't going to let Steve, Ollie, and the rest of the boys die in a missile strike. Not without doing their best to save them.

'It's kind of short notice, Bruce,' said Robertson.

He was a tall man, with sandy blond hair, and the sort of gentle good looks that had probably made him a heart-throb when he was still in the RAF. Like Bruce, after coming out of the services he'd gone into business for himself. Robertson Aviation ran a fleet of three private Gulfstream jets that would fly a small and exclusive clientele anywhere in the world. They didn't compete on price, which was just as well; private aviation was a brutally competitive business, the planes and the fuel were expensive, and most of the small firms were losing money. Robertson competed on security. He was one of the best pilots the RAF had ever had, with the medals to prove it, and even if he didn't fly the planes himself, he made sure the men who did were every bit as skilled as he was. If that wasn't enough to reassure the clients, he could always provide a close protection unit to come along for the ride. DEF provided those men, and the two firms had done plenty of business together over the past few years.

'It's an emergency,' said Bruce.

Robertson raised an eyebrow.

'No questions this time, Jeff,' said Bruce. 'Let's just say I'll owe you a favour.'

'What do you need?'

'A jet to fly over Somalia,' said Bruce. 'I've got two men waiting in my car. They need to make a high-altitude jump over the country, then they can steer themselves home.'

'HAHO?' said Robertson, slipping into an RAF acronym.

Bruce nodded.

'Christ, you're serious, aren't you?'

'Like I said, it's an emergency.'

Bruce had the plan all figured out. There was no way they could make contact with the unit in Somalia. They might be carrying a satellite phone, but MI6 would have that number, and they'd have made sure it was secure. The only way to warn them was for David and Ganju to get to them in person. And the only way to do that was a HAHO – or high altitude high opening – jump.

It was a technique that had been perfected by specialist military units around the world over many years. There were countries where it was impossible to get a team of men in. The borders were sealed, and the coastline secure. But there would always be commercial flights going over a country at 35,000 feet. You'd put your team on board a standard Boeing or Airbus on a regular commercial run, then they'd jump from the cargo hold in mid-flight. If they opened their parachutes within minutes of jumping, they could travel several miles through the air just by tugging on their cords, then drop straight into their chosen destination. At night, a HAHO unit could be dropped into just about any country in the world without anyone knowing they were there.

'What do you need?'

'A Gulfstream to fly over the Somali coast,' said Bruce. 'And two parachutes.'

'Not much then.'

Bruce grinned. 'Like I said, it's a big favour.'

'And, I'm just guessing here, but this one sounds like it's off the books.'

'Unofficial, yes,' said Bruce. 'You, me and the two guys making the drop know about it. Nobody else.'

Robertson thought for a moment, consulting his laptop. 'I've got a Gulfstream II we can use,' he said finally. 'I'll fly it myself.'

'What route?'

'I'll fly down to Lisbon. There's a small private airfield there that's never too crowded, and we have a football manager who is a client of ours who uses it all the time, so it's not going to raise any eyebrows if we register that flight with the air traffic guys. I'll put your two boys down as the close protection unit. From there, I'll register that I'm flying to Lahore.'

'It's a long way round.'

'We have to log every flight with air traffic control, and MI6 keeps a close track on planes coming in and out of the country. I'm assuming that a plane suddenly taking off for Somali airspace is going to raise suspicions. So we need to make it look real and throw them off the scent. Lisbon to Lahore takes you straight over Somalia.'

'How soon can we leave?'

'I'll register all the details of the flight and get the plane fuelled up,' said Robertson. 'Get your boys kitted up, and check them through customs and passport control. We can take off in an hour.'

'Thanks,' said Bruce. 'Like I said, I owe you.'

Robertson drained his coffee. 'They're not carrying anything, are they?'

'No. But can we get some guns on the plane?'

Robertson shook his head. 'It can be done,' he said. 'And believe me it has been. But the rules are so strict on taking firearms on board planes, it needs several days of advance planning. With this kind of notice, it's not possible.'

'I understand. Just get them over Somalia, and drop them off. That's all I'm asking.'

Bruce walked back to the car park. He'd collected a pair of coffees in Styrofoam cups, and handed them across to Ganju and David. 'We'll be leaving in an hour,' he said.

David took a hit of the coffee, letting the caffeine course through his veins. Thirty-six hours ago, he reflected briefly, he'd been reading Peppa Pig stories to the twins, contemplating a day down at the dealership, and looking forward to a long walk with the family on Sunday afternoon with a roast dinner afterwards. And now? He was about to be dropped into an inferno out of the back of a jet. And when he landed – if he landed – he'd be flinging himself into a whirlwind of war and chaos.

It was enough to test the nerve of any man. What would it do to a bloke with a bad spell of post-traumatic stress disorder?

There was no way of knowing.

'You going to be OK?' asked Bruce.

He was looking David straight in the eye. There was a toughness about Bruce. He had the steel core that had made him such an effective parade ground sergeant. Show him a slacker, a whinger or a coward, and he'd chew the sod to pieces and think nothing of it. But there was another side to him. Show him a man with a wound acquired in an honourable battle, and there was nothing he wouldn't do for the guy.

'I'll be fine,' said David sharply.

'I can go by myself,' said Ganju quietly.

'I told you, I'll be OK,' repeated David. 'Probably the best thing that can happen to me. Hair of the dog and all that.'

'Good man,' said Bruce, slapping him on the shoulder. 'Let's get our mates back.'

Thirty-Three

MUSTAF WAS HOLDING THE HOSEPIPE menacingly in his right hand.

Ollie watched it swing through the air, heard its swish as it swirled from side to side, and, even though he held his expression solid and immobile, he could feel himself flinching inside.

He didn't mind taking a beating. A man couldn't come through public school, the Blues, and then the Circuit without learning how to survive the punishment that was inevitable once any scrap kicked off. But torture? That was something different. A test of stamina, fortitude and endurance. A mental contest, in which the strength of a man's mind was put to the test far more than his body. And, in that kind of war, Ollie was never sure how much ammunition he had in his armoury.

'Now tell us the combination,' growled Mustaf.

'I don't have it,' said Ollie.

Mustaf took another step forward. It was two hours now since Yasin had left the room for the second time, and for most of it Ollie had been left alone, strapped to the chair in which he was sitting, with both his legs and his arms bound, but otherwise unharmed. But when Mustaf came into the room ten minutes ago with the hosepipe in his hand, he had no doubt that the beating was about to start.

Play for time, he told himself. Every moment you delay this

gives Steve more time to organise a rescue.

'You'll speak and speak now.'

'Piss off.'

The hosepipe swung again. It was just three feet of hard, hollow plastic, the kind you might find in any suburban garden, but Ollie was well aware of the pain it could inflict. Hosepipes were often used for beatings, by soldiers, by gangsters, or by terrorists. The thickness of the plastic could cut right into a man's skin, digging a channel deep into the blood and tissue, making his nerves boil and pop with pain.

Ollie had seen it done. And it wasn't something any man would want to experience for himself.

'There's no bloody use in threatening me,' he snarled. 'It won't do you any good.'

He looked into the eyes of his opponent, but he could see nothing there, except for the cold, greasy malevolence of a man who had learnt how to enjoy inflicting pain on others.

'Just answer me.'

A second passed.

Then another.

And then the blow fell.

Ollie gritted his teeth and clenched his fists as the hosepipe ripped through the fabric of his sweatshirt then sliced into the skin, thumping into the bone of his third rib. At first Ollie could feel only a numbness, spreading out from the centre of his chest and running up to his shoulders and neck. The nerve endings were seizing up in shock. And then, slowly at first but gradually building in intensity, the pain began. It bubbled up, starting with a stinging around the rib as the blood started to seep out of the cut, then burst inside his brain.

'Fucking, fucking, fuck . . .' He yelled the words, even though his throat was raw and dry.

'Tell us the combination.'

'Piss off.'

Another blow. This one was right above the first, smashing into his body close to the second rib. It wasn't as deep or as hard as the first, noted Ollie in a brief moment of numbed clarity before the next inevitable wave of agony rolled through him. But it didn't make much difference. Choosing between them was like asking whether you wanted your left or right testicle cut off. It was going to hurt like hell either way.

'Bugger, bugger, bugger . . .' he yelled.

The screaming and shouting didn't make much difference. But it allowed him to control the pain rippling through him in wave after wave.

Mustaf stepped back a couple of paces.

The bastard was well-trained in torture, reflected Ollie grimly. He was following the drill, as if he'd been on the same interrogation course Ollie had sat through at Sandhurst. The torturer would threaten you, bully you, then wait. He'd put some blows in, then back off, give you some time to think, then step up the pain again. It was a process of wearing down your resistance.

Your response was just another drill. The box. You were taught to lock yourself up in a mental cavern, think of all the people and places most valuable to you, then retreat inside it, preserving your mental strength, even as your body got shredded to pieces.

There was only one problem, realised Ollie despairingly. It was the same one he'd encountered when he got roughed up by the Africans last year.

There's not much in my box.

Not Katie, that's for sure. He'd cancelled their wedding at the last minute a year ago and, if the woman had been here now, he had no doubt she'd be asking Mustaf if she could have a crack at him as well. Probably with her mother joining the queue for seconds. Not his family either. Ollie's mother had died when he was still a kid, and his father had packed him off to a series of boarding schools, then been furious with him when he'd joined the Army instead of the Navy. There was Lena, the Italian nanny who'd looked after him from his mother's death at the age of three until boarding school started at eight. With her mane of black hair, infectious, flirty giggle, and the scent of boiled sweets that seemed permanently stuck to her, he'd climbed into her bed plenty of times as a child when he couldn't get to sleep. And maybe there was Sandra. She was a hell of minx, no question about that, decided Ollie. A demon between the sheets, and a good laugh when she was out of them as well. But she was devoted to that runt of a boy of hers, and there probably wasn't really space for another man in her life.

If I get out of here alive, I've got to start sorting my life out. Settle down. Jesus, if even Dan can make a start at it with his bar, then I should be able to as well.

'Have you decided to talk yet?' Mustaf was twirling the hosepipe through the air.

Ollie could feel himself wincing again. There were two deep welts where the last blows had gone in. The flesh was red and raw, the nerves still fizzing with pain, and Ollie could hardly conceive of the agony that another blow on top of the existing wounds would cause.

He glanced through the porthole.

Dawn had broken an hour ago. A soft light was flooding out over the calm ocean. It was around seven in the morning, reckoned Ollie. If Steve and the rest of the boys were out there, then they wouldn't attack until night. The compound was too well-defended to risk an assault in broad daylight.

But how many hours until nightfall?

At least twelve.

Jesus, can I hold out until then?

'Piss off,' said Ollie.

But his voice was starting to weaken. Hoarse and frail, the anger was starting to drain out of it, and so was the strength.

He saw Mustaf advance towards him, the hosepipe still in his hand.

Inside, Ollie was retreating into his box. Both Sandra and Lena were in there somewhere, a comfort of sorts, but neither of them was really his, he realised.

And then the blow fell. And as the pain gripped him in its icy embrace, Ollie could feel himself start to pass out.

Thirty-Four

THE HOT SUN WAS STARTING to bake Steve's back. He could feel the sweat beginning to soak through him. But with both the Iranians and the Taliban close by, he didn't feel like removing his body armour, even if it was taking the temperature up by ten degrees.

A scrap could kick off at any moment. And if it did, it was going to be very ugly.

He was keeping the binoculars trained on the hull beached on the cove. It was just after eleven in the morning, and they'd kept the compound under constant surveillance since dawn. Henri and Dan had moved down the coast, investigating whether there was somewhere they could launch an attack on the vessel from the water. Maksim and Nick were scouting to the left and the right of their position, watching for any sign of movement from the other surveillance groups. Meanwhile, Steve and Ian were monitoring the compound, trying to assess its strength, get a fix on the numbers of men inside, find out what kit they had with them, and checking on movements into and out of the base.

Every military base Steve had ever been on, or fought against, had a drill. There was a timetable, one that was stuck to rigidly. Pirates, terrorists, or armies, it made no difference, they all worked to the same basic rule book.

Get to know that, and you might be able to identify the weaknesses.

At eleven thirty, a truck pulled up. It was an ageing Mercedes Sprinter, its white paint covered in a thick layer of dust, and its skin cratered with dents. It stopped by the entrance to the compound, and two men climbed out and rolled big steel drums through the armed gates. Steve made a note of the time, the number of men, and how long it took to complete the delivery. The boat had no fresh water, he reckoned, and this must be the daily supply.

At twelve, a small skiff cruised into the cove, approaching from the west, and pulled up alongside the old boat. Two men on board started unloading boxes of what looked from the distance like food. That's the supplies taken care of for the day, decided Steve: one delivery of water, another of grub. Maybe that's a way in.

'Can we take those?' he said to Ian. 'If we hijacked the truck or the food boat, we could get inside.'

'The same trick we pulled in Afghanistan?'

Steve nodded.

'It's not going to work,' said Ian with a terse shake of the head. 'Look.' He pointed. 'The delivery guys aren't going inside. They just roll up, unload, then piss off.'

Steve wiped the sweat away from his face. 'Then what?'

He waited for a reply. But Ian remained silent, the binoculars trained on the compound. Neither man knew the answer to that yet. All they could do was wait, and keep watching, until a weakness presented itself.

It was just past one when Dan and Henri returned. They'd both been in the water, but as they'd tabbed the mile back to the rendezvous point the hot sun had dried them right out. Dan grabbed a water bottle and put a litre down his throat, then opened up some biscuits, chewing hungrily on a handful.

'So?' asked Ian. 'Can we attack them from the sea?'

'It's going to be hard.' Henri nodded towards the ocean. 'We swam out around the rocks, then approached the rear of the old ship underwater. The bastards have mined the place. There are

238

three narrow channels, which I reckon are used by the skiffs and the supply ships. So long as you know your way through, then you've got a chance. If you don't, you'll probably just blow yourself up.'

Steve glared at the Frenchman. 'We're sick of hearing how we can't do this and we can't do that. I thought you were here for your expertise. My sodding mum can tell us what we can't do.'

'I'm here to stop you throwing away your life.'

'I can take care of my own life, thanks, mate.'

'Easy, Steve,' said Dan. He wiped the sweat and grime out of his face. 'I saw the mines myself, and they are sodding everywhere.'

'Then what?' said Steve.

'We need to wait for Yasin to come out,' said Henri.

Steve paused. 'What the fuck are you talking about?'

'We monitor this compound,' continued Henri, ignoring the hostility in Steve's question. 'He has to come out sooner or later. When he does, we tab up the road and ambush him, then take him prisoner.'

'And what about Ollie?' said Dan.

'He can fight his own way out,' said Henri. 'Or else we can go in and get him afterwards.'

'I hope you're sodding joking,' growled Steve. 'Ollie might be an ugly bastard, and a tosser as well, but he's still our mate. We're not leaving him in there.'

Henri just shrugged nonchalantly. He reached across for one of the rat packs from his kitbag, ripped open the foil covering a chicken pasta bake, then used the spoon he carried in his webbing to start slowly chewing on the food.

'If you are planning to run in there with guns blazing, then that's your decision,' he said after he'd swallowed a couple of mouthfuls of his food. 'You'll all get shot to pieces. It's better to watch and wait for our chance.'

Ian nodded. 'That's what the Iranian and Taliban boyos are

doing,' he said. 'Keeping their eyes peeled, and waiting for their chance. We'll just have to do the same.'

Steve looked towards the compound. He picked up the binoculars and trained them on the deck. He could see the men striding across it, tough and strong. And he could sense that Ollie was in there somewhere, losing hope with every hour that ticked by.

'Shit,' he muttered to himself. They are probably roughing the poor bastard up pretty bad. And his mates are just sitting around here finishing their lunch, and doing sod all about it. Maybe there are reasons for that. But it doesn't feel right to me.

Thirty-Five

THE CABIN OF THE GULFSTREAM II was kitted out with all the luxuries that Jeff Robertson's upmarket clients expected. There were six rows of soft, padded leather armchairs, one on either side of the plane. TV screens were fitted to the back of each seat, with a huge range of films and games, and at the back of the plane there was a small, wood-panelled office with a computer and phone connection. Usually there would be a couple of girls in short skirts serving us cocktails, reflected David, as he glanced from the window at the rough expanse of white sand and blue sea that was all the Gulf of Aden consisted of when viewed from 35,000 feet. But not today. It was just the pilot and the two men in the plane. And any moment now, they'd be checking out. By the back door.

'Ten minutes,' said Robertson from the pilot's cockpit. 'Get yourselves ready.'

They'd taken off from Biggin Hill eight hours ago. It took ninety minutes to get to Portugal, then three hours of hanging around while Robertson sorted out all the paperwork, got their passports checked, and logged the flight to Pakistan with air traffic control. They'd been in the air for over three hours now, flying directly over the Mediterranean, then across Libya and Egypt until they were approaching Somali airspace. Normally, a HAHO drop would be made at night to reduce the risk of detection. Over any normal country, a few guys drifting across the countryside with parachutes open would attract plenty of attention. In Somalia, Bruce reckoned it was safe enough. They'd drop out of the plane over the sea, then steer themselves into the coast; and most of the shoreline was uninhabited. They couldn't risk waiting until darkness anyway. The missile strike could be launched at any time.

They had to get in and warn the boys before it was too late.

Ganju and David had kitted themselves out with American-made MT-1-X military parachutes. The 1-X was specifically designed for HAHO jumps and they'd been lucky to find two at such short notice. The main parachute had a rectangular gliding canopy, allowing it to float long distances through the air, and its high-lift, low-drag profile increased its forward speed, allowing you to get to your target as quickly as possible. The canopy covered 370 square feet, and could hold up to 360 pounds of weight, more than enough for a single man and his kit.

Ganju and David started to get themselves ready. They got out of their civilian jeans and sweatshirts and packed them into their kitbags, then climbed into baggy, light-grey jumpsuits. They strapped on DDT inflatable lifejackets: they were bailing out over water, and if they came down in the sea, they'd need something to keep them afloat. Normally they'd strap pistol belts on top of those, but it was too risky to try and bring any firearms through airport security, so they had to make do with a pair of sturdy hunting knives that Robertson kept permanently stashed in the plane's tool kit. Bruce had supplied them with backpacks consisting of Zainer waterproofed body armour, a first-aid kit, a water canteen, flares and a flashlight, a ballistic helmet and, most importantly of all, a radar that would pick up the signal from Ollie's tracking device. David clipped the pack on to his harness underneath the parachute, making sure the quick-release mechanism was in place so that he could get to his kit quickly once they landed.

'Wind speed north-north-east, twenty-knots,' said Robertson

over the pilot's radio. 'Bail out five miles over the coast, and you should be able to steer yourselves due east.'

Twenty knots, thought David to himself. A fair old gust.

He'd done HAHO drops before, from British Airways planes that were specially adapted for special forces deployments. Up to forty knots was possible, but ten to fifteen was preferable. Too much wind and you'd lose control of the steering.

But they'd just have to take their chances. They weren't going to get another crack at this.

'Two minutes,' said Robertson.

'You OK?' said Ganju quietly.

David paused for a moment before replying. He'd been certain he'd be OK. The dreams that had crept through his mind over the last few months, like a fog crawling over a damp hillside, had lifted at the thought of going back into combat. He'd thought for much of the last twenty-four hours that it might be the cure he needed, like another bump on the head curing someone of amnesia. Now he could sense it didn't work like that. He could feel a fear he'd never felt before: cold and clammy, like a squid wrapping itself around you, it was sapping all the strength and confidence he'd normally draw upon before going into battle.

Everyone was scared before going into combat, he reminded himself. Well, everyone except Maksim, that is. The Russian nutter didn't know about death. But this was different. A fear that started to take control of your muscles, making you incapable of movement.

'I . . .' He didn't know how to finish the sentence.

Ganju looked at him sharply. Then he started to speak, in careful crisp tones.

'We few, we happy few, we band of brothers;
For he today that sheds his blood with me
Shall be my brother; be he ne'er so vile
This day shall gentle his condition:

And gentlemen in England, now a-bed
Shall think themselves accurs'd they were not here,
And hold their manhoods cheap whiles any speaks
That fought with us upon Saint Crispin's day.'

Right, thought David to himself. Some things don't change, no matter how many centuries there might be between battles. Those are my mates down there. And they need my help.

'I didn't realise they taught Shakespeare out in Nepal.'

'It was the only bit of the English class I managed to stay awake through.'

'Right then, let's sodding do this.'

'Oxygen masks,' said Robertson over the radio.

David clamped the tube over his face. Attached to a small bottle of oxygen on his harness, it would allow him to breathe normally while the door was opened on the Gulfstream II; the sudden shock of decompression would suck all the air out of the cabin, making it impossible to breathe without assistance.

'Thirty seconds . . .'

David steadied himself.

The Gulfstream II had a single door, up close to the front of the aircraft and the pilot's cockpit. Ganju stepped forward, unlocked the safety handle, and pulled the door backwards. A huge, swirling gust of air ripped through the cabin, creating a brief, dense fog that was almost blinding. The door flapped and banged against the side of the cabin and for a brief moment David was afraid it might rip straight off. The noise of the two Rolls-Royce engines was deafening, cracking open his eardrums. He checked the altimeter strapped to his wrist. Thirty-three thousand feet.

'Go, go,' Ganju was yelling in his face, pushing him towards the open door.

David started to walk, ignoring the wind swirling around him.

The cold squid was there again. Wrapping its tentacles around him.

'Go, go,' Ganju was yelling.

He jumped.

His eyes closed, then opened again.

Exiting from an airliner is something like trying to ride a giant wave. You have to arch your back to ride the gust of air, the same way you have to ride a wave as it crashes into you, otherwise you'll be knocked over by the force of the blow. David snapped himself into position, emptying his mind, and allowing the drill and training to take control. He counted out three seconds, then four, then pulled the rip cord on the parachute. He could feel the cable flick through its channels, opening up the sack on his back. Other men, he knew, hated that moment, always fearing the day the few yards of life-saving nylon fabric wouldn't open, but David was always relieved when he could finally release the chute, aware that the ordeal would soon be over.

He could hear the whoosh of air as the main parachute and deployment bag shot skywards above him. He took a deep breath from the oxygen bottle, steeling his body for the next shock as his speed decelerated from 120 miles an hour to almost nothing in the space of a few seconds.

The parachute opened up above him.

Up ahead, the Gulfstream was already disappearing into the distance, the noise of its engine fading.

Right, thought David. We're on our own, dropping into Somalia, with nothing but a pair of hunting knives between us. God help us.

As the parachute steadied, he looked down.

The sea down below was a crystal, clear blue. The wind was fierce, but not unbearable. He looked to his left. Ganju had left the plane and was floating two hundred yards away from him. He was signalling to the east. David tugged on the cord. There was a delay of several seconds whilst the canopy of the parachute flapped in the wind, then he started to change direction. Off in the far distance, he could see the rugged, wild coastline. About six miles he reckoned. Checking his altimeter, he saw he was still at 27,000 feet. There was plenty of time to bring themselves down safely.

It took fifteen minutes in total. The parachute was dropping at a rate of a thousand feet a minute, and they were down to 15,000 feet by the time they crossed the shoreline. David was breathing on the bottled oxygen, and that always made him feel slightly giddy, but he was starting to relax and enjoy the view. He saw a couple of ships as they floated across the five miles of sea, but whether any of the sailors saw them, there was no way of knowing. As he looked down, he could see the rugged shoreline of Puntland, an ugly mixture of broken rocks, treacherous coves, and huge stretches of empty, water-starved land. To his left, he could see one twisting road, three miles in at most from the sea. But there were no vehicles. As far as he could tell, this part of the peninsula was completely uninhabited.

Thank Christ for that, he told himself. A couple of blokes with AK-47s could shoot us straight out of the sky.

They were at least five miles inland by the time David guided himself down to the land. His feet skidded and scraped across the dusty, dry ground, before he rolled on to his shoulders, brought himself to a halt, and started wrestling to bring his parachute under control. Ganju was three hundred yards in front of him. David steadied himself, unhooked his harness, then tabbed up towards the Gurkha.

'Welcome to Somalia,' he said, grinning, and slapping Ganju on the back. 'And I'm bloody glad there's no one here to welcome us.'

Ganju looked around. The man had an inner sense for a landscape, David reminded himself. He'd seen it in Afghanistan, and Africa, and he could sense it again now. Ganju had an ear that could tune into the murmurs and whispers of the earth itself, and which could warn of dangers ahead.

'This is a bad, wicked place,' Ganju said, his voice threaded with determination.

'I'm sure you're right,' said David. 'I reckon we crack on then, get our boys out of the soup, then piss off home.'

From his backpack, he unhooked the small radar device Bruce had supplied them with.

At ground level, the signaller fitted to Ollie's tooth had a radius of twenty kilometres. From a satellite being used to guide cruise missiles into their target, it was two hundred kilometres. David peered down at the small screen, waiting for it to boot into life and scan the area for the signal.

They had no way of knowing where Ollie was. Somewhere on the Puntland peninsula, that was all they knew. They'd landed dead in the centre of the region, halfway between Eyl and the border to give themselves the maximum chance of finding him.

A white dot appeared on the screen.

'Got you,' said Ganju.

'How far?' asked David.

'Fifteen kilometres north-north-west.'

David checked his watch. It was just after five in the afternoon. They'd pitched down in the middle of a crater that didn't look as if it had been inhabited since the dinosaurs were roaming the earth. The ground was a sandy red, and only a pair of stubby, deformed trees gave any indication that life could be supported here. He took a swig from his water bottle, and looked straight ahead.

'Let's crack on, then,' he said. 'We can cover that in three hours.'

Thirty-Six

O LLIE SAT ALONE, STARING INTO the blackness.
The blindfold had been strapped round his face at least two hours ago, he reckoned, although it was getting hard to keep track of the time. It was made of a thick, light-blocking cloth, the kind you might use to get to sleep on a plane. Strapped to the chair, he could hear only the gentle lapping of the waves against the hull.

I might as well be dead already, he thought to himself grimly.

Footsteps.

And the sound of a man breathing.

Suddenly a pair of hands were gripping his back. Whether it was one man or two, it was impossible to tell. They were pushing him down. He resisted briefly, but with his arms and legs bound it was useless. He was on his knees, being pushed towards the ground, but then his face was splashing into water. It was all around him. He closed his mouth, cursing himself for not having taken a proper breath before going under, but with no vision, there was no way of knowing he was about to be submerged. He could hear a man shouting something, and they were still gripping his shoulders, but it was impossible to make out what was being said.

The seconds started to tick by. Ollie reckoned his lungs were strong. He didn't smoke and he ran plenty, even when he wasn't on a job. On training exercises in the Blues he'd held his breath underwater for two minutes, and that was a decent result. But he'd prepared for that, taking deep breaths beforehand, splashing his face with cold water, doing everything he could to slow the rate at which his body used oxygen.

Today? Ninety seconds, maximum. That was the most he could hold out for. And at least thirty or forty of them were already gone.

He could feel his lungs starting to ache: a numb sensation, one of the early warnings of impending suffocation. A splitting pain was starting to break through his head, and his eyes were starting to bulge.

Sixty seconds.

Is this it? he wondered. Are the bastards drowning me?

Suddenly, a hand gripped his hair and yanked him upwards. His mouth opened, and Ollie gasped for air, taking a deep, desperate breath, a giddy feeling overwhelming him as the oxygen flooded through his veins.

'Tell us,' roared Mustaf.

'Piss off,' spat Ollie.

He took a desperate lungful of air, aware of what was going to happen next.

Sure enough, his head was plunged straight back into the water.

He held his mouth tight shut. The first twenty seconds weren't so bad. The next twenty were harder: a slow, aching sensation started in Ollie's brain, then spread through his muscles. As he ticked past sixty seconds, Ollie could feel himself beginning to become drowsy and confused. The first signs of drowning. He was fighting it, but he knew over the next minute, he would start to die.

Unless.

Bugger it, I can't even tell them the code. Not until they pull me up.

His lungs were starting to burst. But there was little pain. Just a tiredness that he could already sense might take him away for ever.

Then he was above the water again. His mouth burst open, and he took a huge lungful of oxygen, far more than was good for him, but his body was so desperate for air, it was impossible to stop himself.

'Tell us now,' barked Mustaf.

'Piss off,' roared Ollie.

But already he was wondering if he'd made a mistake. Maybe he should break now, give them the sodding combination. The bastards might well kill him this time around.

Mustaf and another man were pushing at his back. His hair was gripped in their hands, and they were shoving him towards the water. Ollie was kicking back, using what little strength remained in his shoulders, but there wasn't much use in resisting. Get as much air into your lungs as possible, he told himself. No point in wasting it on a struggle you're not going to win.

'Stop,' snapped a voice.

Ollie recognised it at once. Ali Yasin.

'Take off the blindfold.'

Ollie was pulled roughly backwards. The cloth was ripped from his eyes. He blinked furiously, adjusting to the light. Water was dripping down his face, and his breath was short. Right in front of him was the large tub of seawater that he'd been submerged in, and behind, two men standing next to Mustaf. Outside, dusk was starting to fall as the day drew to its close. Yasin was striding towards him, his expression serious.

'I have already told you, I try not to be a man of violence,' he said, looking straight into Ollie's eyes. 'But you are stretching my patience.'

Ollie remained mute and motionless. Say nothing and think nothing, he told himself. Just let the time pass until we hit back at these bastards.

'We have given you a taste of what it is like to drown. Now, we can waste no more of our time on this. If you are determined to die in defence of whoever paid you a few miserable dollars to protect their property, then that is your choice. I will give the command to finish you right now, and I will make sure you do not suffer unnecessarily in the process.'

His eyes bore down on Ollie. 'One last chance . . .'

A pause.

Ollie's mind was working furiously, making a dozen different calculations. There was a note of authority in the pirate's voice that suggested the threats weren't empty. Next time they pushed him under, it would surely be the last.

He looked straight into the pirate's eyes and started to speak.

'Twenty, eighty-five, seventy-two, fourteen, sixty-one . . .'

The words were delivered in a sullen, slow voice.

Yasin nodded. 'Thank you,' he said crisply. 'I had no desire to kill you.' He looked towards Mustaf. 'Food and medicine for our guest.'

The ropes were unbound with the skill of born sailors, men who'd spent a lifetime binding and unbinding knots, and as they were unpicked, Ollie rubbed his hands together, trying to ease the numbness where his skin had been cut. From the hold, another pirate bought out a cup of steaming tea, and a plate of hot food. A large flat piece of bread lay on one side of the tin plate, and next to it a dollop of a stew made from beans, with some kind of meat mixed into it. Ollie leant forward and ate hungrily, using the energy from the food to restore his strength. What the meat was he had no idea, and tasting it wasn't making it any clearer. Let's just hope they haven't captured Steve and put him in the pot, he reflected grimly.

'Here,' said Yasin, handing across a couple of green leaves. 'Eat these. It will help with the pain.'

Ollie struggled for a moment, then he recognised them. He'd been on a course during his time in the Army to identify different drugs. It was khat, a common stimulant throughout the Gulf and

East Africa. A powerful amphetamine, it caused excitement, euphoria and loss of appetite. It was grown throughout the region, and its short stubby leaves released the powerful chemicals directly into the bloodstream when chewed.

If the pirates were eating khat all day, they'll be an even tougher foe than we realised, Ollie reflected. Throughout Africa, soldiers fought high on drugs, and many of them were basically amphetamines. It didn't do much for discipline, but that was never the African fighting man's strongest point anyway. It did, however, do plenty for energy, aggression, and courage. Pirates on khat might keep fighting for thirty hours or more without a break, believing themselves to be invincible. That was hardly the kind of enemy you wanted to get into a scrap with.

'I'm giving up,' said Ollie. 'I'm on a bit of a health kick this month.'

'Eat it,' repeated Yasin.

Ollie could hear no tolerance of dissent in his voice.

He took a handful, and started to chew. The leaves themselves had a mild, plant-like flavour, but there was a bitterness to the stem. It didn't make any difference at first, but as he chewed some more, Ollie could feel his head starting to clear, and a buzz of energy, followed by light-headedness.

He was feeling good. Even if Yasin was about to open the safes, and find there was nothing in them.

'You enjoy that, Englishman, and I'll open these safes. Then we'll find a way of getting you home unharmed.'

Ollie glanced nervously towards the three safes.

Then he looked through the porthole. Darkness had fallen across the ocean. There was a stiffer wind blowing tonight, and the waves were starting to pick up strength, crashing noisily into the side of the hull. Come on, you buggers, thought Ollie, thinking about the unit that was meant to be breaking him out of here. This is the moment to damn well strike. Save my arse in the nick of time. Before the real beating starts.

Yasin was standing next to the first safe, punching in the numbers Ollie had just recited. Mustaf and his soldier were doing the same to the other two. As the door swung open, there was a sly grin on Yasin's face. A man who enjoys his booty, noted Ollie. He's expecting something special in there. Not just thin air.

He steeled himself, taking another deep chew on the khat, knocking back the drug-filled saliva in the back of his throat.

If I'm going to damn well die, I might as well die happy.

The expression on Yasin's face suddenly changed. It was like a cloud sweeping over a sunny hillside before a summer storm, an abrupt darkening that foreshadowed the fury ahead.

'Nothing,' he said, his tone steely. He looked towards Ollie. 'They are all empty.'

Mustaf was already striding towards him, the hosepipe in his hand. Ollie leapt instinctively from his chair, running to the back of the cabin, raising his arms in front of his face to protect himself from the lash of the whip that he felt certain was about to cut into him.

'Koos, koos,' Mustaf was shouting.

'No,' snapped Yasin.

He took two strides forward, grabbed hold of Mustaf's arms, and broke the hosepipe free from his grip.

Ollie was still cowering towards the back of the cabin.

Yasin looked at Ollie fiercely. 'A man is placed on board a worthless cargo vessel, protecting three safes that have nothing in them. The AIS system sends clear signals that there is valuable cargo on board, and all I find is you.' Still looking straight at him, a slow smile started to spread across his face. 'You're not a guard, are you? You're a plant.'

Thirty-Seven

STEVE RESTED THE BINOCULARS. His eyes were growing weary from watching the same spot, and his elbows were numb from digging into the hard, red earth.

'Sod it,' he muttered. 'The bastard isn't coming out.'

He looked across at Henri, Ian and Dan. Nick and Maksim were still a few hundred yards distant, keeping a close watch on the Iranian and Taliban units. All through the early afternoon and evening, they had been monitoring the compound, waiting for the moment when the pirate leader would emerge from his lair, and they could move in and snatch him.

The plan was laid. Ian had rigged up a shaped IED, or improvised explosive device, using techniques developed in Iraq. Some old tin cans were bashed into a concave holder, with some P4 explosive wedged into the bottom, then buried under a mound of sand. As a vehicle passed, the IED would blow, producing a perfectly directed shock wave that should be powerful enough, depending on the quantity of explosive, to push a van or an SUV right over. Once it was toppled, the rest of the men would pick off its defenders with sniper fire, whilst Maksim would rush down and grab Yasin.

Then they'd run like hell.

That was the plan, anyway, reflected Steve. But without the target, it was, as Nick put it with a rare flash of humour, about as much use as an ashtray on a motorbike.

So far there was no sign of the man. And the clock was ticking relentlessly.

'Like I said, he's not coming, is he?' repeated Steve.

'Meaning?' demanded Henri.

'We cut Ollie a deal,' insisted Steve. 'He went in as the bait, and we promised we'd go in and get him out.'

Dan was nodding. 'We've got no idea what the hell they're doing in there, but once they find out the safes are empty, they're not going to be very happy, are they?'

Henri remained silent.

Sod the Frenchman, thought Steve. If he won't come with us, we'll just have to storm the place by ourselves.

'So we sketch out a plan?' said Ian.

Steve nodded curtly. 'Any thoughts?'

'Can you make a depth charge?' asked Henri, looking towards Ian. 'Something that will blow underwater?'

'We've got the fuses and the plastic explosives.'

'Then here's what we do,' said Henri. 'You make me the bomb. It needs to have enough weight and force on it to blow a hole in the hull and shake the vessel, but not so powerful that it blows the whole ship and kills everyone on board. I'll swim under the ship, and put it in place with a timing device. When it blows, it will make everyone on board believe they are under attack from the sea, and we storm the compound from the shore.'

'With any luck, they'll be facing the wrong way, and we can shoot them in the back,' said Dan.

'Can you do that?' said Steve, glancing up at Ian.

'They don't call me the bomb-maker for nothing.'

'Good man.' Steve looked at Henri. At least the Frenchman is coming around to our way of thinking. 'Let's see if we can set the bomb for nine tonight. Nick and I will slip inside five minutes before then, and try to quietly knife the guards at the gate, then as soon as the bomb blows, the rest of you boys can rush inside. We'll have ten minutes maximum to get in there, rescue Ollie and capture the pirate boy, then piss off. Any longer than that, we'll have no choice but to abort and get the hell out of here.'

'It's a big risk,' said Dan.

'I know,' said Steve. His face was twisted into an expression of grim determination. 'And if we had any other choices, believe me, I'd take them. But this is our best shot. So let's just sodding well crack on.'

Two hundred yards to the right, Maksim had buried himself into a small dip in the ground. He was lying flat, his face close to the earth, with a clear view of the Iranian unit holed up another five hundred yards in the distance. He'd been watching them for ten hours now. Time was starting to drag. The unit was stationary through the heat of the day, just watching the compound, observing its movements, but careful not to reveal their own position. In the last hour, however, two men had gone out on patrol. They were scouting the perimeter of the compound, moving carefully through the rugged landscape. Both men were wearing black, allowing them to slip unnoticed through the darkness. But Maksim could see them well enough. And one man was moving closer and closer to his position.

Maksim cursed under his breath.

He'd have moved back to rejoin the rest of the unit if he could. But it was too late for that now. If he started moving, he'd be spotted. There was nothing he could do except wait and watch. He held his breath, and dug himself a little lower into the ground, making himself as close to invisible as he could.

The man was just yards from him now. There was a pistol in his hand, and he was walking straight towards Maksim's position.

The Russian knew there was a decision to make. He could hope the man walked straight past him, and risk getting shot if he noticed him. Or he could attack him now, whilst he could still take him by surprise.

His mind was made up as soon as the question was posed.

Matt Lynn

Maximum, instantaneous aggression was the only way of soldiering he knew.

Like a dog released from a trap, Maksim sprang forward. The hunting knife was gripped in his right hand. The man was just ten yards ahead of him when he started the move, and Maksim was upon him in three bounds. He descended upon his victim like a brutal, bloodthirsty ghost emerging out of the darkness, a vengeful apparition seeking only death. The man squealed once, but he was already numbed by shock, and Maksim smothered his mouth, pushing him straight to the ground, whilst stabbing his blade into the side of the man's throat, all in a single, perfectly coordinated move.

He twisted the knife once, then twice, as if he was removing the core from an apple, shredding open the main artery that ran up into the man's brain. Blood was cascading from the wound, draining the life from the soldier as it seeped into the ground. He bucked, twitched, then died. Maksim slid the knife from the corpse, wiping away the blood on the dead man's chest. He took a moment to recover his breath, then anxiously scanned the arid landscape. He couldn't see anyone, but in the darkness that meant very little. Any moment now they'd come looking for the man. Once they realised he was dead, they'd want revenge.

Maksim rolled the body into the same dip in the land he'd been lying in, then covered it up with stones, earth and brushwood from the surrounding ground. It should at least hide the body until the morning.

He started to tab the few hundred yards back across the hillside to the rest of the unit.

As he approached the men, Steve looked at him. He could see the blood smeared across Maksim's face and sweatshirt.

'I don't know what it is, but something tells me there's been a spot of trouble, Maksie,' he said.

The Russian nodded. 'One of the Iranians found me. I dealt

with the bastard, but the rest of his unit will realise something is up soon.'

Steve turned to face the compound. 'That settles it, then,' he said curtly. 'We're going in. A scrap with the Iranians could kick off at any moment, and even if we prevail, the pirates will just come out and finish whichever of us is left alive.'

Thirty-Eight

ALI YASIN WAS LOOKING STRAIGHT at Ollie. There was a malevolent look in his eyes that he hadn't seen before, a cold, calculating violence, with no hint of pity in it. 'Who sent you?'

Bugger it, thought Ollie. It's about to start up all over again. The torture. The beatings.

Bugger.

He glanced towards the porthole, but there was nothing to be seen there apart from a dark expanse of sea stretching away into the far horizon.

Where the hell are you, Steve West? We had a deal . . .

Yasin reached across to his desk. Underneath, there was a small safe, with a combination lock controlled by a dial. Nothing elaborate, the kind of safe you might find in an office anywhere in the world. He helfted up a steel attaché case, and laid it out flat. Opening it up, he motioned to Ollie to come forwards, then pointed down into the case.

Inside were six metal rings, each one weighing about ten pounds. The metal was a dark blackish-grey, with a rough pitted surface, something like iron.

'Do you know what that is?'

Ollie shook his head.

'Four weeks ago we captured a ship on its way to Japan. We found this on board.'

'So?'

'It's weapons-grade plutonium,' snapped Yasin, his tone suddenly fierce.

Christ, thought Ollie. The pirate is sitting on enough plutonium to blow up half a dozen cities.

'What kind of ship was it?'

'A British ship.'

Ollie glanced nervously at Yasin.

Bugger and double bugger, he thought sourly. The boys over at Six don't give a toss about a few cargo ships getting captured by the pirates. *They want their plutonium back.* But why didn't they tell us?

Ollie was racking his brains, trying to make sense of what he was really doing here. But the khat was still flooding through his veins, lightening his mood, dulling the pain from the earlier beatings, but also making it impossible to concentrate for more than a few seconds at a time.

And concentration is what I need if I am going to figure out what the hell I'm doing here, and how I can ever get out. Unless its going to be in a coffin.

'Now, you may think I'm a stupid man, or at least your masters may think that,' said Yasin, speaking slowly. 'But I can assure you I'm not. British plutonium, and a British guard.' He jabbed a finger straight into Ollie's chest. 'I think you're a soldier, and they sent you to get it back for them.'

Thirty-Nine

DAVID RECKONED HE'D TRAMPED THROUGH some miserable, brutal countries during a career in both the Army and the PMCs. He'd fought for the Army in Ulster, in Bosnia, in Iraq, and freelanced in Afghanistan, Africa, and the Far East. But he didn't reckon he had ever marched across such a scarred, ugly landscape as Somalia. The path was rocky and treacherous, pitted with turns, and drops, and stones, as if the ground itself was trying to eat you.

I can hardly blame the locals, he thought to himself as he trudged forwards. If I was born here, I might take to the high seas and start nicking a few boats as well.

They'd been walking for a couple of hours now and had covered twelve of the fifteen kilometres that separated them from Steve and the rest of the unit. They were moving through the darkness, keeping about five hundred yards away from the main road that twisted through the peninsula. Neither of them wanted to risk any kind of flashlight: on this flat, open, empty land, it would be like sending up a flare into the sky. Anyone might see it and come and attack them. But the moon kept slipping behind a cloud, and when it did, it was hard walking through the pitch blackness, and the rocky terrain presented the constant threat of a twisted ankle.

Any kind of injury, and they wouldn't make it to the rest of the boys. And then they'd all be dead.

'Stop,' hissed Ganju.

David paused. The Gurkha was leading the way. Like all the men in his regiment, he was a natural scout, with an ability to feel his way across the ground that was uncanny. He could inch his way across the most hostile terrain, picking up whispers and hints from the ground that would be lost on most ordinary men. Allied to an instinctive sense of direction, it made him a better guide than any piece of electronic kit. And David never had any doubts about following calmly in his trail.

'What?'

'Just listen.'

David was cupping his ears to the breeze. To the east, he could hear the distant roar of the ocean, but that was at least two miles away, and the sound faint. There was the low whistle of a slight wind rustling the dust, a noise like a persistent cough. Apart from that, nothing. The land was as silent as the moon. And about as welcoming.

'Footsteps.'

'Where?'

'To the east of us, three hundred yards, maybe four hundred.'

David nodded. He couldn't hear a sound, but he'd no more doubt Ganju's word than he would have spat in the face of the regimental sergeant-major back when he was in the Irish Guards. If Ganju said something was up there, then you could count on it being true.

'If we hide, they should pass harmlessly by,' said David.

Ganju shook his head. 'They've a dog with them. I smelt it. They're looking for us.'

'Christ,' muttered David. They had no weapons. No back-up they could call on. And some kind of search party was out looking for them.

The two men laid up behind a boulder. Ganju reckoned the patrol was only a hundred yards away now, and, as the moon peeled out from behind a cloud, he could see them. Two men, dressed in

Afghan dishdashas, Taliban-style. They had short beards, and an ugly-looking bloodhound held on a short string. At a distance, David could see they were carrying AK-47s. No doubt there were handguns and knives concealed beneath their robes.

'They must have seen us landing,' hissed David. 'We'd have been visible for miles around here.'

Ganju nodded. 'And that means they'll keep looking until they find us.'

'What the hell are we going to do?'

Ganju had already drawn his knife. 'They have guns, but we have surprise, and that should make it an even fight.'

They were standing on an empty plateau, pitted with giant boulders. Ganju was pointing to one rock, telling David to crouch behind it. Ganju would station himself five yards further back, behind another giant boulder. 'Make some kind of sound, a cough, anything,' hissed Ganju. 'When they approach you, I'll stab them in the back.'

David took up his position as instructed.

Off in the distance, he could hear the mewling of the dog. They were getting closer. He crouched down low, drawing his knife, listening to the growl of the animal, and the soft scraping of sandalled feet against the dusty, sandy surface of the ground. An indescribable, icy fear started to grip him, something he'd never felt before in more than twenty years of professional soldiering. Usually a heady mix of adrenalin and anger would kick in just before a fight was about to start; his heart would start pumping blood and oxygen furiously enough around his body to banish any nerves, but now he could feel only a mounting dread, and found he was equally fearful of what was about to happen both to himself and to his victims.

Get a sodding grip, he told himself. You're a soldier, here to do a soldier's work.

He coughed once, then twice. The sound was thin, spluttering, but still carried on the night breeze.

The dog barked, and the two men turned. They'd heard the sound clearly enough, and were striding purposefully towards its source. Their AK-47s were gripped in their hands, and their fingers were squeezed tight around the triggers.

They were just thirty yards distant.

Then twenty.

For the next few seconds, David could feel only a morbid detachment from the unfolding scene. Before, a fierce instinct for survival would take control of his body, the way it did for every soldier, guiding him towards survival, but now he didn't care whether the next few seconds ended in life or death.

The two men were approaching the rock where David was hiding. The moon was once again concealed behind the clouds, but even through the brooding darkness he could make out the figures that confronted him. Big and strong, their dishdashas made them appear ghostly. They were standing just five yards from him now, the dog on the short lead sniffing the air. The nose of the animal twitched suddenly, then it started to lunge forward, held in place only by the strength of the man holding the lead. He exchanged a brief word with the second man in Arabic, then loosed off a couple of rounds from his AK-47. They were just testers, David told himself sharply, willing himself to remain still and calm. They just want to tease me out.

He leant against the rock and waited. The fear was starting to evaporate, but David sensed it was still there, ready to lock him down again. We have nothing to fear but fear itself, that was the way the saying went. Well, I'm bloody afraid of it now, thought David bitterly.

From behind his rock, Ganju pounced. He moved with the agility of a panther, springing forward in a single lean, silent motion. His dark skin and black clothes camouflaged him in the darkness, and the complete silence of his movements meant the two men were unaware of his attack until it was far too late. There was a knife in each of his strong hands, both of them curved blades that Ganju had chosen for himself from the selection on the plane, and both similar to the kukri, the deadly knife otherwise known as the Gurkha blade, in honour of the men who fought with it most effectively. Its shape made it most lethal as a chopping and slashing weapon, rather than a stabbing device, and that was precisely how Ganju planned to use it. As he leapt forward, he lashed the blades through the air, slicing the throats of both men from behind.

As Ganju hit the ground, one man fell at his side. The blade had neatly slashed through the skin on the back of the neck, cutting open the windpipe and paralysing the victim. It would be a couple more minutes before he actually died, but he was incapable of anything more than a final coughing splutter of blood before he was finished with his life. The second blade had penetrated its victim's skin lower down, close to the neck, then got stuck on the thick muscle beneath. It had caused a horrible wound, and the man was screaming with pain, but it would not be fatal. He doubled up, dropping his gun, with the blade still stuck menacingly just above his robes. Ganju was just a couple of yards in front of him, still struggling to regain his balance after crashing to the ground. He was vulnerable. And even though he was screaming in agony, the Taliban warrior could sense his opportunity. He flung himself on to the Gurkha, smothering him with his body. Ganju was pinned down on the ground, blood from his opponent's wound dripping on to him.

David rushed forward, grabbing one of the two AK-47s that had fallen to the ground. He clicked the gun into position. The clip was full, and it was pointing straight into the chest of the Taliban warrior. His eyes swivelled round, meeting David's directly, and in his expression you could see that he knew he was dead. There was fear there, and, through the pain and the blood still running from his neck, he was mouthing a few words from the Koran that he hoped might help him when he passed from this world to the next.

David took aim.

It was a tricky but far from impossible shot to kill the man but leave Ganju unharmed.

But then the fog started to descend on him again. He tried to fight it, but it had already gripped him, rendering him incapable of any movement. His finger was frozen on the trigger of the gun.

The man realised what was happening. One thick, strong hand gripped Ganju's throat, whilst the other reached up to release the knife from his neck. He pulled the blade free, grunting with pain as he did so, then prepared to slash it down into Ganju's face.

David willed himself to fire. But his body was paralysed. He could see Ganju looking straight at him, and for the first time he could see only contempt in the eyes of the Gurkha. His life was in David's hands, a man whose own skin he'd saved on more than one occasion, and yet still he would not help him.

Ganju roared, and spat in the face of his assailant. Normally, he fought with guile and cunning, but he had reserves of brute strength he could draw on when the occasion demanded. He hurled himself upwards and punched forwards with his fists. As was so often the case with a Gurkha, the strength curled up inside such a small body took his opponent by surprise, and he wobbled backwards. A fraction of space opened up, and Ganju was quick enough and skilled enough to extract the maximum advantage from it. He rolled, knocking the man's knife from his hand with the movement. The blade opened a tear in Ganju's sweatshirt but left the skin unharmed. Reaching into his boot, he pulled out a short, stubby blade, and in the same action thrust it upwards, cutting through the ribs and into the muscle until the blade connected with the heart. One twist was all it took. The blood gurgled through the man's mouth, choking him, then his heart stopped beating, and he collapsed dead on to the ground.

Ganju wiped the blood from his blade, and tucked it back into his boot.

He stood up and walked across to where David was still

standing frozen to the ground. He took the AK-47 from his hands, and patted him on the back.

David looked into his eyes, his face white, and his lips trembling. 'Sod it, man, I . . .'

'It's OK,' said Ganju quietly. 'It's the dreams, that's all. We all get them. Even in Nepal.'

'No you sodding don't,' said David sourly. 'I'm no use to anyone, am I? Not if I freeze up every time a scrap kicks off.'

David turned away. Behind him, Ganju was picking up the two AK-47s, plus two spare clips of ammo for each gun. He frisked the men, and took the cheap Czech-made CZ-100 handguns he found tucked into their belts. The bodies would have to stay behind, breakfast for the vultures. Slotting the weapons into his webbing, he started walking, looking back towards David. The dog was cowering next to its dead master, but Ganju ignored it: the animal would find its own way home soon enough, and perhaps lead someone to this spot to give the two men a decent burial, but they'd be long gone before then, and there was no need to take the animal's life.

'Come on,' he said quietly. 'We can't leave you here.'

'You might as well,' said David. 'Let the next bunch of nutters finish me off. I'm sod all use to anyone like this.'

'Let me tell you something,' said Ganju.

They were walking in a straight line over the dusty ground. The moon had re-emerged and there was enough light to make out the path for at least a hundred yards ahead. In total, there were only another two miles left to cover, a walk of less than half an hour.

'Among my people, we believe a man is the sum of the experiences he has been through, not just in his own life but in the lives that came before as well. You don't know what your spirit has been through, but you know you have faced up to danger before, and overcome it, and so you know you can do so again.'

'Better to die than to be a coward,' said David. 'I thought that was your motto.'

Matt Lynn

'But a coward is a man who flinches from a challenge. And your challenge is to walk alongside me in as straight a line as you can manage until we figure out a way to overcome this.'

They completed the rest of the journey in silence. The moon was flitting in and out of the clouds, so at times the path was illuminated and at others shrouded in darkness. Through both, they marched steadily forwards, keeping a safe distance from the main road. David felt better for having an AK-47 with a full clip of ammo slung over his shoulder. But he still felt sick with himself inside. He'd let himself down as well as his mates. And, even worse, it would happen again.

'This way,' said Ganju.

It was just after eight by the time they walked through the ridge of hills towards the compound. According to their radar screen, Ollie was three hundred yards away. They could see the lights in the distance, and reckoned that must be Ali Yasin's base. Steve and the rest of the unit would by lying up somewhere, preparing for the assault.

At least we're in time, thought David, glancing up at the stars twinkling in the night sky. The missile strike hasn't kicked off yet.

Suddenly a man leapt up from the ground. He was pointing an SA-80 straight at them.

David peered through the murky darkness. 'Christ, mate, even in this light your ears stick out like a couple of watermelons,' he said.

Nick paused, stunned. Then he laughed. He put his gun to the side, and stepped forward to embrace the two men. 'Sodding hell, I wasn't expecting you two boys.'

He led them quickly back to the rest of the unit. It was a distance of just fifty yards to the small ridge they were hiding behind; Nick and Maksim had taken up forward positions on either side of the unit, scanning the hillsides for any sign of danger.

'Look who's here, boys,' Nick hissed.

'Er, that blonde bird from Girls Aloud who looks like she's well up for it?' said Steve.

'The Domino's Pizza boy with a double pepperoni and a couple of cans of beer?' said Dan.

'Keep wishing, boys,' said Ganju, stepping forward out of the darkness.

It took a moment for everyone to realise who it was. Maksim scurried back from his lookout post, slapping Ganju brutally on the back, and wondering if by any chance he'd brought a bottle of vodka. They explained briefly how Bruce had arranged to drop them into the country by private plane.

'Hold on,' said Ian. 'Something's up, isn't it?'

Ganju nodded. He looked straight at Ian. 'That fax you sent me. You were dead right.'

'Sod it,' muttered Ian, grinding his fists together.

'What the hell's going on?' demanded Steve.

'He sent me a fax from Croatia, detailing the type of signalling device they'd fitted to Ollie,' explained Ganju. 'It's not there for you boys to find him. It's a guidance system for a cruise missile strike.'

It took a moment for Steve to comprehend what was being said. 'A cruise missile strike?'

'The pirates managed to nick a boatload of British-made weapons-grade plutonium,' said David. 'They've been auctioning it off to the highest bidder on the black market. The government is in a state of total panic. They're putting in a cruise missile strike to blow Yasin off the face of the earth – and the plutonium with him.' He paused, glancing around the anxious faces of the men. 'You're not here to capture the pirate. You're just a human guidance system to make sure the missiles go into precisely the right place.'

'We'll all be sodding killed,' said Dan angrily.

'That's why we're here,' said Ganju. 'To warn you.'

'The fucking British,' growled Henri. 'I knew we couldn't trust them.'

'My sentiments precisely,' said Ian.

'Watch it,' muttered Steve. But the protest died on his lips. For once the Irishman was right. They'd been shafted.

'What the hell do we do now?' asked Nick.

'When's the missile strike coming?' asked Ian. He was looking at Ganju.

'No idea,' answered the Gurkha. 'But they'll have an accurate fix on the target by now.'

'They'll be firing them from submarines out at sea,' said Ian. 'Probably in the Gulf, maybe over in the Med. The satellites will guide them home from there.'

'Which means?' asked Nick.

'They'll be coming in tonight,' said Ganju.

There was a brief moment of silence. Each of the men glanced at one another, unsure what they should say or do next.

Eventually Steve nodded towards the compound. 'Looks like we better get in there, boys,' he said. 'This place is going to turn into hell on earth at any moment. Trust me, I've seen the kind of damage a cruise missile can cause. The sooner we get our man out, the better.'

'What about Yasin?' asked Dan.

'Sod him. We grab Ollie, then we get the hell out of here.'

'It's too late for that,' said Henri.

'What do you mean?'

'There's no way we can get in there, find Ollie and get out. The missiles could come in at any moment.'

'I've just about sodding had enough of you, Frenchie,' growled Steve. 'We're not leaving our mate in there to die.'

'None of us signed up for a suicide mission.'

'Yeah, well, that's what we're on,' snapped Steve. 'So we might as well get used to it.'

'Maybe he's right, Steve,' said Ian. 'We have to be realistic about this. Ollie might be beyond saving, but if we piss off now, we might just get out of here alive.'

'In the Spetsnaz, we don't expect our mates to rescue us,' said Maksim. 'If you're dead, you're dead, and that's an end to it.'

'Ollie wouldn't expect us to throw our lives away,' said Dan.

Steve paused. Sod it, he muttered to himself. Maybe they were right. A cruise missile strike? Even with a conventional warhead, no man could expect to survive.

'Would Ollie expect us to go in?' he asked.

The question, he realised, was directed as much at himself as anyone else.

There was a silence that stretched through ten, then twenty seconds before anyone replied.

'I don't know about the rest of you,' said David, his voice threaded with sudden determination. He looked at each man in turn, and, as he did so, he could feel the icy fear that had possessed him start to release its grip. 'But I'm going in.'

Forty

OLLIE REMAINED MUTE, HOLDING HIMSELF steady, ignoring the churning in his gut, trying not to show any trace of fear.

'I show you kindness,' yelled Ali Yasin. 'And in return you betray me.' He turned away, looking at Mustaf and the one remaining guard. 'Search him,' he barked. 'There's some kind of tracking device on the man. Find it.'

Ollie backed away nervously. But he was already against the wall of the small cabin. There was nowhere to run to. No way of defending himself. And no way of delaying the punishment that was now inevitable.

Bugger you, Steve, you tosser. Where the hell are you?

Mustaf advanced towards him, a menacing glint illuminating his dark, shadowy eyes. With his right hand, he lashed the hosepipe forwards, striking Ollie viciously across the thighs. He screamed, fighting back the pain; at the same time, the guard grabbed him by the shoulders and wrestled him to the ground.

'Sod it,' growled Ollie, through gritted teeth. If Yasin's guessed there is a signaller on me somewhere, then he's also going to figure out that an attack on his stronghold could come at any moment. And the better prepared he is, the harder it is going to be for Steve and the rest of the boys to mount an assault. Unless they storm the compound with total surprise on their side, it could turn into a killing ground very quickly. Maybe this battle's already lost.

The guard pinned Ollie's shoulders to the ground. At his side, Mustaf knelt down, leaning into Ollie's face, so close that he could smell the stale, sweaty aftershave on his face.

'You could save us both a lot of trouble, my friend, if you just told us right now where the tracking device has been planted.'

'Piss off,' snapped Ollie.

Mustaf nodded to the guard. He slapped Ollie twice around the face, the blows so hard, his jaw went numb instantly. Then Mustaf started to run his thick hands along Ollie's body, ripping off first his sweatshirt, then his jeans.

Maybe it's better just to die here, Ollie thought grimly. The whole job's gone completely pear-shaped. There's no hope of Steve rescuing me, or of capturing Yasin either. If I could, I'd just tell him to get the hell out of here.

'Believe me, my friend, this is going to hurt,' said Mustaf, a sly grin dancing across his face. 'The way nothing has ever hurt before in your life.'

Forty-One

DAN HAD OPENED UP THE tubs of stealth paint and was steadily applying it to each man. It was a greasy, pale paste, like clear boot polish, and rubbed straight into the skin, but it would suppress any traces of body heat, and that would prevent the guards with their night-vision equipment from spotting them.

That was the theory anyway, reflected Steve, as Dan slapped the paste on to his cheeks and neck. None of us have tried it before. Then again, none of us have tried an assault as crazy as this one before either. If there's anything that might give us an edge, we just have to grab it.

'You look lovely, boys,' chuckled Dan with a big grin. 'I reckon Nick should take some of this stuff to the Swansea nightclubs. If the girls couldn't see him, he might even get a shag.'

'I do allright,' growled Nick grumpily.

'What's the name of your girlfriend again?' asked Steve.

Nick blushed, his ears turning red. 'There's no one steady.'

'In the unlikely event we get out of here alive, I reckon that's our top priority,' said Dan. 'Finding a girl for Nick.'

'I said I do allright, so sodding leave it,' snapped Nick.

Steve glanced towards the compound. It was five hundred yards away across open ground. There were lights beaming down from the boat, and also from the main entrance, but little sign of activity from either the deck or the gates. They'd already mapped out their strategy. Twenty minutes earlier, Henri had set off for the coast, primed with an underwater bomb that Ian had constructed. He'd slip that into position, and set it to explode at nine fifteen precisely. In the meantime, Steve and Maksim would crawl up to the edge of the perimeter fence, cut their way through, and slot the entrance guards from behind with their knives. Nick and Dan would move under the wire, through the channel cut by Steve, and station themselves next to the storehouse they'd spotted to the left of the plank leading down from the ship to the beach. Once in position, they'd set themselves up with the corner-shot rifles. After the bomb detonated, Steve would fling open the gates, and David, Ian and Ganju could rush in, mowing down any opposition they faced. As the pirates realised they were under attack, they'd stream off the boat, allowing Nick and Dan to pick them off. The rest of the men would assemble into a unit and storm the boat.

It was about as desperate as a plan could be, thought Steve. And about as dangerous as well. But right now it was all they had.

'Everyone happy with the drill?' he asked, looking around the faces of the unit.

He knew they weren't. They were all experienced enough – with the possible exception of Nick – to know it was dangerously under-prepared, they were under-equipped, and the odds against them weren't ones that any sane man would accept. No one in his right mind would be happy with the drill. But even if they admitted that to themselves, they weren't going to admit it to each other. In the next few minutes, only camaraderie, guts, and determination would pull them through.

Each man nodded in turn.

'Right then,' Steve said, his voice tense and strained. 'We've got a fighting chance of making this work and coming out of it alive, and sometimes that's the most a bloke can hope for. So let's bloody do this.'

He checked his watch. One minute to nine. They had fifteen minutes to get everything in place before the Frenchman started the fireworks. He nodded towards Maksim, and the two men lay down flat and started to wriggle their way across the ground. Steve had done it plenty of times in training, both in the regular Army and in the Regiment, and in a couple of live contacts as well, but he'd never tried to cross five hundred yards of open ground without being spotted before. They'd rubbed plenty of the dusty sand as well as the stealth paint into their skin and clothes to help disguise their approach, but they still had to keep themselves as low to the ground as possible, with their guns and the rest of their kit slung on their backs, and using just their elbows to lever themselves forward.

Let's hope the guards rely on the night-vision goggles rather than using their eyes, thought Steve. That was the one advantage of technology. Soldiers depended on it too much, and if you could fool the machine, you could fool the man using it as well.

It was a slow, painful crawl. The ground was hard, and there were plenty of sharp-edged rocks in it. Steve could feel them digging into his elbows. His chest and legs were getting scored in hundreds of places as the flinty stones scratched through his clothes, and several times he had to stop to let the dust he was kicking up settle. But slowly he could see the fence coming into view. Three hundred yards turned into two hundred, then one hundred. And the closer they got, the safer they were. A sentry would always concentrate on the middle distance. He wouldn't be looking so closely at the fence itself.

Maksim got there first, two hundred yards up from the main gate. The Russian had more strength in his elbows alone than most men did in their legs, and pulled himself along with ease, slithering across the ground like a predatory snake. He gingerly brushed his hand against the barbed wire, checking that it wasn't electrified or alarmed, then used a sharp pair of cutters to slice open a one-foot-high hole. He crawled through, and by the time Steve joined him, he was sitting up on his heels, his knife drawn and placed between his teeth. With the blade, the stubble, and the greasy paint, his face loomed menacingly out of the darkness, like a night goblin descending onto the earth intent on carnage. 'Let's get the fuckers,' he hissed.

Steve slotted his own knife into position and, still crouching, made his way silently towards the gate. There were two blokes standing guard, both of them big men, more than six feet tall, and weighing a couple of hundred pounds, with AK-47s hanging loose around their chests, pistols strapped to their belts, and night-vision goggles over their eyes.

Steve checked his watch again. Nine thirteen.

They had one hundred and twenty seconds. And then the scrap would kick off.

Henri ran his hands along the outside of the hull. He was fifteen feet underwater, but at this time of night, and this far beneath the waves, there was no light, and he didn't want to risk alerting any of the guards by using a torch. No, he told himself. He'd do this the same way a blind person would. By touch and instinct.

The old ship was in decent enough shape. If it was still sailing the oceans, then its hull would need cleaning, but it would be a few years yet before the rust started to devour it. Even so, there were crevices where the waves had taken their toll. Henri ran his hands along the metal, feeling for a suitable location, then fixed the bomb into place.

The timer was already set.

He turned round and kicked back with his legs. Still underwater, Henri swam a hundred yards, then started heading for the shore. When the bomb went off, the shock waves wouldn't travel far, the force of the explosive would be contained by the water. From here, he could move straight back to the beach and join the assault.

As he broke up through the waves and grabbed a lungful of air, he checked his watch. Nine fourteen . . .

Nick leant back against the crumbling corner of the storehouse.

He paused for a second to collect his breath. He and Dan had crawled across the open ground, sliding through the hole in the wire Maksim had cut, then slipped through the darkness towards the lay-up point. It was a simple, whitewashed structure, made of breeze blocks, with a rough layer of plaster covering the surface. Inside, there was a collection of shipping kit: ropes, nails, planks, paint, all of it neatly stored away.

He slotted the rifle into position.

It was made by Corner Shot Holdings, originally sold to both the Israeli Army and SWAT police teams in the United States but had since been sold to special forces around the world. Made of black metal, it looked much like a standard assault rife. But the front end of the weapon was basically a conventional pistol, which could pivot at an angle where the bayonet would usually go, whilst the trigger was mounted inside the stock. A video screen allowed the shooter to get a good look at the target, whilst remaining hidden from view himself. Nick rested the gun into his hip, and checked the screen. The gangplank was clearly in his sights. Anyone came down, he could nail them in an instant.

He checked his watch. Nine fourteen.

'You ready?' he hissed, looking across at Dan.

Dan remained silent. But a single curt nod of his head told Nick the Australian was prepared for the fight to begin.

Ganju checked the clip on the SA-80 he'd borrowed from the unit, then glanced across at David and Ian. Five hundred yards separated their hiding position from the gates to the compound. As soon as the bomb on the boat exploded, the three men would dash across the open ground and join the main attack.

Hit them from as many different angles as possible, Ganju reflected. Leave the enemy stunned and disorientated, and get the fight over in the first five minutes. That was the only way they had a chance.

'You going to be OK?' asked Ganju.

'I'm buggered if I know,' said David gruffly. 'I'll find out when we go in.'

'Stick close to me, then. I'll watch out for you.'

'I don't need a sodding nursemaid.'

Ganju looked away. That was probably what David did need, he thought. But the man was too proud to admit it. And pride, the Gurkha reflected sadly, had cost plenty of good men their lives on the battlefield.

Steve looked at Maksim.

'Ready?' he mouthed silently.

The Russian just nodded.

Still crouching, the two men approached the gates. They were moving in total silence. The beach was sandy, and that helped; any twigs or stones would have made it far harder to walk without being detected. Any noise, and one of the guards could spin round and spray them with gunfire. They'd be dead in seconds.

Steve advanced steadily. He was ten yards behind the guard now, close enough to hear him breathe. He took three more steps. Five yards. He looked at Maksim. 'Go,' he mouthed.

With one sudden movement, Steve leapt forward. The knife was out of his mouth and clasped in his right hand. He pushed back with his feet, then clamped his left hand hard over the guard's mouth, pulling his head sharply backwards. It was a movement he'd practised dozens of times: yanking the head back made it harder for the victim to cry out, and also tightened up the tendons in the neck, making it easier to get a clean kill with your blade. A muffled cry was stifled by Steve's palm. The man had the strength of an ox, but he was also caught off guard. The knife slipped easily into his neck, cutting deep through muscle and then straight into the windpipe. Steve started to twist, and flicked the blade upwards, severing the main carotid artery that delivered oxygen to the brain. He could feel the man struggle as death arrived with a startling suddenness, but he was beyond resistance. Three seconds after the assault began, the guard was dead.

Steve looked to his side.

The second guard had crumpled to the ground. Maksim was sliding a knife out of his throat.

Steve checked his watch. Nine fourteen.

And thirty seconds.

On schedule . . . so far.

He used the time remaining to assess the gates. They consisted of a simple wood and steel frame, with big chunky padlocks to hold them in place. Steve fished the key from the corpse, and slid it neatly into the lock, turning once.

Then, silently, he started to count down the remaining few seconds.

Ollie had been through plenty of full medicals. He'd taken a fair few beatings at boarding school. He was certain he knew just about every form of humiliation and indignity that could be inflicted on a man's body. But he'd reckoned without a full-body search from Somali pirates. Christ, he reflected through clenched teeth, I'll never complain about an airport search again.

He was lying face down on the cold metal floor. He'd been stripped naked. A couple of buckets of ice-cold seawater had been thrown across him, and one of the big thugs had already probed and searched every crevice in his body.

Mustaf knelt down, leaning close into his face. 'I'll find the tracking device if I have to cut open your stomach and search your intestines,' he snarled.

'Piss off,' snapped Ollie.

He steeled himself for another beating, then another search. At some point, he reckoned he'd break, but he also felt certain they'd execute him once they found the tracking device. I just have to hold out, he reminded himself. So long as there's still a chance of Steve leading a rescue.

The hose lashed into his back. It cut into his skin, then mixed with the icy, salty water, leaving Ollie screaming with pain.

Christ, he swore to himself. Maybe I should just get this over with. A man has to die one day. Why not this one?

And then he heard it. An explosion.

The sound was muffled by the water, the way a cough that started deep within your chest might be. But the boat shook and shuddered, and for a moment it seemed as if the girders and steel plates that held it together had come to life. It heaved and bucked into the air, throwing both Mustaf and his guard hurtling sideways, then down on to the ground.

At sodding last, thought Ollie.

The hosepipe had fallen from the guard's hand as the man was thrown hard against the side of the boat. The shuddering of the vessel made it impossible to stand, but lying on the ground gave Ollie the edge. He slithered across the floor, then grabbed the hose, lashing it backwards, and he was about to whip it into the guard when he realised the man was already unconscious.

Ollie turned towards Mustaf, already picking himself up on the other side of the small room. Still naked, with blood running down his chest and back where the pipe had cut into him, Ollie swung the hose straight into the pirate's face with a force that surprised even himself, slicing open a deep cut that started in the forehead and ran straight down the left cheek into the fat around his neck. Blood was starting to seep from the open wound, and the pirate reached up instinctively to see whether he'd lost an eye.

'Let's see how you sodding like it, matey,' Ollie shouted.

David watched as the explosion kicked a wall of water high up in the air. He could feel some flicks of spray across his face as the water caught on the wind and blew over the beach. The vessel groaned, the metal straining, as it bucked upwards, then fell back into the sand and stone. 'Go, go,' shouted Ganju at his side.

The two men started to run across the open ground. Their SA-80s were gripped tight to their chests, their fingers on the triggers. They covered the distance in just a few seconds, streaking through the gates Steve and Maksim had flung open.

'Forwards, forwards,' shouted Steve.

Up on the deck, there was the sound of shouting, then steady bursts of gunfire as the pirates streamed up on to it, trying to work out where the assault was coming from and how many men were attacking them. From the gates, Steve and Maksim had already opened up with their guns, putting a few rounds into the deck. It was wild, poorly aimed fire but enough to give the boys up there something to think about. A unit of six men was starting to stream down the ramp and on to the beach, their AK-47s on automatic, spewing hot, angry bullets into the air. But Dan and Nick had them in their sights; they released a steady burst of fire from the corner-shot rifles, taking the men out one by one. The bodies crumpled and fell, splashing into the surf, creating pink breakers that mixed white foam and crimson blood.

'It's just like fragging the Jerry in *Medal of Honour*,' grunted Nick with grim satisfaction as he watched man after man fall into the shallow water on the rifle's tiny video screen.

Steve, Maksim, David, Ganju and Ian were still running across the beach, aiming to link up with Nick and Dan behind the storehouse. They were on exposed, open ground, and each man was painfully aware how vulnerable they would be if the pirates could regroup and launch a counter-strike. It would quickly overwhelm them. Bullets were starting to smatter the ground all around them.

Then they heard a shout. 'Stop, stop now,' yelled a voice.

David stopped dead in his tracks. He turned round. A unit of three pirates had dropped down on to the beach. They were advancing with their guns at the ready.

'Get behind the wall,' shouted David. 'Bloody go . . . I'll deal with these fuckers.'

'No, run!' yelled Steve.

'Do as he says,' snapped Ganju. His voice was raised, something that was rare for the Gurkha, and instinctively Steve did as he was told, flinging himself towards the storeroom. David had already dropped to the ground, slamming his SA-80 into position. He could feel the sweat pouring off him, and his hands were shaking. Sodding do this, he told himself grimly. *Or else die right here.*

He slammed his finger into the trigger, releasing a barrage of fire straight into the three men advancing towards him. One dropped immediately, another spun round in agony. But the bullets were still spitting from their AK-47s, chewing up the sand and pebbles all around him. As the man crumpled to the ground, David could feel the adrenalin surge through him, and in an instant years of training kicked in. He felt calm, relaxed, in control: the bullets all around him could kick up the sand but he felt confident none of them had his name on them. Swivelling the SA-80 into position, he squeezed the trigger, slotting two more bullets into the wounded man, then emptying the rest of his clip into the head of the last man still standing.

He picked himself up and started to run.

He flung himself behind the storeroom wall. The rest of the unit was already hunkered down, protecting themselves from sporadic incoming fire from the pirates still up on the deck of the boat.

'Well done,' said Ganju, patting David on the back.

David smiled grimly. 'Good to get back in the groove,' he said.

Steve was looking up towards the boat. There were fifteen, maybe twenty corpses strewn across the gangplank, and more up on the deck, but there was still a unit of men up on the main deck, their guns stuck over the railings, defending their position. There could be at least another ten men to deal with before they got inside to rescue Ollie. They'd evened up the odds but they hadn't won the battle yet.

'What now?' shouted Dan.

'We storm the boat,' said Steve.

Each man looked at him in turn. From the slack, shocked

expressions on their faces, it was clear they all thought he'd lost his mind. There were few more dangerous military manoeuvres than running up a ramp into determined opposition. You created a narrow channel into which the enemy could concentrate their fire and, although it could be successful, casualties were inevitable. It was just a question of how high a price you wanted to pay to achieve your objective.

'All right, all right, you got any better sodding ideas, I'm all ears,' growled Steve.

The sound of gunfire peppered the night sky. Up on the deck, five, perhaps six pirates were putting round after round into the storeroom. They were approaching a stalemate. The pirates had taken too many casualties already to risk coming down on to the beach. But on the boat they could dig themselves in and make their position impregnable.

A stand-off, thought Steve bitterly.

He looked up into the sky. He could hear something. A buzzing sound, something like the static on a car radio that was losing the signal.

It was miles away, he knew that. But he'd heard that sound before, both in training and when he was fighting with the Regiment in Iraq.

A cruise missile.

He slipped a fresh clip into his SA-80, then drew the Russian-built GSh-18 pistol from his webbing, making sure that its magazine was filled with its armour-piercing bullets. He was only going to get one shot at his opponents, if that, and he wasn't taking any chances with his rounds bouncing off protective plates. To have any chance of surviving, a man had to go down each time he pulled the trigger.

'The firecrackers are about to go off, boys,' he said, his tone strained. 'Anyone who's got any sense will probably make a run for it now. But I'm going up that ramp to get our mate out of there . . .'

Forty-Two

HE STILL HAD THE HOSEPIPE in his hand when Ali Yasin burst into the room.

Ollie was standing naked, gasping for breath, after using the hose to whip Mustaf into submission. There was blood on his hands where he'd pummelled his fists into both the guard and Mustaf's faces. Lying at his feet, both men were breathing, but with broken teeth and cut lips, it was going to be a while before they woke up again.

He wiped the sweat from his brow, leaving a smear of blood across his forehead. It had been a short, violent fight, fuelled by intense anger. But when he looked up, he saw the barrel of an AK-47 pointing straight at him.

'Move,' snapped Yasin.

Ollie stood rock still. The boat had stopped bucking and heaving as the impact of the explosion subsided. All around, Ollie could hear the sound of gunfire, and he reckoned the assault had begun. There had been a fierce exchange of gunfire, the start of what Ollie guessed was an attempt at an overwhelming attack, but in the last couple of minutes it had quietened down, and he could hear only a sporadic exchange of shots. Not encouraging, he reflected. On an assault like this one, you'd hope to get the battle won in the first few minutes. Stretch it out, and the odds against you lengthened.

Ollie started to walk forward, looking into the pirate's eyes, but he could see nothing there apart from a cold, calculating fury.

Yasin grabbed hold of his arm, and thrust him forwards. He jabbed the AK-47 barrel into his back, and Ollie could tell from the heat of the metal on his skin that the weapon had been recently fired.

'I said move.'

Ollie remained silent. There was no point in resisting, he judged. Yasin would shoot him if he had to; there were plenty of his men lying dead on the beach already, and he wasn't likely to be in any mood to be gracious towards his enemy. They stepped out of the cabin, then down a single flight of metal stairs that led deep into the hull. The first explosion had knocked out the ship's generator, and there was no light to see by. Yasin clearly didn't need it: this boat was his kingdom, and he knew every inch of its interior.

'Inside.'

Ollie stepped into a dark chamber. It measured ten feet by five. A store locker originally, he reckoned, which had clearly been converted into a safe room. The same way millionaires' mansions had panic rooms built into them – a totally impregnable fortress where they could hide if they were attacked until the police arrived – the pirates had made themselves a safe room to shelter inside if they came under enemy fire.

Yasin switched on a torch.

The room was stocked with tinned food, dried biscuits, and bottles of water. There was a satellite phone in a box, and batteries to power it. The place was kitted out to survive a long stay, reckoned Ollie. Yasin could hole up in here, then use the satphone to call in reinforcements. He controlled dozens of pirate skiffs out in the ocean. Left alone for a few minutes, he could put together a whole armada, and it could be here within the hour.

The AK-47 was still pointing at Ollie. On the table, he noticed the plutonium. Yasin snapped the case shut, then attached it to his left wrist using a chain and handcuffs.

'You make so much as a sound and I'll blow your head off,' he said, looking straight at Ollie.

Henri started to climb steadily up the side of the boat.

He was still wearing his jeans and sweatshirt, but he'd kicked off his boots before first stepping into the water. They'd just weigh him down. He'd hidden his kitbag back at the lay-up point: it, too, was just unnecessary weight. But he'd put the Browning pistol inside a waterproof pouch which was still tucked into his belt. When it came to a fight, as he felt certain it would, he'd need it at the ready.

The side of the old hull was thick with seaweed and slime, and the waves were splashing up around his feet, but there were enough crevices and cracks on its surface to make the climb relatively easy. At fifteen feet, he was far enough up to fling his arms up on to the outer railing and lever himself on board. There was some barbed wire slung around the edge of the boat, but the waves had rusted it, and the sharpness of its spikes had been blunted. The wire snagged his hands in a couple of places, but he ignored the pain and kept pulling himself up. He was halfway along the boat. The lights were all out but through the murky night air Henri could see that the remaining pirates were up front, holding their position against the men attacking them from the beach.

He could see at least six of them, hunkered down behind steel barricades, using their AK-47s to take shots at their opponents.

Careless, he thought to himself. They should know that, for a boat, the real threat always comes from the sea, not from the land.

He advanced another ten yards, drawing the Browning Hi-Power, and releasing the magazine lock and safety catch. The 9mm pistol had an effective range of fifty metres, but these men were only twenty metres away, and that put them well within his range. He only had one clip, but one reason for the popularity of the Browning was that its mag held thirteen bullets, more than most military pistols. And thirteen rounds was more than enough to deal with six men. Particularly when you were shooting them in the back.

Henri crouched down next to a lifeboat, then gripped the Browning between both hands. He chose a target right in the centre of the group of six men. Then squeezed the trigger.

The bullet entered the man's neck from the back, drilling a neat hole straight through the flesh, muscles and vein. His right hand flicked upwards in annoyance, as if swatting away a fly, but in the next half second he realised what had happened. Blood gushed from the wound, but the man was already dying. Henri adjusted his aim, and squeezed the trigger again, controlled the sharp kickback that was a feature of the Browning, then repeated the manoeuvre.

One more man had been killed before they realised what had hit them, whilst another was rolling around clutching his shoulder in agony where the bullet had lodged itself in the bone. The three remaining men flashed round, releasing a rapid, furious burst of fire from their AK-47s. The bullets skidded and thudded off the old steel of the hull, but Henri had already rolled behind the lifeboat, and in the next moment, as the bullets flew through the air, he slotted the Browning back into the waterproof pouch and dropped down into the waves swirling below.

Two hundred yards away, Steve glanced up at the gangplank. He could see a couple of men falling down, and from the angle at which they crashed into the sea, he could tell precisely what had happened to them. Someone had drilled a bullet expertly into the back of their heads.

That meant only one thing. *Henri*.

'Say what you like about the Frenchies,' he said, glancing over to Nick and Dan, 'they know how to shoot a bloke in the back.'

But Dan wasn't listening. Together with Nick, he'd started

running towards the gangplank; there was an opening now, and they had to seize the initiative. The rest of the unit fell in close behind, a tight phalanx of seven men moving in close formation. A couple of shots spat into the sand, but a volley of fire from Dan and Nick soon had the pirates diving for cover. Dan bounded on to the plank of wood that ran down to the beach. He'd slammed his SA-80 into automatic. With Nick right behind him, they were putting down an aggressive barrage of fire, catching two of the remaining pirates by surprise and shredding them in a hailstorm of bullets. The remaining two spun round, but their faces were twisted and fearful. They could tell they were outnumbered, outgunned, and squeezed in a pincer, and they knew enough about fighting to be aware that meant that death was now certain. One man tried to retaliate, releasing a volley of fire from his AK-47, but the second wave of men, consisting of Steve, Maksim, Ganju and David, was already running up the plank, and the man's face and chest were peppered by a sudden assault of bullets that sent him sprawling towards the floor. The second man was starting to raise his hands to surrender, but there was no time to take any prisoners, and Maksim slotted a bullet straight through his forehead before he had a chance to plead for his life.

The guns fell silent.

The seven men were now up on the deck. Henri had run around to the side and up the gangplank to join the rest of the unit.

'Thanks for the help, mate,' said Steve, giving the Frenchman a sharp slap on the back. 'But we're not out of the shit yet.'

Steve looked up.

The missile was flying straight over his head. A Tomahawk.

It was a long, thin white tube, measuring just over twenty feet, like a cigar case, painted white, with two short, stubby wings, less than three metres each, and with stabilisers on its tail. It was powered by a single, subsonic jet engine, and made a low whine, like a small aircraft, but the power plant was designed to make as little sound and emit as little heat as possible, allowing it to evade detection by either radar or night-vision equipment. A Tomahawk would be fired from a submarine and would typically carry a thousand pound warhead, giving it an enormous punch. Some of the newer versions had titanium-encased warheads with a time-delayed fuse, allowing them to penetrate defensive positions then blow them up from the inside, but Steve reckoned the Navy wouldn't be wasting their top-of-the-range kit tonight. All they wanted was a big, dirty bang, enough to kill even the cockroaches, and for that, a plain vanilla cruise missile with a big lump of TNT in its nose would do the job just fine.

So long as it scored a direct hit.

Steve watched the Tomahawk descend but fly clean over their heads. Even with satellite guidance, the missiles were only accurate up to a thousand metres, and this one wasn't a bull's-eye. It landed seven hundred metres inshore. A flash of white light burst into the sky, turning night into day. A fireball blew upwards, and the air was suddenly filled with the noxious smells of charred sand and incinerated explosive. It took a fraction of a second for the sound to catch up, but when it did, the noise was ear-splitting: a brutal wave of thudding, thumping noise that rolled out over the bleak landscape, then gripped and shook you like a Glaswegian drunk intent on starting a fight outside the pub on a Saturday night.

Steve grabbed the railings of the boat. The ground was shaking all around them, as the force of the explosion chewed up the rocks beneath the sand, cutting fissures into the beach beneath them, the way it might during an earthquake. The sea roared and spat angrily below.

'Sodding move,' shouted Steve, above the rumbling din of the explosion. 'There's more of those fuckers on the way. Let's find Ollie and move the hell out of here.'

The unit burst through the ship, but it had been turned into a dark, ghostly wreck, the crew slaughtered in the sudden ferocity of the attack.

Ganju was flashing a torch through the dim interior but there was no sign of Yasin or Ollie. One boy, a teenager, was cowering in the corner of what looked like the main living quarters. His big eyes rolled up towards them, his hands shook with fear.

'We're here to get the British bloke,' yelled Steve, yanking the boy up by the collar and pushing him violently against the wall. 'Now where the fuck is he?'

He could feel the boat shake again, as the aftershocks of the explosion rolled through the ground.

The boy remained mute.

'Where the fuck is he?' Steve jabbed the barrel of his SA-80 hard into the boy's throat.

He shook, then spluttered something in Arabic.

Ian approached them, his Browning drawn. He jabbed the pistol into the boy's left kneecap. 'In Ulster, we took out the knees,' he said, his tone hardening. 'That gets them talking.'

'Hear that?' growled Steve, spitting the words into the boy's face. 'He'll sodding do it as well. Now speak.'

The boy shook his head.

Ian slipped off the safety catch on the pistol. 'I'm counting to two . . .'

The boy just kept shaking his head.

'He's a sodding Ulsterman,' spat Steve into the boy's face. 'Heard of them? A race of bloody nutters. If he says he'll blow your kneecaps off, then believe him.'

The boy spluttered another few words in Arabic.

'Two,' said Ian. He looked into the boy's eyes, but there was nothing to be seen there apart from a mute, uncomprehending terror.

'Sod it,' muttered Steve. 'We'll search the bloody ship.'

'There's no time,' growled Ian. 'There'll be another missile in a minute, maybe less.'

'Do it,' snapped Maksim.

Steve looked around. Dan, Nick, even Ganju were all nodding.

Ian released the trigger. There was a horrible crunching sound as the 9mm bullet smashed the delicate knee bones apart. The boy fell face down, clutching the wound in agony. Ian kicked him hard in the stomach, then knelt.

'Now listen, you little sod,' he said softly. 'A man can live with one leg disabled, but not with two. Not round here.'

Steve turned away in disgust. He's just a sodding kid, he thought to himself.

But as he looked back, the boy was hobbling down the metal staircase. There was a grim, tense smile on Ian's lips as he, Nick, and Dan followed the boy, instructing the rest of the unit to stand guard. They went down a level and shone the flashlight into the dark space ahead of them.

'A safe room,' said Ian, feeling the thick steel of the door.

'Can you blow it?' asked Dan.

'Not without killing the blokes inside,' answered Ian. He looked towards Nick. 'Try the GREM.'

Nick pulled the weapon from his kitbag. They'd picked up the grenade rifle entry munition back at the armoury in Croatia. Originally developed by the Israeli arms industry but adapted by American manufacturers for sale worldwide, it was designed to blast open secure doors at a safe distance, perfect for the house-to-house combat the Israelis were constantly engaged in. Normally, soldiers would fix an explosive charge to a door, but that exposed them to the risk of sniper fire. The GREM consisted of a 1.5 pound grenade, shaped like a flat disc. Fired from a distance of between ten and forty feet, the shape of the explosive device meant the force of the blast was diffused right through the door, rather than just punching a hole straight through it. The door would buckle, then drop off its hinges and collapse.

'Ready,' said Ian, looking across at Nick.

Nick nodded just once. He raised the short, stubby rifle to his shoulder, then waited while the rest of the unit gathered safely behind him. He squeezed once on the trigger. The blast detonated with a dull thud, the door shook violently, then bucked. There was a split-second delay, during which the steel appeared to withstand the blast. Steve shielded his eyes from the flash that accompanied the explosion, and held his breath to prevent the fumes filling his lungs.

Then the door crashed noisily to the floor.

Forty-Three

STEVE GRIPPED THE SIDE OF the boat as the hull shuddered and shook.

Even though they were too deep inside for any light to penetrate, he could feel the wave of heat from the blast and, a fraction of a second later, hear the echoing, booming racket of the explosion.

The Tomahawks were getting closer. Any second now there was going to be a direct hit.

He looked straight forward. The door had dropped to the floor, and there was a cloud of smoke where it had been blasted away. As the fumes started to clear, he could make out the shapes of two men. Ollie, stark naked, stained with blood, and blackened by the explosion of the door-busting grenade. And next to him, a tall, dark man, with an AK-47 in one hand and a metal attaché case chained to the other. Yasin, Steve realised. The bastard they'd come to capture.

'Drop your sodding weapon, pal,' snarled Dan, pointing his SA-80 straight towards Yasin.

The two men stepped out of the small, sealed chamber.

'Good of you to finally show up, chaps,' said Ollie with a rough grin. 'I don't suppose anyone brought a pack of cards, did they? My mate Ali and I were just thinking of getting a game going.'

'We'll save the smart-arse remarks, mate,' said Steve. 'There's a sub out there somewhere firing Tomahawks right at us.'

The unit started to move up the stairs.

Steve helped Ollie, while Dan and Nick kept Yasin under close control. As they came back on to the deck, Steve could see a second Tomahawk had landed two hundred yards closer than the first, kicking up a huge firestorm just five hundred yards in front of them. They ran down the gangplank and joined the rest of the unit. As they did so, Steve could hear the whizzing, roaring sound that was by now becoming eerily familiar. He glanced upwards. The Tomahawk was coming straight down into the sea, three hundred yards to their left. Closer, he thought. Too sodding close.

Suddenly, they were drenched with water and sand. The Tomahawk had landed right on the edge of the beach, kicking up a cloud of spray and debris that covered a radius of five hundred yards from the point of impact. Steve held himself steady, closing his eyes, aware there was nothing they could do until the bulk of the debris had blown its way through the beach. It was like being caught in a rainstorm of sand and water, and by the time Steve opened his eyes again, the hull of the boat was completely covered in a thick, muddy sludge that looked and smelt like raw sewage.

'Everyone OK?' he said, glancing around.

Ollie, David, Ian, Nick, Dan, Henri and Ganju nodded in turn.

Then Steve noticed something. His head spun left, right, forwards and backwards.

Yasin. He was gone.

'The bastard,' Steve hissed under his breath.

'There,' snapped Dan, pointing.

Yasin was splashing out into the water. He'd kicked up his heels and was swimming hard into the rising swell of the sea.

Steve started to run but Dan, then Henri, pulled him back sharply, tugging at his shoulders.

'Leave it,' snapped Dan.

'He's getting away.'

'He knows these waters, and we don't,' said Henri, wiping the thick sludge off his face. 'I reckon there's a dinghy stashed out there somewhere. In the darkness, we've no hope of catching him now.'

'And another Tomahawk could come in at any moment,' said Dan.

Steve remained still. They were right, he knew that. To plunge into the water now was just throwing your life away. He shrugged away the restraining hands.

'Then let's get the hell out of here,' he said, his tone strained.

But Ian was pointing towards Ollie. 'Get the feckin' signaller off your man, then.'

Steve realised at once what he was saying. The cruise missiles were aimed straight at Ollie's mouth.

'I'm sorry about this, mate,' continued Ian, looking at Ollie. 'But we have to get that tracker off you as fast as possible. There's cruise missiles coming straight for it.'

Ollie, still naked, didn't argue. There wasn't any point.

Dan and Ganju were advancing on him. They pushed him down to the ground. David always had a penknife in his webbing, and a pair of pocket pliers was one of its tools. He handed it across to Maksim.

'Is this going to hurt?' asked Ollie.

'Like fuck,' said David tersely.

'I don't suppose there's any chance of finding a dentist, is there?'

David shook his head.

'Then at least make it bloody quick.'

He lay down flat on the ground. Ganju drew a syringe of morphine from his medi-kit and ripped open its packaging. It was designed for use on the battlefield, relieving the pain from a gunshot wound while the choppers came in to medi-vac the casualties. Not for dentistry, that much was for damned certain, reflected Ollie as he watched Ganju inch the needle into his soft flesh around his cheek and start to squeeze.

'That going to work?' he asked anxiously, ignoring the stinging sensation as the needle was pushed too roughly into his skin.

'Sod knows,' said David.

Ollie could feel his cheek growing numb and floppy, then his neck, and then half his chest. David pinned down one shoulder, whilst Ganju gripped his torso, holding him to the ground.

'Sodding move it,' growled Steve, scanning the sky anxiously. 'There could be another missile any moment now.'

'Open wide,' said Maksim, grinning, and flashing the pliers in his right hand. 'In the Red Army we do this all the time. Haven't got any dentists . . .'

Ollie opened his mouth wide. Ian leant over and pointed to the tooth that had been operated on. 'Second molar on the right,' he said.

Maksim snapped the pliers into position. He rested his knee on Ollie's chest, tensed his muscles, then yanked hard. Ollie winced. Despite the morphine, the pain was blistering, like having a limb plunged into molten metal. There was no give in the tooth.

'Give it some sodding welly,' growled Dan at Maksim.

The Russian grimaced. He was the strongest man any of them had ever met, a single ball of tense muscle, but he didn't like having his strength questioned. He paused, wiping away a film of sweat that had collected on his brow and flicking it away with the back of his hand so that it splashed across Ollie's face. He leant into the pliers, and wrenched harder. But even with his muscles straining, and grunting like a pig as he drilled the maximum force into his forearms, the tooth remained rooted to the jawbone.

Ian knelt down. 'We learnt this one in the Maze,' he said quietly. With his right hand, he punched a savage blow into the side of Ollie's face. The man was already close to losing consciousness, and the punch tipped him over the edge. His eyes closed. 'That should have loosened it up,' said Ian, looking at Maksim.

Dan held open Ollie's mouth and Maksim re-attached the pliers. With a brutal heave, the tooth came free. There was blood dripping from the molar. From his medi-pack, Ganju had mixed some water with disinfectant, and he poured it into Ollie's mouth. Henri grabbed the tooth, slotted it inside a half-empty water bottle, and screwed the top back on. He handed it across to Nick. 'I want you to kick this as far into the sea as possible,' he said. 'Aim for the east. The currents are flowing that way, and the bottle will float with them and take that signaller a couple of miles away in no time.'

Nick grabbed the bottle and started to run.

'Just imagine you're Frank Lampard,' said Steve.

'Do that and I'll miss, pal,' said Nick. 'I'm thinking Stevie Gerrard, mate. Someone who actually knows how to kick a ball.'

His right foot collided with the bottle. It spun out into the sea, hitting the waves far enough out to be caught up in the tidal currents.

'With any luck, that bastard Yasin will collect it and find a cruise missile on his arse,' said Ian.

Dan and Ganju propped a still half-conscious Ollie on to his feet and started to hobble forwards. The last Tomahawk had landed in the sea, its explosives quickly extinguished by the waves, but the two missiles that had struck further up the beach had cast burning debris over a wide radius, spreading a pale, ghostly light across the beach. Steve checked that each of the men was standing, then they started to move forwards.

He stopped.

He'd seen some figures moving up ahead of them. Dark, nothing more than shadows in the night. But he was certain he'd seen them.

'There's something there,' he hissed, pointing forwards. He gripped his SA-80, his finger on the trigger.

'The Taliban or Iranian units,' said Dan. 'They'll have come down to see what the scrap is all about.'

'And they'll reckon we have the feckin' plutonium,' said Ian. 'They'll want it from us.'

Steve looked around. There was no cover on this part of the beach. They could retreat into the hull of the boat, but that could easily take another incoming missile. It was another three, four hundred yards up to the ridge of ground where they'd laid up earlier.

Suddenly a shot rang out.

Ganju spun round, dropping Ollie, who fell to the ground.

There was blood gushing from Ganju's thigh, up close to the groin. Dan let go of Ollie as well, and David rushed across to help. He ripped a syringe from his medi-pack and plunged a shot of morphine into Ganju's leg. Dan tore off a strip of his sweatshirt and tied a rough tourniquet round the top of the leg to try and staunch the bleeding. But the crimson liquid was still gushing from the wound. 'Hollow point,' muttered Dan.

David nodded.

A hollow-point bullet was designed to expand on impact, so that the bullet grew as it travelled through soft tissue, causing the maximum damage to the victim.

'Shit,' said Dan. He pulled harder on the tourniquet, while David searched for a bandage in his medi-pack.

'Think he'll make it?'

'Christ knows.'

'Down, boys, sodding down,' shouted Steve, a couple of yards ahead.

The attack was coming from straight ahead of them. Steve, Nick and Maksim rushed forward ten yards, then threw themselves on to the ground, opening up their SA-80s as they did so. They had to put down a wall of steel behind which they could look after Ganju. None of the men had any idea what they were firing at. They couldn't see the enemy, not even smell them.

'Just keep firing,' muttered Steve. 'Keep them pinned down.'

Another pair of bullets chewed up the ground a few yards in front of them.

'Grenades,' said Maksim.

Steve nodded. 'You go right, I'll go left. Get to a hundred yards, then throw.' He looked towards Nick. 'Get Ian and Henri up here and put down some covering fire.'

Steve pulled a grenade from his webbing, tucked it into his right hand, and started to run. He was plunging through the ghostly half-light. They'd been equipped with the L109A1, the standard-issue anti-personnel fragmentation grenade for the British Army since 2001. Weighing 465 grams, it had a fuse delay of three to four seconds, and on detonation would put out a deadly blast of shrapnel. As he ran, Steve could hear a whizzing splitting open the sky: a sound he was starting to grow used to as a ghastly premonition of the carnage ahead.

'Christ,' he muttered.

Another missile.

He kept running, covering a hundred yards, then another. The ground was rough, and a couple of times he could feel himself start to stumble, and he desperately flung out his arms to maintain his balance and keep himself on his feet. To go down now was certain death. He ripped the pin from the grenade but kept it in his right fist for one, then two seconds. Standard training was to release the grenade as soon as the pin was out, since they could regularly detonate on two seconds, but Steve reckoned he'd take his chances. He was only going to get one shot at this. Waste it, and there was nothing left in his locker.

The grenade arced into the air, then disappeared into the darkness. Steve crouched down low and pulled his helmet down over his face. At a hundred yards, the shrapnel from the blast could easily hit him. He steadied himself, preparing both mentally and physically for the shockwave that would follow the detonation.

A single second ticked by.

The blast kicked up high into the air, followed swiftly by a second explosion. Steve permitted himself a brief, tight smile. The Russian had given them the good news at precisely the same time. A double blast. Surely no one could survive that. Steve kept his eyes shut tight and the helmet down over his face, but he could feel the heat of the explosives kicking across the beach, he could smell the flames in the scorched air, and he felt a slither of steel shrapnel lodge itself in his body armour, just below his second rib. A scream ripped through the sky, the sound of a man being torn in two, then a grunt as another man died. Trench-clearing was what they called it on the training fields. Putting grenades into your opponents' positions to finish them off. It was nasty, close-combat warfare, and you had to reckon on having the sights and smells of death all around you.

Steve opened his eyes. But there was no time to see how much damage the grenades had done. Two hundred yards out to sea, another Tomahawk had just detonated. The big, powerful missile had drilled down into the ocean bed, then exploded, creating a muffled, angry blast that seemed to come from within the depths of the earth. A giant wall of water was thrown up into the sky, and Steve closed his eyes while it engulfed him. The force of the water, thick and salty, pushed him down, the way it would if he were standing beneath a powerful waterfall.

Steve opened his eyes again. Blinked, shut them, then opened them again.

Up ahead, a wave had risen up out of the sea. It was thirty, maybe forty feet high.

Christ, thought Steve. A tsunami. And it's heading straight for us.

Forty-Four

THE WAVE WAS MOVING TOO fast, too furiously, for there to be any possibility of escape.

Steve watched for a brief moment, awestruck by the brutal power of the wall of water moving straight towards him. It was like a liquid bulldozer, pushing relentlessly forward, muscling every obstacle out of the way. Get a sodding grip, man, he commanded himself. He turned round, searching desperately for something, anything, he could hide behind.

But there was nothing. Just scrubland, and ridges in the ground.

Steve threw himself to the ground.

Let the water wash straight over me, he told himself. Ride with it, the way you would with any wave.

He breathed in, filling his lungs with as much oxygen as possible, but nothing could prepare him for the liquid assault that was about to begin. The wave rolled straight over him, lifting him clean off the ground, flinging him upwards like a matchstick, then spinning him round. His eyes closed, and he reached out with his arms to try and steady himself, but there was no point in trying to struggle against the thousands of tons of water swirling around him. It dragged him forwards, he had no idea how fast, until slowly he felt its force ebbing, and the grey water turned foamy and white, and he could feel himself falling downwards again.

Back flat on the ground, Steve waited until the breaking waves had drained away before he attempted to stand up. He was soaked through, the cold water clinging to his skin, and there was a thick, dark layer of sludge all over him. He lifted himself up and slowly opened his eyes. The water had extinguished the flames from the earlier missiles, and there was only the moonlight to see by. Even so, it didn't take much light to comprehend the devastation caused by the wave. It had dropped him a hundred yards back from the shoreline. The ground was churned up all around him, with water washing back to the sea in small rivers. The hull of the boat the pirates had used as their headquarters had broken up into a dozen pieces, debris scattered everywhere, and the wire fencing that had enclosed the compound had been washed away.

As he looked around, Steve couldn't see a single man standing. He couldn't even see any corpses.

'Oh, Christ,' he muttered. 'Boys,' he shouted, spitting water and sludge out of his mouth.

Nothing.

'Boys.'

The cry was louder this time, with an edge of desperation to it.

'Sodding hell, mate, I should have brought my surfboard,' said Nick.

The Welsh boy was walking straight towards him. Water was dripping from his skin and clothes, there was sludge all over his face and matted into his hair.

'You don't get waves like that in the Gower Peninsula,' said Steve.

Nick shook his head, water flipping away from him; he looked like a shaggy dog climbing out of a lake. 'Where is everyone?'

Steve kept scanning the beach. The water had taken him a hundred yards from the enemy position they'd been attacking, but it didn't look as if their opponents had survived. One by one the men started to pick themselves out from the mud. Maksim staggered forward first, his clothes torn, followed by Henri, then David, then Dan and Ian.

Even Ollie seemed to be OK. He was still naked, and he was clutching his mouth, but the water seemed to have brought him round and, not for the first time, Steve found himself admiring the endurance of the man. He might not have much sense but he has the strength of a JCB, and that's not a quality in a bloke you can ever underestimate.

Every man of them was still standing – except one.

Ganju.

'Where the sod is he?' asked Steve.

'We lost him,' said David.

His tone was flat, and yet you could hear how worried he was. A wounded man, caught up in that wave? reflected Steve. It didn't bear thinking about. He pulled his flashlight from his webbing but the water had leaked into the batteries. He slammed it angrily to the ground. None of the men's torches were still working.

'Spread out and search, boys,' said Steve tersely.

The unit started to walk out across the beach. Steve checked his SA-80; the weapon was soaked through, and so was the Browning. They might be able to fix them in the next twenty-four hours, but for now they'd have to rely on their knives and their fists. Maksim had already checked the bunker they'd been attacking before the wave struck, but the Iranians had all been killed, struck first by the grenades, then by the wave. It looked as if they had the cove to themselves. Not that anyone would want it. A few hundred miles away, some blokes sitting safely in a sub had sent it back to the stone age, reflected Steve bitterly. And sodding near killed some of their own men as well.

'Ganju, Ganju, where the hell are you, mate?' he shouted as he paced forwards.

Then, fifty yards away, he saw David and Dan standing together, their heads down.

He started to run towards them. But somewhere inside he already knew what he was going to find.

'He's bought it,' said David, glancing up.

Steve took a deep breath, struggling to control his emotions. He'd seen plenty of men fall on the battlefield, and some of them were his friends, but this felt like one death too many. He could feel himself starting to throw up: his stomach was heaving violently, and his guts were churning. He turned round and spat on to the ground, struggling to keep himself under control. A single phrase was echoing around his head.

The best of us . . .

The rest of the men gathered round. Ganju had been whipped up into the wave, and spun round, and the impact had opened up the wound in his leg, tearing out a great gash of flesh, so that the blood had simply washed out of him. On two pints, he would have lost consciousness. On four, he'd have gone. The body only holds eight pints of blood, and once half of it has emptied out of you, you're already dead.

'OK, sod it, boys, let's deal with the body,' said Ian tersely. 'That's the least we can do.'

'What's the Gurkha way?' asked Nick.

'They cremate their bodies,' said David. 'You're meant to wait seventy-two hours, then give them some food to take with them to the afterlife.'

'Well, we haven't got seventy-two sodding hours, have we?' growled Dan.

'Then we'll do the best we can,' said Steve.

Maksim and Nick scoured the beach, picking their way through the debris scattered everywhere when the hull of the boat broke apart, until they found a jerry can of diesel. Steve and Dan arranged the body flat on the ground. Henri prepared some of the food he had in his kitbag and put it next to Ganju, while Nick cleaned his curved knife, the closest thing they had to a Gurkha kukri blade, and placed it in his hands. There was a tear in Nick's eyes as he positioned the weapon, noted Steve, and he could well understand why. But the Welsh boy was just going to have to get used to it. If you couldn't handle watching your mates die, there was no point in becoming a soldier. Which is why most of us soon become desperate for some other life.

'I don't suppose anyone knows what the monks in Nepal might say,' said David, glancing around.

'Good luck, old pal, and let's hope you come back into a better life than this one,' said Steve. 'Or something like that.'

'Right,' said David. 'It'll have to do, I suppose.'

Ian knelt down and poured some diesel over the body, and Henri used a waterproof flint stored in his webbing to bring a spark to life. Each man said his own silent farewell before Ian lit the fuel. The flames licked up around the body, singeing the clothes first and then starting to incinerate the corpse.

David was crossing himself.

Henri and Ian were both mumbling a few words they remembered from the Catholic burial service.

Maksim was standing rock steady, his eyes hollow with shock.

Nick's head was bowed as if in prayer. And his hands were shaking.

Why the hell was it you? thought Steve to himself. If there was one man who deserved to survive this mission, it was Ganju.

The best of us . . .

Thick plumes of smoke were starting to rise up. Steve stood close by, letting them waft over his face. He hated the smell of a burning man; he'd seen blokes killed by flame-throwers, and he'd listened to them being burnt alive as grenades and bombs caught them in their fireballs. But he'd never been up close to a cremation before, and it wasn't an experience he'd ever care to repeat. The cooked flesh, and the spitting of fat and blood, was hard enough to bear in an enemy. In a friend, it was as mournful a sight as he reckoned any man could ever witness.

As the flames died down, he glanced around the beach. Steve wasn't sure he'd ever seen a battlefield so desolate. The ground was churned and sludgy, there was debris everywhere, and the only light came from the flickering flames rising up off his mate. The waves were crashing behind them, and a wind was starting to blow in off the sea.

As he scanned the expressions on the faces of the men around him, Steve could sense the despair that was gnawing at each one of them. They been tricked and betrayed by their own government, used as nothing more than a human guidance system, their lives as disposable as the metal and wire and TNT that made up the insides of a cruise missile. Just munitions to be blown apart on someone else's battlefield.

You couldn't get much lower down the food chain than that.

'Sod it,' muttered Steve to himself. We can't let these boys get downhearted.

He'd seen that happen, and once the spirit was gone, any unit was as good as dead. They were just corpses walking towards the gunfire. There was fight in them somewhere, he was certain of it. They just had to dig it out and they'd be allright.

'Let's cook some grub up,' said Steve, forcing himself to inject some cheer into his tone. 'I'm bloody starving.'

'Right,' said Dan, picking up on exactly what Steve was trying to do. 'We've got a beach. Some food. A couple of tins of beer, and we'd have a barbie going.'

David pulled some of the rat packs from his kitbag, and a couple of tins of the growlers. Henri and Nick collected brushwood blown in from the sea, and broken timbers from the boat, and used some more of the diesel to get a fire going. The men gathered around the blaze, letting its warmth gradually restore their resolve. Ian used his knife to sharpen some wood into small spears, and they skewered the tinned sausages on to them and roasted them slowly. Dan ripped open a selection of pasta bakes, and even though they were wet through, the sachets still heated themselves up, and when they draped the spitting, fatty meat over the top of it, the food was almost appetising.

Ollie, still naked, and bloodstained, was warming himself next to the flames.

'I hate to tell you this, but you look like crap, pal,' said Steve, glancing across at him. 'I mean, even Nick's mum might draw the line at shagging you.'

'Sodding leave me mum out of this,' snapped Nick.

Steve was about to say something. But seeing the way Nick was waving his SA-80 around, and the malevolent look in his eye, he thought better of it. Instead, he glanced across at Henri. 'I hope the British grub's allright for you, mate.'

'I've had worse,' grunted Henri. 'I can't remember when right now. But I'm sure I have.'

'I think they serve these down at Wetherspoon's in Swansea,' said Nick, putting down his gun and shovelling a spoonful of food into his mouth. 'Bangers-and-mash Thursday. All you can eat for a fiver, with a free drink thrown in. Bloody good it is as well.'

'We'll get down there with you when we have a chance,' said Ian, raising a bottle of water, as if in a toast. 'And have a drink to Ganju as well.'

'Do you think he'll really be reincarnated?' asked Nick.

'You come back as the sum of all your experiences,' said Ian. 'The soul, or what the Gurkhas call the *atman*, is immortal; it is just the body that lives and dies.'

'And you believe that?'

'Ganju believed it,' said David. 'That's what counts.'

'I suppose there are worse things to believe in,' said Henri.

'Every man needs something,' said Ian.

'Maybe it's why the Gurkhas are so fierce,' said Nick thoughtfully. 'If dying is just changing your overcoat, then what's frightening about that?'

'Well, if I come back, I hope it's not as a short, ugly Russian,' said Maksim. 'I've been there, done that, and it's not that great.'

'With your experiences, you'll probably be a Moroccan bloke with a kebab shop in Slough,' said Steve.

'And you'll be a bloke selling second-hand Hyundais in Nigeria,' said Ollie, looking up at Steve, chuckling.

Steve grinned. 'You need to get some kit on, sunshine. Before you die of hypothermia – and the rest of us die laughing.'

Nick scuttled away to scour the beach and returned with a pair of denim shorts, a bloodstained orange sweatshirt, and a pair of cheap of trainers he'd reclaimed from one of the pirate corpses. Ollie washed some of the blood off his skin with fresh water, and used Steve's medi-pack to plaster over the worst of the cuts. By the time he'd dried himself over the fire, and put the clothes on, he was starting to look almost human.

'Very fetching, pal,' said Nick. 'But I don't think many nightclub bouncers would let you in anywhere looking like that.'

The unit finished off their food in silence. It was getting close to ten at night, and the night had drawn in completely. There was a half-moon in the sky, and a low, persistent breeze was blowing in from the sea. But the beach was deserted, and so was the ocean. Henri had already scanned the horizon a couple of times with his binoculars, and pronounced himself satisfied that there was nothing out there. They had to assume that Yasin had escaped. And it didn't look like he was coming back with reinforcements, not tonight anyway. Probably reckons we're dead, reflected Steve bitterly. And within another twenty-four hours, he might well be right.

'So what the sod do we do now?' he asked finally.

Nobody said anything.

'Go home,' said Ollie finally. He glanced around the sludge-sodden beach. 'I'm not planning on settling down here, that's for damned sure.'

Ian chuckled softly.

Steve had heard that laugh before. It meant the Irishman had thought of something.

'The British have already tried to kill us once. What do you think they'll do when they realise we've fucked up as well?'

'What are you suggesting?' asked Steve.

Ian was looking out towards the waves crashing against the shore. 'Yasin is out there somewhere with the plutonium still on him. We go and find him, and we get it off the bastard. And then we use that as a bargaining chip . . .'

'For what, exactly?'

'A full pardon for any crimes we might have committed. Complete immunity. The slate gets wiped clean—'

'And a million pounds,' interrupted Maksim.

'Yeah, yeah, Maksie. Plus a crate of vodka, and free tickets to the smartest brothel in Moscow.'

'It's bloody crazy,' snorted Ollie.

'Have you got any better ideas?'

Ollie fell silent.

Steve glanced around the men. It was clear that none of them was impressed. They'd already pitched themselves into one battle with the pirates, and it had been among the roughest, most vicious contests they had ever engaged in. Round two? It didn't look like anyone was up for that. But it didn't look as if there were many alternatives either.

'Death or glory, that's the plan, is it?' growled Steve. Then he broke into a rough smile. 'I like it.'

Forty-Five

STEVE LOVED WATCHING DAWN BREAK over a beach.
    He lifted his head a couple of inches from the kitbag
he'd been resting it on, and took a moment to stare out
into the wild white and blue water straight ahead of him, and to
admire the streaks of orange and gold light that flooded the
horizon as the sun edged into view.

I'd rather be on the balcony of a five-star hotel, with a gorgeous
blonde sleeping in bed beside me, and an Aston Martin DB5
parked in the garage, he reflected to himself. But right now, this
will have to do.

All around, the men were starting to be woken by the piercing,
brilliant sunshine. Nick was scratching himself, Ollie was
struggling to straighten out the ghetto-boy clothes, and Maksim
was digging a pit a few yards away for a crap.

'Make it a bit sodding further back,' shouted David. 'My
stomach's feeling a bit dodgy after those growlers.'

Steve grinned and hauled himself up. They'd put out the fire
when they'd finished eating last night and moved themselves back
another hundred yards into the ridge of higher ground overlooking
what remained of the pirate base. They'd taken shifts on watch,
while the rest kipped down for the night, using their kitbags as
pillows, and the sand as mattresses. They were all exhausted from
the fight they'd been through, and they needed to shut their eyes

and rest their bodies for a few hours before they could contemplate their next move.

Ian rekindled the small fire and fished some soggy teabags out of his kitbag, and within minutes they had a brew going and some biscuits to eat. The tea was salty from the kit being drowned in seawater, and the biscuits were crumbling and flaky, but at least it was food and drink, and it would make them all start to feel like human beings again.

Steve drained his brew, then glanced around at the men. 'So, are we really up for this, boys? Or are we just going to piss off home?'

'We can't,' snapped Ian. 'They'll lock us up. I've done my time in a British jail and I'm not going back.'

'You think they'll jail us?' asked Nick anxiously.

'I think they'll quietly kill us, actually,' said Ian. 'We know about the plutonium, and we know about the missile strike, and I reckon that means we know too much. If we talk—'

'All right, we get you,' said Ollie irritably. He looked across at Steve. 'We haven't got any option.'

'And anyway, Ganju died,' said David. 'We owe it to the man to at least make this mission a success.'

'Right,' said Dan.

'Then we crack on,' said Steve.

The unit briefly inspected their kit. The SA-80s and the Brownings had dried out overnight. They'd need cleaning and reassembling but they should be able to get them working. They checked the clips, and the spare mags. About half had been fired last night, and much of what remained had been damaged beyond repair. They had about a hundred and fifty rounds between them, plus their knives, and if it came to it, their fists. It wasn't much, and it wasn't likely to be a fair fight, reflected Steve. But it would have to do.

The satellite phone Steve had packed in Croatia was still working. An Iridium 9555, it was a tough, durable piece of kit, with a hard plastic shell and, within a waterproof pouch, capable of surviving the drenching they'd been through. He waited for a moment, then punched in the number.

The signal was loud and clear. Somali time was three hours ahead of London. It was just after eight in the morning now, which meant it was only five back at MI6 headquarters, but Steve reckoned they'd have pulled an all-nighter as they tracked the missile strike and tried to assess its results.

'Miss Thompson,' he said, as soon as the call was answered.

There was a pause on the line. Then the sound of a sharp intake of breath.

'You reckoned I was dead, eh? Well, I might soon be, but there's still blood in my veins this morning.'

'What happened to . . .'

'The plutonium?'

'Yes.'

Steve glanced down at a set of coordinates Henri had scratched out in the sand. 'We'll meet you at midnight tomorrow, at latitude 13.2399 and longitude 53.6792. It's about a mile off the coast of northern Somalia. I'm sure the SBS boys can find it for you. We'll have Yasin and the plutonium with us.'

'We don't negotiate, Steve.'

'Then try sodding learning.'

'We—'

'Listen, you'll get your plutonium back. In return, we want an official letter signed by the Home Secretary granting us a full, official pardon from any crimes we might have committed. And we want a million quid in gold.'

'That's black—'

'Blackmail, yes,' growled Steve. 'And considering you fired half a dozen cruise missiles into our arses last night, you're bloody lucky to be getting an offer this good. If you don't like it, we'll just put that plutonium up on eBay and sell it to the highest bidder.'

He switched the phone off and opened its back to remove the

battery. He didn't want to risk it being traced. 'Looks like we're in business, boys,' he said, glancing around.

Their expressions were drawn. They knew they'd just upped the stakes dramatically. And they had precisely forty hours to track down Yasin and the missing metal.

'So where the hell do we start looking for the bastard?' asked David.

'The Bunjani Islands,' answered Henri. 'That's where I reckon he's heading.'

'What the sod are they?' asked Ollie.

'A small strip of islands between Somalia and Yemen. They are about as remote and as desolate as any of the South Pacific islands. Only two of them are inhabited. They have some of the most spectacular deep-sea diving in the world, but only the most experienced underwater experts go anywhere near them. The pirates use them as a refuge and a hiding place. It's the natural place for him to park himself until this blows over.'

'How can we get there?' asked Dan. 'We haven't even got a boat.'

'Then we nick one.'

'Like real pirates,' chipped in Nick.

'I think we've finally found a career Nick might enjoy,' said Ian with a rough grin. 'The careers service back at the Swansea jobcentre should have suggested it.'

Forty-Six

STEVE LAY FLAT ON THE ground, shifting his position to try and relieve the annoying itch somewhere to the side of his ribs. He wiped the sweat off his brow, then looked through the binoculars again. The sea stretched out beyond them, an endless expanse of menacing blue water.

But there was still no sign of a boat. Not one that was suitable for their purposes anyway.

'Christ,' he muttered. This chance is slipping away from us.

They'd tabbed across rough country all through the morning and early afternoon, keeping far enough back from both the sea and the road to make sure they weren't spotted. The first couple of hours were easy enough, but as the sun arced across the sky, the heat grew in intensity until it felt as if they were walking through a microwave turned up to full blast. And as the heat rose, so did the humidity, so that by eleven the sweat was dripping off each man, sapping strength that was already weakened by the intense fighting of the last twenty-four hours. They'd marched due north, heading up towards the tip of the Puntland peninsula. The next village was about ten kilometres up the coast, and they calculated it was there they stood the best chance of finding a boat in good enough shape to get them out to the islands. They could have tabbed back to where they'd stored the boat they'd come in on, but that was at least twenty kilometres, and none of them had the strength or the will left for a march of that distance across hostile terrain.

By three, they'd hit the outskirts of the desolate, dusty port. It consisted of not much more than a few whitewashed shacks, gathered around a rocky cove. There were a few battered old SUVs and pickup trucks, but there was none of the fresh opulence evident in the main pirate strongholds further south. Up here, the people were still making a living from fishing, and, from the available evidence, it was a poor and harsh one. They laid up a couple of hundred yards back from the edge of the village, taking advantage of a mound of rocks to hide behind. Henri had surveyed the port, and although there were a few vessels tied up in the small, natural harbour, none of them looked big or fast enough for what they needed. 'We'll just wait,' he pronounced. 'When the right boat comes into the harbour, we'll take it.'

The waiting stretched from one hour into two and then into three. Steve completed his turn with the binoculars before handing them over to David, then to Dan. As the afternoon dragged on, the heat of the day started to fade, and they could feel some colder air blowing in off the sea. But there was still no sign of a suitable boat. And the clock was ticking closer to the deadline they'd set themselves.

'Maybe this is a sodding stupid idea,' said Ollie, leaning back against a rock and chewing on some dried biscuits from his kitbag. 'How the hell are we going to get the plutonium now? We should have gone home.'

'You've burnt your bridges, pal,' said Ian. 'Like Steve says, it's death or glory.'

'That's bloody nonsense,' snapped Ollie.

Steve glanced at his friend's face, and he could see the anger in the way his cheeks were reddening, but also the disappointment in the way his eyes were rooted to the ground. Ollie had been hoping this job would give him a way back into the Army, or the intelligence agencies, but those ambitions had been broken now. Like most things Ollie had ever wanted, it had been snatched away from him. He'd have to deal with that sooner or later, reflected

Steve. But not today. For now, they just had to crack on, and get this job finished.

'Ian's right,' said Steve. 'If we get their stuff for them, we can write our own ticket, but if we fail, I reckon we'd be better of just disappearing off the face of the earth.'

'We could head down to Spain,' said Dan. 'There are a few places around Malaga where the gangsters hang out and people don't ask too many questions.'

'Or the Philippines,' said Ian. 'There's a few PIRA boys disappeared down that way rather than spend the rest of their lives in the Maze. Informers mostly, boys who knew what we'd do to them if we ever caught up with the bastards. A man can hide himself away on some of those islands.'

'What are the women like?' asked Maksim.

'Cheap,' said Ian with a rough grin.

'And the booze?'

'Even cheaper.'

'I like it already.'

'Too much sunshine for you, Maksie,' said Steve. 'You'd turn bright red and come out in a rash.'

It was past seven by the time Henri finally spotted a boat. It was more a fishing boat than a traditional pirate skiff. A long, thin, metal-hulled vessel, with a powerful outboard motor, it had a wide open deck, with a covered shelter for the captain, and space for supplies down in the hold. It had room for at least a dozen men, more if they didn't mind packing in close together, and looked capable of withstanding fierce weather. Henri took a moment to survey it, then nodded crisply. The boat was fast and sturdy, and that was all they needed. 'Wait another thirty minutes, until it's completely dark, then we'll take it,' he said.

The unit held its position. The boat was anchored five hundred yards out into the harbour. A dinghy took five men onshore, pulling up at the rickety wooden jetty that led into the village. The men headed into one of the buildings opposite. Buying beer, or bullets, or women, decided Steve. Probably all three. Back on deck, they'd left three men. Two of them were chewing bundles of khat, and playing cards. The third was keeping watch, his AK-47 nestling on his lap.

'Here's the plan,' said Henri, glancing around the unit.

Dan and Nick, the two strongest swimmers in the unit, would swim out to the boat and overpower the three men on board. If they had had an underwater pistol they could have used that to shoot the target from beneath the waves, but since Ant hadn't allowed this, they'd have to improvise. Instead, they'd move straight up the side and tackle the men with their knives. Guns would just slow them down. As soon as they'd captured the boat, they'd kick the engine into life then sail down to the next cove. Steve would bring the rest of the unit to the beach and swim out to join them.

'Ready?' Henri asked Nick and Dan.

Both men nodded.

But Ollie was looking at Nick. 'I'll do it,' he said.

Henri shook his head.

'It's sodding dangerous . . .' Ollie warned.

'I need the best swimmers we have, and the best climbers as well,' said the Frenchmen. His tone was terse and final, brooking no disagreement.

'He's right,' said Steve to Ollie.

Henri led Nick and Dan down towards the cove. He'd tied a couple of empty water bottles to some string, and both men could wrap them round their waists to provide some extra buoyancy for the first part of the swim. There was some swell in the water, and the waves were climbing to four or five feet, but the current was with them, and Henri had seen enough of both men in training to feel confident of their abilities.

It was the assault that would prove difficult.

Steve watched them as they slipped into the water. He tracked them for the first hundred yards or so, then lost them as they disappeared below the waves. 'I hope to Christ they are OK,' he said, looking towards Ollie and Ian. 'We've lost one man already.'

A minute ticked by, then another. Steve wasn't sure how long it would take them to swim out to the boat. Three minutes, maybe four. They'd have to come up for some air, but the last hundred yards would have to be completed underwater.

Steve trained the binoculars on the boat. It was a quiet night, with only a few clouds skidding across the sky, and not much wind in the air. The swell was high, however, and the vessel was rocking in the waves. There was nothing to be seen from this distance.

We just have to wish them luck, that's all, thought Steve.

Three hundred yards out, Nick was treading water. The sea was cold. They were still two hundred yards from the boat. Henri looked at him, then at Dan. 'Go under,' he hissed. 'We'll meet under the hull. Wait for my signal, then we all strike at the same time. Remember, if you catch them by surprise, then you don't have to use much force.'

Nick nodded just once. He plunged straight into the incoming wave, then swam furiously. The first hundred yards, he kept his eyes closed, but for the second hundred he opened them. He needed to see everything that was happening. The hull of the boat was looming up ahead of him, a black and dirty lump of metal. Henri was a few yards ahead, Dan a few behind, but Nick just concentrated on powering himself forwards. Underneath the boat, Henri paused, waiting a fraction of a second, treading water whilst he positioned himself close to the stern. He pointed Nick left, Dan to the right, then with a curt hand signal gave the command to move.

Nick could feel his lungs bursting.

He'd been under for ninety seconds already, close to the two minutes he reckoned was the most he could comfortably manage. He swam upwards, bursting through the surface and using the natural momentum of the ascent and the swell of the waves to lift him upwards. His knife was gripped between his teeth. They'd run through this drill before they plunged into the water: grab the ledge and lift yourself over the side in one swift movement. Get it right first time, Henri had warned him; second time around, your enemy will know you're there and have a bullet waiting for you.

It sounded straightforward enough when he was explaining it on the beach. Now that the moment was upon him, however, Nick could feel a tick of panic somewhere close to his heart. Sod it, he told himself. You can do this.

He kicked hard with his legs to propel himself higher into the air, but at the same moment, a wave caught his side, knocking him hard into the slimy metal of the boat's hull. The knife moved a fraction, slicing into his cheek, and he could feel a trickle of warm blood seep back into his mouth. The sea spat upwards, its salt drifting into the wound, making it sting with pain. Nick ignored it, kicking harder with his legs, timing the move to catch the next upwards swell of the water. His right hand reached up, and he clasped it gratefully to the side of the boat, following it rapidly with the left. With a swiftness that surprised even himself, he levered himself upwards until he was on the side of the vessel.

His eyes darted left and right. Henri was already upon the man at the prow, plunging his knife hard into the man's chest. Straight ahead of him, Dan, his face dark and wet from the sea, was flinging himself on to the deck, taking his knife from his mouth in the same sudden movement, and hurling himself towards the two men on the deck. Nick powered down with his arms, throwing himself over the deck in a rolling movement. The two remaining men were struck by panic, their faces confused. They were reaching for their weapons, but it was too late, and Nick could see in their sullen, angry expressions that they were already aware of that. There were big wads of khat in their mouths, and cards in their hands, and a couple of open beer cans next to them, and the AK-47s were a yard or so away from them. Too far. As the man closest to him reached for the gun, Nick fell upon him, plunging the knife hard into his neck.

The blade was wet and slippery, but razor sharp, and it went into the skin easily enough. Nick twisted the blade, opening up a horrible wound through the main artery through which the blood started to empty. The man screamed, lashing out with a fist that caught Nick hard across the side of the head. He was powerfully built, almost six feet tall, thin but with thick muscles in his arms and legs, and the blow was a vicious one. Nick gritted his teeth, absorbing the pain, twisting the knife deeper and harder into the man's neck, until he could slowly feel the life starting to ebb out of him. The blood was flowing freely now, soaking into Nick's clothes, and whilst the next blow still hurt, the strength was draining out of his opponent.

He looked down into the man's eyes and realised he was little more than a boy, eighteen or nineteen maybe, just a year younger than Nick, but he felt no remorse, just a savage desire to end his opponent's life as quickly as possible. Drawing the knife out, he stabbed it back into the neck, and the second blow was the fatal one. The man spluttered once, spitting blood from his mouth, then his eyes closed.

Nick looked up.

Dan was sitting next to his victim, checking that he was dead. Henri was standing over them, the AK-47 he'd taken from his opponent slung across his chest.

'Tough bastards,' said Dan.

'This boat is their only life,' said Nick thoughtfully. 'We shouldn't be surprised if they defend it to the last breath.'

Henri ordered them to tip the three bodies into the sea. He took the wheel, and fired up the engine, steering it back along the coast. Nick grabbed one of the men, and hauled him up to the edge, pushing him out to sea with his fists. As he did so, he looked up towards the coast, then waved once.

Within less than three minutes, Henri had steered the boat to the next cove. The rest of the unit were swimming towards them.

Nick and Dan reached down into the water, hauling out first

Steve then Ollie, Ian, Maksim and David. The men shook the water from their hair.

'I reckon we need to get a brew going,' said Ian. 'I wonder if these pirate boys have any tea stashed anywhere—?'

Henri steered the boat out into the dark ocean. Ian found a small gas burner in the hold, and although there wasn't any tea, there were some coffee grounds, and a small pot. The beer cans the two guards had been drinking from before they died still had some remains left in them, and Maksim poured that cheerfully into the coffee pot.

'Sort of like joyriding,' said Nick, with a crooked smile, as Ian served up the beer-flavoured coffee in the single tin cup they had available and handed it around to the men standing on deck. 'Pretty much a normal Saturday night in Swansea.'

'Except we're not about to smash into the front window of McDonald's,' said Ian. 'At least, I hope we're not.'

Forty-Seven

STEVE SHOOK HIMSELF AWAKE. HE yawned, scratched, then hauled himself upwards. He'd kipped down on a corner of the deck, along with the rest of the men, and although the steel was hard on the body at first, once he got his eyes shut, he'd slept OK. That's the one real secret of soldiering, he reminded himself. Get your eyes shut, and you'll be OK.

'What this country needs is some decent sodding coffee,' growled Ollie.

Dawn was already breaking over the horizon, and most of the men were up. Maksim got the small burner alight, and Dan brewed up the dregs of the coffee left over from the night before, handing around the thick, groggy mixture in the tin cup.

'I'll have the full English, if it's all right with you boys,' said Steve, walking across to join the rest of the men. 'Two sausages, three slices of bacon, a couple of eggs, beans and a fried slice.'

'Sorry, mate, sausages off,' said Nick.

'And the bacon,' said Dan.

'And we've got no eggs,' added Ian.

'Or beans, or bread,' said David.

'Hang on,' said Nick. 'I reckon I've got a growler in my kitbag.'

'It's allright,' said Steve. 'We'll save that that for a special occasion.'

He took a hit of the coffee, then grabbed some of the dried biscuits that Dan had broken open. It was just after six in the morning, and he reckoned they'd been sailing for six or seven hours. The boat had a top speed of about fifteen knots, but Steve reckoned Henri wouldn't have tried to get the maximum power out of the engine. He'd be saving that for an emergency, and the chances were they'd hit plenty of those in the next twenty-four hours.

'Where the sod are we, captain?' he asked as the Frenchman came across to grab a sip of the coffee.

'About two hours' sailing from the islands,' he answered.

Steve looked around. They were out in the middle of the ocean, no land visible in any direction. There were plenty of waves, but none of them more than five feet, and although there was a stiff breeze in the air, the weather was manageable.

'And when we get there?' asked Ian.

'We look around,' said Henri. 'He'll be there somewhere.'

'It's a sodding needle in a haystack,' snapped Ollie. 'We're supposed to be delivering that plutonium by midnight tonight.'

'And you have a better plan?' asked Henri.

That sneer was back in his voice, noted Steve. But the Frenchman was right. There was no other plan, so they'd have to make this work.

'It's our only hope,' he said, glancing towards Ollie. 'If it doesn't work, we'll just keep sailing south. Make our escape and start a new life somewhere.'

The rough breakfast finished, the men took up their posts. Henri was at the bridge, steering the boat, while the rest of the men positioned themselves around the deck, keeping a close eye on the seas all around them. It was dull, monotonous work, and as one hour stretched into two and then three, Steve was struggling to keep his spirits up. What they'd been thinking about last night he was no longer sure, but in the morning light, the task they'd set themselves seemed impossible. He could feel the mission slipping away from them, and his life with it. The garage, he thought to himself. That had been his big payday, the thing he'd worked for, risked his life for, lost some good mates for, and planned to settle down with one day. And now I've sodding well gone and blown it. The same way I blew it with Sam. The same way I keep blowing everything.

He looked down into the sea, losing himself for a moment in the churning waves.

If by some miracle I get through this, I'm starting again. No more blowing anything. I'm done with that.

It was just past ten when Maksim raised his hand skywards. 'There,' he said, pointing straight ahead of him. The rest of the unit crowded around to look. The vessel was clear on the horizon, about half a mile distant, and behind it the faint silhouette of land was just visible.

A pirate skiff, realised Steve, putting the binoculars to his eyes to get a closer look.

It was still seven or eight hundred yards away, but it was heading straight towards them, closing all the time. It was an open-topped vessel, with at least eight men on board that Steve could count. It had a steel hull, painted a chipped, faded green, with a big powerful outboard engine that was leaving puffs of black smoke in its wake. It was built for speed, a rapid-attack machine, no doubt used to bring the raiders to the huge ocean-going cargo ships.

Maksim was lining up his SA-80 on the deck, his eyes squinting in the bright early-morning sun as he tried to get one of the pirates level in his sights. At his side, Nick was lining up his own shot. They loosed off a volley of fire from the assault rifles. There was no question they needed to shoot: the pirates were heading straight towards them, and they didn't look like they were just planning to say hello. But the bullets fell harmlessly into the sea. At this range, with the motion of the two vessels to take account of as well as the distance, you'd need at least a sniper rifle to have any chance of hitting a target. All things considered, it was a task probably beyond even a marksman of Nick's ability.

'Stop shooting,' barked Henri from the bridge. He was swinging on the wheel and Steve could feel the boat swaying as it started to turn. Up ahead, the pirates continued to sail straight towards them, pressing into them, clearly determined to give chase. They were just four hundred yards away now and closing fast.

We've sailed right into their territory, realised Steve. And it doesn't look like they've got much time for trespassers.

'Get your head down, we're heading out,' shouted Henri.

Steve started to run towards him. 'We stand and fight,' he growled.

Henri looked at him, his expression suggesting he reckoned Steve had lost his mind. 'You're bloody crazy. This is their territory.'

'Sod it. We've haven't got the time to search around this bloody ocean looking for our man.' He nodded towards the pirate skiff. 'One of those bastards will know where Yasin is. Capture the sods, then beat the information out of them.'

'Capture a pirate from a fast-moving vessel?' Henri threw his head back and laughed. 'You English really are crazy.'

Ollie stepped forward, the stubble on his face so close to Henri that they were practically touching one another. 'What's the matter here, exactly?' he growled. 'You frightened of a scrap, Frenchie?'

Henri turned to face him, his dark eyes glowering with anger. He pushed Ollie away, and was about to receive a blow in return, when Maksim grabbed hold of Ollie's shoulders and pulled him roughly away.

Straight ahead of them the pirate skiff was closing fast, down to just two hundred and fifty yards. It was scudding through the waves, bouncing over the surface of the water, two men with AK-47s at the ready leaning across its prow, their eyes alert and menacing, tooled up and ready for a fight.

'You fuckers are serious, aren't you?' said Henri, his eyes darting between Steve and Ollie.

'Never more so,'

Henri grimaced. He swung the wheel, and Steve had to steady himself as the boat rocked, the waves crashing into its side. The sound of gunfire was cracking through the air, and as Steve looked across the side of the boat, he could see the men in the skiff were blasting off a few shots from their AK-47s. They were test rounds, designed to establish wind direction, and to let the intruders know what was in store for them. They'd have to get their heads down soon to avoid getting them blown off.

'Die your own way,' grunted Henri.

Steve turned to face the rest of the men.

'Get your cutlasses ready, and haul up the Jolly Roger, boys,' he said with a rough grin. 'It looks like we're going to give these pirates a real scrap.'

Forty-Eight

THE BOAT WAS STARTING TO rock violently as Henri swung desperately on the wheel. As they got closer to the islands, the rocky, craggy shoreline clearly in view now, the waters were getting choppier.

'Go, bloody go,' shouted Steve, his voice raw and hoarse.

The men swung into action with the speed and determination of soldiers who knew their lives were hanging in the balance. Dan, Maksim, and Nick rushed up to the front of their boat, slotting their SA-80s into position, taking cover beneath its metal frame. Ollie took one side and David another, whilst Steve manned the rear. The two boats were now on a collision course, heading straight into each other like a pair of mad dodgem cars, and when the scrap kicked off, it was likely to be a vicious, ugly brawl, from which no man could be confident of emerging alive.

The bullets were starting to fizz and spit over their heads, and to clatter into the side of the boat as the pirates drew relentlessly closer. Steve pulled down his helmet, his expression tightening. The violent motion of the boat made it impossible to take proper cover, and although Maksim and Dan were starting to put down some returning fire into the pirate skiff, it was impossible to contain the assault.

'Let them board us,' shouted Ian, rushing up towards Steve.

'You're sodding crazy,' he yelled, straining to make himself heard above the crash of the waves and the rattle of the gunfire.

Ian was pointing towards the side of the boat. 'We put down a channel of diesel right along there,' he said. 'We play dead, let the pirates come on board, and as they step up to the side, we torch the diesel, and the flames burn the bastards.'

'Burn the boat?' shouted Ollie. 'Then how the hell do we get out of here?'

'The boat will be OK,' snapped Ian. 'It's metal.'

'Unless the diesel in the engine catches fire.'

Steve looked up towards Henri. The Frenchman was following the discussion intently but so far had remained silent. 'Can it work?'

Henri nodded. 'We've a chance,' he said crisply. 'The boat may explode, and we might not be able to put the fire out, but . . .'

'But if you don't want to take any risks, there's no point in getting into a fight,' said Ollie.

'Then let's sodding do it,' said Steve.

Henri rushed back to the wheel. Ollie joined Dan, Maksim and Nick and explained the plan, directing a barrage of fire into the pirate skiff that would hold off the attack for just long enough for the trap to be laid. Steve and Ian dropped down into the hold. There were six jerry cans of diesel stashed close to the engine, each one holding five gallons of fuel. Next to that were two dinghies that could be used as lifeboats, and a stack of flares for emergencies. Steve grabbed a can of diesel and rushed back to the deck. Behind him, Ian rummaged around in the stores and came out with some soap and four empty one-litre beer bottles. The skiff was drawing closer, less than a hundred yards away. Gunfire was rattling out across the ocean. Ian mixed the diesel with the soap, making it stickier, then smeared the thick, gungy mixture all along the side of the boat. He yelled at Steve to do the same. When they'd finished, he thrust a bottle into Steve's hand.

'Much as I'd love to break for a beer, mate, I think we'd better crack on,' said Steve.

'Fill it up with diesel, you feckin' idiot, then rip a strip off your shirt, and stuff it into the bottle,' said Ian. 'It's called a Molotov cocktail.'

Steve steadied his hands and filled two of the bottles, capping them with a strip torn from his sweatshirt. When he'd finished, he looked up anxiously. The skiff was just thirty yards away now, bearing down on them with relentless aggression. The men on board were a savage crew: big men, all at least six foot, with knives strapped to their belts, and ammunition belts slung round their necks like trophies. At this distance, you could see their eyes. Dark and sullen, with a malevolent anger to them, they looked more like pub brawlers than proper soldiers. But that wasn't going to make them any less dangerous, thought Steve. They had plenty of weapons, and this was their turf, and that made them a force to be reckoned with.

'Get them down, get them down,' yelled Ollie at the prow of the boat.

Dan, Maksim and Nick unleashed a volley of fire from their SA-80s, putting round after round straight into the skiff. It was enough to get the pirates ducking but not enough to persuade them to change direction. There was just twenty yards of swirling sea separating the two boats now, and the breakers churned up by the two engines were so close they were touching. The volley bought them just enough time for Henri to finish turning the boat, so that the side smeared with diesel was facing the skiff.

The pirates dived for cover, then returned fire.

The 7.62mm rounds from the AK-47s spat angrily across the deck. Steve glanced towards Henri, then Ian. Both men nodded curtly. They were ready.

'Down, boys, down,' Steve yelled, struggling to make himself heard above the crashing of the waves, the roar of the engines, and the retorts of the guns.

Ollie signalled for the men up at the prow to duck.

They fell backwards, dropping as if shot through their chests, then rolling towards the back of the deck.

'Keep sodding still,' hissed Steve to the line of men now crouching in a row. 'And keep your safety catches off.'

Ian had torn three strips from his sweatshirt to make two Molotov cocktails of his own. He dipped the third in the soapy, sticky diesel, and lit the rag to make a torch strong enough to withstand the spray spitting out over the deck.

'Wait, wait,' hissed Henri.

He'd left the bridge and dropped down to join them. The skiff had drawn up alongside them. There was a clatter of metal as a grappling hook was thrown out. Each man paused, holding his breath, waiting for the inevitable assault. Suddenly there was a roar of gut-wrenching anger as four pirates stepped up, as if out of the water itself, their massive hands grabbing the metal railing and levering themselves on board. Ian dropped the torch into the diesel, and suddenly a wall of flame ignited. The flames from the hot oil leapt into the air, and two of the men fell forwards, their clothes incinerated in the sudden blast. Ian stood up, launching one, then two of the Molotov cocktails. The bottles arced through the air, crashing down into the skiff, igniting in a vicious fireball. At his side, Steve lifted his own two cocktails into the air, and hurled them through the wall of flame. Ollie nodded to each of the men, and, in unison, Maksim, Nick, Dan, David and Henri slammed their SA-80s into automatic, releasing a terrifying barrage of fire. It was impossible to see anything through the thick layer of flame and swirling black smoke, and the heat was unbearable, but from the screams rattling through the air it was clear the lethal combination of fire and bullets was chewing the enemy to pieces.

Steve stood up, ignoring the way the flames were scorching his skin. He ran to the prow of the boat, trying to work out what was happening. Suddenly he was knocked backwards. The flames licking across the deck of the skiff had blown the outboard engine, creating a massive fireball that curled up into the air before it was extinguished by the waves rising all around it. A hole had been blown in the stern, and the vessel was sinking fast. Steve permitted himself a brief, tense smile. The battle had been won. But the war, he reminded himself quickly, was still far from over.

At least six men were dead but two more had leapt into the water and were starting to swim away.

'We need one of the bastards alive,' shouted Steve to the rest of the unit.

Maksim dived straight into the water, disappearing beneath the waves. Steve swiftly followed him, crashing hard into the water, plunging five or six feet under, then emerging to the surface, gasping for air. He looked around. The skiff had already sunk, although not before Nick and David had jumped on board and grabbed some of their weapons, quickly scuttling back to the main boat with their trophies. Maksim was swimming hard after the two escaping men, and Henri had plunged into the water as well, joining the pursuit. The pirates had a start of ten yards, and were heading back towards the island. The seas were growing rougher, and there was a heavy swell in the water, and as Steve used his legs to propel himself forwards, he realised it was going to be tough to catch them. Both Maksim and Henri were gaining fast, however; the Russian had brute strength and determination on his side; and the Frenchman had years of high-quality training, and both of which would be enough, Steve reckoned, to tip the odds in their favour. It took a couple of minutes to close the distance, then Henri managed to grab both men's legs, one in each arm, and dragged them under. Maksim followed swiftly after them, pummelling both men with his fists. The blows were blunted by the water, so he quickly switched to holding their arms behind their backs, twisting them viciously, upwards and around, until one man broke with pain and started to cry out. As he did so, his lungs flooded with water, but still Maksim held him down.

'Alive, Maksie, alive,' shouted Steve as he swam to join them.

Maksim released both men, letting them float to the surface.

One had already drowned. The other, battered by the ferocity of the assault, had lost consciousness.

'Take him back,' snapped Henri. 'He'll live.'

Steve grabbed the man's hair, held him steady between his arms, then kicked his legs and started to swim back towards the boat. It was a distance of just twenty yards. The flames were still burning along one side of the boat where Ian had ignited the diesel, and hot, sooty smoke was swirling in the wind, then hanging low in an ugly, black cloud next to the waves. But the fire was starting to die. With Henri and Maksim following close behind, Steve pushed the one remaining pirate back across the last few yards until David and Ian reached down with their fists and hauled the man up on to the deck.

Steve pulled himself up, and lay for a moment on the deck, panting for breath. He'd learnt plenty about swimming in the last few days, more than he really wanted to.

'You OK?' said Ollie, pulling him to his feet.

'I tell you one thing, mate,' he said. 'Unless it's a hot jacuzzi with a couple of babes in it, I'm not going anywhere near water for months. I'm sick of the sodding sight of the stuff.'

'I'm sure Nick's mum can arrange it,' said Ollie.

'Bloody leave it,' snapped Nick.

Steve ignored the Welsh boy. He glanced around the deck. The flames were still spluttering upwards from one side of the boat, but Ian had laid the trap with the expertise he'd gathered during years in the IRA, and they were some of the finest pyrotechnicians ever unleashed on a battlefield. He'd put down enough diesel to cause a huge firewall, but not so much that the flames lingered. Two of the men who'd died attempting to board had fallen back into the sea, and two more had fallen forwards on to the deck. One of them had been killed by the volley of gunfire, whilst the second had caught fire, his clothes and then his skin set alight, the sticky diesel clinging to him, and sinking like hot coals straight into his chest, incinerating his lungs from the inside. He lay for a few minutes, slowly burning to death, until Dan took pity on him and put a bullet through his chest.

Nick and Dan picked up the two corpses, both of them still hot, and tossed them out into the sea. David was sorting through the kit they'd stolen from the skiff. The pirates didn't travel heavily armed; like special forces soldiers, they depended more on stealth, expertise and precision than heavy weaponry to overwhelm their enemy; although there were five spare AK-47s which would come in handy, some cheap Czech-made handguns, complete with ammo, plenty of knives and ropes, and one rifle David had never seen before.

'What have we got here?' he asked, looking around the rest of the unit.

Maksim stepped forward. He gripped the rifle in his hand, then grinned. It was a smile Steve had learned to recognise in the two years he'd been fighting alongside the Russian, one that said he had just found a new way of kicking off a lot of aggro next time he got himself into a fight.

'It's an APS,' he said.

'What the hell is that?' asked Nick.

'A version of the AK-47, developed for the Red Army's frogmen,' answered Maksim. 'They made them from nineteen seventy-one until the end of the eighties. It was the first underwater automatic weapon ever developed. Bullets don't really work underwater, but this fires a 4.75mm steel bolt. It's got enough punch on it to rip through any kind of frogman outfit and kill a man stone dead.'

Henri took the weapon in his hand, admiring its shape and curve with the practised eye of a man who took his aquatic weapons seriously, and had learnt how to tell the good stuff from the rubbish. 'I've heard of them, but I've never used one before.'

'They were restricted to special forces,' said Maksim. 'The Soviets were desperate for hard currency but they never went as far as selling these. After the regime collapsed, a few found their way on to the black market, sold off by Red Army quartermasters who needed some spare cash.'

'How many rounds?' asked Dan.

'Twenty-six,' said Maksim. He checked the clip. 'There's ten left.'

'Any spares?' asked Nick.

David was rummaging around the kit they'd taken from the skiff. He shook his head.

'It doesn't matter,' said Maksim. 'It's ten more rounds than we started with. With one of these we can do some real damage.'

Forty-Nine

THE PIRATE WAS STILL LYING unconscious on the deck of the boat.

Dan was leaning into his face, trying to revive him, throwing water on to the man, then shaking him violently. Steve checked his watch. It was close to midday; they had less than twelve hours left to find Yasin, grab the plutonium, then sail back to the meeting point. A tight deadline at the best of times. And they still didn't have any real idea where Yasin might be hiding. Or how many men he'd have protecting him.

Some dark clouds were starting to scud across the ocean, the first Steve had seen since they'd dropped into the country. All around him he could feel the wind picking up. The waves were starting to rise, and the boat was swaying. There was a storm coming, Steve reckoned. It wasn't here yet, but it was edging closer all the time. You could smell it in the air and taste it in the salt whipped up by the spray.

'Get him sodding awake,' he growled. 'We need to find out where our man is, and fast.'

Dan slapped him once, then twice, stinging blows that left his cheeks marked, then splashed another bucket of seawater into his face. Groggily, the man started to open his eyes. It took him a moment to realise where he was. His eyes shut, then opened again, Steve noticed.

'Sorry, pal,' he said, standing over him and looking down. 'It's not a dream. It's a nightmare. A fucking scary one, and you're not going to wake up. That clear?'

The man nodded.

He was nineteen, perhaps twenty, reckoned Steve. The leaders aside, piracy was a young man's game. No one they'd fought so far looked more than twenty-five. This one was big and strong, like all the pirates, with large eyes, and hands that were calloused and scuffed from working with ropes. The pirates spoke a mixture of Somali, Arabic and broken English, so Steve reckoned the guy would understand him well enough. If not, a few punches should do the trick: that was a language every soldier understood.

Steve knelt down so that he was looking straight at the man. 'Now, you can make this easy or hard on yourself, mate, it's up to you. We need to know which of these islands Ali Yasin is hiding in.'

The man shook his head.

He was shaking with fear, noted Steve. There was blood around his face where he'd been cut in the fight, but he was ignoring the wounds, just looking pleadingly up at his captors.

'Don't give us any crap about not knowing,' said Steve, his tone harsher this time. 'We haven't got time to piss about, so this is going to turn very nasty very soon if you don't help us.'

At his side, Henri had laid out a chart he'd found in the hold. It showed the sea between the Somali and Yemeni coasts, with the string of Bunjani islands clearly marked out.

'Just point,' he hissed.

The man shook his head. 'Nothing,' he said. 'Know nothing.'

'I've already told you not to piss us around, pal.'

'Nothing. I know nothing.'

Henri drew his knife from his belt and flashed the sharp blade menacingly into the man's face. There was no sun left, the dark clouds now completely covering the sky, but the metal still glinted in the dull light.

'I'm a simple man, I know nothing . . .'

Henri grabbed the man's hand, holding it down on the deck, then stabbed the knife downwards. It sliced easily enough through the flesh. The man screamed out in pain, but Dan and Steve grabbed his chest to hold him steady. Henri twisted the blade, like a corkscrew, chewing up the mess of small bones locking the knuckle and the fingers into place. The man's head slumped forward, his face contorted with agony.

'Nothing,' he muttered, spitting some blood out of his mouth. 'I know nothing . . .'

Steve looked towards the Frenchman. It was a ruthless display of brutality. But there's not much point in being surprised about that, he reflected. Most of the torture techniques routinely used by interrogators in the most brutal regimes these days were first developed by the French during the Algerian war of the late 1950s and early 1960s. Commando Hubert guys would know all the main ways of torturing a man, and probably had a few secret tricks of their own. Henri used his left hand to lift the man's face upwards, then smiled softly. It was important to him that the victim should look into the face of his torturer, and know that he was enjoying himself: that way he would break quicker.

'I can keep doing this until you tell us,' he said.

He twisted the blade again, until you could hear the soft delicate bones of the hand crumble and break. Then he started to slide the knife upwards, putting all his strength into the blade. It scratched hard into the knuckle, making a scraping sound as it cut straight into the bone.

That's one hand that's never going to be raised in anger again, thought Steve. Even Ian looked sickened by the sight. And Steve had never seen the IRA bomber bothered by torture before.

But it looked to be working. And right now, that was all that counted.

'Let me point,' grunted the pirate.

He was fighting back the pain, trying to get it under control for long enough to complete the confession. Henri gestured towards

Steve to lay out the map. He kept the knife hard into the man's right hand. The man leant forward. There were six islands in total, lying at the end of a long stretch of coral reef that started in Zanzibar. They were of varying sizes, but only the island called Chula had any significant population. The finger hovered for a second, then fell upon Koyama, the third of the three rocky stumps of land, and one of the smallest. 'There,' he hissed.

Henri drew out the blade. 'OK,' he muttered. He was studying the chart.

'How far?' asked Steve.

Henri pointed to the horizon. They could see a rocky mountain rising up out of the sea, but that was the first of the chain of islands, the rest would be much further away. 'About three hours' sailing. Maybe less, if we push the maximum power out of the engine.'

'Then crack on,' said Steve. 'We haven't got any time to lose.'

'Get him cleaned up,' said Henri, nodding towards the pirate as he stood up and walked back to the bridge.

Both Dan and Steve released him from their grip. The pirate staggered to his feet. The knife was still dangling from his right hand, the blade deeply embedded, and blood was dripping from the five inches of exposed steel above the flesh.

The man winced in pain and grunted as he used his left hand to draw the blade free. He was holding it in his left hand, starting to lift it upwards. Steve grabbed his SA-80 and pointed it towards him.

'Drop the knife, mate,' he snapped.

The pirate ignored him. With a sudden swift movement, he lashed the blade upwards.

Steve slammed his finger into the trigger of the SA-80 and was about to fire. But he hesitated. There was no need, he realised.

The pirate had stabbed the blade into his own neck. He howled as the knife tore through the skin, then ripped into the arteries below. Blood was gushing from the open wound, but he kept going, attacking himself in a frenzy of self-mutilation. One stab was followed by another, until the blood loss drained his strength and the blade fell from his hand to the deck.

The man fell forward, his eyes closing.

'I guess Ali Yasin doesn't have much time for traitors,' said Steve, after checking that the man was dead. 'He took the best way out.'

He nodded towards Ollie and Dan, and between them the three men lifted the body from the deck and walked towards the side of the boat. Henri had already fired up the engine, and was steering the boat south-east. The seas were growing choppier all the time as the clouds grew darker and the winds blew fiercer. They were steering across the current, and the boat was starting to sway as rising waves buffeted its side.

With a heave, they tossed the body over the side. A wave whipped into the side of the man, then caught him as the water fell down, dragging him with it.

'I tell you what,' said Ollie, as he watched the corpse float away on the rough sea. 'I bet the local sharks are sodding pleased we showed up. Christmas has come early for those boys – if you happen to fancy dead pirate for lunch, that is.'

Fifty

STEVE COULD FEEL DROPS OF rain spitting into his face. It was salty yet warm, another sign of the storm brewing out in the ocean. The waves were getting stronger all the time, making the boat roll in the swell, and as his eyes scanned the horizon for land, he had to peer through a murky mixture of spray, sea and cloud. Even so, the contours of the island were clearly visible some eight or nine hundred yards in the distance. A steep mountain formed the main bulk of Koyama, the remnant of some long extinct volcano, and then it tumbled down into the sea, forming a series of small, well-protected coves. Remote, inaccessible, and easy to defend. A perfect hideaway for pirates.

They've probably been here for a couple of thousand years, he reflected.

'OK,' he shouted back towards Henri. 'Kill the engine. We're close enough.'

If this was Yasin's lair, the pirates would have a man on watch, they could be certain of that. But in the darkening weather, and with plenty of high waves, they should be safe enough. The boat was a greenish-grey, aged by years of use, and it disappeared against the backdrop of rough sea, the same way a tank painted khaki would disappear in the desert.

With the engine dead, Henri let the boat drift on the current. There was no point in putting an anchor down. If they were

349

spotted, the pirates would come out to attack, and an anchor would just stop them making a fast escape.

Steve checked his watch as he gathered the unit together on the deck. It was just after five. They had seven hours left to grab the plutonium and get back to the Somali coast. All the men were wet, both from the rain starting to spit from the clouds and from the spray the bigger waves were starting to kick up all around them. They were cold, and getting hungry as well.

'Just a few more hours, boys,' said Steve, through gritted teeth. 'And then the worst job in the history of the universe will finally be over.'

Dan handed around the single tin cup, freshly filled with some coffee brewed up from the few grounds left, and each man took a sip. The warm liquid started to heat them from the inside and revive their spirits.

'Here's the drill, guys,' said Henri, taking a sip of the coffee. He nodded towards the cove. 'There's a big boat, probably a cargo vessel, anchored in that cove, and from the activity on board, it looks as though that's where Yasin has stationed himself. We need to go in and get him.'

'How exactly are you feckin' planning on that?' asked Ian.

'We could row ashore, then approach from the jetty,' said Ollie.

'Too risky,' said Henri firmly. 'We haven't got the time to get to know the territory, and we can be sure it will be well defended. We'll come in from the sea.'

'How exactly?' said Dan.

'We'll take the two dinghies stashed below, and row up to three hundred yards away from the boat. Then we dive into the water and swim up to the side. If there are guards on the deck, and I'm sure there will be, we use the APS to take them out from under the water. Then we scale up the side and storm the boat.'

Ian chuckled. 'It sounds like Commando Hubert have been taking lessons from the Aussie SASR in subtle tactics.'

'There's no other way,' said Henri angrily.

Steve glanced around the unit. It was high-risk, there was no question of that. They were gambling with their lives, with little idea of how heavily the odds were stacked against them.

'He's right,' he said tersely. 'If we're going in, we need to do it hard and fast. Maximum speed, maximum aggression. Either that, or we forget about it and piss off somewhere to start a new life.'

He looked at the faces staring back at him. He could see the doubts there, but also the determination. They weren't the kind of men to back out of a scrap. Once it kicked off, they were in it until the final whistle was blown.

'I won't think any the worse of any man for backing out,' he continued. 'We all have to make our own choices.'

Apart from the wind and the waves, there was silence.

'Right, that's sorted then. One last scrap, and we're finished. Let's get this sodding done.'

Henri and Dan went down to the hold to get the dinghies, while Nick and Ian got their weapons ready.

Steve looked across at David. 'You going to be OK, mate?'

David paused before replying. He'd been fine in their last two contacts. The fear had evaporated, leaving him as capable a soldier as he'd ever been. He was nervous, but there wasn't a man alive who didn't feel his stomach fluttering before he went into a battle.

'I'm OK,' he said. 'I think the combat has cured me.'

'The mind can play funny tricks,' said Steve. 'The dreams are like a woman, the way I've heard it from Regiment blokes. One minute they're all over you, next they've pissed off.'

'That's just your birds, pal,' said David. 'They bugger off as soon as they know what you're really like. Mine stick around, and usually wait until we've knocked out a couple of kids before they turn moody.'

Steve laughed.

David was going to be OK. He felt certain of that.

'Even so, I reckon you should stay behind.'

'Miss the fun? You're sodding joking.'

Steve shook his head. 'We need one bloke to man this boat. It should be you.'

David shook his head. 'Nick,' he said flatly.

'No, we need him to fire the APS. He's the best shot on the team.'

'He's just a kid.'

Steve put a hand on David's shoulder. 'He has to grow up sooner or later. We can't keep protecting him from the dangerous stuff. And we need someone we can rely on to keep this boat ready for a fast getaway.'

David nodded. 'All right,' he said flatly.

The dinghies were dragged out on to the deck, inflated, and the teams sorted. Steve would take one craft, with Nick, Maksim and Dan. Henri would take the other, with Ian and Ollie. David would stay in charge of the main boat, keeping it ready to fish them out of the water as they made their escape.

'Try and have a nice cup of coffee ready for us as well, mate,' said Steve, as he prepared the dinghy for launch.

'And a slap-up meal,' said Nick. 'We'll be bloody starving.'

Each man equipped himself with a Browning stored in a waterproof pouch, and a spare clip of ammo. There was no point in taking the SA-80s; there was no way of keeping them dry. Nick would take the APS. He'd have liked a couple of practice runs, but with only ten rounds, they couldn't afford to waste any. Maksim had run through with him how it worked. And, as Ollie observed, if Nick couldn't make the shot, none of them could.

They lowered the dinghies into the water, then each man dropped down in turn. The waves were high, four or five feet in places, with swirls of white water breaking on top of them. Steve held tight on to his paddle, nodded to the other three men in his boat, then stabbed the blade into the water, pushing back hard to give them some momentum. There was only a distance of four or five hundred yards to cover until they bailed out, but the weather was ugly, and the currents were cutting across them, making progress hard and slow. Steve could feel his stomach starting to churn as the motion of the waves tugged them up and down. If I'd had anything proper to eat I'd be chucking it by now, he reflected bitterly.

The sky was darkening all the time, and they could see only the contours of the boat harboured in the bay. It was around two hundred feet long, Steve reckoned, a small cargo vessel, with a crane at the back, a bridge at the front, and a flat deck for containers. Just one more of the pirates' many victims. Up ahead, Henri raised a hand, then pointed towards the sea. This is it, thought Steve. The kick-off.

He glanced around at Nick, Maksim and Dan. 'Looks like we're going for a dip, boys,' he said tersely.

Each man nodded in turn but remained silent. No point in saying anything, thought Steve. We all know this might be the last time we see each other.

He took a deep breath, filling his lungs with oxygen, then plunged into the water. It was cold and clammy, but once you got down a few feet, and got your head under the waves, it was at least calmer. As he steadied himself, he opened his eyes, and looked straight ahead. Henri was already underwater, swimming hard, leading the silent convoy of men over the last three hundred yards that separated them from the hull of the boat. As he looked around, Steve could see the stretches of coral, and the colourful fish darting between the twisted, multicoloured rocks, and even in the pale light that struggled down into the sea, he was struck by the natural elegance of the seascape. Great diving, he thought to himself. I might come back here one day. With a couple of Andy McNab paperbacks, a crate of cold beer, and a good-looking girl.

And preferably no pirates trying to kill me.

The grey, barnacled hull of the cargo vessel loomed up at them, like a skyscraper might on the side of the street. It was securely anchored to the reef. Steve reckoned he'd been under about a minute so far; another thirty seconds or so and his lungs would be bursting. Henri raised a hand, then pointed each man towards the position they needed to take up for the attack. As they looked up, through the water they could make out the silhouettes of two men patrolling the front of the boat. Nick's task would be to take them out with the APS. Henri and his unit would scale one side of the boat, using a grappling hook to lift them up the fifteen feet that separated the side of the vessel from the waterline. Steve and his unit would climb the anchor chain, and scale the boat that way.

Steve took up position, and watched Nick ready himself. Henri was already scaling one side of the hull. Nick held the weapon to his shoulder, kicked his legs to hold himself steady, then fired. The bolt flew out of the water, and struck the pirate in the side of the chest with a force that was greater and deadlier than any bullet. The man splashed face down into the swirling water, already dead. In the same instant, Nick fired again, unleashing another bolt, this one hitting the second guard in the back as the man swung round to see what had happened to his mate. The bolt cracked open his spine, pulverising the veins underneath. The shock left him unconscious and he fell forwards on to the deck, rapidly bleeding to death.

Dan started to climb. The chain was wet and greasy, and he could feel his hands starting to freeze and blister on the cold metal. Steve waited in line behind Maksim, with Nick bringing up the rear.

Fifteen yards away, on the other side of the boat, Henri had already scaled the side of the vessel. He lashed a rope on to the railing and dropped it down to the sea, allowing Ollie and then Ian to join the assault. The Frenchman rolled out on to the deck, and drew the Browning from its waterproof pouch. He was halfway along the flat deck, and up ahead two patrol men were already dead, but two more were swinging into action. They were rolling two barrels into the water, aiming in the direction the shots had come from.

Depth charges, realised Henri. Lethal to anyone down below.

He started to run towards them, firing the Browning, emptying the rounds in the clip in rapid succession. One man fell, the next shot missed, then another, before the fourth round found its target. Three charges had already been dropped into the water, however.

'*Merde*,' muttered Henri out loud. He'd shout a warning if he could. But it was already too late.

Down in the water, Steve noticed the first barrel splash over the edge of the deck. It was a simple steel drum, two foot long, but Steve could guess at once it was a depth charge. It was the simplest, most brutal way to deal with an attack by frogmen. A depth charge was a barrel filled with explosive, usually with a barometric trigger that would detonate the bomb at a pre-set depth. The explosion underwater would have limited impact, its force smothered by the water, but it would send out a shock wave that would stun anything in the immediate vicinity. They were developed during the First World War to deal with the threat from submarines, and, in the hands of skilled operators, they were lethally effective. The shock waves from a charge could disable a fully armoured sub. Against a frogman, they would be deadly.

'Sodding move, sodding move,' yelled Steve, his voice raw with anger.

Dan was already halfway up the chain, with Maksim starting to slither upwards. The stocky Russian was swinging up the chain, throwing one arm in front of another like a crazed monkey. As the space opened up, Steve quickly followed, using his hands to shuffle forward, until his feet were free of the water. Just as the waves were spitting up around his ankles, he heard a dull thud, the first charge exploding, followed by another, then another. With a depth charge, there was always a delay, while the shock wave rolled through the water, then a wave would burst upwards. Steve moved as fast as he could, straining his wrist muscles as he struggled to put as much space as possible between himself and the ocean. Dan was already up, and had bundled over on to the side of deck, drawing his gun, and putting some deadly rounds of fire into the men who were now rushing up from the hold to defend the boat. Maksim, too, had scrambled on board.

Steve was shuffling faster, ignoring the aches in his shoulder where he was hanging from the metal links. He looked round. Nick was grabbing hold of the chain, but his hands were sliding off it, and he was struggling to get a grip. Swinging on monkey bars had been part of Steve's basic training, both in the Regular Army and the Regiment: a gruelling, exhausting routine, with a demented sergeant bawling into your ear until you imagined your arms were about to drop off. It was worth it at moments like this, however. Your life depended on instincts drilled into you. Nick didn't have that kind of training. He quite literally didn't know what he was doing.

'Bloody move, Nick,' yelled Steve. 'Just hang on and sodding—'

Steve was more than two-thirds of the way up the chain when the wave erupted, cutting him off in mid-sentence. The sea rose up, a great twisting mass of cold, angry water that lashed into Steve's legs, then smothered him completely. Then another wave followed swiftly afterwards, followed by another, until all three explosions merged into one massive ball of water. He closed his eyes and mouth, hanging on to the chain as he was completely submerged. The water was rushing upwards, dragging him with it, then abruptly changed direction as the wave sank down again with the same lethal force with which it had risen into the air. It was whirling, and Steve could feel it sucking him with it, like a fleck of soap being dragged down the plughole. He was struggling to hold on to the chain, his muscles strained, and his fingers raw with pain as he kept them clamped to the cold metal. The chain itself was creaking as the force of the water yanked it downwards, and Steve fought to prevent himself being taken down with it.

Finally, the water subsided.

Steve glanced back down the chain.

The water had turned into a swirling whirlpool. Nick was nowhere to be seen.

Fifty-One

OLLIE LINED THE MAN UP in the sights of his Browning.
He was crouching down by the side of a metal
lifeboat, his gun stretched out in front of him. A pirate
was running towards him, his AK-47 on automatic, spitting out
bullets that clattered against the metal. Ollie squeezed once. The
bullet struck the man dead in the centre of the forehead, sending
him scattering across the deck, a smear of blood across his face.

Ollie permitted himself a brief, tense smile.

We might be outnumbered, he thought to himself. Out-gunned
as well. But we're better trained. And we've some raw anger in our
blood. And so long as that remains true, we're in with a fighting
chance.

Henri and Ian were crouched down with him, behind the
lifeboat, on one side of the boat. On the other side, close to the
prow, Steve, Dan and Maksim had taken up position behind the
crane at its stern. The thick metal structure gave them just enough
cover to survive the onslaught. All six men had drawn their
Brownings, but they were facing wave after wave of attack from
the pirates who were rushing up from the hold. Ollie counted
eight corpses spread out across the deck, but there were another
dozen or so men still to deal with. The first few had rushed them
blindly, shooting ferociously but with minimal skill and even less
guile, and it had been easy enough to cut them down. The rest had
watched their mates get shot; they weren't about to repeat the

mistake. They were keeping back, taking cover, and planning their next attack.

Ollie looked at Ian. 'What d'you reckon?'

'Don't get pinned down,' said Ian. 'Right now, we've got the initiative. Lose that, and we're done for.'

The deck of the boat stretched for about two hundred feet. Steve's men were up at the top, while Ollie was halfway down. The dozen pirates had retreated behind the bridge, a thirty-foot structure close to the stern, which also housed the main stairwell leading down to the hold. They were taking sporadic shots at their attackers, keeping them pinned down. But it didn't look as if they were planning to rush them again.

They can just keep us penned in here like cattle waiting for the abattoir, realised Ollie. Starve us out if they have to.

'We'll get around the back,' said Henri.

Ollie looked sideways. What the hell was the Frenchman talking about now?

'Use our hands to edge our way along the side,' continued Henri. 'That way we can spring a surprise on them.'

'It's damned near a hundred feet,' snapped Ollie.

Henri shrugged.

Ian nodded. 'I'll cover you.'

'Right, so I'm going, am I?' said Ollie sourly.

'I'd love to,' answered Ian with a rough grin. 'But I might damage my fingernails.'

Ian darted out on deck and grabbed the AK-47 that had fallen out of the hands of the pirate Ollie had shot a few moments earlier. He grabbed the rifle, then spun on his heel. The Irishman was short and stocky, but like a lot of footballers with the same build, he was surprisingly agile, with an ability to swerve and turn that had been learnt from a combination of kicking balls and dodging bullets on the back streets of Belfast. A barrage of fire kicked off from the pirates, spitting and chewing into the metal deck, and then ricocheting dangerously in every direction. But Ian had already turned and was diving back towards the lifeboat for cover, while Ollie and Henri put down a steady stream of bullets from their Brownings, ferocious enough to stop the pirates taking proper aim.

Sweat was pouring off Ian's face as he straightened himself out. He'd taken a nasty bruise to the shoulder when he'd dived. But he had an AK-47, and a clip almost full of ammo. When this scrap turned nasty, that was going to give them some extra punch to put into their enemy.

'Well done, mate,' said Ollie, patting him on the back.

'Not the feckin' shoulder,' winced Ian.

Ollie grinned.

'Go, go,' snapped Henri. He tucked the Browning back into his webbing and started to lower himself downwards, so that just his hands gripped the side of the ship. Ollie followed. He knelt, then gripped. Fifteen feet below, the waves were snarling and angry, the green murky water churning upwards in a fury of swirling foam. Up above, the clouds had darkened further, and the first drops of a rainstorm were starting to spit down. A wind was howling in from the east, gathering strength as it raced over the empty ocean, and you could hear the ship start to creak as the waves tossed it backwards and forwards. Ollie gritted his teeth. This would be hard enough without the boat moving around. With a storm . . .

Forget it, he told himself. It's too late to start thinking about the risks now.

He dropped down, so that his body was flat against the side of the boat, hanging from his hands. Edging his left hand forwards, he followed with his right, and covered the first foot. The metal was wet and slippery, and the rising waves were spraying water up into him. His shoulders were stretching and aching from the strain of supporting his weight. But I'm making progress, he told himself, as he inched along slowly. Just a hundred feet. And then we can shoot these bastards in the back.

Up on the prow, Steve looked anxiously forwards. Along with

Dan and Maksim, he had ducked for cover, protecting himself from the sporadic gunfire down close to the bridge.

'Where the hell is Nick?' said Dan, looking backwards.

Steve scanned the waves breaking all around the boat. 'No sodding idea.'

'What does that mean?' growled Maksim.

'He got knocked off the chain when the charges exploded.'

Maksim turned round. It looked like he was about to jump back into the water, but Steve grabbed him. 'We sort this out, then we can go look for him.'

'He's our mate, we're not leaving him to drown.'

Steve looked out into the sea. The storm was kicking off, with a powerful wind blowing straight into them, and the waves were swirling upwards as the current and the air combined forces. The rain was starting to bucket down, caught up in the gale, and mixing with the spray to blow gusts of water straight into them. Christ, he thought to himself. How the hell is Nick meant to survive out there?

He pushed the thought out of his mind. Concentrate on the battle of the moment, he told himself. That was the first, and in many ways the most important, lesson any soldier had to learn.

'Until we can deal with these bastards, there's nothing we can do.'

As if to emphasise the point, a bullet struck the metal straight in front of them. All three men ducked. The pirates were some distance away, and had taken enough punishment from Ollie's and Henri's guns to be wary of advancing on their attackers again. But this was their boat, Steve reminded himself. They'll have plenty of kit to hit back at us with. They're just waiting for the right moment.

'Then let's deal with them,' said Maksim. 'Then we can find Nick.'

Dan was pointing towards an opening on the deck. It was ten yards in front of them.

'I spent a few summers working cargo boats back in Oz,' he said. 'There's always a way down into the holds.'

'We'll just be dropping into an empty space,' said Steve. He nodded towards the pirates down at the stern. 'Those are the boys we need to deal with.'

Dan shook his head. 'The cargo holds are all connected, in case of an emergency. Drop down there, and we can get to the stern without them noticing.'

Steve thought for a moment. He had no idea whether it would work. But he couldn't think of any alternative.

'We'll give it a try,' he said tersely. Then, glancing towards Maksim, 'You put down enough fire to make them think all three of us are holed up here. We'll see if we can rush them from behind.'

Maksim grunted, slotted a fresh clip into his Browning, took aim, and fired a couple of rounds in the direction of the pirates. If there was one thing the Russian could be relied upon for, reflected Steve, it was kicking up enough aggro to make your opponents believe they were facing a whole battalion.

Dan was already running across the open deck. Steve followed hard behind him, ignoring the rain starting to blow into his face as he flung himself over the few yards. Dan levered up the trapdoor, then plunged down into the darkness. Without hesitating, Steve slipped down through the hatch. There was a simple metal ladder, attached to the side of a steep steel wall. He gripped the rails, and climbed straight down, through five, then six feet. It was completely dark inside the hold, with only the light filtering through the hatch to illuminate the cavernous space, and there was a smell of diesel and rusty metal.

Steve could feel his boots touching something solid.

'Hey, piss off,' snapped Dan. 'That's my sodding head.'

Steve grinned. It looked like they'd touched bottom.

He lowered himself down on to the floor of the cargo hold. He looked around, but it was so dark, it was impossible to see anything apart from the hatch, way above them. The pocket torches they'd equipped themselves with had been ruined in the giant wave that hit them back in Puntland, and they had nothing to light the way.

'Looks like it's the blind leading the blind, mate,' said Steve, as he started to walk carefully forwards.

'Not much change there, then,' said Dan.

Ian looked towards the pirates, then back and across the side of the boat to Henri and Ollie. They were nearly halfway along. As he looked right, he could see Maksim holding his position with sporadic covering fire. But there was no sign of Steve or Dan, or indeed Nick. I hope they're planning something, he thought.

Suddenly, a blast of gunfire raked the lifeboat behind which he was sheltering. He ducked for cover. Then he glanced forwards and saw a man running towards him, hurling some kind of missile straight at him. He crouched, and pulled his helmet down to protect as much of his face as possible. There was a deafening explosion, then a sudden blast of heat as the device detonated a few feet in front of him.

The rain was temporarily vaporised by the force of the blast. As it faded, there was a rattle of metal on metal as hundreds of lethal, red-hot and razor-sharp fragments of shrapnel hurled towards him. At least two clattered into his helmet. Another snagged the sleeve of his sweatshirt, ripping open the fabric and grazing the muscle in his forearm. Ian knew enough about improvised, homemade explosives to assess immediately what had just been thrown at him. A two-litre bottle, he reckoned, stuffed with TNT at the bottom, then topped up with diesel and steel tacks, to create a lethal bomb that would unleash a fireball and a blistering assault of shrapnel. Through gritted teeth, he couldn't help but admire the skill of the bombers. It was a device he'd have been proud of himself.

I don't fancy seeing what they've got for an encore, he told himself grimly.

If I was in charge, I'd soften the opposition. Get them scared. Then I'd kick off with the real fireworks. There's no point in sitting around here waiting to be burnt to death. I need to link up with Maksie.

He glanced up from behind the lifeboat. There was burning diesel right across the deck, and the shrapnel had started smaller fires to the left and right. Ian ran at full speed straight across the deck, letting the flames singe his wet clothes, sliding over the wet surface of the deck. A rattle of gunfire opened up as the pirates spotted him, but by the time it started he'd already disappeared into the black fumes rising from the fires.

'Where the fuck is everyone?' he grunted as the Russian looked up at him in surprise.

Ollie shuddered as he felt the heat of the blast, and tightened his grip on the side of the boat. Henri was ten feet beyond him, moving with the agility and assuredness of skilled marine commando, but Ollie wasn't feeling nearly so confident. As the metal hull groaned and creaked under the force of the blast, one finger slipped, and, as it did so, his hand lost its hold on the salty, slimy surface. 'Bugger,' he muttered out loud. He was holding on by just his right hand, the muscles in his shoulder strained to breaking point as they supported his entire weight.

Henri glanced round. He was motioning frantically; they were so close to the pirates it was too dangerous to speak. Ollie could feel his shoulder starting to give. A wave caught him sideways, its force thumping him hard against the hull, and he could feel the grip in his right hand loosening. He grunted and swung his left fist upwards, his fingers just touching the side of the boat but sliding right off its wet surface. Henri scuttled back, covering the few feet that separated them in a couple of seconds, then, reaching a hand down for Ollie, he yanked him hard, dragging him up.

'Move,' he hissed.

Ollie started to lever himself along. It was only another ten yards or so to the stern. He could hear gunfire rattling across the deck, then another explosion. Waves of thick black smoke were caught up in the swirling wind and rain, blowing straight into him, clogging his eyes and choking his lungs, but he pressed relentlessly on. Ahead, Henri raised a single hand. Ollie paused. The Frenchman nodded to him silently, then both men peered up over the side of the vessel. A group of ten pirates was grouped around the stern, each man equipped with an AK-47. They were looking out across the deck, firing straight into the mess of fire and smoke.

Using his left hand to hold himself steady, Henri drew his Browning from his webbing and held it steady.

He looked towards Ollie. 'On the count of three,' he hissed.

Ollie slipped his right hand into his webbing, and drew out the slim handgun.

'One,' mouthed Henri silently. 'Two . . .'

Fifty-Two

STEVE WALKED STEADILY THROUGH THE darkness.

He had already lost any sense of the distance, and was starting to lose track of the time as well. It was pitch black down in the cargo chambers, and they were wading through pools of stagnant seawater along the bottom of the boat. They had found their way through one door, then another, but it was slow and hard progress, using their hands to feel the way forwards. On a vessel this size, Dan reckoned there would be four separate cargo chambers, each one sealed off from the other. But there was no way of telling for certain. They just had to press on and see what happened.

Up above them, there had been one blast, then another. Steve could feel the boat shaking and, as the first bomb had exploded, he'd fallen straight into the thick, soupy sludge. 'Stay on your sodding feet, mate,' said Dan, hauling him up. 'I've known blokes who can walk home from the pub better than this.'

Steve looked around as Dan felt his way to the next door, and started to twist the lock holding it in place. He could see nothing, but he could smell danger close by. Guns were blasting up on the deck. And something was burning, he felt certain of it. Acrid, scorched smoke was starting to drift through the air. Steve didn't know much about boats, but he knew a bit about engines. And he reckoned he could tell when one had caught fire.

'Christ,' he muttered to himself. If that fire gets close to the fuel tank, we're all done for.

Dan unlocked the door, and as it swung open, both men plunged forwards. They strode steadily through the sludge and darkness, keeping a few inches apart. Suddenly, there was a cascade of sparks, high up, close to the top of the cargo chamber. Steve looked up. Some wiring had blown, creating a storm of flame that tumbled downwards like electric rain. The chamber was briefly illuminated. Steve could see the dark, sea-drenched walls, thick with rust, and also some old crates, with Korean writing on them, which he reckoned were the remnants of the cargo the boat had been carrying when the pirates had captured her.

Something's definitely burning, thought Steve, as he watched the flames lick through the wires. Badly.

Another door. Dan leant into its rotating lock, grunting as he squeezed on the rusty, decayed mechanism.

It started to swing open.

Then Dan paused.

There was a light behind it.

'. . . Three,' muttered Henri, his voice little more than a whisper, barely audible above the roar of the wind and the battering of the rain.

Ollie was holding the gun between his teeth. Both his hands were gripping the side of the boat. He levered himself upwards in one swift movement, putting his elbows on the deck and pushing against the hull with his feet, until the top half of his body was lying flat on the surface of the ship. It was a noisy manoeuvre, but the wind and the rain and the gunfire were on their side: no one heard them, and no one looked round.

There were ten pirates straight ahead of them, all looking forward, their backs turned to the stern. In one simple, well-practiced movement, Ollie dropped the Browning into his hand and took aim. There was no military task Ollie hated more than shooting a man in the back. The least you could do for a man when you were about to end his life was look him straight in the eye. Today, however, there was no other option. And although it wasn't much compensation, reflected Ollie grimly, it did make the task easier. When a man was shot in the back, he didn't fight back, couldn't loose off any last rounds, nor even warn his mates. He just went straight down.

Ollie squeezed the trigger, shifted the gun a fraction of an inch, then fired again.

One man crumpled as the bullet split open his spine. The second man reeled in agony as the round burrowed through the muscles and flesh along the back, and ripped open a chunk of his heart. Blood was foaming from his mouth as he fell forwards.

'Keep firing,' yelled Henri.

Ollie was lying flat on the deck now, using his elbows to support himself. His first two shots had taken down two men, one dead, one fatally wounded. Henri's had been just as effective: one round had been placed straight through the back of a man's skull, blowing away half his brain, and the second had taken out a big enough chunk of neck to put the victim on the ground.

Six men left, noted Ollie.

The men were starting to turn, taking advantage of the split second since their mates had gone down to reassemble and start fighting back. Ollie and Henri were firing in tandem, pumping out round after round into the men facing them. It was impossible to tell who was shooting who; both men were just laying down a barrage of munitions, aware they had only a few seconds during which the momentum of a surprise attack was still with them. Once that moment had passed, they'd be in a fair fight with an enemy with more men, more weapons, and on his own ground. And that was hardly a scrap they wanted to get into.

With the rain soaking him, Ollie fired and fired again, no longer pausing to take proper aim. The enemy was only six feet away; any bullet loosed off from here stood a good enough chance of scoring a kill without having to be aimed with precision.

One man was caught by a bullet in the side of his shoulder, his AK-47 clattering to the deck. Another caught a bullet in the face, blood pouring from the open wound, whilst a third managed to fire a couple of rounds from his gun before two, then three bullets punctured his chest, bringing him to his knees, where a single shot to the heart ended his life.

In a panic, the remaining three men turned and fled the carnage. They were charging up to the prow of the boat, their AK-47s rattling on automatic.

'Go, go,' yelled Maksim. The Russian was pointing straight down towards the stern.

It was a mass of smoke and flames. The fire was getting worse, judged Ian. He'd expected the fireball unleashed by the bomb to have faded in intensity by now, but it was growing in force. As if the boat was burning. Maksim was pointing into the fire, now raging across the centre of the deck. There was movement, and the rattle of gunfire, but through the fumes and smoke it was impossible to make out anything apart from dark, blurred shapes that could be men, or just shadows in the flames.

Maksim was already running straight towards the fire, his Browning drawn, and his finger ready on the trigger.

Ian followed a couple of steps behind, gripping the stolen AK-47 tight to his chest. The Russian was suicidally brave, a man who would run straight into combat, but Ian had learnt to hang back. If Maksie wanted to throw his life away, that was his business; Ian preferred to fight with stealth, and tactics, and not just bull-like determination. But he didn't mind using Maksie as a human battering ram.

Every man has his uses, he reflected drily.

As they drew closer to the flames, the heat was scorching. A fuel tank had caught fire, Ian reckoned, and the burning diesel was creating thick clouds of smoke. Suddenly two figures emerged. Their already dark skin was blackened even further by the flames. Maksim fired twice with the Browning. The first man staggered backwards, then got caught again by the flames that whipped up around him, a howling scream of pure terror erupting from his lips as he realised two things: that he'd caught fire; and that no one was going to help him.

The second man dropped to his knees, wounded in the chest. But from within the swirling fumes, another man leapt out and grabbed hold of Maksim by the neck, yanking his head back hard, and jabbing the barrel of his AK-47 straight into the Russian's throat. It was clear to Ian what he was doing. The pirate could tell he was outnumbered, his mates beaten, and the ship lost, but with a hostage he might be able to negotiate his way out on one of the lifeboats. Ian didn't hesitate; he slammed his finger on the trigger of the AK-47, unleashing a barrage of fire into the man's chest. He was stunned, then killed, before he had a chance to fire back, but the bullets still chewed up his intestines, sending an ugly mix of blood and guts spitting up into Maksim's face.

The Russian tossed the man angrily towards the burning diesel, where the flames quickly engulfed him. 'You could have killed me,' he said, glancing towards Ian.

'I think you can handle that particular task all by your feckin' self,' said Ian sourly.

A blast of gunfire rattled against the door. Dan shoved it open, then ducked behind the wall next to it. Both men drew their guns and waited. Six rounds clattered against the metal, then through the open door, before the man firing the gun realised he was shooting into empty space and released his finger from the trigger.

'Someone's in there,' hissed Dan.

'Thanks, Einstein,' muttered Steve.

Dan glanced round the door. The final cargo hold led through to a cabin designed to hold at least half a dozen men. There were some bunk beds, a cooking area, and a TV with a DVD player attached to it. The electrics on board the ship had been blown out in the explosions that had ripped through the vessel, but there was an oil lamp burning in the corner, and that provided enough illumination to make out the single figure standing at the back of the room with a Czech-made CZ-52 pistol in his hand.

Yasin.

The pirate fired in Dan's direction. He ducked back behind the door.

'Any ideas?' he asked, looking at Steve.

'The motto.'

Dan grinned. 'Maximum speed, maximum aggression, right?'

'That's the one.'

Steve checked the clip on the Browning, then nodded towards Dan. It was a tough manoeuvre. And a risky one. But in the circumstances, it was the best option available to them. Two men should always be able to overpower one. So long as they held their nerve and didn't flinch from danger.

Both men moved simultaneously. Their handguns were gripped tight into their fists, thrust out in front of them. As they jumped into the door space, they fired. There was no time or space to aim, so the bullets cannoned off the back wall and ricocheted dangerously around the enclosed metal space, one of them only narrowly missing Steve's arm. With the bullets still flying through the air, both men pushed through the doorway, standing side by side in a tight unit, their guns stretched out in front of them, pointing straight at Yasin's heart.

'Drop the fucking gun,' screamed Dan, his voice raw with anger.

Yasin hesitated for a fraction of a second. His finger was on the trigger of his pistol, ready to fire, but he was a careful, calculating man, one who knew when the odds were against him, and although he might be able to take down one of the men confronting him, there was no chance of taking out both before a bullet was lodged in his chest. He was a survivor, and, offered the choice between life and revenge, he'd always take the former.

A half-smile played on his lips. 'I thought I'd escaped.'

'There no escaping from us, mate,' said Steve. 'We're like the parking-ticket people. We always catch up with you in the end.'

Ian followed Maksim through the flames. The fire was burning right across the centre of the deck, but by staying close to the right-hand side of the vessel, they managed to squeeze their way through to the stern. The heat was scorching, and their lungs were choking from the black fumes. Both men had their guns drawn, and their fingers ready to fire. Neither of them had any way of knowing how many of the pirates had been killed, or what kind of opposition they might still face.

'Hands in the air,' yelled Maksim as a figure moved darkly through the smoky shadows.

'Christ, Maksie, it's me,' said Ollie.

Ian and Maksim ran forward to join Ollie and Henri. They quickly checked the rest of the deck, but they could see nothing but corpses. The opposition had been dealt with.

'Where's Steve and Dan?' asked Ollie.

Ian nodded below. 'In the hold,' he said.

There was a tight grimace on Ollie's face. 'Let's get down there,' he said. 'I reckon Yasin's holed up somewhere down below, and Steve and Dan should be there as well.'

Ian waved back towards the fire. 'This ship's going to blow,' he said. 'If there's fuel in the tanks, and the flames get to it, then she'll go up like a bomb.'

'Then there's no time to lose,' said Ollie.

From the bridge, a metal staircase led up to the captain's deck, and another led down into the hold. The storm was growing worse all the time, with great gusts of wind blowing hard across the deck, fanning the flames, and sending swirls of black smoke eddying up all around them. The clouds were dropping and visibility was falling. The rain was bucketing down in angry sheets that seemed capable of drowning a man, and the waves were rising constantly, pushing the boat up and down in the swell.

Ollie and Maksim levered open the door to the cabin. The lights had all blown out, and the staircase was shrouded in darkness. Rainwater and spray were spilling from the deck, down on to the stairs, turning them into a small river. As Ollie and Maksim started to plunge down into the darkness, there was a sudden blast. The ship lurched violently, tipping fifteen degrees before righting itself just as suddenly. There was an acrid smell of burning wire and metal, and sparks flew from the cables running down the side of the staircase, briefly illuminating the view with blue and yellow light.

'Something's blown,' snarled Ian. 'This bastard's going to sink.'

Ollie pushed through to the bottom of the staircase. He barged through a small landing, then saw a slit of light underneath the door ahead. Without hesitating, he burst through into the cabin. His gun was drawn, pointing straight ahead.

'If you wouldn't mind putting that away, pal,' said Steve quietly. 'I've been shot at quite enough for one day.'

Ollie grinned. 'Steve sodding West,' he said. 'Just the bloke I'd expect to find hiding out in a pirate's cabin.' He looked across to Yasin. The pirate was solemn, but his expression was composed. He'd handed his pistol across to Dan, but the single metal case containing the plutonium was still handcuffed to his wrist. 'Good to see you again, mate,' Ollie said sharply. He reached out to take the suitcase. 'We'll be taking that.' He yanked hard at the case, but there was no give in the chain.

'The key,' demanded Steve, walking across to join them.

'We threw it in the sea,' said Yasin.

'You're sodding lying, man,' growled Ollie angrily, grabbing hold of Yasin's neck.

The pirate leader remained calm. 'Prove it.'

There was another explosion. The sound rattled down through the cargo hold, and the ship lurched to one side. This time it didn't right itself.

'There's no time to mess around,' snapped Ian. 'Get the fuck out of here.'

Dan jabbed the AK-47 he'd captured from Yasin into the man's back, and started to push him up the stairs. The unit moved swiftly up and back on to the deck. The fires were growing worse, and the ship was listing. Dan and Henri ran to one of the lifeboats, unleashed it from the clasps that held the simple, wooden rowing boat in place, and lowered it into the water. It was buffeted by the high waves, rocking from side to side, and shipping water as it did so, but just about managed to stay afloat. Henri climbed down into the boat, using a rope to hold the vessel in place as he motioned to the rest of the men to join them.

'Quick, quick,' he yelled. 'The ship's going to blow.'

Steve pushed Yasin forwards. Maksim grabbed the man's hand.

'You hold him steady,' he said, looking towards Steve and Ollie. 'I'll blow this off with the AK.'

'You'll take his sodding hand off,' said Steve.

Maksim shrugged. 'So?'

Steve was silent. The Russian was right. They'd come here to get the plutonium, and they'd risked their lives in the process. If they had to shoot a man's hand off, that was a price that had to be paid.

But Ollie was pushing Yasin down towards the lifeboat. 'Leave it,' he said sharply. 'The bugger is coming with us.'

Fifty-Three

THE BOAT MEASURED JUST TWENTY feet by seven, with a curved wooden hull, and two sets of oars. There was no outboard motor, and only the most basic survival kit stashed in a simple metal box close to its stern. Four life jackets, a flare and a whistle, a torch that someone had taken the battery out of, and some empty cartons of food. Not much for seven men to survive on, reflected Steve. But better than getting blown to pieces on a burning ship.

Henri and Dan had taken one set of oars, Maksim and Ollie the other. Steve and Ian were sitting at the back, Ian keeping his gun on Yasin, while Steve steered the lifeboat as far away from the main ship as possible. The flames were smothering the deck now, and the last explosion had blown a chunk out of the hull. Water was shipping through the cargo holds, and at any moment it would reach a critical point, and capsize. That's if it doesn't blow up first, reflected Steve.

The storm waves were four, sometimes five feet high, vicious swirls of water that caught and twisted the oars as the men tried to put a survivable distance between themselves and the burning ship. Rain was lashing across the boat, filling it with water, and the winds were biting into the men's skin, making the water seem even colder. Steve shuddered, and put his head down. Only one thought was playing through his mind. Not hanging on to the plutonium. Not surviving the next few hours. Just finding Nick.

'Where the fuck do you think he is?' he shouted.

Henri was pointing due east, towards the stern of the sinking boat. 'If he got knocked off by a wave from the anchor, the currents should carry him that way.'

Steve started to turn the rudder. The four men on the oars were pulling as hard as they could, but in the rough water it was hard for the blades to get any kind of grip. As they ploughed slowly forwards, Steve was scanning the big waves. 'Nick, Nick . . .' he cried, his voice carrying on the strong winds. But there was no sign of the Welsh boy. It was pitch black now, and with the storm settling in for the night, there wasn't much chance of the moon emerging to light up the ocean. Even if Nick was out there somewhere, how the hell could they find him? In calm weather, in daylight, perhaps. In this . . .

Behind them, there was a loud creaking sound as a section of the ship split away. A mass of sparks flew upwards, and then a plume of burning diesel briefly illuminated the sky, sending puddles of torched fuel skidding out across the ocean. Steve's head was spinning left and right, desperately searching for signs of a body. '*Nick* . . .' he yelled again.

Ian looked up, his gun wedged into Yasin's throat. 'You think there's still a chance?'

Steve ignored the question. The possibility of losing Nick was more than he wanted to deal with right now. 'We keep looking,' he growled.

Steve was steering the lifeboat up towards the stern. The last time he'd seen Nick, he'd been hanging on to the ship's anchor chain, but that was fifteen minutes ago, and conscious or unconscious, he could have drifted a long way since then. Up ahead the light from the last explosion was starting to fade now, and the ocean was turning black once again. The clouds were heavy, the rain was smashing into the men, and the small boat was buffeted by the waves. Their oars were struggling against the rough sea, and each time they made a few yards of progress, the waves pushed them back again. But they were drawing closer to the anchor. The metal chain was creaking as the boat slowly turned on its side. Steve was looking back out to sea, trying to judge the direction that Nick would have drifted when the waves took him. But amid the heaving water, it was impossible to tell in which direction a body might have been washed away. Left, right, up the beach, or out into the ocean, water this rough could take a man anywhere.

He grabbed a flare from the emergency pack, but he was no seaman, and had no idea how to fire it. The last thing Steve wanted to do was waste it. He jabbed it towards Henri.

'Get this up,' he shouted. 'We might be able to see Nick in its light. Or if he sees us, he can shout, or swim towards us.'

Henri turned to look at him, his face hardening. 'It's a waste.'

'What do you mean it's a sodding waste?'

'It's a waste of a flare,' growled Henri. 'We're going to need that to get out of here.'

'That's our mate you're talking about,' shouted Steve. His voice was raw with anger. 'And you're sodding saying the boy's not worth a flare.'

'Forget it,' said Henri, his tone flat. 'He's already dead.'

There was a silence. Nobody said anything. Nobody was rowing. The only sound was the wind howling through them, and the waves rocking up to the side of the boat.

'We're not leaving here without Nick, I tell you,' said Ollie. His face was set in an expression of implacable determination.

'And I'm telling you he's dead,' said Henri with a simple shrug. 'There's no way a man can survive fifteen minutes in this storm. He'll have been knocked out when he fell off the anchor chain. A man can't survive that, not in this shit.'

'Like Ollie says,' snapped Steve. 'We're not sodding leaving without Nick.'

Ian pointed towards the ship, then glanced at Henri. 'How long has she got?'

'A minute, maybe two,' said Henri. 'Then she'll sink.'

'And what happens to us?'

'When a ship that size goes down, it generates a big wave, then a whirlpool. We'll get knocked over, then sucked down.'

Ian's eyes darted between Steve and Ollie. 'We've got more chance of Maksie turning down a vodka in a bar than we have of finding Nick in this,' he said. 'It's time to get the fuck out of here.'

'Not without Nick, I'm telling you,' said Steve.

'Let it go,' said Henri. 'He's a soldier, just like the rest of us. If his number's called, it's called. He wouldn't have expected the rest of us to die . . .'

Steve lunged forwards. He planted a blow on the left side of Henri's cheek. It was well struck, delivered with the force of days of pent-up anger. The Frenchman was taken by surprise, and even though he was a strong man, with a jaw that could have been built from granite, the punch knocked him sideways. Steve followed it with a blow from his left hand, an uppercut that knocked his head backwards, then a blow from the right that connected with the side of his head. Henri was stunned, but far from disabled; he was a formidably built soldier and it took a lot more than three punches to dent him. He kicked back hard with his knees, catching Steve in the chest and knocking the wind out of his lungs.

'You sodding French bastard,' yelled Steve, landing another punch into the man's stomach and following it up with a knee that smashed hard into his ribs. 'I haven't trusted you since the moment I laid eyes on you.'

'Fuck off,' spat Henri.

He was kicking back with his legs, catching Steve harder this time, as both men rolled in the pools of water swilling around the bottom of the boat. Steve bashed into Ian, then Dan, but both men shoved him back. Henri curled his fist into a ball, and smashed hard forwards, and although Steve managed to duck, the blow still caught him on the side of the neck with enough force for him to know there would be a nasty bruise there in a few hours. He lashed out with his right arm just as Henri was about to deliver another blow with his right. The two forearms collided, with a sickening crunch of bone and muscle, but Steve managed to steady himself in time to deliver a sharp punch to the Frenchman's stomach.

'This fight is only just starting, mate,' he spat into Henri's face.

Dan and Maksim had put their oars to one side. Both men stepped towards the back of the boat. Maksim grabbed hold of Henri and pulled him down. Dan reached for Steve's shoulders, locking them between his massive forearms, and pulling him down towards the bottom of the boat. 'You sods bloody stop it,' he shouted in Steve's ear. 'We haven't got the time to start fighting amongst ourselves.'

Ollie had already grabbed the flare that had fallen out of Steve's hand. Pointing upwards, he fired it into the air, so that it detonated thirty yards back from the stern of the sinking boat. Its blue, sulphurous light filled the sky, puncturing the darkness of the storm, and in an instant every swell and dip in the waves was clearly visible. The sea seemed momentarily calmed by the light, and each man looked around, desperately scanning the surface of the water for any sign of a man.

The light started to fade, and the waves returned to their icy, rough darkness.

'She's sinking,' said Ian, nodding towards the ship.

He grabbed the rudder, and began to steer away from the boat. Reluctantly, Dan and Maksim grabbed their oars, and started to row furiously. Henri was still nursing his bruises but had recovered sufficiently to draw his Browning, and hold it steady on Yasin. Steve and Ollie were leaning over the side of the boat, calling for Nick, their lungs raw with the effort they were putting into each shout. But there was no response; just the howling of the wind, the beating of the rain, and the roar of the waves. As each second ticked by, hope was fading. Steve could only look into the treacherous, cold water, aware of its power, and of the way it could lash into a man, knocking the air from his lungs. And he could see nothing there, no matter how hard or how long he looked.

'Nick,' he shouted once more. But the strength in his voice was going.

Up ahead, a light shone out of the darkness. Ian steered straight towards it.

The yards closed. And as it drew closer, they recognised what it was. The boat David had been left in charge of.

A rescue.

In this weather, they needed it, reflected Steve. They had no hope of surviving the storm in this rowing boat. But he could take no pleasure in it. If Nick was lost, and it seemed he was, then he'd just as soon drown in the same seas.

Ian steered the rowing boat alongside the vessel.

'I was starting to get a bit worried about you sods,' said David, chucking down a rope. 'And when I saw the flare, I thought I'd better sail straight towards you.'

Ian grabbed the rope, and held it steady, so that the men could use it to climb aboard.

One by one, Maksim, Ian, Dan, Ollie and Henri grabbed hold of the rope and hauled themselves up on to the small ship.

'We can't keep holding it, Steve,' shouted David. 'Bloody well come on board.'

Steve reached up.

Then he looked back into the dark, swirling water. Behind them, a hundred yards or so, the ship was sinking below the brutal waves. He turned back, reaching for the rope. He could feel the lifeboat rolling violently beneath him, and he knew that without anyone to stabilise it, it wouldn't stay upright in these waters much longer. The spray was kicking up around him, the rain was lashing into his face, and the water spilling into the boat had formed an icy puddle around his feet.

A few more minutes and I'll be dead, he reflected. But as he reached for the rope, he could barely find the energy to haul himself to safety.

Fifty-Four

'WHO'S UP FOR A CUPPA?' asked Nick.

He was walking across the deck, with a mug of coffee in his hands.

Steve's jaw dropped in astonishment. The Welsh boy had changed into some dry clothes and was handing around the tin cup of steaming liquid. Each man was wet through and exhausted, their clothes torn and soaked, and they took the cup gratefully, cradling it in the palms of their hands, letting some of the heat seep through into their blood before putting it to their lips, then passing it on to the next man.

'What the hell are you doing here?' said Steve angrily, looking straight at Nick.

David looked at him in surprise. 'He was swimming around in the water crying for help and blowing his whistle, so I came to fish him out.'

Steve shook his head, half in amazement, half in relief.

'So you've been sitting here, brewing up coffee and having an easy time of it while your mates do all the hard work,' he said, looking at Nick.

'An easy time?' snorted Nick. 'I only tuned the ship's radio into the World Service and just sodding well found out that Liverpool lost two nil to Chelsea this afternoon.'

'Two nil?' said Steve. 'Who scored?'

'Ashley Cole. Twice.'

Steve took a hit of the coffee, letting its warmth flood through his body, then chuckled. 'Christ, we capture the pirate's main man, and Ashley Cole scores for Chelsea. That's two sodding miracles in one day.'

Nick looked towards Yasin. He was standing to one side of the group. No one was holding a gun on him anymore. There wasn't any need. They'd disarmed the man, and he wasn't about to make a run for it. There wasn't anywhere to go. 'Is that him?'

Maksim slapped the pirate on the back and pointed towards the suitcase. 'Our ticket home,' he grunted. 'With a full pardon, and a million to spend on vodka and whores.'

'Cool,' said Nick. 'A real pirate.'

'Well, I'm sodding glad you're allright, Nick,' said Steve. He chuckled again. 'I reckon if we'd lost you on this mission, your mum might not have shagged Ollie again.'

'Now that really would be a blow,' said Ollie.

'Bloody leave it out,' snapped Nick. 'Any more jokes about me mum, and I'll bloody have you.'

'Now, now, boys,' intervened Ian. 'There's been enough aggro for one day.'

Steve checked his watch. It was getting close to nine at night. 'We've got three hours to make the RV,' he said, looking at Henri. 'Think we can make it?'

Henri went up to the bridge and looked out at the worsening storm. 'Only if we sail like the devil.'

The boat turned, and started to head straight into the storm. The waves were high and the rain was still beating into them, but the boat was sturdy enough to stand up to the weather. It was pitching and tossing as it grappled with the big waves, but the engine was turning well, and the pump was heaving out the water almost as fast as it shipped over the side. Henri appeared confident they'd get through safely enough.

Three men were placed on lookout, Maksim up on the prow, and Nick and David at the stern, with an agreement that they'd all switch places in an hour, so the rest of the men huddled together on the small captain's bridge, keeping out of the rain. They used a small gas burner to heat some water and endlessly reboil the few remaining coffee grounds. Yasin remained silent, holding on to the case chained to his wrist. Its metal surface was scratched and stained from the sea, but the contents were still intact. His face was solemn and his eyes sullen, far removed from the confident, swaggering military leader Ollie had first encountered, but the same fierce intelligence was still in evidence.

'What are you planning to do with me?' he asked, after Ollie finally offered him the dregs of some hot, weak coffee.

Ollie reckoned that every soldier deserved to know his fate, and although the world might describe him as an outlaw and a pirate, during the brief period he'd been his prisoner, Yasin had treated him perfectly fairly. Many professional military men he'd encountered would have shot him on the spot.

'We'll be handing you over at twelve sharp,' said Ollie. 'What happens to you then is up to the authorities.'

'Which authorities?'

'The British government,' said Ollie sharply. 'It's their plutonium you stole and tried to sell on the black market.'

'Then I'll be executed.'

Yasin was a brave man, reflected Ollie. Of that, there could be no question. But no man, not even the worthiest soldier, could contemplate his own demise with equanimity, particularly when it wasn't going to come in battle; there was no mistaking the morose tone in Yasin's voice.

'We don't execute people,' said Ollie. 'We play by the rules. That's one thing you can damn well count on.'

'They feckin' do,' interrupted Ian. 'There were plenty of good men executed in the back streets of Belfast back during the troubles.'

'They were murdering bastards,' snapped Ollie. 'Terrorist scum.'

Ian nodded towards Yasin. 'And how do you think they'll

characterise yer man there? A political prisoner? A displaced fisherman?'

'Terrorist scum, like your friend says,' said Yasin. His tone was more reflective than sorrowful or angry, noted Steve. The tone of a man who'd accepted his fate, and was starting to come to terms with it. 'But, really, as I was trying to explain to you when you were my prisoner, rather than I yours, we are just fishermen. You've seen our land. It's bare, and dry, and scrubby. The sea is all we have. The Westerners have stolen all our fish, using their big factory boats, and now all we can do is collect money from the ships that use our waters. We've been left with no other choice.'

'You stole British plutonium,' said Ollie. 'You were selling it to the highest bidder. The Iranians, al-Queda, whoever. They could build a dirty bomb . . .'

'I didn't make the plutonium,' snapped Yasin. 'If the British are so worried about bombs, they shouldn't be making weapons-grade materials.'

'Thousands could die.'

'And my people would starve if I wasn't there to help them. Or would you rather we just lived on handouts of grain and rice from the Europeans and the Americans? We take our fate into our own hands and make our living any way we can. You of all people should understand that.'

Ollie remained silent.

There was some truth to what the pirate said, reflected Steve as he listened to the argument. The world was a hard place, and a man had to find his own place in it. You couldn't spend very long as either a regular soldier or working on the Circuit with the PMCs without learning that simple truth. But although the pirates might have started out as simple fishermen struggling to find a way to replace the living they'd lost from the sea, when you drove through the country itself, you could see how rich they were growing. There were satellite dishes and new SUVs in a lot of the towns. They were growing fat and vicious on the proceeds of their deadly trade, and the easy money would make them greedy and cruel. You couldn't spend very long on the Circuit without learning about that too.

'But those arguments will make no difference to the British,' continued Yasin. 'I'm a threat to them. Even worse, I'm an embarrassment, and for that they'll kill me.'

'You'll be allright, pal,' said Steve. 'Just apply for political asylum. They'll have to take you back to Britain, fix you up with a nice flat, and you'll get a weekly cheque from the social.'

Yasin grinned. 'That doesn't sound so bad.'

'I can fix you up with a few jobs on the black. Cash in hand, and it helps if you're not a stickler for health and safety, which somehow I'm imagining you're not. There's always work for pirates in south London. You'll fit right in.'

Steve drained the dregs of his coffee and walked out on to the deck. They'd been sailing for an hour and a half, and the shift change for the men on watch was long overdue. The rain was still lashing into them, but the waves weren't so high. In the pitch blackness, it was impossible to judge their position, but so long as Henri had the course right, they should be sailing through the narrower strip of sea where the coasts of Yemen and Somalia started to converge.

'Should be a safe enough run now,' said Steve, standing next to Maksim, and looking out into the murky, stormy darkness. 'I'll take over. You get yourself warmed up.'

Maksim shook his head. 'Listen,' he said.

Steve looked out into the darkness.

The clouds were still low, closing in on the horizon, and it was impossible to see anything apart from the swirling waves and the sheets of rain. Whether the visibility was a hundred yards or ten, Steve couldn't tell. It was just one murky, violent snarl of water that came from the sky or the sea.

'I can't see a thing.'

'I said listen,' repeated Maksim.

Steve concentrated on the noises whistling through the night air. The engine was growling beneath them, and the waves were beating against the hull of the boat. There was enough noise all around to stop the devil himself from getting a few moments' kip, and maybe even Nick as well, but nothing that aroused any suspicions.

Steve shook his head. 'Nothing, mate. Looks like a clean run home.'

Maksim nodded upwards. 'A chopper,' he said. 'I'm sure of it.'

Steve looked into the sky. The rain tipped down into his face as if he was standing under a powerful cold shower, but he flicked it away with the palm of his hands and concentrated on peering straight into the clouds. He'd heard plenty of helicopters over the years. There was a throaty, muffled anger to the engines that a man could learn to recognise, in the same way he might recognise the sound of a car or a truck. But right now, he couldn't make out a thing.

'You sure?' he asked.

The Russian shook his head. 'It flashed through the clouds. But in this storm, it could be anything.'

'Keep watch,' hissed Steve. 'I'll tell the others.'

He moved swiftly back towards the bridge.

'Maksie reckons he heard a chopper,' he said, glancing around the unit.

'What sort?' asked Ollie.

'How the hell should I know?' growled Steve. 'He's not even sure it's there. But if someone's on to us, we better make sure we're ready for them.'

'The British?' asked Ian.

'We're already on our way to give them the plutonium,' said Ollie.

'Aye, and we're also asking for a million in gold, and a pardon,' said Ian. 'They might decide it's cheaper, and quicker, just to put us at the bottom of the ocean.'

'They wouldn't—'

'They might,' said Dan. 'But they don't need to come looking for us if they're planning a double cross. We're heading straight for them.'

'We opened negotiations to sell this to the Iranians, the North Koreans, and al-Queda, as well as the Italian mafia,' interrupted Yasin. He was holding up the suitcase full of plutonium. 'They all want this to make weapons, except for the mafia. I reckon they thought they could use it as a bargaining chip. With this under their control, they could blackmail any government they wanted.'

'You think it might be one of those groups, still out looking for it?' said Steve.

'The Koreans and Iranians don't have the ability to get a helicopter out here,' answered Yasin. 'There are plenty of al-Queda groups in Yemen and Somalia, and I know for a fact they were monitoring my camp.'

'We saw them, and fought them,' said Steve. 'Why didn't you do something about them?'

'A man doesn't bother me, I leave him in peace,' said Yasin with a shrug.

'Could they get a chopper out here?' asked Ollie.

Yasin shook his head. 'As far as I know, they don't have any helicopters.'

'That leaves the Iranians,' said Steve.

Yasin nodded. 'They know we've got plutonium, and they want it badly. And they have the largest navy in the whole region.'

'Why are we listening to him?' demanded Dan.

'His life is at stake here as much as anyone's,' replied Ian.

Steve stood up and walked out on to the deck. He scanned the sky anxiously, peering into the clouds and the pouring rain. Suddenly, there was a burst of engine noise, followed by a wide beam of light that arced across the deck.

As he looked up, the Gatling guns underneath the short, stubby nose of an attack helicopter were looking straight back at him.

Fifty-Five

I T WAS ONE OF THE most brutal sights Steve had ever witnessed. Like looking straight into the jaws of death.

The two guns opened up, unleashing a barrage of fire that peppered the deck with lead. Steve shouted at Maksim to take cover, then flung himself back towards the cabin. The rounds were flying all around him, and Steve could feel himself flinching as the cannons roared and wailed.

'Jesus sodding Christ,' he muttered.

The attack helicopter was moving fast through the air, and the pilot could only hold it over the boat for a couple of seconds before it swept back up into the clouds. As the guns fell silent, Steve looked anxiously around. Everyone looked to be OK. Maksim had managed to crawl up to the bridge for cover, and so had Nick, taking shelter from the storm of munitions.

But the chopper would be back, they could be certain of that. The fight was only just beginning.

'What the hell was it, Maksie?' Steve asked anxiously.

'An Iranian version of the Sea Cobra,' Maksim replied, his tone shaky. 'We came across them in border skirmishes all the time.'

'But the Sea Cobra's an American chopper,' said Ollie.

'They sold them to the Iranians before the revolution. They upgraded and overhauled each one, and re-named it the Panha 2091.'

The Sea Cobra was one of the first naval attack helicopters, developed by the Americans in the 1960s, and deployed extensively in Vietnam. It was an ageing piece of kit, but no less deadly for that. It was a light chopper, agile in the air, equipped with three 20mm cannons. Its guns were fitted with 700-round magazines and were capable of up to 650 rounds per minute, although standard procedure was to fire in thirty- to fifty-round bursts. In the right hands, they could deliver a devastating punch.

'What changes did the Iranians make?' demanded Ian.

'Nothing that special. They put in more armour plating, and a new canopy, and they claimed to have put in armoured glass, but they don't really know how to make the stuff so you can still punch your way through it.'

'Armaments?'

'The Gatling guns, obviously. Hydra 70 and Zuni rockets. None of them are guided.'

'But it can still sink the boat?' asked Ollie.

'They aren't going to do that,' said Ian. 'They don't care about us. They want the plutonium. They can't get that if they put us at the bottom of the water.'

'He's right,' said David. 'They'll be aiming to kill all of us then drop a guy down on to the deck to take control of the boat.'

'And with that piece of kit, they've got a bloody good chance,' said Steve. He looked at Henri. 'Can we outrun them? Or evade?'

'A chopper? You have any idea how fast those things are?' The Frenchman shook his head. 'Once the radar locks on to us, we're an easy target.'

Before he'd finished the sentence, there was a burst of noise, followed by a beam of light.

'Dive,' shouted Nick.

All the men fell to the ground, cowering behind the metal of the bridge, their helmets pulled down low to protect themselves. The Panha was fitted with a searchlight, flashing on to the boat like a giant torch. But attack helicopters were daylight weapons, Steve reminded himself, particularly when they weren't fitted with guided or heat-seeking missiles. They had poor visibility and, in this storm, limited capacity to manoeuvre. Maybe that gives us the slither of a chance.

The bullets spat on to the deck, kicking up splinters of shrapnel that flew dangerously through the air. The attack lasted no more than two seconds before the pilot swung the chopper back up into the clouds. Yet in those two seconds it had delivered another hefty blow on the target.

'How long can we hold out?' asked Steve, looking up anxiously at Henri.

'In this tub? A few more minutes. That chopper's just going to chew us to pieces.'

'How do we bring it down, Maksie?' asked Ollie.

'An RPG,' said the Russian with a shrug.

'Right, thanks, mate,' said Dan. 'If we happened to have one spare that would be a really useful suggestion.'

Steve was looking at Ian. 'You wouldn't happen to know about a barrack buster, would you?'

There was the trace of a smile on the Irishman's lips, although it swiftly vanished as they heard the chopper turning and preparing another run. The 'barrack buster' was an improvised IRA rocket, made from steel tubing. They were widely used to attack British Army barracks during the troubles and, most famously, for the mortar attack on 10 Downing Street while John Major was Prime Minister.

'I might.'

'Then you're sodding terrorist scum,' said Steve, with a scowl. Then he grinned. 'A lot of good men never made it back to their families because of those. But if you could rustle one up right now, I might be persuaded to overlook that.'

'Dive,' shouted Nick, louder this time.

The arc of light swept over the boat, followed by the now familiar rattle of cannon fire. The storm was starting to dim in its intensity. The rain was only spitting, and the clouds were beginning to lift. That was making the task easier for the pilot, and this time around he came in faster and lower, swooping just a few feet over the deck, his cannon blasting angry jabs of hot, lethal metal straight into them. A section of the bridge flew away, loosened then crushed by the weight of the fire smashing into it, and even though Henri was swerving the boat left and right, making full use of the waves to toss the vessel around, they were still a simple enough target.

Sod it, thought Steve. We're weakening. And at this rate, we'll soon be dead.

Ian was already hard at work, barking instructions at David and Dan. Usually an IRA bomb-maker would have days to construct a barrack buster but tonight they had just minutes. From the engine room, he ripped out a two-foot length of steel tubing: it was part of the water pump, but they wouldn't worry about that now. He checked that it had grooves on the end; used by engineers to screw pipes together, the grooves would give the munitions inside the improvised mortar grip and direction when it was fired. He had some plastic explosive still packed into his webbing. A cap was sealed on to the bottom of the tube, and the explosive wedged tight inside. A battery and strip of copper wire ripped from the electronics on the engine would serve as a detonator. For a missile, Ian was constructing a lob bomb, a device well known to anyone skilled in homemade munitions, perfected by Iraqi terrorists to use against American heavy armour. Inside the cramped cabin there was a small gas burner that Nick had been using for brewing up the coffee. David ripped it free, released the gas, then used a wrench to lever it open. Ian packed another lump of the soft, damp explosive inside, then fitted a charge that would make it explode on impact.

'Give me some bullets,' he instructed.

David emptied out the mag from his Browning, and Dan ripped open a thirty-round cartridge of AK-47 ammo he'd stolen from the corpse of one of the pirates. Ian tore off a section of his sweatshirt, then stuffed the cotton inside the gas canister. He tipped the bullets into the canister, mixing them up with the shreds of cotton so that they stayed apart from each other. Fired through the steel tube, the device would explode on impact, and the metal canister would blow apart, creating a lethal burst of hot, flying metal. The bullets would detonate a split second later, creating a fizzing, popping series of explosions that would be deadly to either a man or a machine anywhere in the vicinity. Whether they knocked the helicopter out of the sky or killed the pilot made no difference, reflected Ian grimly. Just so long as they brought the bastard machine down into the sea.

Up above, he could hear another round of cannon fire. There was an ominous smell of burning, and the sound of splintering metal.

'OK, let's go,' he said. His voice was strained, bristling with tension.

All three men moved swiftly up on to the bridge. As they looked into the clouds, the chopper had completed its arc and disappeared back into the low cloud, but it would return at any moment, of that there could be no doubt.

'That going to work?' asked Steve.

Ian nodded. 'It might blow us all apart,' he said. 'I've built it too quickly, to be sure. There were plenty of IRA guys died launching barrack busters. The bastards can blow up in your face. But it'll go off with a hell of bang, I can guarantee that much.'

'That's good enough for me,' said Steve. He looked towards Maksim. 'Where's the best place to put it?'

The Russian thought for a moment. 'Straight into the canopy,' he said. 'It's the weakest point of the chopper.'

Steve handed across the launcher. 'Think you can make the shot?'

Maksim gripped the device in his hands. The steel tube weighed in at sixty pounds, and the lob bomb another twenty, making a combined eighty pounds, but for a man of Maksim's formidable strength it was an easy enough task to lift it on to his shoulder.

'A barrack buster's nothing like a regular RPG,' Ian pointed out. 'The cap at its base may well blow out, so keep it well free of your shoulder, or it will take you with it. The kickback will be like getting punched by a JCB, but if you don't hold it steady, the missile won't have a chance of finding its target.'

'What are the chances of the whole thing blowing?' interrupted Maksim.

'You don't want to know,' said Ian with a curt shake of the head.

The Russian stepped on to the deck. He'd been following the trajectory of the Panha on the attacks it had made already. Each time, the chopper dropped hard out of the clouds north-north-east of the boat, then skimmed down close to the sea, opening up its cannons when it was fifty yards out, and blasting the target as it swooped overhead. So far, they hadn't put up any resistance, so there was no reason for the pilot to take any evasive action. By now, he'd reckon he was just picking off pixels in a video game. He'd be getting complacent, and that made him vulnerable.

'We need to get him sideways on, so I can put this into the canopy,' said Maksim.

Henri had salvaged a couple of flares from the boat's stores. He checked they were both working, then gave one to Nick, and another to Steve. 'Get up to the prow, and when you see the chopper, use these. The rest of us will put some fire into the bastard. It should be enough to get him to change course.'

Steve grabbed the flare, and started to run, with Nick alongside him. It was a Greek-manufactured device, probably nicked from one of the boats the pirates had hijacked. A bright yellow canister, fourteen inches long, it worked on a simple pull-cord system, putting a brightly coloured firework up into the sky. Steve ignored the rain and threw himself across the final few yards. He could hear the Panha dropping from the clouds, even though he couldn't see it yet. Next to the stern, there was a metal winch used for the anchor that would provide both men with some basic cover.

'Steady, steady,' he hissed towards Nick.

They crouched, the flares in their hands. The chatter of the cannons opened up and, a fraction of a second later, the furious assault of the heavy-calibre bullets began. Steve could feel his heart stopping as the murderous barrage was launched into them. He nodded once towards Nick. The pilot was flying straight towards the boat just thirty yards above the heaving, violent sea, and as he glanced upwards, he could see the pilot, and the single gunner sitting alongside him. Steve launched the flare right into the chopper. It exploded through the cloud and rain with an intense burst of orange and red light. Right alongside it, Nick's flare burst into the air. It was nothing apart from a shower of sparks, but the shock of it temporarily blinded the pilot, making him veer off course. From the bridge, a burst of gunfire opened up, as Henri, David, and Ian put volley after volley of fire into the Panha. They were pinpricks, capable of nothing more than scratching its paintwork; only a one-in-a-million shot through the glass canopy and straight into the pilot's face would make any difference. But the machine shuddered and jerked as the pilot reacted, then pulled up sharply as the run was aborted. The bullets from its cannons were splattering across the open deck, but none of them were finding any targets. Maksim strode out on to the deck, the barrack buster mounted on his shoulder. The chopper rose up two hundred feet, but instead of disappearing into the clouds, it turned sharply and started dropping again. Its slim, pointy nose, something like a metal snake, was turned sideways on to the boat this time. The pilot had changed his angle of attack, just the way Henri said he would.

Maksim stood steady as the Panha flew straight towards him.

'Fire, you mad bastard,' shouted Steve.

The cannons opened up. The pilot had the Russian in his sights now, and was levelling heavy rounds straight into the man. The bullets were falling like rain, kicking dents into the deck, but still

Maksim didn't flinch. He was watching the Panha, tracking it with his eyes, making minute adjustments to the position of his improvised mortar as he tried to gauge the precise angle of fire that would blast the lob bomb through the canopy.

But still Maksim didn't fire.

'I'm only getting one shot, I've got to get it right,' he grunted.

The bullets were landing all around him.

The Panha flew right over the deck, at a height of just thirty metres. Then it rose, turned, and dropped, approaching from the other side. Steve looked at Maksim. The Russian was wobbling slightly, and there was a puddle of crimson around his left foot. Christ, thought Steve. He's been hit.

From the bridge, Dan ran out to Maksim.

The Russian was struggling to stay on his feet, but Dan propped him up, using his strong shoulders to keep both the man and the mortar steady. The Panha was getting closer. The cannons opened up and suddenly the deck was alive with the sound of metal colliding with metal.

'Steady, mate, steady,' growled Dan.

The Panha was thirty yards away, approaching from the side. Fire was spitting from its guns as it sprayed round after round into its target. Maksim clenched his fists, then gritted his teeth. He watched, waited, ignored the clatter of bullets, and the blood seeping through the side of his boot, and released the detonator. The bomb exploded through the air, amidst a cloud of white sparks and thick black smoke. The barrack buster leapt backwards, narrowly missing taking out half of Dan's cheek, and the cap skidded out across the deck. Maksim was struggling to hold it steady enough for the bomb to complete its trajectory. He grunted, swearing in Russian, as he struggled to hold on to it, leaning hard into Dan, until finally both men collapsed to the ground.

Steve closed his eyes for a fraction of a second. He'd pulled his helmet down low over his face and was cowering behind the anchor, so close to Nick that he could smell every bead of sweat on the Welsh boy's body. Bullets were still skidding across the deck, and the boat was heaving in the high waves.

I'll smell it first, he thought to himself. Either victory or defeat.

The eruption was recognisable the instant it hit his nostrils. The plastic explosives Ian had packed into the lob bomb had no smell, but the bullets inside gave off a pungent, smoky aroma of gunpowder and scorched metal as they detonated. That was swiftly followed by the roar of shrapnel, then the burning smell of the avgas inside the Panhas's fuel tanks igniting. The heat was suddenly scorching, a wave of hot air blasting out across the deck, devouring the oxygen and pushing aside the rain. One explosion was followed by another, then another, each one louder than the last, in a rolling, ugly wave of destructive noise, under the impact of which the boat itself seemed to shake with fear.

Steve could feel a shard of shrapnel hit his helmet, and pulled himself closer to the protective covering of the anchor winch.

One second ticked past, then another.

He knew there was nothing he could do. Look up and he might well lose an eye. He'd find out soon enough whether they'd won or lost.

'Fucking ace,' exclaimed Nick at his side.

Steve opened his eyes. But he already knew from the triumphant tone in the Welsh boy's voice that Maksim's aim had been true.

The chopper was still in the air, thirty metres above the sea and fifty yards past the side of the boat. Flames were licking up from its cockpit, and a trail of burning avgas was spitting down into the rough waves immediately beneath it. The blade was still turning, but it was running only on momentum, as the engine was engulfed in flames. The gap between the chopper and the waves was narrowing by the second and, as the gap grew smaller, both the gunner and the pilot made an attempt to bail out into the sea. But the canopy had been turned into a mess of broken, twisted glass and metal by the lob bomb, and it was impossible for either man to fight his way out before the machine skidded into the rough waves. A plume of smoke rose into the air as the water met with the fire, then the stricken Panha swiftly disappeared into the water.

Steve looked out across the deck.

Maksim and Dan were lying on the ground, sheltering from the battering the cannon had delivered in the last desperate seconds of the fight. The lob bomb had exploded on the canopy, shattering on impact. Some shrapnel had penetrated the chopper, the rest had fallen to the ground. Fragments of scorched, red-hot metal were lying everywhere, and some of the burning avgas had tipped on to the deck, creating small drifts of flame that the rain had yet to extinguish.

Steve ran towards Maksim. He glanced at Dan but the Australian had nothing worse than a few scratches. A fragment of shrapnel had torn through his trousers and put a gash just above the knee, but it was nothing he wasn't capable of cleaning up himself. But Maksim had taken a bullet straight to one of his toes.

Reaching inside his webbing, he grabbed his medi-pack. It was wet through from the repeated soakings it had taken in the past few days but the morphine vial was still intact, and the dressings were damp but better than nothing.

Steve started to unlace the Russian's boot. He slowly slid it down the side of his ankle.

'*Yebat, srat,*' spat Maksim, his face wincing in agony. You didn't need training in barrack-room Russian to know what that meant, thought Steve. The bone in the toe had twisted badly, and there was no way he was going to get the boot off. David had already arrived at his side, and was using his knife to slice open the leather while Steve injected a shot of morphine into the calf.

'Sodding hurry,' muttered Steve. 'He's losing blood.'

'Whoever came up with the phrase 'as tough as old boots' certainly knew what they were bloody talking about,' said David through gritted teeth. He finally managed to jab the knife through the leather, narrowly avoiding cutting the foot again, and tore it sideways, until the sole dropped away. The sock underneath was matted with blood, which dripped out as soon as the leather was cut away.

'Jesus,' said Ollie, kneeling down. 'Maksie's sock. That's one enemy we hoped we'd never be up against.'

'Pull it off,' said David, as he prepared his dressing.

'You sodding pull it off, mate.'

Steve looked up at Ollie with a rough grin. 'You already volunteered, pal.'

Ollie leant forward and gently pulled the sock away. They were all aware that when a man was wounded it was often only his clothes that held bits of his body in place. If you weren't careful, you'd do even more damage removing them. Maksim hadn't taken his boots or socks off for a couple of days, and the foot wasn't in great shape even before the bullet went into it. Bits of skin and flesh were matted into the cotton, and flecks of bone broke away as he pulled the sock free.

'Fresh water,' snapped Ollie.

Steve handed across his drinking water. Ollie splashed it across the wound. The bullet had gone straight through the boot and taken out the third toe. Plenty of damage had been caused on either side, but the sock had stopped him losing too much blood. Ollie rubbed in plenty of disinfectant, ignoring the grunts of pain from Maksim, then wrapped a dressing over the foot. That done, he ripped the sleeve from his own sweatshirt and tied it over the foot, with a strip of plastic on top to try and keep it dry.

'Let's get this bloke inside,' he said.

'A shot of vodka,' gasped Maksim. 'That's what I need.'

'We'll get you the whole sodding bottle, Maksie,' said Steve as he helped Ollie lift him towards the shelter of the bridge. 'I never thought I'd say this, but I think you really do deserve a drink.'

Fifty-Six

'HOW MUCH FURTHER?' ASKED STEVE anxiously.

He glanced up from his watch at Henri. It was five minutes to midnight, local time. They had been sailing for an hour since successfully fighting off the Iranian attack. Maksim had taken shelter under the bridge, and was resting his wounded foot. The other men were keeping lookout, but so far, the rest of the journey had been completed without any more trouble. Which is just as well, thought Steve to himself. We're low on ammo, and even lower on strength. This unit is all fought out. We're not up for any more aggro.

'Four knots,' said Henri, pointing forwards. 'We'll be there soon enough.'

'It's getting late.'

At his side, Ian pointed towards the case of plutonium still strapped to Yasin's hand. 'For that, they'll hang around for a few minutes,' he said crisply.

Steve paced the deck. The storm was calming down as they drew closer to the strip of water that separated Yemen from Somalia. The clouds were still thick and heavy, but the worst of the rain had blown through, and while there was still some swell in the water, the waves were no longer battering the side of the boat.

Get this finished, thought Steve to himself. Then go home and put this behind me once and for all.

He leant against the railing, standing next to David, looking out at the sea. He'd always loved the water. When he was a teenager in Bromley, he'd sometimes borrow a car with a few mates and drive down to the east Kent coast, towns like Whitstable and Herne Bay. He would look out into the horizon and immediately sense how much freedom there was out there, how much adventure, and how a man could get himself a share of it if he just unmoored himself and pushed his boat out into the waves. It had been on one of those weekends, with his mate Jeff Campbell, that they'd both decided to join the Army rather than put up with any of the dead-end manual jobs they'd been offered down at the Labour Exchange. And every time he stared into the ocean, with a moment of quiet to himself, he was reminded of that teenage boy, and of how little he'd really changed since then.

'You OK, mate?' he asked, looking at David. 'I mean, the dreams . . .'

David nodded. 'They're gone. If anything good has come out of this mission, it's that.'

'They could come back. I've heard of blokes that's happened to.'

'If they do, maybe I'll just have to come out on another job with you blokes.'

Steve grinned. 'There aren't going to be any more jobs. This is the last one.'

'You said that in Afghanistan, mate. And in Africa. It was bollocks then, and it's bollocks now.'

Steve looked into the water. There was a break in the clouds, and a thin beam of moonlight was starting to light up the ocean, catching the foamy breakers on top of the waves. There was some truth in what David was saying, he didn't mind admitting that. The adrenalin and excitement kicked in every time they headed out on another mission. He loved the vintage cars up at the dealership in Leicestershire. There wasn't anything much he'd rather do than mess around with old Austin-Healeys and Jaguars, and he was sure he could make money at it one day as well. But it didn't get the blood up in the way one of these jobs did.

'It's different this time,' he said. 'Watching Ganju catch it really brought it home to me. If we carry on like this, we're all going to wind up dead, and where's the sense in that?'

'One minute,' shouted Henri from the bridge, before David could reply. 'Get yourselves ready.'

Steve glanced inside. Ollie and Ian were talking to Yasin. Nick and Dan had drawn their weapons, and were checking their clips were full of ammo. He pulled his own Browning from his webbing, and suggested to David that he did the same. They'd discussed it between themselves, and agreed that they couldn't trust MI6. Layla and the rest of them had been willing to sacrifice their lives once to get their plutonium back, and there was no reason to think that they wouldn't do so again.

'There,' shouted Nick, from up by the stern of the boat.

Steve glanced forwards.

There was a light shining out across the ocean, about a hundred yards away. Henri shut down the engine, reducing the boat's speed, so that it could pull up alongside the British vessel. Steve leant over the edge, looking straight ahead. It was a thirty-metre fast motor cruiser, the kind you might see berthed in one of the smarter Mediterranean ports, usually with a fat old guy at the wheel and a blonde on the sun-lounger. They clearly weren't using a Royal Navy vessel, he noted; this operation was still completely off the books, and the fewer people knew about it the better. Even the Navy couldn't be trusted.

'Steady her,' shouted Nick, back towards the bridge.

Henri killed the engine. The boat was still drifting, bobbing on the heavy waves, but it soon slowed down. The cruiser was right alongside them. A flashlight fitted to its prow turned on to them, its powerful beam punching through the gloomy darkness. Steve stared straight into it. He could see four, then five figures standing on the deck, but all of them were wearing black waterproof anoraks and woollen hats, and at this distance, it was impossible to make out who they were.

'Bring Yasin up here,' shouted Steve.

The pirate marched up from the bridge, towards the centre of the boat. His shoulders were sagging slightly but there was still a quiet dignity to the way he held himself. Ian had snapped a pair of plasticuffs – the simple plastic handcuffs used by armies around the world – on to his wrists. Maybe he is a condemned man, the way he thinks he is, thought Steve to himself. They won't arrest him and put him on trial, that's for certain. Too embarrassing. Maybe they'll put a bullet through his head. Maybe they'll turn him loose. Either way, you can't fault the man's courage. He's not a bellyacher or a whinger, and you had to admire him for that.

'Hold it there, mate,' said Steve.

He looked across to the cruiser. On its deck, Steve could now make out both Ant and Dec, and alongside them Layla. Next to them were two men he didn't recognise. Both tall, burly, dressed in black, they were carrying SA-80s. He felt a stab of anger in his chest as he looked at Layla, but he soon dismissed it. This was no moment to let emotions cloud your judgement, he reminded himself. Get the job done and get out of here. That's all that matters.

'You have our plutonium?' shouted Layla. Her voice carried easily over the ten yards that separated the two boats.

'You have our money?' shouted Steve.

She nodded curtly.

Steve could see her saying something to Ant and Dec but couldn't catch the words.

'Put down your guns,' she said, looking towards their boat.

Steve could hear Maksim growling behind him. The Russian had hobbled out of the bridge and was holding himself up with a stick, his gun already drawn. 'I'd sooner tip a bottle of fresh vodka into the sea,' he muttered.

'Do what she says,' said Steve.

'I'm buggered if I'm putting down my gun for that bitch,' snapped Ollie.

'For Christ's sake, man, use your head for once,' said Steve. 'We make the transfer, then piss off.'

Both Ollie and Maksim were scowling but there wasn't any point in arguing. One by one they put their guns inside their webbing. They could draw them quickly enough if anything went wrong, but they couldn't expect Layla to complete the deal if they were all pointing weapons at her.

The two armed men pushed out an aluminium walkway. Steve and Nick grabbed hold of it, and fastened it to their own vessel. The storm might have abated, and the moon was now bathing the ocean in a pale, silvery light, but there was still plenty of power in the waves, and the walkway creaked and groaned as its metal frame was locked into position. Layla started to walk across, holding on to the railing. Ant and Dec were close behind. From the bulk of their anoraks, he reckoned they were packing some kit. Maybe Brownings. Maybe even SA-80s. They didn't trust anyone, that much was clear.

Steve reached out a hand to help Layla aboard.

'I'm glad to see you've recovered your manners, Mr West,' she said, looking straight into his eyes, with a light smile playing on her lips.

'Somebody has to keep up standards. And it isn't going to be you.'

Layla ignored the remark. She stepped down on to boat, looking around at the men staring back at her.

'Is that him?' she asked, gesturing towards Yasin.

'The pirate?'

'Yes.'

Steve nodded.

She took a step closer, examining Yasin with an air of wary appreciation, as if he were a dangerous animal in a zoo.

Steve walked across and pushed the pirate a step forward. 'The case is what you want.'

'I recognise it.'

She turned towards Dec and nodded. He stepped forward, and put down a black plastic sports bag. From the way he was carrying it, it was obviously heavy. He leant down and unzipped it, pulling out a single gold bar.

'There's your money,' said Layla.

'I'll check it,' said Steve.

He knelt down. Gold was currently just over £700 an ounce. A million pounds was 1,500 ounces. The standard gold bar stored by central banks, and traded by bullion dealers, weighed four hundred ounces. There were four bars in the bag.

'We rounded it up,' said Layla. 'That's actually one point one million pounds at today's spot price. With government finances the way they are, that was hardly an easy decision. But we didn't want there to be any hard feelings.'

'No sodding chance of that,' muttered Steve.

He picked up a bar, and handed it across to Maksim. Russia was a gold-mining country, and the currency was so weak when Maksim was growing up, it was widely used instead of money. He was the man most likely to know whether it was real or not. They had none of the kit they would need to check it properly, but gold was one of the heaviest metals, and just by holding it in his hand, Maksim could make a fair assessment of its worth.

'It's allright,' he grunted.

Layla drew an envelope from inside her coat and handed it over to Steve. Opening it up, he could see that it was official Home Office stationery. It simply stated that the eight named men were officially pardoned for any crimes they may have committed, up to and including the date of the letter, and was signed by the Home Secretary. Steve nodded, and passed it across to Ian. Once he'd read it, and decided it was Ok, none of the others needed to take a look. Ian was the most suspicious bloke any of them had ever met, particularly where the British government was concerned. If it got past him, it was allright with the rest of them.

'A deal's a deal,' said Layla. 'We've kept our side of the bargain. Now you should keep yours.'

Steve nodded towards the pirate. 'He's yours.'

Ant and Dec moved swiftly across the deck. Ian and Ollie stood aside, and the two men grabbed Yasin by the shoulders. They started to push him towards the walkway that would take him back to their own boat, and met with no resistance. Layla tracked them with her eyes, then looked at Steve.

'The plutonium and the pirate leader, Mr West,' she said. 'An unexpected bonus. We might use you again.'

'Call any time you like,' said Steve sourly. 'I never hold firing a couple of cruise missiles up my arse against a woman.'

Yasin put one hand down on the railing to the walkway.

Then he lashed out with a brutal suddenness.

The strength of the man took everyone watching by surprise. His right fist collided with Ant's chin while his left punched straight into Dec's jaw.

And the plutonium had dropped to the ground.

Fifty-Seven

OTH ANT AND DEC WERE sprawled out on the floor. Dec, at least, was a strong, fit man, noted Steve, but Yasin had muscles like a rhino and could probably bring down a building with a well-planted punch. Taken by surprise, neither man stood a chance.

From inside his pocket, Yasin pulled out a knife. Its blade was only six inches long but it was sharpened to perfection, and with the kind of force the pirate was capable of putting into a stab, it would be simple enough to kill a man with it.

The plasticuffs had clearly been severed earlier, and so had the chain securing the plutonium to his wrist. Steve wasn't sure what had happened yet, but he'd seen Ian and Ollie talking to the man only a few minutes earlier and he reckoned they'd cut both the man and the briefcase free. And, right now, he couldn't blame them for a moment.

Layla started to move. Her hand had slipped inside her black, padded coat.

Reaching for her gun, reckoned Steve.

But Yasin was too quick for her.

He moved with surprising agility for such a big man, closing the few feet that separated them and grabbing her by the neck. For a woman, she was strong. Steve knew that from personal experience. But she was no match for the pirate. He yanked hard, pulling her head back with his left hand, whilst with his right he put the blade to her neck. The metal was pressed hard into the lightly tanned skin, so close that it would take only the most minute increase in pressure to draw blood. A single flick of his wrist and she would die.

Up on the cruiser, the two men in black outfits pointed their guns straight towards Yasin. But they knew they couldn't fire without killing Layla. One by one, Steve and the others pulled out their own weapons.

The case was still on the deck.

Steve walked across to pick it up.

Ant and Dec pulled themselves up off the ground, their eyes darting anxiously between Layla and the two armed guards back on their own boat.

Steve offered the case to Ant. The older of the two men, he judged him to be the more senior. And also the most callous.

'Here's your plutonium,' he said roughly. 'Now get the fuck out of here.'

'We're not leaving without her,' said Ant.

Layla was about to say something. But Yasin was holding her throat too tightly, and if she moved the muscles in her neck, the blade was going to cut into her.

'She's a hostage,' said Steve. 'If we give her back to you, your boys up there will blow us out of the water. We'll look after her, and we'll drop her at the next port. She'll be fine.'

'I told you we're not leaving without her,' said Ant angrily.

'Listen, sunshine, either you want this plutonium or you don't. If you want it, you'll do what I say. If you don't, then sod off.'

Steve could see Ant exchanging glances with Dec. They were making a calculation, that much was obvious, and it didn't take them long to crunch the numbers. Their orders were to bring back the plutonium. Nothing else mattered. Layla was expendable.

Just the way we were.

Ant nodded crisply and reached out a hand.

Steve placed the case in it.

Without a word, the man turned and started to walk back up the gangplank connecting the two boats. Ollie, Nick, Ian and David had all turned their guns on the cruiser. The guards up there could start a scrap if they wanted to, reflected Steve, but it would turn into a bloodbath. And not one they were likely to win.

Dec followed Ant, glancing only once at Layla.

'Contact us as soon as they drop you off,' he said. 'We'll make sure you get picked up.'

There was a look of terror in her eyes. But it was still impossible for her to speak.

Henri fired up the engine. Nick ran forward, unhooked the gangplank and cast it back towards the cruiser. The engine started to churn up the water and the boat began to move, powering gently into the big waves. At its side, they could hear the roar of the far more powerful engines on the cruiser. It turned ninety degrees then disappeared into the distance.

It's done, thought Steve to himself. Well, almost. One more thing.

'Let her go,' said Steve, looking across towards Yasin.

The pirate released her. She burst free from his grip, her hand reaching back inside her jacket. But Steve grabbed hold of her wrist then slipped his own hand inside her coat. The back of his palm brushed her breasts but he ignored that and pulled out a compact Sig Sauer P230 handgun. He took out the eight-round magazine and slotted it into his pocket, then handed back the weapon.

'I should have known you'd team up with him,' Layla said angrily, pointing towards Yasin. 'You're all just criminal scum.'

'Freelancers is the word we prefer,' said Steve sharply. 'We work for ourselves, and no one else.'

'You're working with a pirate.'

'We got your plutonium back, didn't we?' snapped Steve.

'I'm not interested in a discussion with criminals. Just take me to the nearest port. *Now*.'

The motor cruiser was already out of sight. They were moving steadily, navigating the basin between the coasts of Somalia and Yemen that would eventually take them up towards the Suez Canal. The moon was shining brighter now, and whichever direction you looked in, you could see only the sea stretching towards the horizon. There was no land in sight. Nor was there any sign of any other ships. As you gazed out, you could feel the loneliness of the ocean, its isolation, and its emptiness.

There's no law out here, thought Steve. No one for her to turn to. We can do whatever the hell we like.

'There are debts to be paid.' He was looking straight into her eyes as he delivered the sentence. They were hard and unyielding, suggesting only contempt for the men who'd taken her prisoner. Men whose lives she'd been planning to sacrifice.

'What do you mean?' she snapped. 'You've been given what you asked for.'

Steve took a step forwards, the menace in his posture unmistakable.

'There's a mate of mine, a Gurkha, and a sodding good man, with a family back in Nepal that depended on him, and because of you he's not coming back from this job,' said Steve. His voice was flat, unemotional, but with a tone of finality to it.

At his side, Ian handed Steve a Browning. 'You've always been a bit squeamish about executing women.'

'Not this time.'

Layla took a step back. The cold arrogance in her eyes had disappeared. For the first time, she looked afraid. What was about to happen to her had just struck home, but she was still struggling to comprehend it.

Her eyes darted towards the bridge. 'Henri . . .' she cried out.

But the Frenchman just looked at Steve and gave a curt nod of the head.

Steve took the handgun, flicked the safety catch in his right hand, and started to lift it.

'Steve, no,' she cried.

He lifted the gun so that it was level with her face. 'This is for Ganju.'

The bullet was precisely placed in the centre of her forehead. There was no malice in the shot. It was put where it would end her life as quickly and painlessly as possible. She staggered backwards, a look of fearful incomprehension written on her elegant features. Steve held the gun steady. He was about to deliver the second bullet, the double tap drilled into him by Regiment training, but his heart wasn't in it. Blood was starting to pour down her face, and she was choking violently. Suddenly, she fell forwards, cracking her head viciously on the metal deck, shuddered, then stopped moving.

Ian knelt down, picked up her wrist, and checked for a pulse.

'She's dead,' he pronounced simply. He nodded once towards Dan. The two men picked up the body, walked to the side of the boat and slung it out into the water. It fell with a splash, sank, then started to resurface.

'The sharks are welcome to that bitch,' said Ian, watching as the corpse was caught up on a wave and started to drift away. 'That's if they don't count it as eating one of their own kind.'

As Ian and Dan walked back to the centre of the deck, Yasin was shaking hands with each man in turn. 'As I told Ollie, in Somali we are known as *badaadinta badah*, saviours of the sea,' he said. 'I think that applies to you gentlemen as well.'

'We're in the same trade in the end,' said Steve, shaking the pirate's hand. 'Buccaneers.'

'And damned good ones as well, I reckon,' said Ollie.

From down in the hold, Dan had bought up an inflatable dinghy, kept in storage in case of an emergency. He was using the pump to blow it up. Ian pulled one of the gold bars from the sack and handed it across to Yasin. 'Honour amongst thieves, pal,' he said. 'You've earned this as much as we have.'

Yasin held the bar in his hand, allowed a half-smile to curve his lips, then handed it back.

'There's plenty of gold in these seas,' he said. 'You keep it, and make sure you never need to come back to these waters. I don't mind outwitting the Royal Navy, but I don't want to come up against you boys again.'

'That's one thing that won't happen,' said Steve. 'We're out of this game for good.'

'I've heard old pirates say that,' said Yasin. 'But the sea never forgives, never forgets, and certainly never lets go. There's always one more voyage.'

Dan and David were lowering the dinghy down into the water. There was only one paddle, and nothing in the way of supplies apart from a couple of bottles of water. The storm had mostly blown through, but the waves were still high, and it was a long way back to the coastline.

'You going to be OK?' asked David.

'We have a saying amongst our people. If you are born into the ocean, you won't die in it.'

He pushed back with his strong forearms, and launched the dinghy into the oncoming waves. Stabbing the paddle into the water, it took a moment to stabilise the craft, and another to sniff the wind and decide on his direction. But once those tasks were completed, he picked up speed, riding skilfully over the waves and disappearing into the darkness that lay over the horizon.

Steve watched him go. Travel the world, meet new people, and sometimes shoot them, that's what they say about this line of work. But I never thought I'd be adding the most fearsome pirate in the Somali Basin to my list of mates.

He turned round and walked across the deck.

Henri had gunned up the engine, steering the boat north-east. They were heading straight into the wind, and there was still plenty of swell in the waves, but the rocking of the boat was no longer worrying anyone. They were just pleased to be alive. And to have got the job done.

'Where to?' said Henri, looking round from the wheel.

'Majorca,' said Steve.

'I heard there's a dammed good Aussie beer bar there,' said Ollie.

'About time somebody mentioned getting a sodding drink,' said Maksim.

Steve slapped Henri on the back. 'Full steam ahead, captain. We owe you a cold one.'

'We might even have a French lager for you, mate,' said Dan, with a rough laugh. 'That's if you don't mind drinking piss . . .'

Epilogue

D AN PUT DOWN A TRAY of beers on the table. 'I've chosen a drink for each bloke,' he said. 'From what I can modestly claim is the finest beer bar in the whole of Spain.'

'The whole of the damned Med,' said Ollie, raising his empty glass.

'The world,' cheered Nick.

'Shut up and hand over the drinks,' grunted Maksim.

Dan nodded proudly. He pushed across a bottle of Baltika Russian beer for Maksim, with the inevitable double vodka chaser; a bottle of Hobsons Mild, brewed in Shropshire, for David; a pint of Warrior, from the Welsh brewer Evan Evans, for Nick; a bottle of Badger Ales Golden Champion for Ollie, brewed down in Dorset close to where he went to school; a pint of Everards Tiger for Steve, the local Leicestershire beer he used to drink with his uncle when he was discussing buying the vintage car dealership from him; the inevitable pint of Guinness for Ian; and a bottle of Trois Monts, widely considered the best French beer, for Henri. 'And a bottle of Oz's finest Toohey's New for myself,' he said, putting the bottle to his lips. 'If ever a bloke deserved a drink, it's us lot today.'

Bruce Dudley slapped a bottle of Glendronach single malt down on the table, then unrolled a wad of fifties and handed them across to Nick's mum, Sandra. 'Keep the beers coming, and tell those ladies to keep dancing,' he said with a wide grin.

Steve sat back in his chair, took a long hit of the beer, let the alcohol seep into his bloodstream, and allowed himself to relax for the first time in what seemed like weeks.

From the Somali coast up to Majorca had been a long but smooth ride. It was a distance of 2,800 nautical miles, up through the Suez Canal, then along the Egyptian coast, through the Med, and across to Majorca. Even with Henri pushing the boat up to 20 knots, and manning it in shifts so they could sail twenty-four hours a day, it still took them six days. None of the men minded. The weather was good enough, and they were all exhausted from the battles they'd been through, and welcomed the chance to rest. Henri had pulled in briefly at one the ramshackle ports up the coast from Port Sudan, just before you crossed into Egyptian waters, and paid cash for supplies of food, water and fuel from one of the many merchants who made a living supplying the drugs and weapons to smugglers that sailed these seas. They weren't the kind of men who asked any questions. From an internet café at the port they'd managed to get a message back to Sandra that they were on their way home and that Nick was OK. Apart from that, they didn't stop, they just kept on sailing through the days and nights, getting plenty of rest, and eating the simple meals they managed to cook in the cabin.

By the time they pulled the boat into the small cove just down from Dan's Beer Bar earlier that day, they'd all recovered from their ordeal. Maksim's foot was healing well, and he was starting to walk again. They made their way up to the bar, only to find that Bruce Dudley had flown in to welcome them all back, and that Sandra had managed to persuade some of the girls from the club in Cardiff to fly over to spend a few days working in the lap-dancing bar she and Dan were creating. The men washed, showered, put on some fresh clothes, ate plate after plate of burgers and chips to get their strength back, then gathered in the back bar, where Dan was laying on the beers, and Sandra's girls were laying on a pole-dancing show.

'A full pardon from the Home Secretary himself,' Bruce Dudley chuckled to himself, looking at the single sheet of paper that Steve still had safely tucked away inside his jacket pocket. 'We could certainly have some fun with that.'

'A feckin' riot,' said Ian. 'I'll keep a copy of that in case they ever try and send me back to the Maze.'

'Not for me,' said Steve firmly. 'You don't need any pardons when you just stick to running a vintage car dealership. Not unless it's from the Revenue anyway.'

Up on the stage, a black girl called Pearl was striding up the pole as the opening bars of Shirley Bassey's 'Goldfinger' boomed out over the loudspeakers. The club had been fitted out since they'd last been here, and the guys had done a good job, noted Steve. It was smaller than the club in Cardiff where Sandra worked, but classier as well. There were three poles, each with its own stage, and ten booths of black leather seating arranged in semi-circles. There was a long bar, selling shots and champagne, as well as Dan's formidable range of beers, and behind it in neon lights the slogan Dan had been talking about as they slogged their way through Africa last year. 'Ice-Cold Beer, Red-Hot Girls. You Lucky Bastards.' It still brought a grin to Steve's lips every time he looked at it.

'A toast,' said Bruce, standing up, and nodding to the bar girl to bring over a fresh tray of beers. 'To the best sodding military unit in the world. Afghanistan, Africa, and now Somalia, Death Inc. always comes through in the end.'

Each man cheered, then downed their beers.

'And to the mates who didn't make it home,' said Steve, raising his bottle.

'To Jeff,' said Ollie.

Each man raised his bottle.

'To Chris,' said Dan.

'And to Ganju,' said Nick.

The bottles were all drained, and swiftly replaced. On the second pole, a blonde called Alycia was starting to strut to the opening chords of 'Walk This Way'.

'We're looking at theme nights,' said Sandra as each of the boys ripped the caps off the fresh bottles, or blew the froth from their pints. 'Any ideas?'

'Bloody fantastic,' said Ollie. 'I reckon we should all choose one. I'll take the nurses.'

Sandra gave Ollie a playful squeeze. 'Nurses, Ollie babes. I think I might be able to sort something out for you. You might even get a private dance.'

'Christ,' spluttered Ollie. 'I am one lucky bastard.'

'Biker gear for me,' said Steve. 'Babes in leather. What could be better than that?'

'Playboy Bunnies for me,' said David. 'I'm a man of simple and obvious tastes, and there's no need to change that now.'

'Whores,' said Maksim. 'And tarts.'

'I think that's pretty much a given, Maksie,' said Ian. 'What sort?'

Maksim shook his head, as if he didn't understand the question. 'So long as there's beer and women, why should I care?'

'What about you, Ian?' asked Steve.

'Me? Oh, I don't know.'

'Nuns,' said Henri.

Ian grinned. 'Aye, a bunch of girls stripping off their habits. That would be quite something.' He chuckled and finished his beer. 'And you?' he continued, looking up.

'For a Frenchman, that's easy,' said Henri. 'If the girls just wear a dab of Chanel No. 5, then that will suffice for me.'

'That's what I like,' said Sandra. 'Some class . . .'

'What about you, Nick?' said Steve, looking towards the Welsh boy.

'Not Nick,' snapped Sandra bossily.

'Mum,' protested Nick.

By some strange twist of lap-dancing logic, which Steve hadn't ever been able to figure out, Sandra would never allow her son to get a dance from any of the girls.

'Don't try it on, lovely boy, you're not interested in that sort of thing,' she said sharply, at the same time rubbing his hair affectionately. 'Now, let's get those girls back on the poles.'

Sandra strode away, and reappeared a few moments later, ready for her own twirl on the stage. Whilst Alycia dragged David away, and Pearl grabbed Henri for a private dance, Sandra reappeared in black lingerie, which offset her naturally blonde hair and her full red lips. After high-kicking her way through 'Like a Virgin', she took the rest of her kit off to 'Careless Whisper', reducing the unit to stunned silence with the moves she'd devised for the song's long sax solo.

'I'd say she's a keeper, mate,' said Steve, looking across at Ollie. 'I don't imagine your ex-fiancée could do anything like that.'

'Not unless you got her a new Amex card,' chortled Ollie.

After a few more beers were sunk, and a few more dances uproariously cheered, Sandra pulled Steve away. 'A word,' she whispered in his ear.

'A private dance?' said Steve. 'I knew you'd get tired of Ollie soon enough. Nice enough bloke but basically a tosser.'

Sandra gave a curt shake of the head, and even with half a dozen beers already swilling around inside him, he could tell there was something on her mind. Something serious.

'What?' he asked.

'While you were away a woman came in here looking for you.'

Goldfrapp's 'Ooh La La' was kicking off in the background. Steve's attention was briefly distracted by the sight of a seriously gorgeous brunette called Jasmine taking to the pole dressed in thigh-high black leather boots and a red corset. When he saw Sandra glaring at him, he reluctantly brought his attention back to her.

'She was blonde and pretty,' continued Sandra.

'I'm sorry I missed her then,' said Steve with a grin.

'She left you this.' Sandra handed him an envelope, then walked back across the club to join the rest of the party.

Steve looked down at the envelope.

There were plenty of girls it might be. He'd knocked around with a few blondes over the years, and most of them were pretty, so long as you didn't mix up that word with stunning. But he recognised the handwriting on the envelope. There was only one blonde that belonged to.

Sam. Probably the only women he'd ever loved.

He took a deep breath and walked outside. It was a cool evening, with a light breeze rustling through the air. The tables and chairs on the outdoor patio were all neatly arranged, but the work on the main building hadn't been finished yet, and the place was still empty. Steve pulled up a chair and sat looking out at the ocean. He'd never really known what the term soul mate had meant, hadn't even thought about it much if he was being honest, but that was what Sam was. A woman he could imagine sharing every day with.

Except he hadn't heard from her since the day Ollie had shot her brother. He deserved the bullet as richly as any man Steve had ever met, but Sam disappeared straight afterwards, and Steve hadn't heard from her since.

Hadn't expected to.

And although he didn't think he'd ever completely stop hoping, he couldn't imagine she'd ever want to see him again either. Even if she had said she loved him.

He looked down at the envelope. It was a simple manila cardboard-backed package, the kind you'd use to send a document. What it might contain he couldn't imagine. With his fingers, he started to rip it open, but he could feel a ripple of fear somewhere close to his heart as he did so.

Christ, man, he muttered to himself. You've just been to hell and back, and you lived through that. What's scary about a letter from a bird?

Inside was a single sheet of paper.

'Bloody hell,' he said out loud.

It was a birth certificate. Recording the birth of Archie Sharratt, in London, on 15 August 2010. The son of Samantha Sharratt. And the father's name?

Unknown.

But not to Steve.

He looked out into the ocean. The waves were crashing into the cove. Inside, he could hear a Coldplay track kicking off on the dance floor, and the roar of Maksim cheering. August this year, he thought to himself. Nine months after the African job. Nine months after I last saw Sam.

It's my boy.

No other reason why she would have left this for me. She must have been pregnant when we parted. And she must have named the kid after her dead brother.

A father, thought Steve to himself. After the way my dad and I fought over my decision to join the Army, instead of going into banking like my brother, I never thought I was cut out to be a parent. And certainly not like this.

'You allright, old boy?'

It was Ollie. Together with Nick he was standing right behind him, both men pulling up chairs for themselves, but Steve was so lost in his own thoughts, he hadn't heard them approach the patio.

He handed over the birth certificate.

Ollie glanced at it, whistled softly in surprise, then handed it across to Nick.

'Sodding hell,' he said eventually.

'Very profound, mate,' said Steve. 'I knew I could rely on you for some insight.'

Nick put a hand on Steve's shoulder, looked thoughtful for a second, then handed across his bottle of Warrior ale. 'Jesus, mate, you're a dad.'

Steve took a swig on the beer. Not bad, he thought to himself. Then he looked back towards the sea.

'He'll be better off without ever knowing me,' he said finally. 'Sam's a great girl, and she has plenty of money. They'll be fine.'

'What are you saying?' asked Ollie.

'That I'll leave them be. She hasn't left any kind of address, or any contact details, and she didn't even tell Sandra her name. She doesn't want to see me. And she's right. I'll just be trouble.'

'A boy needs a dad,' said Nick. His voice was suddenly forceful. 'My old man pissed off before I was born, probably didn't even stay the night.' He nodded towards the club room. 'I mean, I love me mum and that, but . . .' His voice trailed away, as if he'd lost the thought.

'Meaning what exactly?' said Steve.

'I think what Nick means is a boy needs a father,' said Ollie. 'So you should try to find them.'

Steve thought for a second. Then he grinned, and finished the bottle of Warrior in a single gulp.

'I think for just once in your lives, you boys might be right,' he said with a sudden grin. 'I mean, the poor little sod can't go through life with a wanky name like Archie, can he? We need to get that sorted.'

The Weapons

The weapons, techniques, and military units described in this book are all accurate as far as possible.

Commando Hubert: France's Commando Hubert is widely considered the finest unit of combat swimmers – or *nageurs de combat*, as they are called in France – anywhere in the world. The unit was formed in 1947, with a base at Hyères near Toulon. It's first task was clearing the thousands of mines still scattering French coastal waters after the Second World War. It first saw serious action in the Suez crisis in 1955: Hubert troops joined up with the French Foreign Legion to storm the canal, then clear it once it had been taken. Since then, Hubert has taken part in French military operations around the world. Probably its most famous operation was the sinking of the Greenpeace vessel *Rainbow Warrior* in 1985, but its men have also fought in the Lebanon and Bosnia. They have even been deployed in Afghanistan: Hubert soldiers are expected to turn their hands to missions on dry land as well as sea. Commando Hubert is still headquartered at the Toulon military base, and is a key component of French special forces. The selection is brutally tough, with only six to eight men 'badged' every year, officers included. Like other special forces units, standards are never compromised; if not enough candidates make the grade, then no one is admitted.

The Quds Force: The Quds – or Jerusalem Force – is a formidable player within both Middle Eastern politics and Islamic terrorist groups but operates entirely in the shadows. It is was created as a special unit with Iran's Army of the Guardians of the Islamic Revolution during the Iran-Iraq War as a special forces group charged with training terror groups to strike at Iran's enemies. It operates entirely outside the country's own borders. Reports by intelligence experts to the US Congress put its numbers at around 15,000 men, although no one really knows the true size. It has been implicated in operations in Afghanistan, in Iraq, in forging links with al-Queda, and in supplying weapons and training to Hezbollah in the Lebanon. American generals have consistently blamed it for meddling in Iraq, supplying insurgents and capturing hostages as a way of stepping up chaos within the country, both to keep it weak and to increase Iranian influence.

Taurus PT 24/7: Forjas Taurus, based in the Brazilian city of Porto Alegre, is a manufacturing conglomerate involved in metals and construction, but its weapons division has grown rapidly to become one of the largest, and certainly most respected, arms manufacturers in South America. It made its first revolver in 1940 and started exporting sidearms in the 1960s. The PT 24/7 pistol was introduced in 2004. A small, high-impact handgun, it fires 9mm munitions, and its magazine can hold from 6 to 17 rounds depending on the model and the calibre of the bullets used. Its ergonometric design is rated for its superb handling: the grip on its polymer frame makes it an exceptionally easy weapon to hold and fire. In the US, the Taurus retails at around $500, making it one of the more expensive handguns on the market, but most mercenaries would certainly consider it well worth the price.

Heckler and Koch K P-11: Developed by the German manufacturer in the 1970s, the P-11 was one of the first genuinely effective weapons both above and below water, making it a perfect weapon for marine special forces. It uses an electric firing system to shoot a lethal dart, and it is both quiet and accurate enough to be used in any combat situation. The P-11 has two main parts, a barrel cylinder with five watertight firing tubes, and a handle that holds two batteries that power the tubes. It was widely ordered by European and American special forces but the high cost of its maintenance – it has to be sent back to the factory to be reloaded – means that it is only used very rarely.

GREM: The grenade rifle entry munition was originally developed by Rafael Advanced Defence Systems, the main Israeli authority for developing new weapons, and was then manufactured by the American conglomerate General Dynamics. One of the trickiest tasks for any military unit is blowing down a well-defended door. The soldier is likely to be greeted by a hail of bullets. The GREM is a special application grenade that can be launched from a standard M16 or M4 rifle at a distance of up to 40 metres – far enough away for the attacker to take cover. The flat shape of the charge diffuses the explosive energy around the door, so that it quite literally drops off its hinges. In 2005, the US Army included the GREM on its list of the ten most important military innovations of the year.

SA-80: The SA-80, standing for 'small arms for the 1980s', is a British designed and produced assault rifle that first went into production in 1985, and became the standard firearm for UK forces. It replaced the ageing L1A1 SLR, the British variant of the Belgium-design FN FAL, a weapon known as the 'right hand of the free world' for its ubiquity among NATO forces during the Cold War. It fires a NATO-standard 5.56 x 45mm bullet, and has a 30-round magazine. After coming into service, however, the weapon was widely criticised for its poor reliability: magazines would drop out without warning, and it was prone to jamming. Even so, more than 300,000 of the rifles were produced for the

British Army. In 2001, it was replaced with the heavily modified SA-80A2, which was widely regarded as a big improvement on the first version. Even so, there are very few mercenaries who would make the SA-80 their first choice of weapon over the Russian AK-47 or the American M-16.

Corner-Shot Rifle: Like many of the world's most sophisticated weapons, the corner-shot rifle was originally developed by Israeli army officers, although it is now manufactured by an Israeli-US company based in Miami. The idea is very simple: a weapon that allows a marksman to pick off his opponents whilst remaining behind cover himself. It takes a pistol and mounts it at the front end of the weapon, with a pivot halfway along, with a sixty-degree hinge. A video camera and firing mechanism is fitted further down the weapon. The marksman swivels the tip of the gun round the corner and takes aim using the video camera. The range and accuracy of the shot depend on the kind of pistol fitted to the weapon: on the standard version it has an accurate range of around 200 metres. Corner-shot rifles have been sold to armies around the world, and also to police forces. They aren't the most precise or powerful guns in the world but they are an effective way of dealing with an enemy whilst remaining out of danger yourself.

GSh-18 Pistol with PBP AP Ammo for Special Applications: The GSh-18 has been described as 'the most lethal handgun' in the world, and with good reason. It was designed to defeat the body armour that is now commonplace among soldiers. It was designed in the late 1990s by the KPB Equipment and Design Bureau in Tula. In the tradition of Russian arms manufacturing, the initials are taken from the names of the designers, in this case Gryazev and Shipunov, who are probably better known for their aircraft cannons. The gun can fire conventional 9mm rounds, but really comes into its own when fitted with the PBP AP ammo. A standard bullet won't make much impact on steel, or body armour. The PBP

AP is a very hot version of a 9mm bullet, with a steel core, and capable of high-impact speeds. The heat allows it to start burning its way through the armour, whilst the hardness of the steel completes the task. In tests, the handgun could blast through 8mm steel plate, or Class III body armour. But the GSh-18 is also light and compact, allowing it to be carried as a concealed weapon by policemen, secret service agents, and soldiers. Its polymer stock makes it very light, weighing just 580 grams without a magazine. There is no conventional safety button, just a tiny lever integrated into the trigger.

APS Underwater Assault Rifle: The APS, or *avtomat podvodnyy spetsialnyy*, is a derivative of the legendary Soviet assault rifle, the AK-47. It was designed by the Russian arms engineer Vladimir Simonov, and when manufacturing began in 1975 it was the first automatic underwater rifle to go into mainstream production. The Red Army wanted to counter the threat from frogmen. Conventional bullets are highly inaccurate underwater, and have a very short range, even if the gun is waterproof. So instead, the APS fires a steel bolt, 5.66mm wide and 120mm long: it is, in effect, a long, thin dart, with a blunt end designed to cause maximum damage on impact. The barrel isn't rifled, but the projectile is kept on target by the hydrodynamic effect of the firing mechanism. The APS could be used both above and below water, although above water its effectiveness was limited to a range of about 50 metres. The rifles remained in production until the late 1980s.

Stealth Paint: Because surprise is one of the most important military tactics, stealth technology has always been a key part of weapons research. Stealth fighter jets have captured the headlines, but plenty of effort has gone into making infantry less visible as well. For example, the steel of many gun barrels – the AK-47 in particular – glints in the light, so new alloys are being developed to dull their appearance. Stealth paint is a development of that

433

research. Night-vision equipment works by detecting body heat: against a green backdrop, any hot object, such as a human body, flashes up red. In response, scientists have developed heat suppressors. Special fabrics have been developed to reduce heat signatures, creating what the US Army calls the 'stealth poncho'. They use particles called cenospheres – tiny, hollow spheres of aluminium and silica (a chemical combination of silicon and oxygen) that are woven into the fabric. Stealth paint takes that a step further, creating a cenosphere-based body paint for the face and hands that doesn't block perspiration. Any soldiers using concealing technologies have an immediate advantage over their opponents, particularly when launching a surprise attack at night.

Tomahawk Cruise Missile: The Tomahawk is a subsonic cruise missile, designed by the American defence manufacturer General Dynamics in the 1970s. The Royal Navy started buying the missiles in the mid-1990s. It has a modular design, allowing it to be fitted with a variety of power plants and warheads: its flexibility has helped make it one of the most widely used missiles in the world, capable of delivering both conventional and nuclear payloads. It is long and thin, like a cigar tube, with short and stubby wings, and a three-piece tail fin. It is 5.56 metres long, or 6.25 metres with a booster rocket for extra distance, and has a diameter of 0.52 metres. It is capable of travelling up to 2,500 kilometres with the right configuration, and has a top airspeed of 550mph, similar to a conventional civilian jet. It can be fired from land but is most often used as a submarine-launched missile. The Royal Navy first used Tomahawks in the war in Bosnia, and subsequently deployed them in both Iraq and Afghanistan.